What people are saying about …

An Open Heart

"*An Open Heart* is a page-turning combination of loss and redemption, along with a glimpse into the spiritual realm that shouldn't be ignored."

Lisa Harris, author of the Christy Award finalist *Blood Ransom*

"*An Open Heart* is rich with international, spiritual, and medical intrigue. Who better than Harry Kraus, a doctor with great wisdom in spiritual matters and intimate with his setting, to pen such a fascinating novel? This is a thrilling read!"

Hannah Alexander, author of *Keeping Faith*

Praise for …

A Heartbeat Away

"Harry Kraus knows how to put a reader's heart through the ringer. Fast-paced, suspenseful, and emotional, *A Heartbeat Away* kept me reading late into the night, eager to know where Tori Taylor's new heart would lead her. This one's a keeper!"

Robin Lee Hatcher, bestselling author of *Heart of Gold* and *Betrayal*

"With romance, hospital politics, and life-or-death action, *A Heartbeat Away* will grab your attention and command you to try to wrap your mind around the fantastic idea of cellular memory and how it could affect a person's inner life and outer actions."

Serena Chase, *USA TODAY*

"A transplanted heart comes with a double dose of nightmares for its recipient and is the catalyst for danger, romance, and lives forever changed. Riveting and poignant with breath-catching twists, surgeon Harry Kraus offers masterful storytelling and 'grace from the cutting edge.' A perfectly prescribed read!"

Candace Calvert, author of ECPA bestseller *Code Triage* and *Trauma Plan*

"*A Heartbeat Away* is a medical thriller brimming with suspense, mind-blowing twists, romance, and a spiritual message that reaches deep into the soul. Harry Kraus has masterfully crafted another dynamic story that will keep you reading late into the night. Highly recommended!"

Mark Mynheir, retired homicide detective and author of *The Corruptible*

"An intriguing, fast-paced, compelling story that had me glued to the pages and raises the question, can we pass along the essence of who we are? Can you change someone's eternity from beyond the grave? Fascinating medical questions with a riveting plot. Highly recommended!"

Susan May Warren, award-winning, bestselling author of *You Don't Know Me*

"Writing with the authority of a physician, Harry Kraus takes us inside the world of medicine to meet a surgeon who needs a heart transplant … in more ways than one. This is, without a doubt, Dr. Kraus's best novel yet."

Richard L. Mabry, MD, author of *Lethal Remedy* and the Prescription For Trouble Series

"Harry Kraus is as skilled with a pen as he is with a scalpel. *A Heartbeat Away* is a compelling, page-turning story that surprised me at every turn. And it is ultimately a beautiful picture of the depths of the human heart when God is allowed to reside there."

Deborah Raney, author of *Beneath a Southern Sky* and the Hanover Falls Novels

"I don't normally read medical suspense novels. But I read this one. And once I started, I couldn't stop. *A Heartbeat Away* is a great read. It has everything I want in a book. And it's based on a premise I've never heard of and found utterly fascinating. Do yourself a favor: get this book!"

Dan Walsh, bestselling and award-winning author of *The Unfinished Gift, Remembering Christmas,* and *The Discovery*

AN OPEN HEART

a novel

HARRY KRAUS

David C Cook®
transforming lives together

AN OPEN HEART
Published by David C Cook
4050 Lee Vance View
Colorado Springs, CO 80918 U.S.A.

David C Cook Distribution Canada
55 Woodslee Avenue, Paris, Ontario, Canada N3L 3E5

David C Cook U.K., Kingsway Communications
Eastbourne, East Sussex BN23 6NT, England

The graphic circle C logo is a registered trademark of David C Cook.

The website addresses recommended throughout this book are offered as a
resource to you. These websites are not intended in any way to be or imply an
endorsement on the part of David C Cook, nor do we vouch for their content.

This story is a work of fiction. Characters and events are the product of the author's
imagination. Any resemblance to any person, living or dead, is coincidental.

Unless otherwise noted, all Scripture quotations are taken from
the King James Version of the Bible. (Public Domain.)

LCCN 2013935961
ISBN 978-0-7814-0535-5
eISBN 978-1-4347-0604-1

© 2013 Harry Kraus
Published in association with Natasha Kern Literary Agency,
PO Box 1069, White Salmon, WA 98672.

The Team: Don Pape, Dave Lambert, Amy Konyndyk, Renada Arens, Karen Athen
Cover Design: Nick Lee
Cover Photos: Shutterstock, iStockphoto

Printed in the United States of America
First Edition 2013

1 2 3 4 5 6 7 8 9 10

071213

For the faithful staff at Kijabe Hospital

ACKNOWLEDGMENTS

Special thanks to Angela Elwell Hunt for providing helpful information about lovable, drooling mastiffs.

1

Jace Rawlings, MD, sat in the damp Kenyan jail with his back against the stone wall. He leaned forward, his once-defiant posture erased as he slumped in defeat. He looked at his watch. His fall from prominence as a much-sought-after cardiothoracic surgeon in Virginia to the sweaty holding cell in equatorial Africa had taken exactly thirty-seven hours, twenty minutes.

Another inmate, one of some thirty-odd men in a fifteen-foot square cell, leaned against him and smiled through green juice dripping from his chin. Jace recognized the man's striking mix of Arabic and African features—he was Somali, and his vice was khat, the addictive stimulant plant chewed for pleasure.

Jace counted. He was one of thirty-four men being held in this cell at a Kenyan police station in Uplands, a town on the edge of the Great Rift Valley. Perhaps he should be thankful for the crowded cell. The sun would soon set, and at their present altitude, just under eight thousand feet, human flesh would provide the only defense against the cold.

The Great Rift Valley etched a ragged scar from the Middle East through the top half of the Dark Continent, parting Africa in much the same way as the corrupt politics, tribalism, and poverty divided its people into haves and have-nots. Renowned for its rich animal life, Africa spread a veneer of beauty over a landscape of blood, military rebellion, and HIV.

Jace averted his eyes from a man relieving himself into a bucket in the corner of the room. The overpowering odor indicated the single waste bucket was at least half-full.

Not half-empty as his estranged wife would have seen it. He winced as he thought of her, and in spite of being an ocean away, he could feel her judgment over his current predicament. *Always trying to save the world, aren't you, Jace? Well, look where it's gotten you now.*

There was one window in the cell, a good eight feet from the ground, opening to a sky colored by the setting sun. The walls were unpainted stone, drab gray except for a brown section of mud beneath the window. Jace heard a whistle outside and the unintelligible sounds of a tribal tongue. Two prisoners jumped to their feet. One stretched high and grabbed the window bars, trying to see out as his feet scrambled up the muddy stripe on the wall.

A moment later, the prisoner dropped back to the ground, holding a small black plastic bag retrieved from the other side. He ripped it open and smiled as he pulled out fresh chapatis, the fried-bread staple famous in Kenya.

A fist dissolved his smile. The man dropped to his knees as a flurry of blows bloodied his face. The chapatis now belonged to a muscled man whose wild look of determination warded off any challenge. Jace studied the new owner of the bread. He wore a shuka, the traditional dress of the Maasai tribe. His earlobes dangled, pierced with holes large enough to accommodate a plump carrot. The man sat against the wall next to Jace. *I must look like the least likely threat to his prize.*

The occupants of the room seemed to be settled along tribal lines. The dark-skinned, wide-nosed Luos gathered at the far corner. Others with lighter skin and sharper features kept to themselves. Jace recognized them as Kikuyus, the tribe of Kenya's president. Jace, the room's only mzungu, or white person, huddled in a corner with the rest of the minorities: a few harsh-tongued Somalis and the chapati-bearing Maasai.

He closed his eyes. *Think, Jace. How are you going to get out of this?*

If-onlys crowded out hope. If only he'd upgraded to first class, maybe he wouldn't have arrived so sleep deprived, and his reactions would have been quicker. If only he'd let someone else pick him up at the airport instead of agreeing to drive a friend's Land Rover. If only that last goat hadn't tried to cross the road. He slipped his hand into his suit-coat pocket and closed it around a small wad of shillings, the local currency. If only he'd been willing to pay the bribe, he could have avoided the whole mess.

He should have known that the crowd that gathered around his Land Rover would have sided with the locals. "He was speeding," they had all agreed. Kikuyu mamas with colorful clashing sweaters and headscarves. Barefoot children pushing roasted corn beneath his nose, hoping for a sale. An old man on a donkey cart had rubbed his gray chin-stubble and nodded with apparent wisdom. "Shouldn't race on our roads." Everyone claimed it was Jace's fault.

The goat had broken from the herd on the side of the road at the last moment. Jace, who knew his speed was slow compared to the matatu drivers who had passed him on the road, had had no time to respond. He'd slammed the brakes, but nailed the goat. *Crunch*. An unforgettable sound.

Nor could Jace dislodge the image of the goat. Gray and brown splotches over a base coloring of white. A gray patch in the center of a brown circle. Right before impact, Jace had thought, *Looks just like a target.*

He shouldn't have stopped.

Stopping had caused all the problems.

A boy claiming possession of the goat had demanded ten thousand shillings. Jace wasn't aware of the current market price for goats, but he was sure that the boy had jacked the price at least fivefold after seeing the color of his skin and the newness of the Land Rover. At that point, Jace let his determination—a quality his wife called stubbornness—rule. He wasn't about to cave in to that kind of extortion.

A police officer arrived. "I am authorized to mediate a solution."

Jace shook his head. "His goat should not have been in the road."

The officer smiled. "Give him something for his trouble." He eyed the Land Rover. "My mediation fee is two thousand shillings."

Jace shook his head again.

The officer drove Jace's Land Rover to the Uplands Police Station.

If only Jace had paid the bribe. If only.

He slumped against the wall as the chill and his fatigue began exacting a toll. But despite his predicament, he steeled his resolution. He had right on his side.

But this was Africa. As they say, TIA. *This is Africa.* He smiled. Yes. Africa. After twenty-two years, he was home.

Mzee Simeon Okayo's forehead wrinkled beneath a white afro. Behind him, a four-story hotel under construction dwarfed his small *duka* advertising herbal cures for HIV. As a town elder of Kisii, Okayo was respected and feared.

For more than fifty years, Okayo had practiced traditional witchcraft, serving a clientele both common and elite. He feared he might need to move his shop soon, but so far, the large Nairobi construction firm responsible for building the hotel next door had been unwilling to cross him, fearing a further slowing of their progress. If you could call the inertia surrounding the five-year project progress. He looked at the trees lashed together, forming a tenuous scaffolding that surrounded the building site, a curious mix of traditional and modern. He shook his head. Another worker had fallen to his death just last week. No surprise to the witch doctor. They should have been paying him for protection.

He'd spent most of the day planning a cleansing ritual. It seemed the body of a Kisii tribesman was refusing burial. Two hearses carrying the body had attempted the one-hundred-fifty-mile journey from Nairobi, heading for Kisii, a bustling town nestled in the hills of southwestern Kenya. The first became hopelessly mired in mud. The second was sideswiped by a speeding matatu—a bus—and ran into a ditch, dumping the red, black, and green casket onto the roadside in the process. Okayo planned to chant, dance, and sprinkle a secret mixture of herbs over the colorful coffin to pacify the soul of the dead.

But a call from a minister of parliament in Nairobi had diverted his plans, demanding that he assist in another more urgent matter. A matter to be managed with discretion. He smiled. At least this business could be accomplished from his shop. He would not have to change into business attire and work in the presence of the minister. Although he moved with ease between the two worlds, he much preferred the simplicity of animal skins rather than a three-piece suit.

He moved about his one-room shop with methodical slowness, selecting seeds from one large basket, bones from another, and a dark liquid from a hollow gourd. His "office" appeared disorganized to others, but to Okayo, everything was in the perfect place.

Behind a glass counter lay his most valuable medicines. On a marred wooden table, a note was fixed to the back of an aging cash register: "Current prices set by management."

The outside of his little duka was coated with a thick slathering of orange paint. Green lettering on the wall next to a solitary window advertised the most frequently used services. Communication with the dead. Relationship consultation. Cancer treatments. Cure HIV. Break curses. Send curses.

Across the street, a woman selling soapstone carvings cackled over daily gossip and hoped a white tourist would buy. "Looking is free. Come into my shop. Special price for you."

Okayo spent several minutes mixing a dark powder and then poured it into a glass bottle. He rolled a newspaper photograph and slid it, too, into the bottle. He inserted a cork and lowered himself onto a stool in front of his shop, leaning forward over a small charcoal fire. He muttered a series of words in his mother tongue, then heated the bottle, waving it above the glowing coals. When the powder began to smoke, he screamed and threw the bottle against the rutted clay roadside.

A curious tourist across the street fidgeted with a large bag and began to lift a camera—but halted when Okayo met her gaze.

He turned his attention back to the mess at his feet. "Be free," he whispered.

Beneath his feet, smudged with black powder and laying among the shards of glass, was a photograph cut from Nairobi's largest newspaper, *The Standard.* A man wearing a white lab coat. A caption read, "Dr. Jace Rawlings, US heart surgeon, to return to Kenya."

Jace awoke with a start, his face stinging. He touched his cheek and looked into the face of his attacker, a large Kenyan with his hand raised above his head.

Jace covered his face with his arms and felt himself being lifted to his feet. There was something wet on his lip. Jace touched his nose. Blood. He tried to focus. More blood dripping on the floor at his feet.

A bare lightbulb hung from the ceiling behind his foe—a dark, menacing silhouette with breath worse than burnt rubber. "Take off the coat."

Jace slipped his hand into his pockets. The shillings were gone, no doubt stolen while he slept. He hesitated. Too long. The shadowy figure hit him again, knocking him back against the wall.

He heard laughter. No one would come to the rescue of the rich mzungu. "Here," Jace said, pulling his arms from the coatsleeves. "Take it."

Jace slid down the wall, his face throbbing. He pinched his nose, feeling the grit of bone against bone. The ache was horrible, but he needed to stop the faucet that painted the floor between his feet.

A few minutes later, with the flow reduced to a few drops, Jace looked up to see the man modeling his new jacket, grinning through crooked teeth like he'd won the lottery.

Don't they even give a man a phone call in this place? You can't be jailed for an accident, can you?

There had been no arrest. No judge or magistrate. Simply an angry officer bent on leveraging some jail time for a bribe.

Jace thought about his luggage in the back of his friend's Land Rover. At the last minute before leaving the airport, he'd covered the three large trunks with an old carpet fragment so they wouldn't attract attention. In Kenya, anything of value visible in a vehicle was fair invitation for thievery.

He closed his eyes but couldn't sleep. The pain that enveloped his face had robbed him of that. He eyed the bucket in the corner. Soon, he would have to take his turn. Jace didn't want to think of that. How could he relieve himself in front of these men?

A few minutes later, he had a new problem. Cold. Without his jacket, he'd begun to chill. He looked at the lone window. The sky was just beginning to lighten. Hopefully, the day would warm up once the sun cleared the horizon.

He hugged himself as footsteps echoed from the hallway beyond the holding cell. An officer appeared, this one younger and slimmer than the one who'd brought Jace the night before. He read from a clipboard. "Mr. Rawlings."

Jace struggled to his feet. He stared for a moment at the man wearing his coat, a vain attempt to call attention, hoping the officer might notice. He knew the rules of this place. Treat the police like they were the bosses. Don't resist. "Yes, sir," he answered.

The officer slammed a club against the bars at the front of the cell, hitting the fingers of an old man clutching the bars. "Back away. All of you," he said. The old man stumbled away, wailing and holding his hand. "You," he said, pointing his club at Jace. "Come here."

Jace nodded and stepped forward. The officer unlocked and opened the door.

"You're free to go."

"I can go? What about—"

"The matter has been settled."

Jace wouldn't argue, though he didn't understand.

The officer handed Jace his keys. "Your vehicle is parked behind the station."

Outside, cool air greeted Jace. The sky to the east was brilliant with orange and purple hues.

Jace found the Land Rover, and his luggage was undisturbed. Amazing. He was just starting to drive across the nearly deserted lot when he saw a Kenyan boy running across the parking lot toward him. He braked to a stop. The boy carried a goat, which he set down just before arriving beside Jace's vehicle. The goat scampered off a few feet until the rope the boy held drew tight. Jace stared at the goat. White with gray and brown splotches. A gray patch in the center of a brown circle. Like a target.

Jace's mouth fell open. "What the—"

Now Jace recognized the boy. The one who had tried to charge him ten thousand shillings for a dead goat.

The boy's eyes were wide with awe, a clear white section completely visible surrounding the dark iris. "You touched my goat."

Jace shook his head, trying to remember. Yes, he had knelt over the goat at the scene. The goat had been bleeding from the nose and mouth and had taken one last gasp before jerking into the stillness of death.

The boy reached out to place his palm against the window next to Jace's face. "You are a magic man."

2

Heather Rawlings awoke with a start and reached across the bed. It had been a month since she'd asked Jace to leave, but she still thought of it the same way. *Jace's side.* As many days as they'd been separated, and she couldn't bring herself to sprawl into his space. She pulled a pillow, *his*, to her face. A moment later, she rose and took the pillow to the hall closet and stuffed it above a stack of blankets on the top shelf.

She plodded to the kitchen and flipped on the drip coffeemaker. She'd hoped that time away from Jace would bring clarity to her thinking. Instead, her loneliness only accentuated her confusion.

Coffee in hand, she flipped on her MacBook and clicked the Get Mail icon. Nothing from Jace. Not that she'd expected him to give her updates.

The last months had been a whirl. She'd fallen into media attention as the wife of the man who'd saved the governor. She'd watched Jace enjoy the limelight, struggled to trust him when the papers brought accusations, stood by him through rehabilitation from a head injury, and then asked him to leave when he seemed intent on running away to Africa to escape his troubles.

She stood and paused at the window, looking at the sun reflecting off the daffodils. Jace had swept into her life on a spring morning just like this. They were freshmen at a small Christian college in western Virginia. She'd landed a work-study job in the office of the dean of men, part of a program to help financially needy students pay for tuition. Heather had been raised in Mozambique as part of a missionary family. She'd made a few friends in college but was having a hard time relating to the other freshmen girls. All they seemed to talk about was boys, clothes, and celebrities, and she had no experience with any of those things. After seeing poverty, the results of civil war, and the devastation of HIV, she didn't understand American television or the preoccupation with all things material. Her suitemates' only concern seemed to be that the shopping available around the school was paltry compared to the malls in northern Virginia, where their fathers worked in lucrative law practices or the government.

That's why her interest was piqued when Dean Welty walked out of his office escorting a young man. "Heather," the dean said, "Mr. Rawlings needs a copy of the school brochure entitled *Stewards of a Green Earth*. You'll find it in the information-packet materials."

"Sure," she responded. Heather retrieved the pamphlet and handed it to the student, who offered a smile above an untidy goatee. He wore a pair of jeans, a ripped T-shirt, and a pair of blue flip-flops. His hair was a tangle of beautiful curls.

"Time for penance," he said, clutching the pamphlet.

"Penance?"

He rolled his eyes. Blue as the Indian Ocean on the Mozambique coast. "Ask him," he said, nodding his head toward the dean.

She watched the young man disappear, measuring his proud stance and muscular shoulders as he walked. When she looked at the dean, he was studying her. "Stay away from that one, Heather. He's trouble."

"What did he do?"

"Seems the MK thinks he's still in Africa. A raccoon was making noise outside his dorm room, upset a garbage can. So he took his bow and arrow and shot him." The dean shook his head and chuckled. "Right in the middle of campus, like it was hunting season or something."

Heather put her hand to her mouth to hide a smile before stepping to the window to look out over the campus from their third-floor office. Daffodils were in bloom. She watched until she saw Mr. Rawlings bound down the concrete steps and onto the lawn. *MK?* She uncovered her smile. *He's a missionary kid?*

She looked back at the dean. "He killed a raccoon?"

"Skinned it in the dorm lounge. Said he wanted to cure the hide to hang on his wall."

What was the dean expecting her to say? Didn't he understand that she was an MK too? She selected a word she imagined coming out of one of her suitemates. "Barbaric."

"Exactly. I've assigned him a five-page paper. A response to reading our policy." He turned to go back into his office. "Could you be sure he hands it in by Friday?"

"I can follow up," she said. "What's his name?"

"Jace. Jace Rawlings."

She sat back at her desk, with the memory of Jace's blue eyes still fresh. *You killed a raccoon with an arrow?*

She smiled. *I'll bet I'm a better shot than you.*

Zombie-like from two nights on a plane and a third in a Kenyan jail, all Jace wanted was a bed. Well, maybe a shower and a bed. It took him thirty minutes to travel from the jail to Kijabe, the home of Kijabe Hospital and Jace's alma matter, Rift Valley Academy. He'd made arrangements to rent a small house, and after picking up a set of keys from the station hostess, he parked the Land Rover in a carport and made quick business of unlocking first the barred external metal door and then the regular wooden front door of his new dwelling.

He walked from room to room, taking it all in. Sparsely furnished. Small kitchen, sitting area, two bedrooms, and a bathroom. He'd turn one of the bedrooms into a study. He nodded. Far from his spacious home in Virginia, but adequate. Out of habit, he opened the refrigerator. The welcoming committee had stocked a few basics. Milk, butter, cheese, and some hamburger meat. A carton of eggs sat atop the kitchen counter, and a gift basket adorned a small kitchen table. Sugar, tea, coffee, and a small jar of a dark-red jam.

He stopped in front of the bathroom mirror. Deep purple had settled below his left eye. He held a tube of Crest toothpaste at arm's length and shut first one eye, then the other. *Vision okay.* He gently touched his nose, forcing himself to palpate deeply enough to ascertain the bones were straight beneath the swelling. There was a subtle offset pointing toward the left. His eyes watered with the pain. Leaning over the sink, he took a deep breath and steadied one hand over the other, gripping the bridge of his nose. He paused, testing his resolve. He'd once taken a karate class in college. There he had learned to shout the *kiai,* the scream to harmonize or focus your energy during a physical fight. He looked away from his own image and began an energy-focusing scream, starting guttural and low and rapidly rising in pitch and volume. He pulled down hard. Bone grated against bone. In an instant, an involuntary scream replaced the *kiai*. Tears rolled from his eyes and mixed with fresh blood dripping onto the white porcelain sink.

Electricity jolted through his face. Beyond the scream, silence. For a moment, the room darkened. Jace dropped to his knees, aware only of pain, throbbing and rhythmic, threatening to take over all other sensory input. His next conscious thought burst from somewhere behind his eyes. *Breathe!*

He'd been holding his breath. *Open your mouth. Take a breath!*

Involuntarily, he obeyed.

Gently, with trembling fingers, he explored the length of his too-soft nose. *Better.*

He found ibuprofen, took four, and then added two extra-strength Tylenol from his toiletry bag.

In spite of the pain, he found himself chuckling. *Just like the old rugby days at RVA. Welcome back to Kijabe.*

Kijabe carried a weight of memories for him, both wonderful and horrifying. He would face them in time. For now, his head felt slow, his thoughts fighting their way forward through a fog of sleep deprivation. After a shower, he surrendered to the coma of sleep, not caring that it was morning in Kenya. Readjusting his clock and remembering Africa would have to wait.

But deep, renewing sleep remained elusive. A strange bed, threadbare draperies that let in too much light, and troubling images kept Jace tossing. He remembered feeling so bone-tired after a full day of rugby at the Blackrock tournament that his body refused to relax and sleep. When he did drift off, pain in his face prompted him to imagine he'd just been tackled and forced into a faceplant on the dry ground in midfield.

He rolled over and covered his face with a sheet to block out the light. But he could not stop thinking. Images of the Kenyan boy's palm against the window and echoes of his voice quickened Jace's pulse and moistened his sheets with perspiration. *You are a magic man.*

Could I have misinterpreted the goat's condition? Maybe he wasn't dead, only suffering a brief concussion. Maybe the goat I saw this morning wasn't the same one I ran over.

His mind inevitably churned out images of his father, mother, and sister in Kijabe. A mind beginning to process a boatload of pain, buried by years away from Africa. His father wearing bloody scrubs home and smelling of antiseptic. His mother chasing the baboons from her watermelon patch. His sister laughing.

His sister's sickening cry.

Sleep came in fits and starts, much like their family's old Toyota pickup. Full speed for five minutes. Then flooded and stalled.

He spent the remainder of the morning squeaking on the old bed until an incessant pounding in his head became recognizable as someone at the door.

He pulled on a shirt and a pair of jeans, glancing at himself in the bathroom mirror before trudging toward the front door. Bed head. Three-days worth of chin stubble. Face shiny with sweat. *Welcome to Kijabe, Dr. Rawlings.*

He fumbled with the locks on the doors. Outside were three Kikuyu mamas bearing large baskets of vegetables. He smiled in spite of the interruption. The vegetable ladies. Women selling vegetables door-to-door had been part of the local culture since missionaries had first come to Kijabe in the early 1900s.

A woman in an orange-and-red-striped sweater broke into a grin that would make any dentist cringe. "Remember me? I sold mangos to your father."

He hadn't been in Kijabe for a day, and already he was seeing the shadow of his father. Jace shook his head.

"And how is Dr. Rawlings?"

"I'm—" He halted, realizing they were speaking of his father. "He's retired now. Lives with Mom in Florida."

The women began unloading their baskets, displaying fruits and vegetables on the concrete stoop.

Jace shook his head. "I don't have any local money now. Someone stole my shillings."

"Take what you need. We will come next week for payment."

He selected three mangos, a pineapple, two tomatoes, lettuce, a half-dozen potatoes, an onion, zucchini squash, and a few fat stalks of broccoli. When he was done with his selections, his counter was covered with food.

The vegetable ladies loaded their baskets and trudged slowly down the path leading from Jace's stone-block house. With bulging baskets on their backs and long straps adjusted to lie across their foreheads, the women leaned into their loads. Jace could only imagine the strain they were putting on their cervical spines.

He had just shut the door on the vegetable peddlers when another knock sounded.

This time, an older gentleman with a generous waist and a larger smile held out his hand. "Karibu, Daktari," he said. Welcome, Doctor.

Jace shook the man's hand. It was meaty and calloused. "Jace Rawlings."

"I'm John Otieno." His dark complexion and wide nose revealed his Luo tribal affiliation. "I'm a hospital chaplain. We'd heard rumors that you would be here today."

"Pardon my appearance. It was a long journey."

"Of course." Jace had heard of Otieno's reputation. His love of the patients, including the often-harder-to-love Somali tribe, was unparalleled. He was known to spend hours holding hands with family members in the small surgery waiting area or serving tea to the mother of a sick child. On the pediatric ward, Chaplain John was known to carry a puppet to coax a child into conversation. He prayed with the dying and wept with the survivors, raised shillings to pay a poor patient's bill, and had a laugh as deep as the color of his skin. He had no agenda to convert the lost. His only mission was to love. And because of that, conversions followed as naturally as smoke follows fire.

The chaplain seemed to hesitate.

Jace sighed. "Would you like to come in? I think I saw some tea in a welcome basket around here somewhere."

"That would be kind."

Jace poured water in a saucepan and flipped on the gas burner. He added an equal volume of milk and sprinkled in a few tea leaves.

"It's been a long time since I made Kenyan chai."

The chaplain laughed. "It will be fine."

They made pleasant conversation as the tea began to steep. Chaplain Otieno asked about Jace's family, a cultural prerequisite to any real conversation.

Jace filled two mugs with the steaming tea and added three heaping teaspoons of sugar to each. Jace had learned early in life to drink tea like a true Kenyan. Light with milk, sweeter than sweet with granular sugar. Like drinking the milk left in the bowl after Cinnamon Toast Crunch cereal.

"I remember you as a child," the chaplain began. "I wondered if you would ever return after…" His voice caught. He looked away and cleared his throat.

Jace nodded. "Yeah, well, I'm back."

"You want to do heart surgery in Kijabe, is that it?"

The question came out as a tentative exploration. A doubt of Jace's intentions, perhaps?

"That's the plan." Jace sighed. "If I can ever get my equipment through customs. My heart-lung machine is being held at the airport." He shook his head. "The customs guy had no idea what it was worth, didn't even know what it was. All he saw was a chance to make a few shillings."

"With the money it will cost to start up your program, I could feed an entire orphanage for a year, pay the staff, and dig a new well."

Jace nodded and forced a weak smile. He had expected resistance, but not from the head chaplain. And not in the first conversation. He should have known. Rationing of care in a poor environment was a way of life. He proceeded forward, keeping his voice gentle but steady. "But it wouldn't save the life of a child with a heart valve destroyed by a strep infection."

"No. It would save fifty children."

Jace pushed back from the table. "You came to welcome me?"

"Yes." He paused. "And to know you, young Rawlings." His eyes rested on Jace's.

Jace felt exposed. Vulnerable. As if the old man saw into his soul. He shifted in his seat and sipped his chai. Memories of chai time at RVA came to him. Every day at ten. Chai and mandazi, the donut-like fried bread they dunked in the tea.

The chaplain also sipped. "Will your wife be joining you?"

"She's not much for air travel." Jace didn't want to explain. "Perhaps in time."

"Why have you come back here?" Otieno paused, waving toward their meager surroundings. "I've heard that you were quite wealthy. Why would you give it all up to come here?"

Jace regurgitated the automatic response. "To explore starting a heart program for—" He looked up at the chaplain. His face reflected compassion. Perfect peace. And disbelief in Jace's story. Perhaps he knew better.

"You are running."

Jace set down his mug. Too hard, spilling precious tea onto the table. "You've been talking to my father."

"He is my friend."

Jace held up his hands. "Look, I'm not my father. Sure, I'm a surgeon. I want to help the Kenyan people, but I'm no missionary."

"Your father seems to think—"

"I'm sure he has his opinion of why I returned to Africa."

The old chaplain nodded slowly, wrinkling his forehead and blowing out a noisy breath through large lips. He stayed quiet for a moment longer. "Perhaps you wanted to set things right with your sister."

"Some things can't be made right."

"Your father believed in God's forgiveness, Jace."

"My father isn't standing in my shoes." Jace walked to the sink, gazing out through the barred windows toward the Great Rift Valley. This was incredible. In one short visit this chaplain had managed to pick the scab of Jace's deepest pain. This was a test. They'd sent Otieno to sound out his resolve. And Jace had failed the test. He'd come out looking like anything but the altruistic surgeon he wanted them to see.

Before the chaplain could answer, Jace turned. "Look, I'm sorry. I'm tired from a long trip. Perhaps another time."

The chaplain nodded. He dropped a heavy hand on Jace's shoulder as he stood to leave.

For a long time after the chaplain left, Jace felt the weight of his hand. It was a familiar feeling. One he'd run from before.

Guilt.

3

With a second shower, Jace began feeling almost normal. At two in the afternoon, he ventured out for a walk around Kijabe, hoping to see a colobus monkey or two. Colobuses were shy, traveled in families, and were characterized by contrasting white and black color. They had shorter black hair on their backs, long white beards, and tufts of long white hair on the tips of their tails.

Kijabe. For him, the place had been a boyhood paradise. Camping out in the forest, sleeping under the dusting of the Milky Way, chasing zebras on his motorcycle, watching his father operate, playing rugby, hiking to the hot springs, climbing the loquat trees, and sucking sweet fruit. But mostly, it brought *her* back to him. Everywhere he looked his sister peered back, teasing him with memories of fun, sibling mischief, and her crazy laugh. Part of him liked thinking of her. Maybe the chaplain was right. Maybe it was time to make peace.

But some things could never be made right. So he walked around the dusty paths crisscrossing the little town, thinking of Janice, but avoiding the dark edges of that memory.

By four o'clock, he had exchanged money at the hospital business office and become acutely aware that he was ravenous. It had been days since he'd had a decent meal. When had he last eaten? Breakfast on his British Airways flight from Heathrow had been something approximating a ham-and-cheese quiche, a small muffin in cellophane, and a fruit cup.

He left the hospital on foot and headed to the nearby stretch of small shops, or dukas, butcher shops, and local hotels. These weren't hotels in the American sense. What they were, and what Jace needed, was a place to sit and enjoy Kenyan cuisine.

He found what he wanted at Mama Chiku's. He entered the small restaurant through a tangle of beaded strings hanging over the doorway. There were six tables, four of them full. The decor was clean but far from uniform. Plastic tables and chairs, colorful non-matching tablecloths, vases of gaudy artificial flowers and framed pictures from nature magazines provided the ambiance. This was authentic Kenyan. Local produce served hot with a smile. Just be sure the water comes from a sealed bottle. Or safer yet, drink the unique-tasting Coke from a Nairobi bottling company.

The stew Jace ordered was filled with cabbage, potatoes, and fresh carrots. Jace had sukuma on the side, a spinach-like vegetable prepared with onion and finely chopped tomato. Jace dragged ugali, the white starch similar to thick hominy grits, through the stew with a folded chapati. After two plates, he polished off three samosas, the triangular fried dough filled with spicy meat, before pushing away from the little table. For Jace, this was comfort food at its finest, the food of his childhood. Every taste evoked memories of family meals, with his father sharing story after grue-some story of surgical triumphs over illnesses long ignored. To Jace, these stories were normal. Only when they had dinner guests and his mother shushed his father did Jace realize his family was unique.

When Jace had finished his meal and paid the equivalent of two dollars (which included a nice tip), he noticed a finely dressed Kenyan elder sitting at a corner table sipping chai. When he caught Jace's eye, the man stood and made his way slowly to Jace's table.

"Hello, Dr. Rawlings. Welcome to Kenya."

Jace studied the man for a moment. Tall, wiry, closely cropped white afro, dark blue business suit, and a face so wrinkled it looked like it had experienced two lifetimes of trouble. But for two large loopy earlobes stretched with traditional piercing, he could have been a distinguished African-American businessman.

"Hello," Jace responded, taking the man's hand. "I'm sorry, I don't believe I know—"

"Dr. Simeon Okayo," he said. He looked at the dishes on the table. "You enjoy our food."

"I grew up eating this," he said, leaning back into his chair. "It's been a long time."

"We have business. May I sit?"

What business? Was he a new doctor at Kijabe Hospital? Jace nodded. "Sure." He pointed to an empty plastic chair.

The man retrieved a small bottle from his pocket. He held it up, gently shook the white powdery contents, and offered it to Jace. "Take it. Dissolve it in a cup of water. Soak a cloth in the water, and place it against your eye. It will draw out the color."

Jace touched his left eye. The good food had distracted him from his pain. He took the small container and held it up to the light. "What is it?"

"An herb. Your Western instructors would not have taught you about this."

Jace eyed the man with suspicion. "You came here to see me? How did you know where I'd be?"

"It is not hard to track a new mzungu. All the villagers know who you are. The children will come asking for help with their school fees soon enough."

Jace smiled. Some things never changed.

"You will be meeting with the minister of health tomorrow."

"Why?"

"The minister is the one who paved the way for you. Your state government contacted the minister about your interest in assisting us."

Jace swallowed uncomfortably at the mention of his own government. He didn't want the Kenyans to be biased against him from the start.

The old man smiled. "You cannot hide in Kenya, Dr. Rawlings. You've been in our news. I've known for months you were coming."

Jace chuckled at the man's exaggeration. "I've barely known it for that long myself. You couldn't have—"

"I understand your twin sister asked you to come."

Jace felt blood drain from his face. He hadn't told anyone in Kijabe about his sister contacting him. He shook his head. "That's impossible."

"Relax," the old man said, chuckling as if he were talking about something mundane. The weather. Sports. "Your sister told me to expect you."

"No!"

The African gentleman looked around to the other customers as if to say, *Don't mind the crazy American.*

"Look, I'm not sure what you want with me, but you've got some crazy ideas. What you're suggesting is impossible."

"You are reluctant to admit she contacted you." Okayo shook his head. "I wouldn't expect any less from an American doctor. Miracles can be explained by science, reality is only what you can see and touch, and the dead don't speak from beyond the grave."

Jace shook his head and whispered, "It's impossible." He looked up at the man. "My returning has nothing to do with her."

"Yes, yes," he said with a flip of his bony hand. "You also have a rational reason, don't you? The heart program."

"Yes."

"Of course." He spoke like he didn't believe a word of what Jace had said.

Jace stared silently at the empty plate in front of him, feeling a twinge of indigestion and wishing he hadn't eaten so much.

The old man continued. "If your sister is trying to reopen communication with the family, I'd think you'd be wise to listen."

Jace stayed quiet.

Simeon Okayo spoke again, this time dropping the sarcasm. "Twins share so much more than the same human house for nine months, Jace. You go about your life and your work, but Janice is never far from your thoughts." He reached for Jace's shoulder. "She touches every part of your life, Dr. Rawlings. Even now."

Jace stood. "I think you don't know me." He took a step away from the table, his eyes on the doorway. "About tomorrow. I've only just arrived, and I want to get settled, see the operating theater here, make a materials list—"

The old man held up his hand. "The minister of health won't be kept waiting. I'll have a car pick you up at ten."

"And just who are you, Mr.—"

"Dr. Okayo." The old man smiled. "I do consultant work. Sometimes for the parliament. Sometimes for others."

"Why would he want to meet with me?"

"You are a valued specialist. A rarity in our country. The minister only wants to be assured that your loyalties are in the right place."

"I'm here to help the poor."

Dr. Okayo nodded. "Then you won't have any trouble from us."

Jace swept aside the beaded strings at the front entrance.

Simeon Okayo called after him. "Oh, Dr. Rawlings. Use the remedy. I want you to look your best for the minister." He cleared his throat. "And do try to stay out of jail."

Jace stared at the man. He knew about last night? What was this? Another test? A warning of some sort? We are watching you?

Instead of taking the bait, Jace exited into the equatorial sun.

Slowly, he walked up the rutted dirt road, not understanding what had just happened, and now acutely aware of the eyes of everyone he passed. Judging him. Sizing up the heart surgeon. He didn't want to be the center of attention. He'd had enough of that back in Virginia, where he'd been hailed as the one who'd saved the governor's life but later condemned by the same media.

For stealing the governor's wife.

4

Jace collapsed into a deep sleep at eight. Merciful solace without troubled dreams.

But at three thirty in the morning, he stared at the ceiling, wide awake, with an internal clock struggling to reset. Predictably, his mind regurgitated snippets of conversations, unable to digest the nuances of cross-cultural communication. One thing he understood. He was being watched. Judged. And he'd traveled around the world only to find that his colorful past had tagged along for the ride.

After a few minutes, he realized the futility of remaining horizontal. He sat up, noticing the small towel he'd moistened with a solution of the herb Dr. Okayo had given him. He lifted the hand towel from the bed, curious that the once-white material now contained a circle of purple. He'd tried the remedy the night before, mixing the potion and placing the moist towel over his face as he drifted off to sleep. He hadn't believed in the herb but wanted to try it out of respect for the local culture. *When in Rome.* Oddly enough, though, the pain in his face had disappeared during the night.

He walked to his little bathroom to wash his face. He looked in the mirror and traced the edge of his cheek with his index finger. *Strange. I look normal.* The bruising had vanished.

He straightened, at a loss for an explanation. He rubbed his finger against the bridge of his nose, gently at first and then with additional pressure. No pain. He shook his head and added the event to a growing list of things from this trip that he couldn't explain.

I'll have to ask him for another sample of that herb. Maybe I can get a lab to analyze it back home.

He made Kenyan coffee, dripping the first cup straight into a mug emblazoned with the logo for a popular little blue pill. To Jace, this coffee, grown on the hillsides of Kenya's tallest mountain, was the best in the world.

He drank it black and strong and let the liquid dance across happily awakening tastebuds.

At the small kitchen table in the stillness of the night, Jace questioned his motives. Was he, as the chaplain accused, on the run from his past?

Or was he running toward his past?

He sipped his coffee, feeling a sudden loss. Not many weeks ago, Heather would have shared this morning ritual.

Without her, his loneliness seemed palpable. He'd made mistakes. She'd lost faith in him. Four weeks ago, after too much media speculation about his relationship with the Virginia governor's wife, Heather had asked him to move out.

Jace had begged her to come with him instead. Start a new chapter away from the pressures in Virginia. But she couldn't see beyond the damaging gossip of the supermarket tabloids.

It was a media circus that he found himself helpless to refute, since he remembered almost nothing of the events they reported. To Heather, his amnesia seemed too convenient. Unlike the events preceding his accident, he clearly remembered waking up in the hospital. He lifted his hand to his scalp, reliving the memory.

The first sensation that day had been pain, a gripping headache that began at a point deep inside his skull on the right and spilled out over his scalp like ants escaping an anthill. He could feel every one of their six legs as they marched forward, spreading their misery to his spine. He opened his eyes and tried to lift his hands to his head, but someone restrained him.

Heather. He'd recognized her petite hand in his immediately.

"What's wrong?" he whispered.

"Jace. You're awake." Her voice trembled. "I thought I'd lost you."

He tried to shake his head but the pain prevented him. "Where am I?"

"The hospital. You were in a car accident and had surgery to drain blood that was pressing on your brain."

She pulled his hand to her lips. He studied her face. She was relieved. Crying. But behind her tears, he felt something else ... *doubt?*

"Jace. Tell me what happened."

"I—I don't remember."

"You can tell me."

He searched her eyes and strained to remember. "We were at the movies."

"That's right," she said softly.

"Are you okay?"

"Jace, I wasn't in the car with you."

He squinted at her. Pain. Fuzzy thoughts. Again, in her eyes, he saw something else. Behind a mask of relief, he saw a flash of pain. "But, we—" He hesitated, trying to remember. "Who?"

Her gaze hardened. "Anita Franks," she said, spitting out the name that had come between them. She gently laid his hand back on his chest. She kept her voice low and leaned forward over him so that he could not avoid her eyes. "So tell me, Jace. Just what were you and the governor's wife doing out so late together?"

"I. Don't. Remember."

Her eyes bored in on his for a moment until she broke her stare, looking off, turning away, wiping her eyes with her hand.

He'd recovered rapidly from the accident, but the memory of that fateful night seemed to be permanently erased.

"How convenient," Heather had said.

In the end, the newspapers splashed their speculation, and Jace's once rock-solid marriage began to crack.

"Come with me to Kenya," he begged her.

But Jace recognized that look of pain in Heather's eyes. She wouldn't come. Claimed she *couldn't* go with a man who wouldn't come clean.

Jace couldn't stay. But it wasn't so much what he needed to leave behind as what he needed to find in Kenya again. Beginning alone was his only option. He needed a fresh start. A new canvas. And enough paint to make a difference in the world.

The problem with Kenya was that every memory brought his sister back into view. As twins, they had been inseparable. So alike but so very different. And never were their differences cast into such sharp contrast as the spring before their high school graduation.

Janice was frustratingly optimistic, wildly positive about life. She could see good in everything. If Jace and his teammates lost a rugby match, she said, "It will help the guys focus. They won't be overconfident for the upcoming tournament." If they had a flat tire that delayed their travel, she was sure they'd been spared a worse catastrophe. "We could have been in an accident." Her optimism was inseparable from her faith. She accepted every-thing, good or bad, as a gift from a loving heavenly Father. For Jace, a young man of common sense and science, her attitude was a simplistic cop-out.

But what happened to Timmy O'Reilly tested even Janice's posi-tive bent.

For everyone around Kijabe station, Timmy's arrival had been a special gift. Abandoned at the hospital after birth, this little Kenyan boy was adopted into the home of Matt and Tina O'Reilly, the mis-sionary neighbors of the Rawlings family. Unable to have children of their own, Matt and Tina joyfully opened their lives and wrapped Timmy in love and acceptance. He was boy to the core, and soon there were backyard campouts, scraped knees from an encounter with an angry skateboard, a broken window from a line drive, and a collection of African porcupine quills that Timmy scavenged from the forests around Kijabe. One afternoon, a few months before Jace and Janice's high school graduation, eight-year-old Timmy con-vinced Janice to pitch fallen grapefruit to him so he could practice his baseball swing.

With every successful thwack, Timmy laughed harder. After hitting twenty or so slow, fat pitches, Timmy was covered in a fine, sticky mist of citrus, and the smell of sour fruit hung thick in the afternoon humidity. Janice changed her tactic, winding up in an exaggerated fashion to give him the old Rawlings heat. "Try this," she said, launching a fastball over a makeshift home plate of banana leaves.

Timmy swung and missed. Once, twice, and then a third time the yellow fruit whizzed past and rolled under a hedge of bougainvillea. "Give me another chance."

Janice held up her hands. "Hey, sport, I'm all out."

Timmy scampered to the flowering hedge and knelt on hands and knees. His head disappeared under the hedge.

A moment later, Timmy screamed. High and piercing, the kind of scream that could only mean pain or terror.

Janice ran to him. "Timmy, what's wrong?"

"Sn-snake," was all he said.

She grabbed his feet and pulled. He had three double-pronged bite marks—face, neck, and right arm.

Janice winced. Black mambas were known to strike multiple times when cornered. She called for help. For anyone. For God.

Timmy's mother responded.

Timmy covered his eyes with his hands. "Everything is blurry." He squinted at Janice. "Two Janices," he said.

Janice stood and watched Tina running toward the hospital with Timmy cradled in her arms.

He was dead within minutes.

Dr. Rawlings found and killed the snake an hour later. Without antivenom, the black mamba bite was often fatal. In Timmy's case, he had such a high dose of venom that it caused cardiovascular arrest within fifteen minutes.

Why did Timmy O'Reilly die?

For lack of antivenom.

Why was there no antivenom?

Because Dr. Lloyd Rawlings had decided not to stock it. The antivenom was too expensive and went out of date too quickly to justify stocking the expensive vials. They could treat a hundred cases of malaria for the price of one dose of antivenom. In a small mission hospital, difficult choices were made every day. They were always trying to stretch a dollar further than ever intended.

And Timmy paid the price.

Two days later, as the population of Kijabe shed enough tears to launch a boat, Timmy O'Reilly was laid to rest.

Jace found his sister in her bedroom, her arms locked around her knees, sitting in the center of her bed, numbly quoting a verse from the book of Romans. "All things work together for good." Over and over, as if the blind recitation of words would take the pain away.

Jace took on the role of encourager but felt inadequate for the task. Janice had always been the one to see the silver lining. But words, however sincere—even the Bible—couldn't penetrate Janice's sorrow. Her pain was emotional. The words were aimed at her intellect and fell short, rain on ground too crusty to absorb.

Jace took the part of Job's wife. "Curse God and die," he said. "I hate Him for what He's done."

His words shocked his sister from her agony. "Don't hate Him, Jace. He loves us. *Loves us*," she said. "I'll never understand this." She paused, wiping her eyes. "But I know God is still good."

She stood and pulled Jace into a bear hug. "Take it back, Jace. You don't hate Him. You can't."

But he did. He couldn't see beyond her tears. He couldn't bear the O'Reillys' sorrow.

He hated the mission hospital for being underfunded and his father for not being able to purchase the medicine that could have saved Timmy.

He closed his heart to his sister's words. If God was good, He sure had a funny way of showing it.

Jace and Janice plodded on. There were only a few months left before graduation. Then Jace would leave Africa. Leave the pain. Go to college in America and find a new life. He wanted nothing more in the few days that remained to him in Africa than to focus on his friends and make a few last good memories.

He had no idea how much pain was in store before he would make his escape.

At ten a.m., surprisingly prompt for the Kenyan culture, a well-dressed man driving a Toyota Land Cruiser pulled into the lane outside Jace's little house. Jace looked through the bars over his kitchen sink to read the emblem on the driver's-side door: Ministry of Health.

Jace opened the door as the man approached. He was young, dressed in a dark blue suit with a white shirt and black tie. He held out his hand. "I'm Samuel, John Okombo's driver."

Jace shook the man's hand firmly, alternating with a grip of his fingers and sliding into a grip of his thumb, a traditional Kenyan handshake. "I'm Jace Rawlings."

Samuel nodded. "I am to take you to see the minister." He handed Jace a business card.

Jace wore a blue blazer, a dress shirt, a red patterned tie, and khakis. From the looks of the driver, he might have underdressed.

"Please sit in the back. It is safer."

Jace nodded and obeyed. He was glad not to have to drive himself. He didn't want to repeat his last performance behind the wheel. As they pulled away, he studied the little card. "Hon. John Erastus Okombo, MP, Ministry of Health." A Luo name, Jace thought. The Luos, the third-largest tribe, were often at odds with the Kikuyu, and often had last names beginning with O. Kikuyu was the name of the largest tribe in Kenya, and their last names often began in K, M, or N.

The trip to the edge of the capital city of Nairobi took just under an hour. Often traveling in excess of 120 kph, Samuel wove in and around the traffic with rally-car enthusiasm. Jace remembered how he used to amuse himself as a boy on road trips by counting donkey carts, bicyclists clinging to the rear of unsuspecting trucks, or anything else remarkably African. Often he and Janice would count the number of men urinating at the roadside. She always joked after she saw another one. "Okay, now my day is complete." On this trip to Nairobi, Jace smiled as he counted five.

As they entered the city, the driver turned right on James Gichuru Road to connect with Ngong Road, a major Nairobi artery.

"Going the back way?" Jace questioned.

"We have a stop to make first."

The driver offered no explanation, so Jace just watched from the window and stayed quiet. At every stop, street vendors selling everything from roasted corn to pirated DVDs of in-theater movies hawked their wares. He had once purchased a Rolex knockoff for his father for Christmas from a vendor on the street. The guy was wearing twenty watches, walking up and down the street, pausing at every stopped driver to display his collection. It cost Jace seven hundred shillings, about ten US dollars. Jace just shook his head. Some things never changed.

The driver turned right off Ngong, heading for Kibera.

Jace wrinkled his nose. Kibera was Nairobi's largest and one of Africa's most famous slums, home to over a million people. A typical dwelling in Kibera was made of sticks and mud and had corrugated metal roofing, without electricity or running water. Located on a slope near the heart of Nairobi, Kibera was a politician's nightmare. Open sewage, disease, prostitution, and HIV had all found a home.

The driver pulled up in front of a small shop displaying hundreds of pairs of used shoes on the ground. He motioned to a young boy, spoke in rapid Kiswahili, and handed the child fifty shillings. Samuel looked at Jace. "He'll watch the vehicle. Come," he said. "Minister Okombo wants you to meet someone."

Jace followed Samuel down a muddy street, careful to step over a black serpentine stream smelling of a mix of human sweat, sewage, and burning charcoal.

Samuel squinted into the midday sun. "Watch for flying toilets."

Jace knew the term. The lack of running water, the paucity of Porta-Johns, and the danger of going out to the few long drops at night had given rise to the common practice of defecation into black plastic bags. The bags were then thrown in a stinking heap, sometimes in a trash pile, sometimes on a roof, but, every time, somewhere as far away as the donor could pitch it. Thus, the "flying toilet."

Jace nodded soberly. "Thanks. I'll keep an eye out." He stepped past two youths who knelt at the roadside, each with a glue bottle shoved up his nose.

The driver kept walking, ignoring the shopkeepers offering to show their products. "Stay close, Daktari."

In a few minutes, they arrived at their destination, and Samuel knocked on a wooden door. "Hodi," he called. Jace recognized the typical Kiswahili request: "May I come in?"

From inside, a weak voice, answered "Karibu." Welcome.

The door opened after someone struggled for a few moments with two locks. Inside was a darkened one-room "apartment." Jace paused to let his eyes adjust. A table, two plastic chairs, a bed, and a small desk crowded out any walking space.

The woman wore too much makeup. Red lips and an immediate smile. In broken English, she said, "You brought me customer."

The driver held up his hand. "Hapana!" No!

The woman frowned and stepped back, sizing Jace up. Her face looked Kikuyu, but she wore tight jeans and a blouse whose missing buttons exposed too much. "We could be friends."

Jace looked at his hands, suddenly wanting one of those gel sanitizer bottles. He looked around the room, contemplating African sexual viruses, and retreated toward the center of the small hut.

Samuel talked in rapid Kiswahili to a woman and a girl of about sixteen. After a moment, the woman nodded. The girl stood and stepped toward Jace. "Dr. Rawlings, this is Beatrice. The minister of health desires your opinion of her condition."

Jace was on the spot. He hadn't even brought his stethoscope. "What's the problem?"

The woman spoke in English. "She is always tired. Always coughing." She held up two small clear bags containing white tablets.

Jace inspected the bags. On the outside of one, someone had written, "digitalis." On the other, "furosemide." Medicine for heart failure.

Jace ran through a list of questions, probing the girl's history. Before he'd heard the end of the story, he'd made a preliminary diagnosis. "Here," he said to the girl, "sit here."

Beatrice sat on the edge of a small bed. Jace took his hand and laid it on her sternum. She had a remarkable murmur. For this one, he did not need a stethoscope. He placed his ear against her back and asked her to breathe and then examined the veins in her neck.

"She's in heart failure," he said. "How far can she walk?"

The mother answered. "Only across the street. Then she's gasping for breath again."

"Who is caring for her?"

"We take her to Tumaini clinic, here in Kibera. A doctor comes once a month."

He looked at Samuel and then at the mother. "She needs some tests. Possibly surgery. For now, I want you to increase this medicine. Instead of one pill twice a day, take two pills twice a day. It will help get rid of the fluid in her lungs."

"Thank you."

Samuel spoke quietly to the woman. "Minister Okombo will arrange for her treatment. Perhaps Dr. Rawlings can see her again in Kijabe."

They walked out along the same path, again ignoring the offers from the shopkeepers.

Jace was almost certain the young woman's aortic valve had been severely damaged from an untreated strep infection. The girl had gotten sick six months ago, had a sore throat, but didn't see a doctor. After a few weeks, the sore throat went away, but she became weak and short-winded, unable to complete even menial tasks without gasping for breath. Without a valve replacement soon, the girl faced worsening heart failure and eventual death.

Once back in the Toyota, Jace shook his head. "That's a tragedy back there. She needs heart surgery, and sooner rather than later." He paused, wondering. "Why did the minister want me to meet this woman?"

Samuel nodded, his forehead wrinkling and his eyebrows lifting in concern. "Can you help?"

"Maybe. If we can get our equipment through customs. If I can find the right staff for an ICU. If I can convince the administration at Kijabe Hospital that it is worth the risk. An open-heart program is very expensive."

"In Kenya, we are used to facing obstacles."

Jace nodded.

His talk with the hospital chaplain the day before had convinced him that his dream might be difficult to implement. Jace knew only too well that money would be the issue, and the trade-offs would be heartbreaking. Save one child with valvular heart disease or treat five hundred cases of HIV?

He thought of Timmy O'Reilly. Money had always been the issue at the mission hospital. Spend the least money to serve the most patients. Do what you can. Some patients are going to die. Give up the sickest to save the most.

Is that how it was always going to be in Africa?

The driver shifted into reverse. "We need to go. The minister will be expecting us soon."

5

The contrast between the Kibera slums and the opulent Ministry of Health offices highlighted a common problem in Kenya: the fat get fatter as the poor beg at the gates of the rich.

The Honorable John Okombo held out his hand as Jace and Samuel approached. "Karibu, karibu," he said. Welcome.

First impressions came quickly. Okombo was an impressive man, to be sure. Sharp features, a gray suit, and generous lips that hinted at a smile. But what struck Jace was the sheer size of the man. He was Shaqesque, towering above them. Jace's hand disappeared in Okombo's, and his voice caught in his throat. "An honor to meet you."

"Sit." Okombo gestured to a leather couch.

Jace looked around, taking in the oil landscapes, tropical palms in huge decorative planters, and a Persian rug. He sat next to a bronze sculpture of an elephant that served as the base of a table lamp.

"Governor Franks told me to expect you."

Jace studied the huge man for a moment. Nothing like starting by dropping the name of a famous friend. "You know the governor?"

The MP chuckled. "I've done business with Stuart. Kenya and Virginia have much to offer each other." He smiled to reveal even rows of gleaming white teeth like two opposing teams lining up across a gap.

Jace nodded, thankful that Minister Okombo continued.

"He owes you a great debt, Dr. Rawlings."

Jace looked up at a Kikuyu woman wearing a short skirt. When she leaned forward in front of him, she displayed more flesh than an American teenager at a Britney Spears concert. She set a tray on the coffee table and began pouring tea into china cups. "Chai, Daktari?"

"Thank you." He reached for a cup. "It was an honor to serve Governor Franks."

"An honor?" Okombo leaned forward. "You have a strange way of showing your loyalty."

Jace straightened. What was this? Another powerful Kenyan flexing his muscle? A test? "Don't believe everything you hear." He hesitated. "Or read in the papers. Our media is more concerned about opinion than truth. Vice, not virtue, is what sells papers."

"Opinion is all I have, Dr. Rawlings."

Jace stayed quiet, hoping the man would reveal his agenda.

"Scandal seems to follow you."

"A misunderstanding. Nothing else." Jace set down his cup. "Why should this be of concern to you?"

Okombo shrugged, feigning nonchalance. "I need to know everything about my associates, don't I? You've come to practice medicine in my country. Things are different in Africa. This knowledge will help secure your loyalty."

"I am committed to principle. Morality. Surgical excellence."

"Interesting," he said, slurping his sweet chai with vigor. He looked at the steaming liquid. "The British taught us to like what was under our noses all along." He smiled. "The best tea in the world is grown right here in Kenya." He laughed. "Have you ever seen a Brit drink a cup of tea? They were always critical of the width of the African nose," he said. "But they have such pointed beaks that it is difficult for them to get their nose into a tea cup." He imitated a clumsy attempt to sip tea, bumping his nose onto the opposite rim of the china.

Jace shifted, his pants sliding across the rich leather cushion.

"You've seen the girl in Kibera?"

"Yes."

"Share your opinion with me."

"Aortic stenosis, heart failure. Likely a valve destroyed by an untreated strep throat. Without surgery, she will drown as her lungs fill with fluid."

"Swimming without jumping in the pool."

"So to speak."

"I want you to fix her." He paused. "We have thousands more just like this one."

"I am far from having a program up and running."

"Perhaps you could do it at Kenyatta."

The Kenyan National Hospital. The place had a horrible reputation. Jace wanted a place to practice far away from government bureaucracy and inefficiency. "I would like to open a program in Kijabe." Jace paused. "You have a few other heart surgeons. Why don't you lean on them?"

"The few Kenyans who have left our country for training and returned have gotten a taste for the lifestyle of the West. They want to operate in Kenya, but prefer private practice, where they can charge Western prices, over practice at our government hospital. I am hoping that you will be different. The few surgeons we have prefer their private cases at Nairobi Hospital, while the cases stack up at Kenyatta. At least half the patients die just waiting in a queue for surgery."

"If my interest was money, I would have stayed in Virginia."

Okombo poured himself another cup of chai. "If I know that you will serve the poor and charge only a small fee, I can smooth the way for your equipment to get through customs." He paused. "You know it was me who approved of your intentions to begin such a program for the poor."

"You have my sincere appreciation."

"The heart surgeons who practice at Nairobi Hospital will be upset if you begin doing private cases." He shook his head. "I'm not interested in facilitating a turf war."

Jace took a deep breath. "Offering open-heart surgery for a few private patients in Kijabe could finance medical help for the poor there. My interest in private patients would only be to help defray the high cost of the program, not to pad my wallet."

"How altruistic. But I'll warn you. If Kenyans know that a famous American heart surgeon is available in their country, they will find a way to knock on your door."

"So be it. Did you invite me here to warn me?"

"We should be friends, Dr. Rawlings. I need to know what your intentions are. Without my office's blessing, your program is dead."

The minister stood, his massive bulk towering over Jace. Whether he meant to intimidate or not, he used his size effectively.

"Can I count on your help?" Jace asked.

"Can I count on your discretion?" Okombo countered.

"I've never been one to speak about my life or my business publicly. Perhaps if I had, I could have countered some unfortunate media assumptions."

"Is that meant to encourage me? If you won't protect your own reputation, how do I know you will protect mine?"

"I'm only saying that I know how to keep my mouth shut."

"Fair enough, Daktari." Okombo sat again, and his voice was softer, almost pleading. "The young woman that you have seen in Kibera. I want you to help her."

Jace was about to offer his assurances that he would try when the minister spoke again, this time in a whisper.

"She is my daughter."

6

Jace stared out the window at the passing Kenyan countryside, his eyes recording but not digesting the images. Rolling hills, colorful dukas, people glistening with perspiration, feet dusted with Africa. As he headed back to Kijabe, he rehashed his encounter with the parliament minister and felt a familiar unpleasantness: the sense that he waded through a bog of emotion. The Honorable John Okombo had his own designs for Jace, and that added another click of tension in Jace's quest. It was as if every new encounter ratcheted the spring a little tighter.

He loosened his tie and laid his coat beside him on the seat, glad that his driver had left him alone to his thoughts. He wiped the sweat from his forehead and wondered if his efforts would be rewarded. Ever since his arrival, it seemed everyone had questioned his motives, calling attention to past scandal, past relationships, and past pain. In a way, he understood. The white man almost always had a selfish agenda for Africa. The land and the people had been raped of resources and ruled for expansion of personal power.

Why should they think that the American doctor would be different?

Because I am, he thought.

He wished to start anew without the attention that came with treating the rich and famous. Like the governor of Virginia.

He wanted to treat anyone. Anyone except the daughter of a Kenyan politician. But at least this time, it seemed the politician wanted to stay far away from the limelight. This wasn't a ploy to gain media attention.

What was it he was expecting to find? From Chaplain Otieno to the mysterious Dr. Okayo to the Honorable Minister Okombo, everyone seemed to be warning Jace to stay in line. And he hadn't yet met with the medical director or medical staff of Kijabe Hospital. They had responded positively to his suggestion that he come and evaluate possibilities. But how long would their support last after they saw the real cost of running a heart program?

Jace wished Heather had come. She'd been a fixture in his life since college, two missionary kids finding their way as strangers in their own country. Everyone said they were a perfect fit. Now, after years of familiarity, he missed her presence. Not so much the passion of emotional intimacy but the longing for some anchor as he faced a new world of challenge. Maybe that's why she'd asked him to leave. He'd loved the fact of her presence more than he'd loved *her.*

Had there *ever* been more? He had stumbled along an easy path, avoiding pain by keeping short reins on the strings of his heart.

Nonetheless, his loneliness was as present and as certain as a physical pulse. At least, that's the way it struck him—as a rhythmic ache.

What he longed for at the core was a human connection. He supposed that was every person's want, but for so long, he'd accepted a counterfeit. He'd slid into success, but he'd let admiration take the place of intimacy fostered by transparency.

And transparent was just what he couldn't be, so admiration would have to do.

He smiled at the memory of the boy and his goat, the picture of the boy's hand pressed against the glass. *Do I fancy myself a magic man? What am I outside my ability to heal?*

The Land Cruiser turned down the road leading from the highway to Kijabe. *What am I doing here? Fooling myself that I can make a difference?*

An answer came, but not one he would admit to anyone just yet. *My sister asked me to come.*

Heather Rawlings coaxed the two-hundred-pound mastiff up on the table. "Come on, Bo. Time for the brush."

She pushed a rebellious strand of blonde hair behind her ear and laid a towel on her shoulder. The towel, a kitchen towel in a former life, was now formally dubbed a drool towel. She used it to wipe away drool slingers from the walls after a session with Bo.

As she worked, she talked softly to the gentle giant. "There, doesn't that feel good?"

While other women in the upscale Richmond suburb might have craft rooms for hobbies such as painting, Heather had converted their large laundry room into a grooming-feeding station to support her dog-walking business. She had started three years ago, needing to do something other than provide arm dressing for her cardiothoracic-surgeon husband at social functions. The dog walking came to her naturally. She loved animals, and after taking care of a friend's beagle while they were on vacation, she thought, *Why not?* It was the most practical of solutions. She got her exercise and got paid to do it.

Even Jace seemed pleased, except when she talked about it at parties.

Bo was her Monday, Wednesday, Friday, ten o'clock. Because of his size, she always walked him solo. In the afternoon, she tripled up with a pair of Maltese and a miniature schnauzer. She took Tuesdays off completely and had only one appointment for a German shepherd on Thursday mornings.

Heather's cell phone sang out the theme to the Pink Panther. She looked at the screen. *Mom.*

"Heather," her mom began with a sigh. "Have you heard from Jace?"

"Mom," she said. "I'm not exactly expecting him to call."

"But certainly he'd—"

"I asked him to leave, Mom. He's not likely feeling much obligation to me right now. Besides, he just arrived yesterday. He probably hasn't had a chance to get a phone or Internet connection."

"I'm rethinking this. Maybe you should have gone with him."

"Don't start. I needed time to figure things out."

"What's to figure out? It's been all over the news."

Now Heather sighed. The last two months had been a whirl of attention, most of it the kind she despised. So much had been said about Jace, accusations that he was unwilling or unable to talk about.

It seemed all their conversations in the last month had ended with raised voices and frustration. She'd finally come to the conclusion that if she was to discover the truth, she needed to do it with space away from her husband.

What she hadn't anticipated was his sudden departure for Africa.

"Let's not go there, Mom. I know what the media says. I'm just not sure."

"The only thing I'm not sure about is whether we ever knew who Jace Rawlings really was."

"Well," she said, pulling a wire brush through the coat of the mastiff, "that's what I intend to find out."

"Maybe you should come to Florida for a while. Your father would love to spend some time with you."

"I can't. I've got the dogs."

"The dogs, the dogs." She spoke with a rising and falling singsong. "You wouldn't have to do that. You don't have to work at all. Jace made enough to keep you from—"

"Mom, I *want* to do this. I'm doing something. I like it. It's good for me."

More silence and a heavy sigh.

Heather began to scratch Bo behind the ears. "Look, I'll call you if I hear from Jace."

"Okay," she said. "You do that."

The call ended. Heather's mom wasn't much for prolonged good-byes.

She snapped a leash to Bo's collar and walked him back to his owner's home, conveniently only two doors down. Mr. Robbins loved Bo, but his arthritis kept him from giving the dog enough exercise. Heather put Bo in the backyard, latching the tall redwood fence behind her.

She collected the mail, intrigued by a manila envelope without a return address postmarked from Richmond.

Inside, at the kitchen table, she opened the envelope and slipped out a three-page document. It seemed to be a photocopy originating from a medical examiner's office.

She read the title with a growing discomfort. *Autopsy Report: Anita Franks.*

Why would someone send me this?

Anita Franks. The name alone was enough to bring bad feelings. The now-deceased woman had been the governor's wife. A woman with a passion for helping Virginia's farmers.

And apparently a passion for Heather's husband.

Heather scanned the document. Most of it was anatomic, listing injuries. She wrinkled her nose at the description. The state's first lady had been struck by a car while she knelt at the side of a Richmond street tending to Jace.

Heather peered into the envelope. Nothing. The only item inside had been the autopsy report, with no explanation as to who'd sent it.

Looking at the pages again, she saw two lines highlighted in yellow. The first was a toxicology report. Her blood-toxin screen was positive for ketamine.

Heather shrugged. She'd heard of ketamine somewhere, but it didn't register as important. The second item made her shudder.

"Vaginal vault contains evidence of recent sexual intercourse. Motility of sperm place the timing within two hours of death."

Jace? Just what went on that night?

That night, Heather lay awake as her mind seesawed between the Jace she knew and loved and the mystery that seemed to surround him since his accident. She clung to the former and drifted to sleep remembering their first "date." It was a week after their first encounter in the dean's office.

Jace had handed her his assignment. "Could you see that Dean Welty gets this?"

"Sure." She studied his eyes and hesitated. "The dean told me what you did."

"So I suppose you think I'm cruel for stalking cute little innocent furry animals?"

"I think you should have left him by the trash cans. No one would have known."

"I wanted the skin."

"I have a leopard skin."

"You?"

"I grew up in Mozambique. I had it hanging on my wall at home. I brought it with me to school, but when I met my suitemates, I decided it best to leave it in the bottom of my trunk."

"Don't tell me. They're vegans or something."

She giggled. "Or something."

He looked at the paper in her hand. "I'm sure the dean will get a kick out of this."

"He told me to stay away from you. That you were trouble."

"Because I killed a raccoon?"

"Maybe he knows more about you than I do."

He twisted a lock of curly blond hair beside his ear. "Let's just say I carry an American passport, but I don't seem to fit in my own country."

She nodded. *I know exactly how you feel.* "We're having a suite charade night tonight. We're supposed to invite a guest. Would you come?"

"Will you show me the leopard?"

"Promise not to tell the vegans?"

He laughed. "Deal."

She held out her hand. "I'm Heather."

"Jace," he said, shaking her hand.

"I know." She smiled. "I think I'll introduce you as the great white hunter." She laughed with him. "All the raccoons on campus have heard of you."

7

The following day Jace awoke at six a.m., a clear sign he was making progress on resetting his clock to African time. He brewed strong coffee and wondered if adjusting his Western mind-set to the pace of Kenya would be as easy. *That's a joke. I'm not sure I could ever be patient enough not to resent the pace of change here.*

At ten, Jace knocked on the office door of Kijabe Hospital's medical director. Blake Anderson, MD, was a wiry blond Aussie with sideburns that sloped down his ruddy cheeks and met the corners of a mustache so long that Jace couldn't tell if he had an upper lip at all. He spoke a Kiswahili greeting with a strong down-under accent. "Karibu, mate!"

Jace held out his hand. "Jace Rawlings."

"Good day to ya. How's the head?" he asked with a chuckle. "I'm always in a cloud the first week back from home furlough."

"I'm adjusting." Jace shrugged. "I'm anxious to see the place."

The medical director pointed to a stack of papers. "Here's your orientation packet. Our formulary is limited, but better than the government's district hospitals. Here's your pager," he said, handing him the device.

"Wow. I was hoping I'd seen the last of this in America."

"Yeah, well, we'd all rather do without the night business, wouldn't we, mate?" He handed Jace a sheet of paper. "This," he said, "is the call schedule. I left you off this first week so you could get your feet on the ground. Your first call is Monday night."

"Call?" Jace looked at the paper. "I didn't anticipate much call until the heart program was up and running."

Blake raised his bushy eyebrows and stared at Jace. "Good joke. I like a bloke with a sense of humor." He paused before proceeding without a smile. "Everyone here does his or her share of call. Since you were a board-certified general surgeon before you did heart surgery, you'll be on the call schedule for general surgery. Perhaps later if the heart program gets off the ground and is busy enough to justify taking you off the general surgery call, we'll let you take cardiothoracic call only." He chuckled to himself as if to say, *We'll see if that ever happens.*

Jace felt a stab of anxiety. *General surgery? How long has it been since I even saw an appendix?*

"Dr. Rawlings?"

Jace looked up, suddenly aware that he'd been staring blindly at the call sheet. "Look, Blake, I thought we had an agreement about setting up this program. You talked to the minister of health. You even talked to the airline about my extra supplies. I thought everyone was on the same page about the heart program."

Blake smiled. "Of course. But things move slowly here. I can't afford to house a capable surgeon for months while the wheels start to turn."

Jace forced himself to return a weak smile.

"Shall we take a tour?"

Jace followed quietly as Blake entered the long main hospital corridor and wove through a sea of patients. They seemed to be everywhere. Standing, sitting on wooden benches lining the halls, sitting on the floor, leaning in through the windows, and crowding the doorframes. There were Kikuyu mamas carrying babies on their backs in cloth slings called kangas. Somali women with head coverings peered out through slits revealing only glimpses of dark eyes.

Blake edged past a series of stretchers lining a hallway leading to the X-ray department. Two men with bloody faces and twisted limbs looked back at Jace and muttered something in Kiswahili.

"Sorry about the crowding. Seems we've just had a bit of a road traffic accident."

Jace nodded and plodded along behind him. The smell was a mix of human sweat, urine, and iodine. *Funny. The smell is exactly the same as I remembered it.* "I used to come down here and watch my father operate. It's like nothing has changed."

Blake chuckled and kept moving. "Here's the lab. We can do basic chemistries, blood counts, urine analysis, malaria smears, amylase, liver functions, bacterial cultures, and HIV testing. The crew is quite good at identifying TB."

"May I see the blood bank?"

"This is it," he said, pointing to a single refrigerator. "There is no separate room for the blood bank."

The blood bank is a refrigerator. Jace scratched his head.

"Let me show you our new HDU, the high dependency unit. Not quite an ICU, but getting there. It's just up the ramp here."

They walked up the long sloping hallway. Because there were no elevators, the hallways were long and graded so you could push a stretcher up a series of two long hallways to go from first to second floor.

Could I really do open-heart surgery in a place so primitive it doesn't have an elevator?

Blake showed Jace around the HDU, introducing him to the nurses and pointing out supplies. The monitors above the beds looked modern but were already a few generations behind the ones he'd used in Virginia. Jace squinted down the row of patients.

The medical director smiled. "Bed one is a head-injury patient from a road traffic accident. Bed two has cerebral malaria. Bed three is an HIV patient who presented with a perforation of the bowel from typhoid fever. Bed four is a chest injury from a hippo. Bed five is a patient who had esophageal cancer and a resection." He paused. "Welcome to Africa."

Jace took a deep breath. It was clear that, as a general surgeon, he'd be expected to pull his weight. And he knew that if he didn't, he wouldn't likely swing the staff in favor of letting him do open hearts. He offered a weak smile in response, aware that he felt nothing positive. What did he feel?

Scared. Alone.

He was in the deep end of the pool and had forgotten how to swim.

That afternoon, Jace sat at his computer, happy to have gotten his Internet connection. He needed to send some emails back home. His first message was to Heather.

Heather, arrived safely, but my equipment is hung up in customs. I could have predicted this. I didn't want to bribe the official, so here I am in Kenya without my bypass pump.

I did meet with the Kenyan minister of health. Hopefully, he will grease the wheels and I'll get my stuff. I also met with the Kijabe Hospital administrator. They want me to do general surgery until things can be sorted out with the heart program. I'm not sure I remember anything about general surgery. I'd better learn fast. I picked up a book at the library to help.

I've been thinking a lot about us. I've never been one to analyze feelings and relationships, but perhaps this space will help me figure things out. I miss you. Strange, this place feels like home.

Jace

Jace clicked Send, then sighed and reflexively traced a small scar on his scalp. The bony indentation for a burr hole was filling in and soon would be hard to find. *Two months,* Jace thought. *Enough time to recover from drainage of a subdural hematoma.*

Two months. A whirlwind of change, recovery, physical therapy, seeking approval to start a heart program, and securing donated equipment—details that fell magically into place like dominos tumbling down a line. The speed of the change amazed him, and he'd entertained thoughts that someone very powerful was pulling strings on his behalf. But in the end, he shoved those thoughts aside and wished his memory would return. But because those memories eluded him, Jace hid from the media and wondered if his own questions would ever be answered.

In two short months, bone had reached out to bone to link and repair the small defect in his skull. *But will my marriage ever heal?*

Will I ever remember?

8

Heather Rawlings sat in a booth in the Robin Inn, a restaurant in the west end of the Fan district of Richmond, enjoying the four-cheese ravioli and the company of longtime friend Gabriel Dawson.

Gabby looked up from her salad. "How can you eat that stuff and maintain your figure? If I ate like you, I'd weigh three hundred pounds."

"Then you could ask Dr. Marks to operate on you."

"That's not the way I'd like to get his attention."

Heather laughed. "You know my schedule. I need to wear a pedometer some week. I must do thirty miles a week with the dogs."

Gabby set down her fork and leaned forward. "Okay, honestly, how are you doing? The buzz in the OR is that Jace left you high and dry in a sudden need to get back to Africa."

Heather took a deep breath. "Not exactly true. He had a sudden need to get to Africa, yes, but I'm the one who decided it was best to separate."

"You?"

She looked down and nodded. "After the accident, things just weren't the same between us. It was like everything that he'd spent so many years building didn't mean anything to him anymore. Here he has this successful cardiothoracic practice, patients who practically worship him—"

"Tell me about it, sister. I've seen the old ladies practically slobbering over him."

"Then, he gets out of the hospital and starts talking about the poor Kenyans without a heart doctor."

"A close call with death can change your priorities."

Heather shook her head. "It was more than that. It was mystical. In the end, he said his twin sister asked him to come back."

"Twin sister? I didn't know Jace was a twin."

"Nobody around here did." She chased a lemon section around her water glass with a straw, stabbing the fleshy fruit to release the juice. "Family secret."

Gabby raised her eyebrows. Her voice was laced with sarcasm. "Okay."

"I need some professional advice."

"You need a psychiatrist," Gabby said.

"Funny. I need an opinion from someone who knows cardiac anesthesia."

Now Gabby's eyebrows lowered in seriousness.

"I know you worked with Jace a lot. He told me you were his favorite pump tech."

"Flattery, my dear, will get you nowhere unless you're picking up the tab."

Heather took a paper out of her purse, the name of the drug she'd copied off Anita Franks's autopsy report, and slid it across the table to her friend. "What do you know about this drug?"

AN OPEN HEART · 75

Gabby wrinkled her nose. "Why do you want to know about ketamine?"

"I just want to know. What is it?"

"It's an anesthetic drug. We use it all the time." She shrugged. "I use it in combination with a few other drugs when I'm sedating pediatric cases."

"Did Jace use it for his patients?"

"Maybe not Jace himself, but I'm sure he saw us using it on his patients."

"Is there any reason to have ketamine in the blood if you weren't having an operation?"

"Why are you asking this?"

Heather took a deep breath and kept her voice low. "I'm just trying to find out some information. Someone sent me a copy of Anita Franks's autopsy report."

"Somebody?"

"Anonymous. It was weird. I just got this envelope in the mail with no return address. Apparently, someone wanted me to see some things about her autopsy report. They photocopied it and highlighted a few items. The first one was that she was found to have traces of ketamine in her blood."

"That's weird." Gabby stared off.

"What is it?"

"I've heard reports that ketamine can be slipped in a drink to use as a date-rape drug."

Heather swallowed. Hard. "That may go along with the second thing that was underlined on the report." She hesitated. "You can't tell anyone about this, okay? I'm not even supposed to know this stuff."

"Someone obviously thinks you should know."

"The report said that Mrs. Franks had evidence of sexual intercourse within two hours of death."

"So the governor and his wife are still young. Just because—"

"Gabby, the governor was out of town. He wasn't anywhere close to his wife that night. It was all over the news. He was in Williamsburg at a trade summit, meeting with some Kenyan leaders about exporting tobacco or something."

"What are you saying?"

"Nothing. I'm just trying to find out what this means. And why someone would want me to know this."

"You think Jace had something to do with—" Gabby halted, her hand to her mouth. "Come on, Heather, Jace would never do something like this."

"I'm not sure I know what Jace is capable of anymore. I want to believe in Jace." She paused. "Maybe this will erase my doubts."

"How can you doubt him? Just look at the guy. He wouldn't need to sedate anyone to get them into bed. Just one look into those blue eyes ..."

"Yeah, thanks for the encouragement."

"Hey, I'm just saying what you already know in your heart. Jace was straight as an arrow. He wouldn't cheat on you. And if he did, he wouldn't need to use ketamine." She paused and reached across the table. "Come on, Heather, Jace is a believer, right? He wouldn't—"

"So you think being a Christian keeps you from cheating on your wife?"

"It should."

"Jace is from a missionary family. I made assumptions about what he believed just because of the family he came from." She sighed. "But Jace has always been quiet about his faith. I'm not sure his parents' faith ever took."

"He's a good guy."

"Being a good guy is different from having true faith."

Gabby released Heather's arm. "I'm going to pray for him. I think you need to give him the benefit of the doubt."

"So why the media speculation about Jace and Anita?" Heather quoted a newspaper tabloid, "'When the cat's away, the mice will play? Anita Franks out with husband's heart doctor.'"

"I don't read that crap." Gabby took a bite of salad and spoke with her mouth full. "What does Jace say about it?"

"That's the strange thing. He claims he has no memory of that evening. The accident erased it all." Heather snapped her fingers. "How convenient. He is seen coming out of a downtown hotel with the governor's wife, and he doesn't even remember."

Gabby frowned. "What happened that night?"

"All I know is the little Jace will say combined with what I got from the police. Jace was driving our car away from a downtown hotel with Anita Franks when he was broadsided by a drunk driver. Jace was knocked out. Apparently, Anita called 911 and pulled Jace from the car. She was kneeling over him when she was struck by another vehicle, a VCU student going home after a late night studying."

"He did have brain surgery. Maybe you should give him a break."

"Maybe the injury just prevents him from lying to me anymore."

"Heather!"

"I don't know what to believe—" a sob interrupted Heather's words. "I *want* to believe in him, Gabby. I want to believe in Jace and me like we used to be."

Gabby squinted. "Then *believe* him, Heather. He's had plenty of opportunities to stray in the past, but he's always made it clear that he's a one-woman man."

"Then why is someone sending me this?" Heather asked, pointing at the paper.

"I don't know."

Heather reached across the table and crumpled the paper before burying it in a Bottega handbag. "I don't know either, but I'm going to find out."

That evening, Jace left his small flat in search of the Anderson house, where he'd been invited for supper. Blake said he'd invited a few of the other staff, including the general surgeon, so Jace would have a chance to meet them face-to-face. *The other general surgeon.* He remembered how the medical director had emphasized *other* as if reminding Jace of his expected position.

Jace's path took him below the hospital and along the dirt road beside the only place on the station Jace had avoided since his arrival: the Kijabe Station cemetery.

Located right next to the hospital, the cemetery was a small memorial to missionaries, local Kenyans, and a few unclaimed patients along the way. *Convenient location,* Jace thought. *If I have to do general surgery, my patients won't have far to go to make it here.*

He paused at the back of the hospital, where a parking lot abutted the field next to the cemetery. A footpath cut the corner to a series of houses below the cemetery but took Jace through the center of the tombstones. The dirt road, to the right, skirted the border of the cemetery. Hesitating, Jace focused on the other side. *This is crazy. I should just walk straight through.*

He took a step, then two, and felt his heart quicken. With a boldness in his stride he did not feel, he veered off the path and stopped at a small, flat memorial stone in the second row back. The little stone marked the one event that caused even his sister's faith to falter. *Timmy O'Reilly.* A small cross was etched above the dates of his birth and death. *Only eight years old.*

In the weeks following Timmy's death, Janice's faith, however battered, emerged with a renewed hope. From that point on, she seemed to be living with a palpable longing for heaven. For Jace, the pie-in-the-sky by-and-by seemed akin to shoving your head in the sand. Life was hard. Period.

But Janice, more than anyone else he'd ever known, seemed to live in an awareness of her own yearning to be free of earthly restraint. That yearning colored everything she saw, even the evil, with a rose-colored optimism.

"Look around," Jace told Janice one afternoon as they walked down the hill from school. "Poverty. AIDS. Corruption. Death of innocent children. Where is God?"

She looked up from the rocky path. "He's in the pain, Jace." She paused, her face taking on that faraway look he'd come to expect.

"But one day, all of our tears will be wiped away. All of our pain will be gone."

Back in the present, Jace heard a twig snap and turned to see a large man rising from behind a memorial stone. As the man approached, he recognized the chaplain, John Otieno.

Otieno's eyes were glistening as he held out his hand. "Daktari Rawlings." He looked down at the memorial stone. "All of us remember Timmy."

Jace wasn't prone to flagrant displays of emotion but struggled to find his voice behind the walnut in his throat. Instead of speaking, he just nodded.

The chaplain unfolded a sheet of paper from his coat pocket and laid it against the stone. Then he shaded the paper, rubbing with the edge of a pencil, lifting the image of the cross from the stone to the paper. He stood in silence for a moment before handing the paper to Jace. "The O'Reillys wanted this to be the only message on the stone."

The chaplain smiled as Jace struggled to find his voice. "Uh, sure." All he could see was the image of his sister's little wooden cross as flames devoured it in his vow not to serve the God it represented.

John Otieno nodded. "Kind of changes everything, doesn't it?" He turned to go. "You take care, Daktari." With that, he turned and walked down the path to the opposite end of the cemetery.

Jace didn't follow. He wasn't ready. Not yet. Instead, he walked through the tall grass to the place the chaplain had been kneeling a few moments before. There was another flat memorial stone.

Jace read the inscription. Mary Otieno. The dates revealed that she had died a dozen years ago, at age five. *The chaplain's daughter?*

Somehow, it didn't surprise him. Death in Africa was so common. A family that had not suffered an untimely loss was the exception, not the rule.

Common, but so unfair. Why does suffering have to mark this land?

He looked at his watch. He was going to be late. He looked down the path that stretched through the remaining stones. *No, not today.* Instead of heading through, he turned around and backtracked toward the road.

What was I thinking, passing through this place of death?

John Okombo hated using the phone. He much preferred a face-to-face confrontation, where he could use his size to his advantage. But the phone was a necessary tool. He dialed and listened. As he waited, he twirled a hand-rolled Virginian cigar in his fingers, a small gift in anticipation of a huge deal he had made with Virginian politicians.

On the other end, he heard Simeon. "Jambo, sir."

"You did well."

"You refer to the American doctor?" Simeon asked.

"Of course."

"You sound surprised. I told you he would respond to my call."

"Have you made the other necessary arrangements?"

"Yes. It will be untraceable. I have a friend in the Mungiki. He is only too willing to carjack a wealthy westerner."

The MP shook his head. He didn't like working with the Mungiki, a radical political-religious cult, but he did like their efficiency. "I want you to call it off."

"Call it off? But payment has been made. It won't—"

"Delayed, not canceled. I have need of the doctor."

"Not your heart, I hope." Simeon chuckled, and Okombo could hear something rattling. He imagined the witch doctor shaking bones in a jar, working on some new incantation. "If you are having problems, I may have an answer for you here."

"No, no, not for me, my friend." Okombo hesitated. "Someone else needs him. After he is done, your Mungiki friend can make the American disappear."

"Fine, fine. I'll make the change."

"Can you assure his safety until I call you again?"

"Security and prosperity. An expensive proposition. It will cost you, Mr. Okombo."

The MP drew hard on the cigar and blew smoke rings at the ceiling. "Put it on my tab."

9

Jace looked around the table laden with a Western feast of chicken, potatoes, rolls, and salad. To his right sat Ellen and Dave Fitzgerald— the *other* general surgeon in Kijabe. To his left and across from him sat Blake and Kim Anderson. Beside Kim was Sue Watkins, a nurse educator in the Kijabe Hospital school of nursing.

Blake extended his hands to Kim and Jace. *Great,* Jace thought, *another honored Christian tradition. We get to hold hands.* He remembered how during high school, he used to try to sit next to a pretty girl, anticipating this very thing. But that wasn't the case now. Hiding his discomfort, he took Blake's and Dave's hands. Blake smiled. "Jace, would you pray for our meal?"

Jace blinked. Pray? *Of course, pray! Out loud. Now.* He opened his mouth. Nothing. His mind was blank. It had been years since he'd been put on the spot for what must have been a routine spiritual duty here in Kijabe. Surely he could pull this off. He looked around the table. All participants had their eyes closed. He cleared his throat.

Before he could begin, his conscience assailed him. *What a poser! You fraud!*

What could he do? He'd heard his father do this a thousand times. But how could he explain that what was routine to his father hadn't worn off on him? How could he say it? It just didn't "take"?

Jace cleared his throat. As he began, a memorized childhood prayer fleeted across his mind. *I can't say that!* He looked at the others, whose heads were bowed reverently, waiting for him to begin. Of course, he could do this. He paused. His memory did not fail. He would have to use the old prayer. "Dear Father, thank You for Your great blessings and the provision that has been set before us. Bless this food and may we use it in Thy service." He hesitated again, this time for extra spiritual emphasis, the way his father had, before adding in a sober bass voice, "Amen!"

Jace felt a stab of embarrassment. *Stupid! Why did I say "thy?" I never talk that way.* He'd just revealed his lack of Christian maturity to the boss. *Fine work, Jace.* He felt like he'd just shown Jeff Gordon how fast Jace's VW Beetle was off the line. He wanted to excuse himself, but the damage was done.

He avoided their eyes and loaded his plate. Meals like this would be a rarity in coming weeks as he fended for himself in the kitchen.

Kim Anderson had a delightful Australian accent. "Well, Dr. Rawlings, tell us about your family. Do you have children?"

Jace looked up from his plate, now heavy with chicken and mashed potatoes. "No, no kids." It was a sore spot for Jace. But what was an irritation for Jace was an unrelenting ache for Heather. He felt Kim's eyes on him, waiting for more. "My wife stayed at home." He cleared his throat. "For now," he chuckled. "I guess she wanted to see how things would go." He smiled. "How about you?"

"Three girls," she said. "But they are eating with friends."

"So," Dave Fitzgerald started, "I hear back in Virginia, you're the surgeon to the stars."

Leave it to the surgeon in the group to be direct.

Jace shrugged. "Don't believe everything you hear."

"Don't be modest. CNN reported that you saved the life of your governor."

Jace wished attention would turn elsewhere. If they knew about the governor of Virginia, they had to know about the swirl of controversy that followed. The Internet had made the world too small and uncomfortable for those wishing to hide in anonymity. "The governor is a fine man, a friend. But he is no more worthy of having a competent surgeon than the people of Kenya are."

Blake nodded. "Well said."

A shrill beeping interrupted the conversation. Dave excused himself to use the phone.

Jace took a bite of chicken; it was certainly different from the tough Kenyan chicken he remembered from his childhood. He chewed, happy that the focus was off him for now.

A minute later Dave came back to the table, shaking his head. "I need to eat and run, I'm afraid."

Blake nodded. "What's up?"

"A triple treat," he said, laughing. "Head injury, perirectal abscess, and an old mzee who hasn't been able to urinate all day." He paused. "Say, if you're willing," he said, looking at Jace, "I could use your help."

Jace thought about the problems. He wasn't a neurosurgeon. He wasn't a urologist. But he had drained a perirectal abscess during his general surgery internship, and he was comfortable doing open-heart surgery. Certainly he could figure out a way to lend a hand. Selfishly, he wanted to observe Dr. Fitzgerald on the job before he faced the same problems alone during his first night of call. Jace nodded. "Sure."

Dave grunted. "Eat fast."

Ten minutes later, Jace trailed Dave as they walked into the casualty department. Dave walked fast, and Jace felt as if he were a medical student again. They met an intern, Margaret Mwaka. "Show me the head-injury patient first," Dave said.

The Kenyan intern was professional and controlled. "Over here," she said, pulling back a curtain. "Twenty-eight-year-old male thrown from the back of a pickup truck. Arrived conscious with a GCS of fourteen. We got a chest X-ray and C-spines and saw no fracture. Ten minutes after arrival back in casualty, he blew his right pupil and GCS dropped to six."

"Is theater ready?"

"Waitin' on you."

"What else do we have?"

She pointed at an old man in a shuka, traditional dress for the Maasai tribe. "Hasn't been able to void all day. Bladder palpable at his umbilicus. Nurses tried a Foley and failed." She moved to the next stretcher. "This gentleman has a large perirectal abscess."

"Set our urinary retention patient up in recovery room. I'll show Dr. Rawlings here how to get a catheter in while you prep the trauma patient for the burr holes." Dave looked at Jace. "Think you can drain the perirectal abscess while we do the head trauma?"

"Sure." Jace spoke with feigned confidence and followed the seasoned general surgeon to the theater.

Dave didn't look convinced. "How long's it been since you've done any general surgery?"

Jace shrugged. "Residency."

"Do you want me to get the intern to drain the abscess?"

"No. I, uh—I can do it."

Dave nodded. "Okay. I'll be in the next room if you need help."

Jace changed into scrubs and watched as Dr. Fitzgerald deftly placed a Foley catheter using a flexible metal stiffener, resulting in over a liter of urine.

The surgeon nodded. "Normal capacity of the male bladder is around 450 ccs. This guy will need to keep the catheter for a few days to let the bladder muscle recover. We'll likely need to do a prostatectomy to help his flow." He paused. "Do you have any experience in prostatectomy?"

Jace shrugged. "I've never even seen one."

"I guess I'll just have to show you how." His voice was pleasant, but his expression gave a clear message: *Worthless subspecialist!*

As Dave went off to start the head-trauma patient, a nurse came out of the second operating room. "I have the patient's spinal in. We are ready for you to drain the abscess, Dr. Rawlings."

Jace wished he'd had a chance to look the procedure up. He took a deep breath. *Hey, I can do cardiac valve surgery. How hard can this be?*

He followed the nurse into the room to see the male patient up in stirrups as if he were ready to deliver a baby. At least the problem was obvious. An angry reddened swelling looked ready to burst. Jace nodded at a scrub assistant. "I'm Dr. Rawlings. First day," he added, shrugging.

"My name is Michael. The scrub sink is out there."

Jace stepped back into the hall and began scrubbing his hands at the sink. In a moment, Dave Fitzgerald joined him. "This ain't heart surgery, Jace. You can stop scrubbing now."

He felt his face flush. He stepped to the door. *Wow,* he thought. *If only my cardiothoracic surgery partners in Virginia could see me now. Big American heart surgeon draining a perirectal abscess.* He chuckled at the irony. Surgery could be humbling stuff.

He pushed open the swinging door. *It's just a test, Jace. They want to see what you're made of.*

He positioned himself between the patient's legs, and the assistant handed him a knife. *Thank God for an assistant who knows what to do.*

He felt the skin, tense and stretched over the abscess. He stood with the knife poised over the skin. *Here goes nothing.*

He stabbed the skin, releasing a large amount of pus. He smiled behind his mask. *Just like riding a bike.*

He stood looking at the operative field for a moment, saying nothing. The tech asked. "Would you like to irrigate?"

Sure, that's the next step. "Irrigation," he said.

He irrigated the wound and applied a gauze dressing. Standing back, he mused how as a heart surgeon he had dreamed of coming to Kenya to do open-heart surgery—high-tech, critical operations. Yet here he was doing what many surgeons would consider the most basic and useful of operations: the evacuation of pus. His dreams were being downsized, one notch at a time. First, an overnight in the local jail, suspicions of local Kenyans inside and outside the government, and now, an opportunity to operate at last—and what do they give him to do? *Butt pus, the bane of all surgery.*

He walked out and washed his hands again before walking into theater number one. There, Dave Fitzgerald was instructing the intern over a sleeping patient.

"The dilated pupil indicates increased pressure inside the skull, likely from a bleed. Where do you make the first burr hole?"

The intern was confident. "Temple area, above and in front of the ear."

"Which side?"

"The side with the dilated pupil."

"Correct. What if both are blown?"

"On the side with the pupil that blew first."

"Okay. If you don't find blood at the first burr hole, where do you drill next?"

"Occipitoparietal."

"The third hole?"

"Frontal, at the hairline."

"Excellent. What's the prognosis?"

"If we are quick to drain the blood before there is serious damage, the reversal of symptoms and the recovery can be very rapid. If all we do is a burr hole, the intervention is quite minor. He could be normal in a week or two."

Jace listened intently. *Yes, I know that from personal experience.* He wished for a piece of paper. He needed to be taking notes. The intern knew more about head trauma than he did. The last time he'd treated a head-trauma patient, he was an intern at the University of Virginia—and there, they had a CT scan to show the surgeon exactly where to drill. Here, out in the middle of remote Africa, the surgeons had to rely on physical findings and the patient's clinical course in order to decide when and where to drill. Without the advanced technology available in the West, the surgeons in Africa had to be *better* than their American counterparts. That thought was new for Jace.

His gut tightened. How would he ever be able to face everything that came through the casualty doors when he was on call? Who was he fooling? Certainly not himself.

When the surgery pair started drilling the first burr hole, Jace was mesmerized. He raised his hand and explored the tender scar well hidden beneath his hair.

It had only been eight weeks since he'd been the patient in an identical operation.

An hour later, after the lights in the operating theaters were out and the orders were written, Jace exited the hospital beneath the expanse of the African sky. He felt out of control. He longed for cardiac cases, where he knew what to expect and where he enjoyed ruling his small kingdom. But here, he felt alone and on unsure footing. *Why does everything have to be so hard?* He raised a fist to the sky.

And listened.

Around him, a chorus of crickets faded to background noise as he tilted his head, turning an ear to a silent, mocking sky.

There were no answers beyond the accusations in his own mind—the guilt that drove him, occasionally with the sharpness of a surgeon's scalpel, but always with a dull emptiness asking for satiety that never came.

Then suddenly, he laughed. Not from joy, but from the irony of a tiny speck that dared lift a fist in the face of the universe.

And Jace knew, as certainly as he understood the complexities of the physical heart, the muscle he'd dissected a thousand times, that the heartbeat of his soul had faltered along the way.

He'd been avoiding a confrontation with the source. He lowered his fist and slowly opened his hand, watching an involuntary twitch and pushing aside a doubt about his readiness.

Beneath the twinkling of the night sky, he again turned toward the cemetery.

A few minutes later, he entered the graveyard via the dirt path leading from the hospital parking lot toward the housing units on the other side. As was so typical for Kijabe, cool wind rose from the floor of the valley and swept across the edge of the Rift Valley escarpment, battering the leaves into rhythmic applause. The grass was tall and needed cutting, something that would be done by hand with a Kenyan sickle. Gravestones, mostly small, some leaning as if they were burdened with age, stretched in rows on either side of the path. Rows of dead patients. Rows of the missionaries who came to serve on the African continent, lives given unfairly and prematurely to malaria, typhoid, and Rift Valley fever.

This, to Jace, was the ultimate slap in the face. What kind of divine message was this—that sacrificing a life for God would mean the loss of loved ones in return? Parents had come to Africa, filled with glorious hope of converts; instead they had buried their children.

He slowed his pace, aware of the moonlit shadows of tree limbs dancing on the ground in front of him. They swayed to a funeral march. Two-thirds of his way through the field of death, he paused, looking at the branches of a eucalyptus. Hands lifted high toward a distant God.

Jace turned, his heart quickening. He moved forward, his legs parting the tall grass. Ahead of him, and to the right, a blur of fur startled him. A mongoose had been digging at the foot of a grave-stone. He took a deep breath and continued, counting the stones from the edge of the path.

At twelve, he stopped and leaned over a flat stone. He knelt in the tall grass and began to brush away the dirt from its surface, his hand trembling.

"Janice Elaine Rawlings," he whispered, tracing the letters with his finger.

"O-okay," he stuttered. "I've come back. Now what?"

Twenty meters from the edge of the cemetery, Lydia Otieno leaned over the kitchen sink and squinted at the outline of a dim figure in the moonlight. "John," she said. "I think you'll want to see this."

The chaplain rose from his chair, switched off the kitchen light, and stared out beyond a row of bougainvillea. In the cemetery, a solitary figure knelt over a grave marker.

"It's Dr. Rawlings," he said softly.

His wife nodded and placed her hand on her husband's shoulder.

"The battle is beginning," he whispered. "We need to pray."

Other than the day of her burial, this was the first time Jace had dared visit his sister's grave, had dared to confront his painful past.

He didn't know what to expect. A voice perhaps? Another vision?

Instead, what he experienced was an amplification of the jumbled noise he'd carried around for so many years. Guilt. His parents' loss. He cupped his hands over his ears and rocked forward, with so many voices echoing within him. His father's voice. *All things work together for good. His ways are higher than our ways.* Platitudes that spoke to the mind but not the heart. Janice's scream as she fell.

He shook his head in a vain attempt to silence the memories. "Janice. I'm so sorry, I'm so sorry, I—" his voice cracked— "am sorry."

A world away in America, he had pushed hard in pursuit of career and professional reputation. As long as he did, his guilt withdrew into the background, a nuisance, nothing more. But all of that changed when he met Anita Franks. Something about her brought Janice to his mind. She was fresh, different from Heather, and apparently open for play. And so, guilt slipped off its background perch and began an assault for recognition.

He wouldn't have recognized that he'd planned a medical mission to Kenya to soothe his conscience. But it wasn't always easy for Jace to see the obvious.

The grave marker in front of him was flat, with little to distinguish it from the others. But for Jace, it seemed to loom like the Washington Monument over the Mall.

"Dr. Rawlings."

Jace recognized the bass voice of John Otieno and looked up.

"I live just over there and saw you. Is everything okay?"

"Sure." He stood. He wanted away from the big man, but the chaplain stood between Jace and the way back out of the cemetery. He stepped to the side, but John moved to block him. Jace sighed and looked back down at the grave marker.

"I remember Janice," Otieno said. "I used to chase her out of the hospital after hours. She was always hanging around watching your father."

"From the time she was in the first grade, she always said she wanted to be a surgeon."

The chaplain nodded and smiled.

"She wanted to come back here, be a missionary surgeon."

"And you?"

"My desire to enter medicine came later in life. In college."

The old chaplain chuckled. "When you were here, all we heard about was Jace and rugby. We thought you'd anchor the first American team in the World Cup."

Jace smiled and looked at the large Kenyan. A fine spray of wrinkles dignified his face. Whatever wear and tear his skin showed, he'd earned the right to wear it through years of hard work and his share of tears over the troubles of his people.

"This is it, isn't it, Jace?"

"It?"

"The reason you came back." He knelt beside the grave. "The answer is right here."

Jace choked on the apple in his throat and swallowed hard. "Janice asked—" he paused, then rephrased his thought—"would have wanted me to do this."

10

When Jace finally went to bed, his mind refused to rest. He thought about all he'd seen in the operating rooms, especially how deftly the surgeons had dealt with the intracranial bleeding for the head-injury patient. And that brought back a mental rehearsal of all that led up to his own similar injury not long before.

He'd been on call the night governor Stuart Franks felt sudden chest pain and collapsed at a fundraising dinner for Virginia's Special Olympics. By the time Jace was called, the governor was clearly in a fight for his life. Jace walked past the bodyguards on his way into an ICU room crowded with two nurses, a respiratory therapist, and two cardiologists.

Dr. Robert Hawthorne looked up. "Hey, Jace, thanks for coming."

Governor Franks was fifty-five, overweight, and lying in a tangle of monitoring cables and drainage tubes. He was unresponsive except for the rhythmic rise and fall of his chest with the mechanical ventilator. His blood pressure, recorded on the monitor, was seventy systolic.

Cardiologist Hawthorne pointed at a portable echo machine at the bedside. "He's had a massive MI. I cathed him, was able to open up a 90 percent LAD lesion and a second 80 percenter of the circumflex. Problem is, he's developed an acute mitral regurgitation. Seems to have ruptured attachments to his mitral valve."

The second cardiologist, James Green, nodded. "With maximal pressors, we just can't get his pressure up to snuff. He's barely staying out of heart failure. As it is, we had to sedate him and put him on the ventilator just so he could be oxygenated."

Jace studied the monitor screen on the ultrasound machine. Slowly, he replayed the video. "Wow. Look at this," he said, pointing at the screen. "You can see his mitral valve leaflets just flopping in the breeze, totally uncoordinated."

"He needs a new valve. Tonight. I'm afraid he won't last the night if we let this keep on."

Jace took a deep breath. "Agreed. Has anyone talked to his wife?"

"On and off all evening," Hawthorne said. "She's in the waiting room with her husband's chief of staff, Ryan Meadows. Come with me, I'll introduce you."

The cardiologist led Jace down the hall from the ICU to a private seating area that they used for patients' families. When he pushed open the door, Jace peered in to see a young, fit, bottle-blonde Anita Franks leaning forward and holding hands with Ryan Meadows. Jace's first thought was that this was the governor's daughter.

"Mrs. Franks," Dr. Hawthorne began, "I'd like to introduce you to Dr. Rawlings. He's a heart surgeon."

This was the wife, then. She released the hand of the chief of staff to reach out to Jace. "Anita Franks." Her voice trembled. "A surgeon?"

Jace nodded. "Your husband's heart attack has damaged his mitral valve, the valve between the main pumping chamber, the left ventricle, and the left atrium, the chamber that receives the blood back from the lungs." Jace unfolded a laminated card he kept in his coat pocket and pointed. "Here," he said. "The heart attack has injured the valve so that it is now incompetent. What that means is that blood is allowed to flow in two directions across the valve instead of just one."

Anita Franks nodded.

"Instead of allowing blood to flow only into the main pumping chamber, the left ventricle, blood sloshes back and forth across the valve, so that extra blood is pushing back out into the lungs." Jace paused, searching her face for clues of understanding.

"That's why he's having such a hard time breathing?"

"Exactly." Jace sat across from the duo so that he would be at eye level. "We need to replace the valve with a mechanical one."

"When?"

"As soon as possible. The heart doctors are doing everything they can, and your husband's heart is failing. I fear that if we don't replace the valve soon, we may lose the only window of opportunity we have." Jace paused again. "Without surgery, he may not survive the night."

"And with surgery?"

"I won't sugarcoat it. This is very risky. But I'd give him a fifty-fifty chance with surgery."

Anita looked at Ryan.

He touched a graying sideburn of his perfect hair. "It's your choice, Anita."

She squirmed and tugged at the edge of a too-short skirt. "I have to give him the chance." She looked at Jace, her eyes pleading. "Do what you have to do to save my husband."

On Monday, Jace went to the hospital early and found his assigned intern on the Wairegi ward, the men's ward named after a generous male patient. Dr. Fitzgerald had divided his service, handing Jace a few post-op patients so he could share the load.

Jace looked into the bright face of his intern, Dr. Paul Mwaka. Paul held out his hand. "I hope that you will allow me to assist in heart surgery."

Jace found himself chuckling. "I only hope we'll be given the chance." He paused, looking at a stack of charts. "Can you introduce me to the patients?"

Paul nodded and lifted the top chart. Lean, mostly legs and lungs, he was built like he'd be at home running a marathon.

As they worked through the list, Jace couldn't help noticing the reversed role. He was the attending surgeon, but the intern was teaching him. Fortunately, Paul was experienced, and Jace deftly stepped around his own lack of knowledge by assuming the role of teacher: He questioned the intern. But instead of testing him, Jace was learning.

The first patient on their rounds had had prostate surgery the day before. Jace felt his gut tighten. He'd had a total of one month's training in urology years ago during his own internship. "Do you want to stop the bladder irrigation?"

Paul shook his head. "Not yet. We'd better wait until the urine isn't so red."

"And what might happen if you stop the irrigation too soon?"

"The catheter may get clogged with a clot, causing the bladder to leak through the suture-closure."

Jace nodded as if he'd known the answer all along. "Of course."

The intern handed Jace a chart. Jace reached for it with his left hand, and the chart slipped from his grip and landed on the floor, opening the two-ringed binder and spilling the papers. As Paul hurried to collect the papers, the intern apologized. "Pole sana," he said softly. *I'm so sorry.* It was Kenyan custom. Apologize even when it's not your fault.

Jace rubbed his left hand. He'd been through rehabilitation. He'd come a long way, but a slight residual weakness remained in his grip strength. He pushed the next thought from his mind. *I'm ready.* He didn't want to consider the next accusation that assaulted him. *What if I drop an instrument at a critical moment during surgery?*

Almost without thinking, Jace felt and traced the scar on his right scalp buried beneath his hair. When he became conscious that his intern was watching him, he turned away.

Jace's left hand twitched, but he quickly covered the jerky movement by clasping his hands together. Had the intern noticed? "Shall we see the next patient?"

That evening, Jace picked up the phone in his small flat after the second ring. He'd been waiting for business on this, his first night of general surgery call. The book on his lap was open to a page describing treatment of sigmoid volvulus, a common condition in Africa where the colon twists on itself, causing an emergency obstruction.

"Dr. Rawlings."

"Ah, Dr. Rawlings, I'm glad to find you at home. I'm calling from the customs office at Jomo Kenyatta International Airport. I believe we have some of your equipment."

Jace sighed. "Yes."

The voice on the other end spoke with a Kenyan accent. Although firm, he spoke very softly, another Kenyan distinction. "We have made an assessment of value on the equipment. We are authorized to release it to you after payment of an import tax."

"How much?"

"Five hundred thousand shillings."

Jace shook his head. *That's over five thousand dollars!* "Look," he said. "I've talked to the minister of health. He told me he would help me get my equipment through customs. The equipment was donated at no cost to me. It has no value except to the needy patients of Kenya." Jace sighed. "Do you have the letter from Compassion Industries? They donated the equipment and arranged to have it air-freighted to arrive with me."

The man laughed. "Of course I have the letter."

"It explains that the equipment is used and is of no retail value."

"I understand how the system works, Dr. Rawlings. Your hospital devalues used equipment over a few years so that they will not be taxed. But this does not mean that the items have no value in

Kenya, correct? Also you will earn a great deal as a result of using the equipment. I know this equipment is for heart surgery."

"Yes. Heart surgery on those who cannot afford to pay me for the service."

The man on the other end of the phone scoffed. "We cannot keep such items in our warehouse forever. The storage fee is five thousand shillings a week."

"Please," Jace found himself begging. "I cannot pay such a fee. Talk to the Honorable John Okombo. He will vouch for me." He winced at his own words. Truthfully, he *could* pay the fee. He had the money. But it was the principle of the matter. His father had passed that Rawlings stubbornness on to Jace: *If you pay the bribe, it will only make it worse for the next doctor trying to help.*

More laughter. "Dr. Rawlings, Minister Okombo is the very man who told me to reduce my fee to five hundred thousand bob."

Jace hesitated. Was this a bluff? If he caved to such a demand, would more money be exacted in the future?

"Next week, the cost will be 505," he said. "You may pick up your equipment between nine and four on business days."

Jace was about to speak, but realized that a click had signaled the end of the call.

Jace looked down at the book on the table in front of him. *I came here to do hearts, not untwist locked colons!*

Do I dare ask the hospital to help me get my equipment through customs?

He shook his head to answer his own thought. No, that would certainly end the program before it began.

The phone rang again.

He lifted the receiver. "Dr. Rawlings."

"Dr. Rawlings, it's Paul. I have a patient in casualty with free air."

Again, his gut tightened. Free air was medical lingo for a perforated intestine or stomach. They called the air free because it was not confined to the intestinal tract. It had been years since he'd handled any such problem, and in residency, he always had an attending to hold his hand. Now *he* was the attending, feeling like the captain of a ship without a rudder.

Jace took a deep breath. "I'll be right there."

11

Heather lifted the schnauzer onto the table and scratched him behind the ears. "It's okay, buddy. Dr. Meadows just wants to look at you."

She'd shown up to walk one of her afternoon regulars, a miniature schnauzer named Skippy, only to find him listless and vomiting. Before walking a pair of Maltese, she had brought Skippy to the vet.

Dr. Steve Meadows frowned. "The blood tests show an elevation of amylase."

Heather squinted. "And that indicates …"

"Pancreatitis. This breed is prone to it. Maybe little Skippy got into the trash and ate some fatty food of some sort." He paused, stroking the silver-gray coat of the young animal. "Every time he eats, the pancreas has to work, so we'll have to force him to fast for a few days. I need to keep him here with an IV."

"I'll let his owner know."

Dr. Meadows smiled. A row of perfect teeth. He brushed his hand against hers as she held onto Skippy's collar. "How are you doing?" He seemed to hesitate before adding, "I heard your husband left for Africa."

She nodded. "Who told you?"

"My brother. Ryan is the political one in the family. He's the governor's chief of staff."

She studied his blue eyes. They were soft, caring. She wasn't sure how much to say. "I'm okay."

He nodded. "Do you like tea?" He pointed to a shipping box in the corner. "Ever since my brother made friends with the Kenyan leaders, I'm swimming in this stuff."

He lifted a smaller green box from the larger corrugated one. "Here," he said. "I'm serious."

She accepted the gift. "Thanks."

"Ryan told me about you."

She felt her face flushing. "What would he know about me?"

The veterinarian shrugged. "Thought your husband was a fool for leaving."

She thought about telling him that the separation was her idea, but didn't. Maybe it wasn't such a bad thing if he thought she'd been abandoned. Instead, she offered a polite smile and stayed quiet, gripping her box of Kenyan tea.

He scribbled something on a clipboard chart as an assistant entered. Heather took a step toward the door.

Dr. Meadows stopped her with a gentle touch of her shoulder. "Take care. You can call me for an update on Skippy tomorrow."

Inside the operating theater, a fifty-one-year-old Kenyan was being put under anesthesia. Outside, Jace Rawlings stood at the scrub sink and tried to calm his runaway heart. Other than draining the peri-rectal abscess, this would be his maiden voyage as a surgeon since his accident. To make things worse, his intern had abandoned him to see another patient in casualty.

He scrubbed each finger with a bristle-brush, working up a rich brown iodine-based lather. He held out his left hand and frowned behind his mask. A fine tremor had returned.

He'd called the Fitzgerald house to get some advice from the experienced general surgeon on station, but had talked only to his wife. Dave was in bed, having been up late operating the last three nights. Jace told Ellen not to bother him. He'd call if he needed him.

He felt sweat on his brow in spite of the night's sixty-degree temperature. Because of the high altitude, Kijabe temperatures plunged when the sun dove below the horizon. He looked through a window in the door separating him from his patient. *What are you doing? You've never operated on a patient like this alone. You are a cardiac surgeon. What do you know about this?*

He was well trained, he tried to reassure himself. Surgery was surgery. If he could replace a heart valve, he could do this. He backed into the room holding his hands in front of him. Unlike back in Richmond, here he was expected to gown and glove himself, something he did awkwardly, contaminating one gown in the process. When the scrub tech, a young man named David, saw him struggle, he assisted in gloving Jace.

When they had the first pair on, David held up a second pair. "Better double glove, Dr. Rawlings." He paused. "HIV is everywhere."

Jace nodded and felt his gut tighten another notch.

A few minutes later, with the abdomen of the sleeping patient prepped and draped, Jace found himself throwing out a silent prayer. *Help!*

"Knife." Jace held out his hand and accepted the scalpel. *I can do this.* He guided the blade across the abdomen starting just under the sternum. A red stripe followed the knife. He touched an electric-pencil cauterizing instrument against the bleeders.

He worked on, opening, identifying a hole in the ileum, tying, resecting, irrigating, sewing, and closing. At every step, when he hesitated, the scrub tech quietly helped by handing him the instrument or suture he needed. Jace was humbled. Rescued.

Later that night, Jace sank into the only soft chair in his small living room, fighting emotion that he thought he'd conquered in training. Self-doubt had set up camp on his doorstep since his accident, and he wondered where the confident Jace had gone. *Instead of just putting his bowel back together, should I have brought out the proximal end as a stoma? Will the anastomosis hold together? I should have called for the surgeon's advice. Pride!*

Who am I fooling? he thought as he gripped his trembling left hand. *Did I come here because I feared I'd fail in Virginia with everyone watching?*

Jace fell into a fitful sleep at midnight, only to be called at three a.m. by his intern again. "Dr. Rawlings, I am admitting a girl who is in florid heart failure."

"Sounds like a medical problem," Jace responded, rubbing sleep from his eyes. "Why are you calling me?"

"She is very weak. She can barely talk. Her pressure is low."

Jace sighed. "How's her oxygen saturation?"

"I'm not sure our monitor is picking up properly. It reads seventy."

"She needs to be intubated, put on the ventilator."

"I'm not sure she will survive the night. She is very afraid."

"She'll need a pressor drip. Does the hospital have dopamine?"

"Yes."

"I still don't understand. Why aren't you calling the medicine doctor? I'm a surgeon."

"I know, sir. But she came in asking for you. She said that she's your patient."

"My patient? There must be some mistake."

"It's no mistake, sir. She is from Kibera. A girl named Beatrice."

12

The Kijabe Hospital casualty department was a sixty-by-twenty-foot rectangle filled with stretchers separated by old curtains. Jace found Beatrice Wanjiku on a stretcher, sitting bolt upright, sweat beading off her slick dark skin.

It took one look, a ten-second assessment of the ABCs—airway, breathing, circulation—and Jace knew she was in trouble. Life-threatening, in-your-face, I-can't-get-my-breath trouble. In his time as a cardiothoracic surgeon, Jace had watched plenty of people who looked better than this go south and die in a hurry.

He looked at a nurse. "This patient needs to be intubated now. Do you have a crash cart somewhere?"

"It is just there," she said, pointing to a wooden cart on wheels in the corner of the room.

He laid his stethoscope against Beatrice's back and moved it up and down, listening to her shallow and labored breathing. To his intern, he said. "This is classic for wet rales. They go most of the way up her back." He pointed to the veins in her neck. "Here," he said, "she has jugular venous distention up to the angles of the jaw. You will not see a better example of heart failure."

Paul nodded. "I was able to start a small IV in her hand."

"Give furosemide 80 mg. stat. We need to chip her out."

Paul's expression told Jace he didn't understand.

"Sorry, I'm using slang. We need to cause her to get rid of extra fluid. We say that's making her dry like a potato chip, so we say *chipping her out.*"

The nurse frowned.

Jace understood the dilemma. In Kenya, potato chips were called crisps. In Kenya, if you asked for potato chips, you'd get what Americans call fries. "Okay, we'll call it *crisping her out.*"

Jace assembled supplies, preparing to slide a breathing tube down into his patient's trachea. That way, when breathing became too hard for her, the machine could do the work. From the looks of his patient, he didn't have much time.

Jace looked at the nurse again. "I'll need some sedative. Do you have Versed and fentanyl?"

"I will bring them."

Jace stood beside his patient and explained, "You are wearing out, Beatrice. You will die soon if we can't support your breathing."

Her eyes widened. "Help me," she whispered.

"I'm going to give you something to relax you. You won't remember."

Jace instructed the intern, gave the IV medication, and placed a mask over the patient's mouth. He used an inflatable bag known as an Ambu bag to push oxygen into his patient's lungs. Then, after the patient was no longer fighting, he slid a metal laryngoscope blade into her mouth, pushing the tongue to the side. He stood by his intern at the head of the bed, staring down through the patient's open mouth toward her feet. "There," he said, "can you see the vocal cords? Slide the end of the tube through there."

Paul slid the tube into place and inflated a balloon-cuff to keep air from escaping around the tube. "I'm in."

"Good job. Let's get her up to the HDU. Call the medicine doctor. I want all the help we can get to stabilize her."

The next morning, it took two hours of phone calls to finally get the Honorable John Okombo on the phone.

Jace looked at his watch. "Thank you for taking time to speak to me."

"Dr. Rawlings, my pleasure."

"Did you know that Beatrice was admitted to Kijabe Hospital last night?"

He heard a faint "Excuse me" and the cessation of background noise. He imagined the MP was stepping away from the ears of others at the mention of his secret daughter. After a moment, Jace heard Minister Okombo's strong bass voice spoken just above a whisper. "I was unaware. How is she?"

"She's in heart failure. The damaged valve is worse. She is alive because a machine is forcing oxygen into her lungs."

"Do everything, Daktari. I'm indebted to you."

Jace decided to play hardball with the politician. He might never have this kind of leverage again. "I need my equipment."

"I told customs to release it to you."

"Yes, for five hundred thousand shillings. I don't have funds for such a bribe."

"Bribe? This is an import tax."

"For a donated, used item? The pump has value only for your people."

"I've already instructed them to give you a fair price. They assured me that they could have asked for much, much more."

"I spent the night at her bedside adding and adjusting her meds. Beatrice may need surgery soon. If we can't stabilize her, there will be nothing I can do without my equipment."

"Surely, to an American heart surgeon, our tax is like buying weekly groceries. I know you would make this amount in one surgery at home."

Jace frowned. The MP was right. He *could* afford it. It was a matter of principle. But at that moment, Jace wasn't sure if the MP was bluffing or if, in fact, he was bluffing himself. *Would I really let my patient die if I could save her for five thousand dollars?*

He knew the answer. He would move heaven and earth to save this girl if he had to. To lose a patient because of a political battle would be beyond unethical. But he needed the politician to believe that Jace would do just that. After all, tough decisions to limit care were made *every day* in Kenya.

He hesitated. "Beatrice may not last long. I'd hate it if she didn't make it because of lack of equipment. Should I transfer her to a heart surgeon in Nairobi?" He tapped on the phone. "Or maybe you could arrange an air evacuation to South Africa?"

"You are a more than capable surgeon. Moving her could be risky."

"My hands are tied."

"Pay the fee. I'll see to it that your equipment arrives."

"Drop the fee, and I'll do what I can to convince the hospital to take her as our first open-heart case."

"Don't play games with my daughter's life."

"Exactly," Jace responded. "Don't play dangerous games with me. I've lost many patients before. But have you lost a daughter?"

The MP huffed.

"Even if I get my equipment, there are still many hurdles."

"But you will try?"

"If I get my equipment."

Jace listened as the MP's voice became muffled. It sounded as if he had covered the phone with his hand while he engaged in a cascade of rhythmic cursing. After only a few seconds, he heard a clicking sound and the dial tone.

His appeal to the MP was over.

In Richmond, governor Stuart Franks sat behind his massive oak desk staring at the medical examiner's report. He looked up at his chief of staff, Ryan Meadows, and slapped the paper. "Who knows about this?"

"Just the folks down at the medical examiner's office. They released it to me only because I pressured them. I told them I represented you. Since it's officially a medical record, it can be accessed only by next of kin."

"And why has it taken so long for this to come to my attention?"

Ryan walked away. "Look, Stuart, I've sat on this for weeks. No one else knew. The police weren't investigating a homicide." He sighed. "I didn't want to tell you until you'd gotten back on your feet yourself."

The governor sighed. It had been a long road back. First, he'd had the massive heart attack and emergency surgery, then a postoperative stroke and pneumonia. Only this week had he been able to work a full day without napping. He knew his friend had his best interest at heart.

"I don't want the media getting hold of this." He shook his head and sighed. "I'd always hoped they were wrong about Anita." He ran his fingers through graying hair. When he looked up, his assistant was standing in the corner, looking out over the grounds of the governor's mansion. "I messed up, Ryan. I let my political drive take time away from her."

"She supported you, Stuart. Don't be so hard on—"

He lifted his hand to cut him off. "I should have been there for her. After her miscarriage, things were never quite the same."

Ryan poured himself and the governor two fingers of Maker's Mark Kentucky bourbon. "Do you understand what the report implies?" He lifted a glass to his lips. "Anita was raped. Ketamine is a powerful anesthetic."

"So she might have been innocent after all?"

"Did you trust her?" He tapped the top of the red wax-dipped bottle.

The governor looked away. "I don't know." He paused. "I wanted to believe her. I'd always hoped the media speculation was due to distortion from political enemies."

"And so maybe it was. But this ketamine takes her death to a whole new level."

"How is that?"

"If someone gave her ketamine as a date-rape drug, perhaps she was still groggy. Sure, she was hit by a passing motorist, but did the drug affect her ability to get out of the way?"

"You're suggesting homicide?"

Ryan shrugged. "Think about it, Stuart. Who has access to anesthetic drugs?"

"A heart surgeon."

"Who else was with her the night of her death?"

The governor walked around his desk and poured a second drink. When he spoke again, his voice was etched with anger. "You say you were protecting me by not sharing this with me sooner?"

Ryan's voice quivered. "Of course, sir."

"Stupid!" he said, spitting bourbon from his lips. "Stupid, stupid, stupid! By sitting on this information, you let Jace Rawlings slip away."

"What do you want me to do?"

"Keep this away from all other eyes. I'm going to talk to the chief of police and the attorney general. I want a DNA match on the semen found in my wife, proof that this was Rawlings."

"The man's made his escape."

"Some altruistic mission," Franks huffed. "He was running away."

13

That afternoon, Jace stood at the bedside of Michael Kagai, the patient with perforated bowel on whom he'd operated the evening before. Jace looked up when he heard his name.

"Hey, Jace, heard you were busy last night. Welcome to Kijabe." Dave Fitzgerald smiled.

Jace nodded. "Thanks." He handed him a chart. "Would you mind looking over this?" He gestured toward the patient in the bed. "I'm a little new at this general surgery stuff."

Jace watched as Dave leafed and *hmmed* his way through the chart, making short comments to himself. "Free air … perfed bowel … primary anastomosis." He handed the chart back. "Better check his HIV status and cover him with Cipro. Perforated ileum from typhoid fever is twenty-five times more common in HIV-positive patients than in the regular population."

Jace made a note. "Sure."

Dave moved closer and spoke to the patient in fluent Kiswahili. The patient responded and wrapped his hands over his chest. Dave then spoke again and the only thing Jace could pick out was "HIV."

"Whenever you order an HIV test," Dave explained, "you need permission. The test comes with counseling."

"Why did he do that, wrap his arms around his chest?"

Dave smiled as he walked away. "I told him you were a famous heart surgeon."

"What did he say?"

Fitzgerald mimicked the patient's actions. "He's protecting himself from you."

Jace mumbled, "Good idea." He walked up the hall toward the HDU, where he found his intern fumbling with an ultrasound probe. Paul pushed the machine toward their young heart-failure patient.

Jace placed the ultrasound probe over Beatrice's chest to evaluate her heart function. As he did, he taught his intern, Paul, how to interpret the images. "Here is the aortic valve. It's almost nonfunctional. See the blue and red color here? It shouldn't show flow both ways across the valve." Jace pushed a button to freeze the image, then moved the cursor over the wall of the left ventricle, measuring the thickness of the muscle. "See, it's too thick, hypertrophied as a result of working too hard."

"Her oxygen is better than last night," Paul said. "What do you think about an operation to replace the valve?"

"She needs it for sure, but I'm not sure we're ready. I still need my equipment, and that's only the first step. If I can get my equipment through customs, I'll need to ask my pump tech and a cardiac anesthesiologist to make an emergency trip. They told me they would if I could get everything ready." Jace sighed. "It takes a lot of blood to do this sort of thing. I'm not sure the blood bank is up to it."

Paul nodded. He smiled and added. "We are a people of faith at this hospital, Dr. Rawlings. I've seen God do miracles."

Jace stayed quiet. He'd asked God for a miracle only once.

And God hadn't come through.

So Jace hadn't been on close speaking terms with Him since.

He studied the chart a minute longer. "Give her an additional dose of Lasix tonight. If she looks better tomorrow, we may consider removing this ventilator."

Jace walked back to his little rented house hoping that God would hear Paul's prayers, but not daring to believe.

He replayed his conversation with the MP. It would be so much easier if his first case wasn't such a high-tension production. If he operated and failed and Beatrice died, the minister of health might force the program to shut down, defeating Jace before he could really test the waters. It might be best to drag his heels a bit. The heart program would be safer if Beatrice were to die without an operation than if Jace tried something risky and failed.

But Jace couldn't allow himself to travel far down that path. His training, his whole orientation, was to push as hard as he could for as long as he could with whatever means available in order to save a patient's life.

And with that approach, sometimes he lost. But when he did, he could still move forward, knowing that he'd given everything he could.

He sighed. *Why did his first case have to be a politician's daughter?* He'd had his fill of cases involving politicians. Invariably, memories of his other recent high-profile case came into focus. Looking back, he wished he'd never performed surgery on Stuart Franks.

Jace Rawlings stripped off his gown, pulling the disposable covering into a wad inside his sterile gloves, and threw it in the trash. The governor was still on the operating table behind him—critical, but at least alive. Jace thanked his staff and looked at the anesthesiologist. "Thanks, Joe. I'll see you in the ICU in a few minutes. I need to talk to the family."

He found Anita Franks sitting in a private, quiet room along with the governor's brother Bill and the governor's chief of staff. "Good news," he said. "We're all done."

Relief broke across their faces. Hugs were shared. Jace stood back and relished the moment.

"I had to replace the mitral valve. The operation went fine, but the governor still isn't out of the woods. Remember, it was an infarction that got him into this condition in the first place. We've only just now gotten him stabilized. It is going to be hour by hour for the next few days."

Anita stood. She was taller and slimmer than Heather, Jace thought. And certainly more youthful than the overweight governor. She brushed blonde strands of hair behind an ear pierced with two small gold rings.

Before he could react, she pulled him into a hug, gushing her thanks. When she pulled away, Jace saw a photographer just outside the privacy area, snapping away. *Paparazzi.*

Jace hurried to close the door to the intruding photographer.

Ryan Meadows shook his hand. "Would you like to talk to the press? We've arranged a room on the second floor for media updates."

Jace shook his head. "Not yet. Let's see how the night passes." He paused. "Just tell them the operation went as planned, but the governor is still considered critical."

He walked out, aware that cameras were clicking. His hug with Anita would make the front page of the *Richmond Times Dispatch*.

Jace awoke in Kijabe to the squawking of the ibis. He showered and was almost finished dressing when he heard pounding on his front door. He looked out the front door's inset window. A familiar Toyota Land Cruiser with the emblem of the Ministry of Health sat in the gravel driveway. He opened the door, leaving the metal bars in place, and found himself across the bars from two uniformed officers.

The first held up a badge. "Kenya Police. We've been instructed to bring you in for questioning."

Jace unlocked the bars. "On what charge?"

"Extortion of a government official. Bribery."

Jace sighed. He knew arguing with the officers would get him nowhere. They were pawns of someone in the government intent on making his life miserable. "Come in," Jace said. "I'm almost ready. Would you like some chai?"

The officers smiled. "Asante." Thank you.

Jace fixed the sweet milky tea and set three steaming mugs on the table.

"An American knows how to make Kenyan chai?" The taller of the two officers took a sip.

Jace nodded. "Kenya was my first home." He paused and shook his head. "But it seems Kenya doesn't love me anymore."

They sipped their tea and talked of an upcoming rugby World Cup match.

In fifteen minutes, Jace followed them to the vehicle. "This belongs to John Okombo. Did he send you to get me?"

"Our department is suffering. We have limited vehicles. Minister Okombo was kind enough to lend us his." The officer's large smile of perfect white teeth gave Jace the impression that he'd been handed the standard bull. *Of course Okombo sent you. He wants to show me how powerful he is.*

Jace stayed quiet during the trip, enduring yet another version of African NASCAR. They took him all the way back into Nairobi to a police station off Ngong road.

As they entered the two-room facility, Jace paused to let his eyes adjust. Either the electricity was off or they hadn't paid the light bill. The room was dark, dusty, and contained only a desk and two wooden chairs. A uniformed man with black hair and a well-trimmed moustache sat behind the desk. The men who had accompanied Jace greeted him with a nod. "Captain."

"So this is the American heart surgeon."

Jace squinted.

"Why is it that you insist on cluttering up my day, Dr. Rawlings? Certainly we have better things to do than to sort out your problems."

"I'm not sure what you're talking about."

"You are accused of bribing a government official."

"Ridiculous." Jace studied the men and pondered his next step. Ask for an attorney? He needed more information. He'd heard from his father that as long as you let the official feel like the big man, and didn't try to argue, business would go smoothly. He decided to try. "With all due respect, Captain, I would like to know the exact nature of your concerns. Perhaps I can clarify the issue for you."

He raised his voice. "Bring the recording."

A third officer entered the room carrying a small cassette player and set it on the desk in front of Jace. The captain pressed a button and Jace heard his own voice. He recognized his conversation with the minister of health.

"Drop the fee and I'll do what I can to convince the hospital to take her as our first open-heart case."

"Don't play games with my daughter's life."

"Exactly," Jace responded. "Don't play dangerous games with me. I've lost many patients before. But have you lost a daughter?"

The captain snapped off the tape.

Jace cringed. They were making him out to be an uncaring jerk. He wanted to scream. *That's not the way I meant it!* Instead, he forced himself to remain composed and meet the gaze of the uniformed man.

"Our beloved minister of health is under the impression that you are trying to escape paying an import tax. It seems you are leveraging the life of a young woman."

"Sir, I was only pleading with Minister Okombo to drop the fee so that I can get to work. How can I pay thousands in taxes when the equipment will be used not for financial gain, but to serve the poor of Kenya?"

"The situation does not sound so simple. Minister Okombo says he sent the girl to you, hoping for help. Instead, all he gets are threats."

"I've been misunderstood."

"Have you? It seems the tape speaks for itself."

"I will be glad to operate on the girl if I can get my equipment and the necessary staff to help. I was only hoping a man as powerful as Minister Okombo could use his influence to help me out. I would never put money in front of a patient's life."

"Perhaps you can explain why the tape sounds as if you are doing just that." He hesitated. "Or do I need to forward this tape to a judge?"

"Please, sir—surely you understand my desire to keep this out of the courts. That would certainly delay the heart program. I will pay the fee if I have to. I said those things so that Minister Okombo would understand that I am not a pushover. I wanted to make him believe that I believed the stakes were quite high for not getting my equipment through customs. It's not like it's the first time I've been to Kenya. I grew up here. I know how things work."

"Why don't you explain it to me?"

Jace hesitated. "Sometimes it is difficult to tell the difference between a legitimate tax and a bribe."

"You think our customs official was asking for a bribe?"

Jace stayed quiet. *Yes. Of course it was a bribe.*

"Losing Kenyan lives is a high cost to pay for your games." He looked at the officers. "Why don't you take Dr. Rawlings to a holding room until I can contact Minister Okombo? If he is comfortable mediating a solution without the courts, so be it."

Jace wanted to argue, but sensed it would only aggravate the men. An officer grabbed Jace by the upper arm and led him out of the room. Outside, he took Jace across the gravel parking lot and shoved him through a high metal gate into a fenced enclosure. The holding room turned out to be a ten-by-ten-foot section of gravel bounded by a ten-foot solid metal fence topped with razor wire.

Jace sat in the corner and leaned against the fence.

There he waited for the next three hours, with only a rectangle of sky to occupy his thoughts.

Jace had had little trouble with the law. His only other point of reference for dealing with public officials had left him suspicious and wounded. His mind slipped back to an afternoon shortly after he'd operated on Virginia's governor. He'd been in the hospital making his rounds when, as he passed the waiting room, someone called his name. He looked up to see Anita Franks and two men he assumed were security. "Hi, Mrs. Franks. Your husband looks a little better today."

"Thanks to you."

He studied her a moment. She'd aged in the last two days, but was still very much a woman dressed for the public. "How are you doing with all of this?"

She took a deep breath. "Got a year?"

He forced himself to chuckle. "You do need to leave the hospital occasionally. The team is taking good care of your husband."

She nodded. "I do need to get out." She hesitated. "Would you go with me? I'll buy you lunch. It would mean so much to be able to thank you."

"It's not necessary, really."

"No, but I want to."

He checked his watch. "I have to be in my office for clinic in forty-five minutes."

"Perfect," she said.

In ten minutes, in spite of his misgivings, he sat across from her at a table at a local delicatessen. It took only moments to find himself enraptured by her charm.

"You're staring," she said, returning his gaze.

"You remind me of someone."

"An old girlfriend, perhaps?"

He shook his head. "Maybe it's just your hair." He looked down. "My twin sister had hair just like yours."

The sun was past its peak when Jace heard the rumblings of a diesel truck, tires crunching against gravel. A moment later, the gate rattled, so Jace stood and brushed the dirt from his khakis. His throat was dry, and his back ached from leaning against the fence.

The gate opened, and a guard said, "Come with me."

Jace followed the officer to the back of the truck. The man pulled up the sliding door to reveal the crated equipment Jace had brought from Virginia. Alongside his equipment sat a dozen other boxes, each bearing the markings of biotech companies.

"Minister Okombo wanted me to allow you to inspect your equipment before shipment to Kijabe."

"But I thought—"

The captain's voice sounded from behind him. "The minister of health wants you to understand a gesture of goodwill."

Goodwill? You've just kept me locked up for three hours in the sun and you want to talk to me about goodwill? Jace nodded. The big man needed to be in control. "How thoughtful."

"My men will escort you back to your hospital. Your equipment will be on the way, right behind you."

Jace wasn't sure which would be worse: doing without his equipment, or being indebted to a corrupt politician. He locked eyes with the police captain. "What about the import tax?"

"Evidently, it has been taken care of. Minister Okombo only gave instructions to have you escorted back to Kijabe." He paused. "Good day, Dr. Rawlings."

A mental image of the MP hovered in Jace's mind. *He must have orchestrated this whole thing just to prove to me that he was in charge. What will this madman do if I operate on his daughter and she dies?*

14

Heather pushed the shopping cart up the aisle, fighting an annoying pull to the right from a wheel that wanted to roll only half the time. Maybe it was just getting her back for loading it down with two large bags of dog chow.

She was sniffing the end of a ripe cantaloupe when she heard her name.

"Heather?"

She looked over to see Lisa Sprague, a twenty-something reporter from the *Richmond Times Dispatch*. Lisa had done a local interest piece on Jace just after he'd operated on Governor Franks. She'd done a balanced job and hadn't joined in on speculation about Jace and the governor's wife.

Heather glanced at Lisa's cart. Fresh fruit, yogurt, vitamin water. Lisa wore what appeared to be athletic gear, as if she had just stopped in on her way to the gym. Heather had known Lisa first from their church, but at this moment, she viewed Lisa as one of *them*, the media who had been so unkind to Jace.

Heather forced a smile. "Hi, Lisa."

"I was just thinking of calling you," she said. "Is it true what I heard about Jace, that he's off on a mission to Kenya?"

"I wouldn't exactly call it a mission, but yes, he's off."

Heather turned her cart away. It was time to act busy.

Lisa didn't take the hint. "I was hoping to do a follow-up story, maybe include something about his trip."

Heather shook her head. "No," she said. "No interviews." She tried to focus on picking out a few tomatoes, but Lisa stayed at her side.

"I could help," Lisa said.

"Help? The paper hasn't exactly been friendly." Immediately, Heather regretted her sarcastic tone.

"I'm not interested in gossip," Lisa said. "I was thinking a positive story about his work in Kenya would do some good."

"No," Heather responded. "I can't do that now."

Lisa hesitated, then leaned closer and said in a confidential tone, "I'm not like the others."

Heather took a deep breath. "Look—I'm sorry. It's just that things have been a bit stressful." She lowered her voice. "You want to help?"

Lisa nodded.

"Then pray for my husband. The last thing Jace needs is a story painting him as some hero."

"I will," Lisa said. She stepped back. "You know, we were friends before I did the story."

"I remember."

Lisa retrieved a business card from a small leather purse and handed it to Heather. "If I can do anything else, just call."

"Thanks."

A minute later, in the checkout line, Heather threw in two Reese's Peanut Butter Cups, an impulse buy. The candy carried memories of her first date with Jace.

The two of them had sat in the back of the dorm lounge on folding chairs, trying to make sense of the game going on in front of them. Fellow students acted out advertising slogans, imitated famous TV and movie actors, and laughed about American politicians and their wayward ways.

Heather and Jace smiled politely.

And didn't get any of it.

Jace leaned over and whispered in her ear. "Want to sneak out?"

She nodded.

A minute later they were walking down the hall heading for an exit. Heather playfully punched his shoulder. "Wow," she said, "I thought I was the only one on the planet who hadn't heard of Seinfeld."

"Yeah, planet America." Jace halted. "Whoa!"

She stopped with him in front of a candy machine. He was staring at the options.

"Of everything we had to do without in Kenya, American chocolate was the thing I missed the most," he said. "I learned to like these when visitors would bring them as gifts." He fished several coins from his pocket. "My treat."

He smiled when they made the same selection. Heather unwrapped the Reese's cup. "Whenever someone would come to visit us in Mozambique, this is what I would ask for."

Jace fed more money into the machine and pushed the buttons again. "Here," he said, "take one back to your dorm room for tomorrow."

"Big spender," she said.

They walked slowly across the lawn in front of the administration building, a red-brick monstrosity with three-story white columns in front. Jace touched her shoulder. "Do you ever feel like you don't fit in your own country?"

Heather's response was fast. "All the time!" She studied him for a moment, wishing she hadn't responded so fast. *I'll scare him away*, she thought.

Jace smiled, easing her fear. "I carry an American passport. But I've lived most of my life in Africa. When the guys talk about cars and football, I feel like I've landed on another planet."

"Exactly."

"I remember," he said, "when we first got back, my father said he was going to take me to McDonalds so that we could experience American culture." He laughed. "But I was so embarrassed. He tried to order chips and the lady behind the counter didn't understand he meant fries."

Heather nodded. "I did the same thing."

They walked quietly. The grass was wet and she saw that they both wore flip-flops. Not the expensive leather variety, but the kind you can buy at the Dollar Store. "What do you miss?"

"Rugby." They sat on the concrete steps. "You?"

"I used to help the young women in my village by applying a traditional white paste mask. Once they taught me how to do it, they thought it was fun to have me do it for them. It was made by mixing crushed bark from a bush with water. They thought it would lighten their skin."

"And make them look like the beautiful American?"

Heather felt herself blush. She let his comment pass. "Okay. There has to be something else besides rugby."

Jace looked away, and she watched as his lower lip began to quiver. He quickly pressed his fist to his mouth. "I miss my sister," he said.

"Tell me."

"My twin," he said. "Died." He hesitated. "And it was all my fault."

Back in Kijabe, Jace found his intern in the HDU sitting behind the nursing station desk, a chart open in front of him. He was dressed in a pressed white lab coat and wearing a tie that barely came halfway down his lengthy torso. He looked up with surprise. "Dr. Rawlings. I've been paging you all day."

"Sorry, Paul. I've been in Nairobi." He lowered his voice. "It seems one of your politicians is playing games with me. I may need your perspective to help me understand."

The intern nodded.

"First tell me about our patients."

They walked to Beatrice's bedside. She was off the ventilator and breathing oxygen from a facemask.

"Habari?" Paul asked. How are you?

"Nzuri." Fine.

Jace understood the interchange, and understood also that the answer to *Habari?* was always *Nzuri*, even if the patient was taking her last breath. He needed specifics. "How is your breathing?" he asked.

"Better." With her accent, it came out sounding "Bettah."

"Do you have an appetite?"

"They won't feed me."

Paul explained. "I wasn't sure what you would want."

"If she's hungry, feed her. We need to maintain her nutrition so that she can withstand an operation."

The patient's eyes widened. "An operation?"

"Perhaps," Jace said. "We still need to do a lot of preparation."

"You are the doctah," Beatrice said.

Jace smiled at her accent and her attitude. Letting the doctor be in control was an attitude Americans had abandoned in the last decade in search of patient autonomy.

"Would you like me to talk to your parents?"

"My mother," she said, looking down. "But she is poor, unable to come here."

"How about your father?"

"I don't have a father."

Jace frowned. "Everyone has a father."

"Of course," she responded, folding her arms in a protective posture across her chest.

Subconscious body language? She is protecting herself from my knife.

Beatrice continued. "I've had biology in school, Dr. Rawlings. I know I have a father."

"Do you know him?"

"My mother has had many customers. It could be anyone."

Wow, Jace thought. Beatrice had pulled herself into a protective cocoon. She spoke of her unknown parentage as if she were reporting the evening news.

He looked at the line of her jaw, her lanky frame, the long legs and fingers. He could see the imprint of the man claiming to be her father. *Her father is rich, easily able to pay for her operation, and she doesn't know.*

Jace rested his hand on her shoulder. "You have to have some idea."

"Ideas disappoint. I'm doing all right on my own. I'm going to school. I want to be a nurse."

Jace smiled in admiration. This one was strong. A tree tested over and over by life's wind. Instead of dying, she'd sunk her roots deeper in response to suffering. "You're going to make it."

"You will help me."

He swallowed. *I hope so.*

He nodded, trying to convince himself. He walked away with his intern, hoping he could live up to his patient's expectations.

The duo finished rounds. Jace was particularly pleased that Michael Kagai, his bowel-perforation patient, seemed to be recovering. There was no fever, and he had even taken sips of chai without problems. And for the first time, Kagai didn't wrap his arms around his chest at the sight of his surgeon.

Jace opened his chart and looked at a lab result. HIV positive. Dave Fitzgerald had been correct. Predictably. Jace pointed the result out to the intern and asked, "Have you discussed this with the patient?"

"Not yet. I'll do it in the morning. I need time to discuss starting him on antiretroviral therapy. I can't just drop this bomb on him and move on."

"He's married?"

Paul nodded. "Two wives."

"They will need to be counseled as well."

"Of course." Paul shook his head. "I'm sure he didn't get it from them."

Jace looked up in response to the sound of boots. One of the guards from the front entrance approached. "Dr. Rawlings, there is a truck out front. They say they have a delivery for you."

Jace smiled. "Yes," he said. "Come on, Paul, we've got a heart program to start."

The parking lot of Ukrop's grocery was the last place Heather expected someone to show off their surgical scar, but she was a surgeon's wife, after all, and that put her at risk for listening to and looking at all manner of scars of Richmond's finest patients. She was struggling to get the overloaded shopping cart to travel straight ahead in spite of the weight and a sticky wheel, when a bleached blonde in a low-cut dress came to her aid.

The woman, who appeared to be about Heather's age, grabbed the front of Heather's cart without asking. "Let me help," she said. "Where to?"

"Just over there," she said, pointing to a silver Chrysler minivan. She shrugged sheepishly. "Thanks. This is just too heavy today."

Together they wrestled the uncooperative cart to the back of the van. The woman turned. "OMG!" she exclaimed, actually voicing the initials of a popular texting phrase. "You're Dr. Rawlings's wife. I recognize you from your photos on his desk."

"Yes, well, I—"

She lifted a pair of gaudy sunglasses from her face to reveal lashes thick with mascara above brilliant blue eyes. "Honey, you're way more gorgeous than your picture."

Heather was about to respond, but the woman barged ahead.

"Your husband saved my life!" At that, she grabbed the front of her dress and pulled it even lower, revealing a red lace brassiere.

Heather glanced around the parking lot before settling her gaze on the woman's ample cleavage. Blushing, she noted a fine scar that began at the notch above her breastbone and plunged further south than Heather was comfortable inspecting.

"Go on," the woman coaxed, "look closer. You can barely see it anymore."

Heather cleared her throat and straightened, cautious to position herself on the opposite side of the cart lest her newest acquaintance pull her face forward for an up-close and personal view. "Wow," she muttered. "I wouldn't have noticed."

"I had a heart transplant," the woman beamed, opening her arms and allowing her hands to flop outward as if to say "ta-da!"

Before Heather could respond, the woman continued. "My two-year anniversary with my new heart is next week," she bubbled. Then, placing her hand on her hip, she added, "Since my transplant, my fashion sense is entirely new. Before I got this heart, I would have been wearing a blue business suit."

She paused just long enough for Heather to muse that a conservative suit might have been more appropriate.

"I've always had the goods to wear something like this," she said, cupping her breasts quickly before smoothing the front of her dress over her hips. "But I wouldn't dare." She winked. "Now that my new heart has given me a new lease, I don't care what anyone thinks." She leaned across a bag of dog food. "What's Dr. Rawlings like at home? It must be so exciting married to a heart surgeon. And I'll bet he keeps you in the finest clothes."

Heather clutched at the collar of her plain white blouse and cleared her throat. She opened the back of the van. Maybe if she started loading the groceries, her husband's patient wouldn't dump any more of her story.

The woman grabbed a bag of dog food.

"You don't need to do that."

"The point is that now I can. But you should have seen me before your husband's knife. I couldn't walk across the room."

Heather quickly emptied the cart and slammed the door a little harder than she'd meant. "Thanks again. Excuse me," she said, wheeling the cart away to a cart collection area a few spaces away.

She tried to not make eye contact with the woman, hoping to avoid hearing more of her story. But when Heather returned, the amazing-scar transplant woman stood behind her van, smiling. As she opened her mouth to speak again, Heather raised her voice and said in one breath, "I'm so sorry, but I'm late for an appointment, thanks again for your help." She practically jumped into the minivan and started the engine, checking the rearview mirror for her assailant. Thankfully, she had moved on.

As she drove slowly across the lot and then out into traffic, Heather found herself on the verge of tears.

Is this my only identity now? The wife of the famous heart surgeon?
She sniffed.

What did I expect? Who else am I? The dog-walker?

Who am I without Jace?

She'd fought being swallowed into Jace's identity, but in Richmond, wherever she was recognized, it was the same. She was the surgeon's wife.

And with Jace gone, where did that leave her?

That evening, Jace spent two hours examining the equipment. But he didn't understand. In addition to his cardiopulmonary bypass pump and a few monitors, there was a new endoscopic ultrasound device, arterial line monitors, two new pulse oximeters, an entire box of unopened Swan-Ganz pulmonary artery catheters, a portable suction machine, and a cardiac defibrillator with small paddles for intraoperative use directly on the heart muscle. He looked at Paul. "I packed this, this, and this," he said, touching the boxes. "The rest of this, including this endoscope and ultrasound equipment, has been added by mistake."

"Maybe Minister Okombo is behaving like Joseph."

Evidently, Jace's confusion showed. His intern continued. "Remember when his brothers wanted grain? Joseph sent them away with grain and put their money in the tops of their sacks as well." He pointed at the boxes. "Maybe Minister Okombo has an interest in helping your program succeed."

"He wants something. As I recall, Joseph was testing his brothers. Maybe this is another test. I'll have to notify Minister Okombo of the items that aren't mine."

Jace stood. "I need to talk to the powers that be. Beatrice is better for now, but the only way to save her long-term is with surgery. And I'm not sure everyone around here will be happy to see this kind of surgery being done here."

Paul shook his head. "Why wouldn't they want you to operate on Beatrice?"

Jace sighed. "It's not just about this one case. It's about the whole program. When I first asked the hospital administration about starting a heart program, they gave me a provisional 'go-ahead' with a plan to revisit the issue after a few cases to see how the program impacts the hospital."

"Oh, they will see. We can save thousands! Who wouldn't want that?"

Jace appreciated the intern's optimism, but could only shake his head. "If you knew all the misery we'll attract if we open this program, you wouldn't ask."

15

Governor Stuart Franks looked across his desk at Ryan Meadows, his chief of staff. "Look, I've talked to the attorney general. Extraditing Jace Rawlings on any charge is going to be complicated and would require the cooperation of the State Department. What we need is more evidence."

"We've got the autopsy report. What more would they want?"

"DNA evidence." He picked up a letter opener, a gift from the NRA, with a handle made from a white-tailed deer antler. He used the blade to clean beneath his thumbnail. "Fortunately, DNA is fairly easy to get."

"Easy?"

"Sure. Kleenex. A beer bottle. A cigarette. Even an envelope that he licked."

"Dr. Rawlings doesn't smoke."

The governor ignored him. "What we need is someone to collect the evidence."

"And if we get it, then what?"

"Then we'll make a case for the cooperation of Kenyan authorities to extradite him."

"If he's helping their people, they may be reluctant to give him up."

Stuart Franks wiped the blade of the letter opener on his pants. "We've just made a multimillion-dollar trade deal with Kenya. I don't think they'd want to jeopardize our relationship."

Ryan nodded. "I made quite a few friends during our tobacco trade deal. Do you want me to get them involved to collect the evidence?"

The governor shook his head. "I don't want to approach anyone in Kenya till we have the evidence in hand." He stood and looked out the window over the lawn. "Maybe we can arrange for someone else to visit Mr. Rawlings."

Jace watched as Blake Anderson draped his stethoscope around his neck. "She sounds better," he said. "Not so wet."

"For now," Jace said. "But she won't stay compensated for long. She needs a valve."

The medical director waited until they were in the hallway outside the HDU before he spoke again. "This isn't the timeline we discussed. We talked of fundraising, installing new equipment in our HDU, maybe furnishing a new operating theater. The heart program needs to be instituted with full staff support or the whole thing will collapse. You have to give our African nurses time. If they don't own this program, it will go nowhere."

Jace kept his voice low. "This girl is going to die without an operation."

"So send her to Nairobi. That's what we've done for years."

"Kenya's minister of health wants her here."

"And what business is this of his?"

Jace hesitated to answer, but after a moment, he decided he needed to confide in the medical director. "Look, the girl is his daughter."

"What?" The Australian shook his head. "Are you crazy, mate?" He touched the side of his mutton-chop sideburns. "We need a nice quiet case to get this program started."

"No one knows about his connection to the girl."

"And if you lose her, what then? The MP will see to it that we're shut down."

"He's been supportive."

"You don't understand Kenyan politics. It's all about scratching the backs of the powerful."

"He waived the import tax on my equipment. In fact, when I called to tell him that I'd received a few items that I'd not brought along, he informed me that it was a gift. And we're not talking small-dollar items. The endoscopic echocardiogram unit alone is at least fifty grand."

"My point exactly," Blake said, lowering his voice. "How long have you been working on this?"

"Two months."

"And your equipment? How does donated equipment get here so fast?"

"Compassion Industries took care of the donation and the air freight."

"And only a few weeks for the Ministry of Health to approve a new program? Don't you find that the least bit unusual? Nothing in Kenya moves that fast."

"I just thought the timing must have been right. I mean, what's to decide? There's a huge need here, and I offered to come and bring what I needed. So I just think the Ministry of Health stamped it *approved* without another thought."

"Or maybe, just maybe, someone powerful was pulling strings behind the scenes. Maybe the MP even manipulated the donation of your equipment in the US." He paused. "Maybe the MP brought you here to do his daughter's operation."

"Ridiculous. He couldn't have known she'd need it."

"Don't be so sure."

"Okay, maybe I did think it was moving fast. But everything lined up so neatly that I just felt it must be right."

"You think God had something to do with it," Blake said.

"Maybe I wouldn't be bold enough to put it in those words, but … yes, maybe God wants me here, so He worked it out."

"Why would the MP just give you extra equipment?"

"He wants his daughter to survive."

"Nothing comes free here."

"He wants me to operate on his daughter."

The medical director sighed. "He wants to control us."

Jace massaged his forehead. "Look, I asked him about moving her to Nairobi. He won't have it."

"He's put us in a corner."

"This is what I came to do," Jace said.

"I hope you like pressure." Blake Anderson combed his moustache with his fingers. "'Cause you ain't seen nothing yet."

That evening, Jace answered a knock at the door to find the chaplain, John Otieno, holding up a small black plastic bag. "Dr. Rawlings, my wife sent some fresh chapatis."

"Thanks."

The chaplain seemed to hesitate. "I was hoping we could talk."

Jace motioned him in. "Sure. I'll make tea."

John sat in a kitchen chair that groaned under his weight. He watched as Jace went about boiling water and milk and adding black tea leaves and sugar. "I hear you are planning to go ahead with the heart program. This is sooner than I expected."

"Perhaps sooner than I expected as well. But I still need a few things to fall into place before I can commit to doing our first case."

"Perhaps there are other obstacles of which you are not aware."

Jace raised his eyebrows and looked at the man. The chaplain was sober, touching his curly white sideburn as he stared at Jace. "Such as?"

"You will need the chaplaincy office to bless this work before beginning. I'd hoped I'd get a chance to talk with you further before you barged ahead without consulting us."

"I was unaware of the need." Jace paused and stared at the large man. "I had the preliminary approval of the administration and staff before I came to this country. I didn't realize that your department also needed consultation."

The chaplain smiled. "Jace, of course you can go ahead with your program and ignore us." He folded his hands. "But what I'm suggesting is that your way will be so much easier if you operate inside the mission of our hospital."

"Mission?"

"The work of Kijabe Hospital is more than an outreach to sick bodies. It is an outreach to heal the souls of men." He paused and accepted the mug that Jace set in front of him. "My job is to make sure everyone is on board with this approach."

Jace sipped his chai. He didn't really feel like discussing his personal spirituality. Or lack of it.

"Why do you want to start a heart program here?" Otieno asked.

"There is great need in this country."

"So why not offer your services at Kenyatta? Why Kijabe?"

The surgeon shrugged. "This was my home."

"So you admit that you do not have a burden for the souls of your patients?"

The language was a put-off for Jace. Christianese, he called it. Just what was "a burden for souls"? Jace took another sip before answering. "I am not interested in the inefficiency of the Kenyan government hospital system. I am not interested in using a private Nairobi hospital that fleeces the rich. I want to help the poor. Is that burden enough for you?"

"I am concerned that we all be on the same page."

"The same page? What exactly are you referring to?"

"Our orientation has to be a concern first for the eternal destiny of the patients."

"My concern is the physical health of my patients. I'll leave their souls in your hands. How about that?"

"That isn't good enough."

"What do you expect of me?"

"All of the doctors in this hospital are deeply committed to spiritual ministry. That's the way it is done here."

"And why is the way I practice your business?"

"The patients' well-being is my business. I'll not have Kijabe Hospital losing its focus. If all we do is treat the physical body, we lose our distinctive. We will just be another humanistic outreach."

"You will try to stop me if I press on while limiting my work to the physical?"

"I am here to encourage you to think about the eternal. Life is short, Dr. Rawlings. What can you give them, twenty years? Thirty?" He pushed back the kitchen chair. "A life given over to Christ is affected for eternity. That's the perspective we want to preserve at Kijabe."

"Perhaps I can keep my patients alive physically so that your team can prepare them in other ways."

"For me, it boils down to motivation. Why do you want to do this work?"

Jace shifted in his chair. "I want to help Kenyans with heart disease. Particularly ones who can't afford to pay private-practice costs."

"But why? I've been watching your adventure. You endure the games of politicians, the dangers of a new culture, the suspicions of those you came to serve with. Why put up with all these hassles?"

"I'm not sure what to tell you." He held up his hands. "I want to help."

"Most who give up so much are motivated by gratitude." He paused and looked across the kitchen table at Jace. "Or guilt."

Jace wasn't sure how to respond. Or even whether he should respond. He couldn't seem to make his eyes meet the chaplain's, so he stood and walked to the stove and added chai to his mug.

John Otieno spoke with a soft voice. "Jace, the work we do at Kijabe Hospital is 'get-to' work, not 'have-to' work." He stood and set his empty mug beside the sink. "It's the difference between grace and wages."

"I get that. I've heard the song."

When the chaplain looked confused, Jace added. "You know, 'amazing grace, how sweet the sound.'"

"I know it well. But the concept seems lost on you. You are striving, performing."

"I'm a surgeon. That's what I do."

"A wise man once told me that grace is God at work. Legalism is me at work. The difference isn't in the work; it's in the motivation."

"And you can take a spiritual scalpel and expose what is in my heart? How can you presume to know what motivates me?" Jace turned away. "Maybe I don't know myself." He paused and turned slowly back to Otieno, whose large hands were folded in his lap like a child praying. "Can I count on you to bless the work, even if you do not know the motivation? The work is needed."

"I have other concerns, Jace. Kijabe Hospital is known for compassionate, Christ-centered care. When the public hears that the famous, colorful, American heart surgeon is at work here, their opinion may change."

"So you're really worried about me tarnishing the hospital's reputation."

"It is my place to be sure that spiritual ministry is not hampered."

"Shall I pack up and go home? Is that what you want?"

"What I want is for you to understand why you are working so hard. Are you trying to earn God's favor? For what sin are you trying to atone?"

Jace shook his head. He'd heard enough Christian language. *Why not speak plain English instead of presumptuous, pious phrases?*

But the last phrase did make him think. *Some sins deserve punishment.*

When Jace didn't respond, the chaplain turned toward the door. "I'll let myself out. Enjoy the chapatis."

16

Jace opened his computer and clicked on the "Get Mail" icon. After watching the twirling emblem for a long minute, he saw that he'd finally gotten a reply from Heather. The message was brief. And too polite.

Glad you're safe. I hope that your time away is all that you need it to be. I know you want to figure things out between us. I've been thinking about the way it was in the beginning. We were young and full of hope, and determined not to end up like the rest of American couples who grow apart instead of together. So where did we go wrong? Can we find that hope again? I know if things are going to work for us, I need answers. Transparency, Jace. I need to know what was really going on between you and Anita Franks. I hope you get your equipment soon. If I know anything about you, you'll feel lost without it.

Maybe that's part of the problem. For the last decade your identity has been your ability to be cool when hearts were in crisis. Well, Jace, maybe this is a heart crisis of sorts for us.

Stay safe,
Heather

Jace shut his laptop and sighed. If only *he* knew what had really been going on with Anita.

Had anything been going on? Had he slipped from comforting a patient's family member into something else entirely? Had he crossed the line into dangerous territory with another man's wife?

He knew that at one time, not too long ago, he had dreamed of doing just that.

It had begun innocently enough. An accepted invitation to talk, over lunch. Hands brushing, lingering a little beyond the friendly graze. A hug after walking her to her car. Comfort offered to a friend.

Then, in a parking lot outside the hospital, he'd handed her a card with his private cell number. He remembered the look in her eyes: *You are special to me.*

"Thanks. I won't misuse this," she giggled. She leaned forward to offer him a friendly hug and her cheek touched his.

He inhaled her perfume. He felt heat. And desire.

A male voice interrupted their good-bye. "Mrs. Franks. Your car is waiting."

Jace looked up to see the stern face of Ryan Meadows.

"Oh, Ryan, you remember Dr. Rawlings? We were just saying good-bye. He tells me the governor is progressing."

"Of course."

When Anita turned away, the chief of staff met Jace's eye and kept his voice just above a whisper. "Step carefully, Doctor."

Jace didn't reply. He didn't need to. His conscience was screaming the same warning. Instead, he nodded at Ryan and watched as he took the first lady's arm, escorting her to a waiting limousine.

Ryan helped Anita into the limo, then climbed in beside her.

Once alone and behind the tinted windows, Anita turned to him. "Drink with me." She poured golden liquid from a crystal decanter.

Ryan sighed. "This has turned out so different than I'd imagined." He watched the surgeon, still standing there, as they drove away. "For a while, I found myself imagining what would have happened if the governor hadn't pulled through." He looked back at Anita. "Then maybe we could have stopped hiding."

"Is that what you want?"

"I want to be with you. You know that."

"Well, that's a little impossible right now, regardless of what we might want. And I'm not about to break the news to the governor when he's in the hospital."

"I get that, Anita. But it doesn't stop me from wanting more."

She brushed his hair away from his forehead. "Nor me."

He drained his small glass, enjoying the burn of the alcohol in his throat. "You should be careful. The local media is starting to speculate about you and your husband's doctor."

"You're jealous."

"Should I be?"

"Ah, Ryan. Always lurking in the shadow of the governor."

"It wasn't so long ago that *I* was touted as the party's pick for their candidate." He smiled. "That's when you made your first play for me. When you thought I was going to be the governor." He tapped his finger against the window, where a honeybee clung to the outside surface. "Maybe I would have made Stuart my chief of staff."

She shook her head. "He wouldn't have done it. Too proud."

"Too proud to imagine his wife looking elsewhere? He's a pig."

"He's your boss."

He leaned over and kissed her earlobe. "Don't remind me now. He's still in the hospital. Anything could happen."

That evening, Jace made a long-distance call to Gabriel Dawson. "Gabby, it's Jace Rawlings."

"Dr. Rawlings, the infamous African heart surgeon?"

"Very funny."

"I didn't expect to hear from you so soon."

"I didn't expect to need you this quickly. Gabby, I've got an urgent valve replacement to do. I'm going to need you sooner than I'd thought."

"So how's it going? Is everything set?"

"I'm working on that." He paused. "So how soon do you think you can come?"

"I have some time off coming my way, but I'll have to ask Evan. He makes the schedule."

"I already talked to our cardiac anesthesiologist. Dr. Martin marked off the week after next."

"You're serious. I'm supposed to just drop everything and fly to Africa?"

"We talked about this. You said—"

"I'll make it work, Jace. You sound stressed."

"It's been a little crazy. I had quite the adventure getting my stuff through customs. And everyone around here seems to want to size me up and figure out why I'm doing this."

"So how is your sister?"

He paused. "That's not funny."

"What do you mean? Heather told me that the reason you left was because your sister had asked—"

"She told you that?"

"We're friends, Jace. We went out to lunch. I thought it must be special. I didn't even know you had a sister."

"My sister's dead."

"Oh, Jace, I'm sorry. W-when?" she stuttered. "I mean, Heather just said—"

"She died a long time ago. When we lived here as kids."

"You're scaring me. Why would Heather say something like—"

He sighed. "Look, it's complicated. I'm not crazy, okay?"

"What's going on, Jace? If you expect me to come all the way to Africa to lend a hand, I need to know."

Jace began to pace, using the full length of the stretchy phone cord to walk around his little kitchen. "I'll explain everything when you get here."

"No, Jace, I'm staying in Virginia unless you tell me."

He ran his free hand through a tangle of uncombed hair. "Okay," he said, starting slowly and picking his words carefully. "I'll admit, this sounds a little crazy."

"Try me."

"It was during my accident. I don't really remember much about it." He paused.

"Heather told me as much."

"But I have one memory that I've been reluctant to share. I don't know how much Heather told you about my sister."

"Apparently, not everything. I didn't know she was dead."

"She died just before we graduated. We were twins," he said, "very close."

"Jace, I'm sorry."

"After my accident, well, I had some sort of vision. I guess that's what I should call it. I saw my sister. I remember her face as I was lying on the side of the road. She leaned over me and said, 'Come back to me, Jace.' Clear as anything. She was crying. I know it sounds weird, but that's what got me started thinking I was supposed to do something else with my life."

"Other people say you're running away from trouble."

"Heather?"

"She's worried about you."

"Yeah, well, it seems everyone is worried about me." He reached the end of the phone cord and turned around again. "What do you say, Gabby? There's no way I can start this program without a good pump tech."

"Are you sure you're ready for this? What you just told me is creeping me out a little."

"I'm okay. If it makes you feel any better, it creeps me out a little too."

He heard her sigh into the phone. "I'll talk to the boss. If he says I can go, I'll work it out with Dr. Martin."

"Thanks." He breathed a sigh of relief. "I'm not crazy, Gabby."
Am I?

Simeon Okayo considered himself a modern professional. This, of course was in stark contrast to his dress, a tribal garment accented by a necklace of bone. He prided himself in his fluidity. He was as comfortable in a three-piece suit walking the halls of government in Nairobi as he was in the traditional garb he wore in his little duka in Kisii.

Tonight, he had reason to worry. The evening before, the elders in a neighboring village had blamed nine women suspected of practicing witchcraft for the lack of development in the area. Two of the women had been hacked to death, three burned alive in their homes, and four had escaped into the forest.

His anxiety wasn't new. Witch doctors were feared for their power, loved for their blessing, and blamed for economic hardship. So far, his political ties had allowed him a bit of protection, but ties to men in power always came at a price.

Of course, politicians didn't think spiritually. They wanted control. Curse this opponent. Assure this victory. But Simeon knew that the spirits demanded a resolution when a curse had been put in play. Someone wanted Dr. Jace Rawlings to die. A blood price had been purchased. But now, delays. Perhaps an animal sacrifice would provide a temporary delay on the spirits' demand for blood.

He stepped around his shop's floor, one ear attuned to the street and one listening for the chirp of his cell phone. Outside, a drunk threw aside a plastic cup and propositioned a young woman. The man's mind must have been buzzed from the effects of chang'aa, the illegal brew so popular in the slums and villages of Kenya. Simeon wished for a sip of the fermented maize drink himself, hoping to stuff away his worries of the spirits' unrest, but he wouldn't buy it from a street vendor. The cheap drink boiled in metal drums was often contaminated by methanol and had earned a reputation as poison because it caused blindness. Simeon would purchase his stock from a friend in the Mungiki, the cult-like political group who owed the witch doctor more than a few favors for the protection he offered.

His cell phone sounded. He looked at the screen. *The MP.*

"Jambo," he said.

"You shouldn't leave messages with my secretary," Okombo said.

"How else am I to reach you? You do not answer your phone."

"I will call you when it is time."

"I am worried. The spirit world requires balance."

"Don't worry. My need of the doctor will end soon. Then you can have your balance."

"It's not that simple. You asked me if I could get the American to come."

"At the request of the governor's office."

"That's not important to me now. I talked to the dead. I called Dr. Rawlings to come. Now the spirits will demand blood."

"Soon, Simeon. Surely you are powerful enough to—"

"Tell your friends to stop the witch hunts. They killed five yesterday."

"They are not my friends."

"You have influence."

"So do you. You're the one communicating with the dead. Ask them to help you."

"You do not understand." Simeon sighed. "I'll offer a substitute. But they will still be thirsty."

"I'll be in touch."

17

When Gabby didn't find Heather at home, she circled the neighborhood until she found her striding along beside an animal that looked more like a bear than a dog. She passed the duo, parked on the street, and got out to tag along, positioning herself with Heather between her and the monstrous beast.

Heather brightened at her approach. "Hi, Gabby. I didn't expect to see you."

"What is that?"

"Bo? He's a mastiff."

"I thought you said you were a dog-walker," Gabby said. "That's no dog."

The animal seemed to be setting the pace. Gabby struggled to keep up in her heels. "Could you slow him down?"

"I'm doing the best I can." Heather held on like a water-skier as the mastiff pulled her along.

Gabby slipped off her shoes. She jogged to catch Heather again.

"We need to talk."

"So talk."

"Like this?" Gabby resumed jogging, juggling two shoes and her handbag.

"Welcome to my world."

Sweat began beading off Gabby's forehead. Richmond's clear sky offered no relief from the bright sun. Gabby reached for the leash and pulled hard with Heather. Bo looked back and miraculously stopped.

"There. I'm going to Kenya," she said. "I want you to go with me."

Jace's initial excitement over the possibility of getting his heart program up and running gave him hope that he might soon be taken off general surgery call. That hope dissolved when Dave Fitzgerald insisted that Jace scrub on a prostatectomy so he could learn the technique.

Jace felt like an intern again. Each step was accomplished under Dave's instruction.

"Here," he said, "slip your finger in behind mine."

Jace obeyed.

"Feel that? That's the right plane. Now work your finger back in and forth around the gland. Push more against the gland so the bladder won't be injured. It's all done by feel."

Everything Jace did in cardiac surgery was done with the tissues exposed so that he could see every step. Now he was being asked to operate by feel. *Like my life*, Jace thought. *It's like I'm feeling my way ahead through darkness.*

"I've arranged to have a cardiac anesthetist and my pump technician come to initiate the heart program."

Dave didn't respond. "Let me feel what you have." He lowered his hand into the pelvis and after another few moments, he lifted a prostate gland out of the bladder. It was white and the size of a small apple. "There," he said. "You'd better get this operation down before you think about cardiac surgery."

"I've already lined up the first case."

"We'll see." He held out his hand to the surgical tech. "Chromic," he said, asking for a suture. "The capsule needs to be oversewn along the superior edge for hemostasis. I'll show you this time. Next time, you're on your own."

"Will you assist on my valve replacement?"

"Look around, Jace. Do you really think we're ready for heart surgery?"

"Sounds like you've already made up your mind that we're not."

"We've yet to see how these heart cases will affect our ability to continue giving the level of care we currently embrace. One case is going to demand lots of blood, theater time, and the retraining of our staff." He sighed. "I'm not sure we have the resources."

"The medical director has signed off on it."

"Look, the whole staff agreed to the program on a trial basis. To let you do a few cases and see what kind of impact it has on our resources."

"But you're not convinced."

"You should know by now that I won't keep my opinions to myself. We have enough problems just doing the present load without taxing the system even more."

"So you were outvoted."

"Apparently."

"Blake is in agreement to proceed with the valve."

"Blake seems to think a politician has backed us into a corner. Just because the staff goes along with this first case doesn't mean the program is a go." He paused. "Close the bladder in two layers of running zero chromic. Imbricate the second layer over the first."

With the instructions given, Dave stepped away from the operating table and stripped off his gown. "How much blood do you need for one open-heart case?"

"Ten units."

"Yeah," the surgeon responded. "Sometimes it takes days to just find one suitable unit, so good luck with that." He picked up the patient's chart. "Maybe you're a bigger man of faith than I thought."

Dave exited the room, leaving Jace to close the bladder alone. *A bigger man of faith? Or just a man with a crazy dream and no faith at all?*

"Look, I've thought about it," Heather said. "One of the reasons I didn't go to Africa was because Jace needed space to figure out his life. That hasn't changed." She lifted a glass of sweet tea to her lips. She thought about the conversation she'd had in Ukrop's parking lot. *I've got a life outside my surgeon husband.* "Besides, I've got responsibilities here."

Gabby sat across the kitchen table from her friend. "I know. I understand. But it would be so much better for me if you'd come."

"I've been thinking about something. I want you to do me a favor," Heather said.

"Sure."

"I want you to get a sample of Jace's blood."

"What?"

"I talked to a friend down at the medical examiner's office. He said that they could use a sample of Jace's blood to do a DNA test to see if it matches the semen sample found in Anita Franks."

Gabby winced. "You can't be serious. Jace would never—"

"I'm not sure of anything anymore," Heather interrupted. She stood and started to pace around the island in the kitchen. "Why else would there be ketamine in her blood? Who else would have access to that kind of drug?"

Gabby shook her head. "I shouldn't need to defend him to you. You should know he's not capable of rape."

"I know that," Heather responded. "But maybe, just maybe, he's a fallible man, and in a moment of weakness, he fell into the clutches of a seductress." She paused. "I hate doubting him, but … he refused to explain what he was doing that night."

"You said he didn't remember."

"That's his story."

"Collecting evidence should be a police matter."

"The police aren't investigating Anita Franks's death. It's being considered an accident."

"Do they know about the ketamine?"

"I don't know." Heather raised her hands. "I'm not even sure why *I* know. But someone wanted me to know this stuff."

"So what if they find a DNA match? What then? Are you going to go to the police with your findings? Turn in your own husband?"

"No. I'm doing this for me. I want to prove he's innocent."

"Or guilty."

"I don't want that, Gabby. I want to believe in my husband again. Maybe this will help."

Gabby took a deep breath. "So you're saying maybe this will prove it to you."

Heather bit her lower lip. "I hope so."

Gabby reached for her hand. "One more try," she said.

"One more—what?"

"Go with me, Heather. Work it out with Jace, face-to-face."

Jace plodded out of the hospital lobby and into the night air. He needed to walk. To think. And spend some time under the expanse of sky.

He'd always been the doubter. When Janice credited God, he credited circumstance. When she acknowledged divine insight, Jace claimed human wisdom. When they met an obstacle, Jace saw obstruction; Janice, opportunity.

He walked away from the hospital, along a dark path leading through an informal soccer field. There, away from ambient light, he looked at the heavens, a mantle salted with a million stars and the brilliance of the moon. Unlike back in Richmond, where only the brightest stars could be appreciated, under the African sky he could study the Milky Way, seen on edge as a stripe of heavenly white dust.

There, under the enormity of the starry host, Jace felt alone.

Small.

Stripped of the accolades of his cardiothoracic colleagues or appreciative patients.

Facing opposition from hospital staff, threats from politicians, and questions about his motives from the chaplaincy, Jace puffed up his chest.

I'll show them all.

I can save Beatrice from heart failure.

I can …

He raised a fist to the sky.

18

A few days later, Jace stood in a sea of Africans, pressed together as one mass, their eyes all focused on the scene unfolding on the other side of a wall of glass. He was in Jomo Kenyatta International Airport, watching with the others to see if their loved ones would be the next to escape customs and walk through the opening from the baggage claim area into the expansive foyer leading to the parking lots beyond. Here, in the group, there was no respect for personal space. Everyone pressed together to see. It was one mass of sweaty, colorful humanity, all jockeying to get a glimpse of the people on the other side of customs.

Jace waited for Dr. Evan Martin and Gabby Dawson, both critical members of his open-heart team. Jace had worked with Dr. Martin for the better part of the last decade. He was a no-nonsense, get-the-work-done kind of guy, a gadget lover who always had the latest technology. He was what Jace would call an *über*geek, but also the kind of doctor you wanted in your corner when the deck was stacked against your patient. To Evan Martin, every patient was important. Money, title, or fame meant nothing to him. He'd been in Jace's corner when he operated on the governor of Virginia and on hundreds of others of lesser fame but equal importance to Evan.

From his vantage point, Jace could see the passengers collecting bags and heading to the customs officials. He stood on his tiptoes to see over a Kenyan woman wearing a tall hat. The British Airways flight from Heathrow had landed, and the first passengers, bags in tow, were just starting to filter out past the customs officials. He was anxious to see his friends, but even more anxious to see if his hunch was correct: it would be just like Gabby to convince Heather to come along. And what a delight it would be to show her his boyhood home.

He saw Evan first. Tall and slender and lacking a tan, he stood out among the other passengers waiting beside the serpentine conveyor belt carrying the bags. He saw Gabby next.

But no Heather. His heart sank.

I should have known.

When Evan and Gabby walked into the airport lobby, Jace was careful not to show his disappointment. "Karibu Kenya," he said. "Welcome to Kenya."

He hugged his friends, feeling for perhaps the first time since arriving in Kenya that he had true comrades to share his misery. He found himself suddenly on the edge of tears. *Wow,* he thought, *I hadn't realized how alone I really felt until now.* He brushed away a tear. "This way," he said. "I hope you guys had a good flight."

Jace looked over his shoulder at the other exiting passengers.

Gabby's voice broke into his brief daydream. "She didn't come, Jace. I tried to convince her."

Jace forced a smile. "You thought I'd expect—"

"Of course," she said. "I know *you*."

He nodded and looked at his friends. "You don't know how glad I am to see familiar faces."

Gabby raised her eyebrows. "What, is your boyhood home different than you remembered?"

"Let's just say that I've gained a new appreciation for how difficult it is to get anything done in this place." He locked eyes with them again. "It's so great to see you."

Evan checked his watch.

"We're eight hours ahead of Virginia here," Jace said.

"I wasn't checking the time," Evan said. "This is an altimeter. Did you know Nairobi is just like Denver? Both mile-high cities. Cool."

Jace smiled. *The gadget guy.*

Evan surveyed the mass of people crowding around them, shouting out offers to carry their luggage. "What have you gotten us into?" he said, smiling.

"Oh, you have no idea," he said. "No idea."

The following week, Jace gathered in the operating room with Gabby and Evan. The occasion: the eve of the maiden-voyage open-heart case at Kijabe Hospital.

Evan sighed. "It's going to be awfully crowded in this room."

Jace pushed the anesthesia machine back six inches. "This is the biggest room we have."

Gabby frowned. "There's a gap beside this window pane. A fly or mosquito on your sterile field could spell disaster for your patient. The whole operation would be for nothing if she gets a valve infection."

Jace took a blue towel and shoved it in the crack. "That should do for now."

Evan did a three-sixty while touching each piece of equipment within arm's reach. The arterial line monitor, his endoscopic echocardiogram, an EKG monitor, and a drawer full of cardiac meds. "Tight, but doable. Remind me to check with pharmacy. We seem to be a bit low on fentanyl."

Gabby leaned across her silver pump, the heart-lung machine. Tomorrow, it would whirl, extracting blood from the patient's right atrium, oxygenating it, and pumping it back through a cannula inserted in the patient's aortic root. "What's the blood availability?"

"Still need two more units. What is your blood type?"

"No, no," she said. "I'm already short of breath because of the altitude."

"I'm B positive, compatible with the patient," Jace said. "I gave one unit three days ago. I'll give another tonight."

Evan frowned. "Do you think you should? We need you at one-hundred percent, Jace."

"What choice do I have?"

"You can't bleed yourself for every case."

"This isn't every case. It's our first."

"Exactly. Look, I'm O negative. I can give," Evan said.

Jace nodded. "We'll both give." He looked at the clock on the wall. "They're expecting us in blood bank."

Evan shrugged. "You're asking a lot. First we donate our time, our skills. Now you want me to hemorrhage too."

Jace smiled. "We've got exactly twelve hours. Let's get this done."

That night, Jace approached the bedside of Beatrice Wanjiku. In a wooden chair next to the bed sat a woman Jace recognized as Beatrice's mother. Her mascara was streaked, and her sweater was buttoned up to her chin, a concession to seeing her daughter in a church hospital.

"Dr. Rawlings," the patient said.

"Hi, Beatrice." He took her hand and nodded at her mother. "Nice to see you again."

Beatrice forced a smile. "Tell her not to worry. I'm going to be okay."

The parent-child relationship in reverse. Beatrice seeking to comfort her mother.

"We have a good team," Jace said. "We have every reason to be optimistic."

Beatrice looked at her mother and spoke in Kikuyu, their tribal tongue.

Her mother answered, her questions punctuated with sobs.

Beatrice looked at Jace. "She says it is not possible to open the heart. She knows the heart is needed to pump my blood."

"Tell her that we have a special machine that will take over the function of your heart and lungs during the operation." He paused. "Will she understand?"

"I will help her." Beatrice began a long explanation in Kikuyu, gesturing toward her chest, tracing a path with her fingers up toward her neck and then turning down around her left breast. She closed and opened her fist. The pumping heart.

Her mother shook her head.

Beatrice frowned. "She says she will be praying."

"That's good, right? She agrees then?"

"No. My mother isn't a religious woman. She says this only to impress you. She wants you to think she is a good woman."

"She cares about you."

"She is a prostitute. She cares about her next drink."

Jace sighed. He knew Beatrice was right, and her insight and lay-it-all-on-the-table approach were both alarming and touching. She'd obviously been forced to grow up fast, and as happens with so many dysfunctional families, the roles of parent and child were reversed and messy. "Many people talk of God when they are facing crisis." He looked down. "It's natural, not a bad thing." Jace felt odd offering an opinion about spirituality. He cleared his throat. "What about you? Do you pray?"

"I pray every day that God will help me escape my life in Kibera. Escape my life with a woman who embarrasses me."

Jace looked at Beatrice's mother. "She is concerned. That ought to mean something."

Beatrice shook her head. "She came to take me home. She says we cannot afford an operation."

"Don't worry about the money. Someone has offered to pay your bill."

Beatrice spoke again to her mother, gesturing again, opening her hands in front of her. The two talked for a few minutes with Beatrice's mother becoming more and more animated.

Jace watched, unsure how to proceed. "If you leave, you will die."

"My mother wants me to see a doctor in Kibera."

Jace pulled down on Beatrice's gown, moving the neckline lower to expose a series of burn scars on her upper chest. "The doctor who gave you these?"

"Yes." Beatrice sniffed and her eyes were glistening.

Jace studied her. She appeared to be trying not to cry. "The traditional healers have nothing to offer you."

Beatrice shrugged. "You won't convince *her*. She feels it is impossible to open the heart without causing death."

Jace sat on the edge of the bed and faced his patient's mother, studying eyes that glistened with tears. "I will make your daughter well again."

Slowly, over the next twenty minutes, with Beatrice interpreting, Jace explained all he could to help the mother understand.

Finally, she agreed. Jace stood again.

Beatrice caught his hand as he turned to leave. "Dr. Rawlings," she said, her voice thickening, "I'm so afraid."

"I will be with you the whole time," he said. "I won't let you down."

He wished he could say more. He wished he were like his father, who always had an encouraging Bible verse to share. But he was empty. So he squeezed her hand and walked away, out into the main hall where he saw the chaplain standing with the other members of his team. "Dr. Rawlings," he said, "we are gathering in the chapel to pray on this eve of such a momentous day for Kijabe hospital."

Jace nodded, making eye contact with Gabby. She would be all over this. She wasn't noisy about her faith but wasn't exactly quiet, either. She constantly told Jace about the answers to her prayers.

He followed the chaplain into the small chapel and stood in a circle with the staff members who had gathered there. He recognized a few of the theater nurses and two hospital administrators, along with the medical director, Blake, and Dave Fitzgerald.

Jace nodded at Dave without speaking. *Who twisted your arm to be here?*

Jace would have been more comfortable without fanfare, without ceremony, but this was the Kijabe way. Significant events did not pass without acknowledgment, often a formal meeting, a speaker perhaps, but at least a formal prayer.

Blake led the little circle. "We have come a long way in a short time. From the time Dr. Rawlings contacted us, equipment was donated, the Ministry of Health approved our request, and these gracious members have donated their time. So we mark this day with a prayer of thanks and a plea for God's healing, guidance, and mercy." He looked over at Jace. "Comments, Dr. Rawlings?"

He cleared his throat. "I'd like to thank each one of you for your support. We've got an early day tomorrow. Let's get some rest." His eyes met Blake's. "After the prayer, of course."

The nurses and Chaplain Otieno chuckled. "Of course," Otieno said. "I will lead in prayer."

He began softly, pleading for God to continue his blessings on the ministry of Kijabe Hospital. When he got around to praying for

Jace, he placed his hands upon Jace's shoulders and moved so close that Jace could feel his breath blowing across his forehead. "Take this man. Use his mind and his hands for your glory," he asked.

The chaplain's hands were heavy. Jace could not imagine a man with hands so hot and so heavy. Just as Jace's knees began to buckle, the pressure lifted.

Had he imagined it?

He reached up and touched his shoulder, where only moments before the chaplain's meaty hand had rested. *It's hot.*

Jace shook his head. *Just my imagination.*

After the chaplain's prayer, amens were shared around the circle. Each member gave Jace a vigorous handshake, an affirmation of their support.

Even Dave seemed to have been won over. "I'll be there at six sharp."

Jace thanked everyone again, and the group broke up, each one exiting the chapel into the cool night. He said good night to Gabby and Evan and strode off to his little home, knowing that sleep would be difficult.

That night, Beatrice's mother refused to leave, sitting on Beatrice's small hospital bed in the women's ward, amid all the other patients. For Beatrice, sleep was difficult enough, as it was hard for her to breathe while lying flat on the bed. That had something to do with her heart failing, Dr. Rawlings had explained.

Sometime after midnight, her mother curled against Beatrice, stealing her warmth and further disrupting her sleep with her snores. Her mother told her she wouldn't leave her on the night before her big day, but she knew her mother had no other place to go. If she did not sleep with Beatrice, she would find a patch of ground beneath a tree outside—or worse, find the company of a stranger.

Beatrice didn't want that. Besides, it comforted her, having her mother there. At least she could tell herself she had a mother who cared.

There, in the night, with the sounds of her mother's snoring and the busy steps of the nurses caring for the other patients, Beatrice pulled her mother's arm around her like a blanket. *She does care, doesn't she?*

She arranged for the American doctor to see me.

That must mean that she has some powerful friends.

Or is my father secretly watching me?

It was a mental game she'd played, growing up without a father. She imagined that he was someone special. She would look at herself in the small hand mirror her mother had given her one Christmas and try to see her features in the men who visited her mom.

Could it be the man who brought Dr. Rawlings to me? He dressed in a suit and drove a big vehicle for someone important. Did he arrange for my care?

In the early hours of the morning, Beatrice's nurse stopped by the bed.

"Child, you should sleep."

Beatrice nodded.

The woman had a kind face, with muddy brown eyes and a Kikuyu name like hers. "Afraid?"

"Yes," Beatrice whispered.

"Close your eyes. I will pray."

Beatrice obeyed. And as the woman prayed and stroked her hair, she imagined her mother was the one who was touching her, that her mother was the one who prayed with such vibrancy that Beatrice found herself believing things really could turn out okay.

The next day, work began for the open-heart team at six. The patient was brought down, a central line was placed, an arterial line inserted, sterile fields opened and prepared. IVs were hung, antibiotics dripped, the patient anesthetized, and the skin prepped. By nine, Jace stood at the scrub sink and tried to exorcize his self-doubt. It had been months since his last open-heart case. But what was mere months in time seemed a world away.

As he lathered his hands and arms, instead of a prayer to God, he whispered his sister's name. "Okay, Janice. Here we go."

A few minutes later, as he stood with the scalpel poised above his patient's sternum, Gabby spoke up after clearing her throat. "Dr. Rawlings," she said, using his formal title since they were in front of staff. "I'd like to begin with a prayer if that's all right. It's a historic day for this hospital." She hesitated. "And for Kenya."

Jace nodded. *Couldn't hurt.*

Gabby began. "Dear Father, we commit this precious life to You. Watch over her and all the staff. Help us. Guide Dr. Rawlings's hands. Bring healing. We promise to give You all the glory."

Jace closed his left hand into a fist during the prayer, hoping to quell a twitch. When Gabby finished praying, he echoed, "Amen."

He glided the scalpel over the skin, separating the brown skin to reveal a layer of yellow fat beneath. Then he picked up the pencil cautery and applied it to multiple small dermal and subcutaneous bleeders. He then bluntly worked the tip of a scissors beneath the sternum, freeing the soft tissue from the undersurface of the bone. He took a sternal splitter and a mallet and split the sternum. Back in Richmond, he would have done this with a pneumatic saw, but in Kijabe, he did it the old-fashioned way.

In a moment, the lining around the heart was opened and retracted and the patient's heart was exposed. Across from him, Dave Fitzgerald shook his head. "Man, this is so cool."

"Nothing like the human heart." Jace looked at Gabby. "Let's set up the heart-lung machine."

As many times as Jace had done this, he was never without amazement at the process. Large bore tubes were sutured into place in the aorta and right atrium, the heart was cooled, and the pump started.

Gabby sat behind her silver cardiac bypass pump, a queen happy in command central. "You know what they say," she bantered.

Jace knew what was coming. "Okay, Gabby, what do they say?"

Gabby rolled her stool, staring at the machine in front of her. "What is the fastest way to a man's heart?"

Dave Fitzgerald shrugged. "Through his stomach."

Gabby laughed. "Between the fourth and fifth ribs."

Jace smiled behind his mask. He spoke to Gabby, his tone suddenly serious. "Venous line's to you."

She understood the notation. She opened the line. "We're on bypass."

A heart-stilling medication was infused directly into the heart. This cardioplegia, as it was called, was high in potassium, causing paralysis of the heart muscle cells. The patient was now alive, but without a beating heart. Little blood circulated through the lungs as the heart-lung machine oxygenated the blood as it went through the pump.

Jace went to work, opening the heart, removing the old diseased valve and placing a new one in its place.

While they worked, they fell into routine. Jace discovered that, as on a bicycle, everything came back. He placed sutures with the precision of a watchmaker. Fingers blurred in a flurry of knot tying.

"Gabby," Jace teased. "I'm sure we can find you a nice Kenyan young man to convince you to stay. I'd bet that one of my Maasai friends would pay twenty or thirty cows for a woman like you."

Gabby huffed. "Only thirty?"

After forty-five minutes, the heart was closed again, and they began a rewarming process. When the patient's temperature was within a few degrees of normal, Jace asked for the internal paddles to shock the heart. He looked over the drapes at Evan Martin. "What's wrong?"

Evan shook his head. "This girl is so sensitive. I've had her on next to no anesthesia."

"I'm operating on her heart and she's not under anesthesia?"

"Chemically paralyzed, that's about it."

"Just give her something to keep her from remembering. Here she is being suspended between life and death. It could be pretty freaky for her."

Awareness.

Darkened passages, a sudden bright light, like looking into the sun, but different. She had no need to shield her eyes.

Did she have eyes?

Weightless, floating, hearing, seeing, feeling, but not embodied. Away from the light, she tried to focus. *That's me down there. That's my heart.*

I'm dead.

My doctor doesn't know. He doesn't seem concerned. He jokes with the woman about getting a husband.

Beatrice looked on with a strange sort of detachment. *My heart. My chest pried open by steel jaws. But I feel no pain.*

So I must be dead.

Can I travel? Move?

Thought seemed to move her around the room. She reached out to touch a pole laden with IVs, but her hand passed *through* it. She tried again. Same result. She touched the surface of a monitor, then pushed her hand *into* it.

Inventory time.

Is this heaven? Hell?

In between?

Alive?

Dead?

Up.

A thought took her through the ceiling, passing through wiring, rafters and roof. Warmth of the sun.

Down.

Instantly, a descent back through the building and into a damp world of worms and dirt, darkness and cool.

Cold, but temperature did not affect her. She had no desire to warm herself.

Up!

Inside again. She looked at the monitor. No activity. She'd grown accustomed to the sound of her own heart while in the HDU. She'd awoken several times in fear, only to comfort herself with the rhythmic blips of her own heart. *Alive!* She'd imagined herself in a little car, riding along the green road of the monitor's glowing line. She would bump, jump, and skip from hump to hump, using the small swellings to vault her over the jagged pointy cliffs, land, and jump again.

But not now; the monitor was dark except for a silent horizontal line running from left to right. The squiggles of life, the treacherous road of bumps, hills, and cliffs were flattened in the crush of death.

Right.

Through the walls to hover in a small waiting room above her mother slouched in a plastic chair.

An empty woman without hope, crying a prayer into her hands. "She is all I have."

She looked closer, seeing not just her mother, but *inside*. A battle. An invader. Not spiritual, but a violence nonetheless. And no one else in the room seemed to notice. Swirling, gnawing, the color of deep red, not blood, but something foreign, circling, attacking, enveloping.

Weakening.

The AIDS virus.

Beatrice just knew. Her mother's cough, the continuous fight with diarrhea, the glistening of her forehead with fever. It was the African prostitute's destiny, a lifetime virus left in deposit for ten minutes of flesh pressed against flesh. It was a payment for pleasure, with pain the currency.

Beatrice knelt in front of her, taking her head in her hands, first letting them pass through, and then concentrating on resting on the surface.

Her mother jerked upright, staring wildly at the other people in the little room.

She studied the people in the room. *I can see through them.* Some were glowing white, some dull. She looked at a man with a glowing white heart. In his hand, a leather-bound book seemed to captivate him. *A Christian?*

Her mother seemed to push into Beatrice's touch. *She can feel me.*

She willed her mother to relax. *I'm here.*

"*Beatrice,*" a male voice echoed. *From inside me?*

She looked to see a body wrapped in a glow, light streaks that bent, swirled, and *moved,* hovering just above the skin. If it could be called skin at all.

To say handsome would have been a vast understatement. He was the most beautiful creature she'd ever seen. Tall. Muscled. Light shooting from his fingertips, trailing like a flare as he gestured her closer.

But then she saw his eyes. Dark, ominous, and small, windows into blackness.

She drew back. Away!

She moved into the operating theater again, not wanting to go with the creature.

But he followed, up, down, mirroring her movements.

She looked at the monitor. Silent.

She watched as Dr. Rawlings placed what appeared to be two spoons on the heart. *My heart.*

"I have a message for you to give to Dr. Rawlings."

He doesn't have a mouth, but he communicates his thoughts with me. She wanted to get away.

Dr. Rawlings spoke calmly. "Charge to fifteen." For a moment, she stared at her surgeon. *Is his heart white?* Beatrice wanted to see.

The woman behind the silver machine, adjusting a dial on the machine's face, had light streaming from her chest. She twisted the knob before speaking. "Charged."

Crisis.

The surgeon depressed a button on the handle of the spoon.

The monitor blipped once, twice, then the glowing green road of hills, bumps, and cliffs began to tent up the once-flattened line.

Beatrice dropped.

Darkness.

Jace positioned the spoon-like paddles directly on the heart muscle. "Charge to fifteen."

The point of crisis. The critical point to move from the still heart to restoration of heart function.

Gabby responded, "Charged."

Jace discharged the paddles. The heart quivered, beat once, twice, and then dropped into a regular rhythm. Clockwork.

"Okay," Jace said, "let's dial back the pump." He paused, studying the heart. "Looks like we need volume. Give me one hundred."

Gabby responded, "One hundred … in!"

Jace looked over at Evan. "What's the echo look like?"

Evan studied the ultrasound screen. "Valve looks good."

"Amazing," Jace said. "Great job, team."

Dave Fitzgerald nodded. "You pulled it off, Jace."

"Dial back the pump another fifty percent. Let's get out of here."

19

Jace spent the first eight hours after Beatrice's surgery doing what surgical interns call "sitting hearts." From a chair pulled up to the bedside, he watched every beat of the heart on the monitor, noted every cc of urine, calculated every drop of IV fluid, and graphed blood pressure to identify trends.

There at her bedside, Jace could rest, at home in the environment of electronic beeps, the mechanical whine of the ventilator, the smell of antisepsis, and the sight of a spaghetti-tangle of IV tubing and monitoring lines. There, as in the operating room, Jace was focused, happily distracted from assaults on his conscience.

But it was there, after hours of tedious concentration, that his mind began to drift. He remembered waking up in an ICU not so very different from the one he now sat in. But that had been a world away.

That day, he had struggled to open his eyes against lids thick with sleep. *Did someone tape my eyes shut? Where am I?*

Another sensation grew, pushing him into consciousness. *Pain!* Throbbing, itching, poking up his scalp with a thousand needles inside his skin.

Something is burrowing its way across my scalp.

Light. Fluorescent tubes behind a lattice covering. Voices. Beeping.

Beeping too fast for my heart.

A female voice. "Dr. Rawlings?"

He strained to lift his hand and saw that it was connected to a clear plastic tube. *I have an IV.*

What has happened to me?

My throat is sore. He explored the dry cave of his mouth with his tongue. He attempted to close his mouth, but found that impossible. Something blocked him. *A tube. Am I intubated?*

Someone has to kill the animal inside my head.

A female voice again. *Janice?*

Am I dead?

His next thought terrified him. *Was my father right? Am I in hell?*

He explored a few inches around his hands. A bed. Another tube. A railing.

"You're in the hospital."

A face floated above him.

"Call his wife. I think he's waking up."

A touch on Jace's shoulder brought him back to the present. It was Paul Mwaka, his intern. "Dr. Rawlings, why don't you go take a break. I'll oversee Beatrice's care for the night. I'll try to wean her from the ventilator."

Jace rubbed his eyes. "Okay." He stood and took a step toward the door. "You'll call me if you have any concerns. Any at all."

"Of course."

Jace walked away, his eyes seeing the rocky path in front of him, but his mind still heavy with recollection of his own ICU stay. In the hospital, he'd awakened to a cloudy reality, unsure how he'd gotten there and what events had led him to the point of being in a car with the governor's wife. And yet, from within the confusion was a new vision for a radical change in his life. From the haze of unclear memories, he'd experienced the real sense that his sister wanted him back in Kenya.

That's when Jace began a delicate walk, holding the hand of sane reason on one side and the not-so-comfortable hand of mystical experience on the other. That's all he knew to call it. He wouldn't have described his calling back to Kenya as spiritual, exactly, but he knew it also wasn't entirely rational. He'd opened his eyes in the ICU with a vision of his sister leaning over him and imploring him to return.

It wasn't the kind of thing he could share with the doctors back home. They'd think he was coming unglued.

And Jace wasn't so sure they were wrong.

That night, in a late celebration of sorts, Gabby Dawson and Dr. Evan Martin joined Jace at his house for supper. Jace had picked up takeout from Mama Chiku's. That meant hot stew, chapatis, ugali, and the spicy meat-filled dough pockets called samosas.

"I wish I had a few cold Tuskers to share," Jace said. "I'd like for you to be able to sample Kenyan beer, but Kijabe is pretty much a teetotaler kind of town."

Evan sat at the table laden with local food. "Against the law?" He looked at his watch. Not waiting for Jace's reply, he added, "Did you know we're nearly a mile and a half over sea level here? I'll bet all our patients are a few points down on their oxygen saturation."

"Reports from the gadget guy," Gabby said before asking Jace again, "So drinking is against the law?"

"Not a written one exactly. More of an expected way for the missionary community to behave."

Gabby chuckled. "So when did our Dr. Rawlings decide to start painting inside the lines?"

Jace sighed. "Recently," he said, pausing uncomfortably. He wasn't good at offering prayers, but felt something was needed. He looked at Gabby. "Would you say grace?"

She nodded and bowed her head. "Dear Father, thanks for this food we are about to eat. And thanks especially for watching over Beatrice and our team. I pray Your continued guidance for Jace and for Your hand of healing to rest upon our patient. In Jesus' name, amen."

They filled their plates. The trio fell silent as they sampled the local fare. Soon, approving grunts and "umms" followed.

Jace dragged his ugali through the stew, the customary way to eat the thick white starch. "So you think that's what got me here?"

Gabby looked confused.

"God's guidance," Jace suggested. "You asked God to continue to guide me. I guess that means you think I'm following His lead."

She sighed. From satisfaction or anxiety, Jace wasn't sure. "I hope you are, Jace. Something big has obviously happened to you. If anyone was ever on the professional track to stardom back home, it was you." She gestured around the little room and its sparse furnishings. "Now look at you. You live here, of all places, and are giving your services away."

Evan leaned forward. "I think traveling all the way over here to help you entitles us to the inside story. There are all sorts of rumors back in Richmond about why you left. Some say you're running. Others talk of a Damascus-road experience."

Jace frowned. "Damascus?"

The anesthesiologist nodded. "The Christian-hater Saul turned into Paul the apostle on the road to Damascus where he saw a bright light and heard a call from Christ." He gestured, palms up. "*Damascus-road* refers to a turnaround of similar proportion."

"I'm not sure my experience was so spiritual."

"So what?" Evan asked, helping himself to another hot samosa. "If it isn't spiritual, are you running from something?"

Jace hesitated.

Evan probed again. "Did you cheat on your wife?"

"That's not your business."

"I think the fact that I came all the way over here to make sure you find the success you desire makes it my business. I need to know who I'm working for here. Why are we doing this? To appease your conscience?"

"I love my wife."

Evan stared down his longtime friend. "So you weren't having an affair with the governor's wife?"

Jace set down his fork and gripped his left hand to cover up a tremor. He shook his head. "I really don't know."

"Don't tell me," Evan replied with sarcasm, "Heather didn't buy it."

Gabby interrupted. "Of course she didn't buy it. You lost your memory. How convenient."

"It's the truth."

"Tell me what you remember, Jace," Gabby said softly.

He took a deep breath. "Anita Franks was an intriguing woman."

"Stop it, Jace," Evan interrupted. "She was gorgeous. Everyone could see that."

"Okay, she was gorgeous. And interested in me. We shared a meal or two, mostly just professional stuff, me filling her in on her husband's progress. But …." He paused. "I got the feeling that she was unhappy in her marriage. She talked about the governor. He was never home, didn't treat her like he used to, that kind of thing."

Jace's friends sat and met his gaze, saying nothing.

"We never did anything."

"Jace," Evan said, "you were seen with her exiting a downtown hotel."

"That was the night of the accident." Jace moved his hand across his scalp, tracing a long scar. "I don't remember."

"Did you want to have an affair?" Gabby asked.

"Look, what I wanted isn't relevant. You saw Anita Franks. What testosterone-bearing male wouldn't want her, at least at some level? The proper question is, am I capable of giving in to desire like that? Could I really throw away what I had with Heather for lust?"

"You're worried that you did?"

Jace answered slowly. "I've entertained my share of worry." He paused. "I thought about Anita. Heather and I fought about her all the time. I didn't sleep with her. At least not until …" He halted. "I don't know what I did during that last visit before she died."

Gabby pushed back from the table. "There's something else you should know, Jace. Anita Franks had an autopsy by the medical examiner. There was evidence of recent sexual intercourse just prior to death."

Jace felt sick.

"There's more. Her serum tested positive for ketamine."

"Ketamine? Why ketamine?"

Evan coughed. "I use it all the time in the OR. But recreational use?"

Gabby shook her head. "Not recreational exactly. Ketamine is used for date rape."

"Date rape?" Jace stood up and began to pace. "You don't think that I …"

Evan Martin tapped the tabletop. "Don't jump to conclusions, Jace. I think the presence of ketamine actually helps you."

"And how is that?"

"You say you think Anita Franks was interested in you? Interested in an affair?"

Jace shrugged. "She was pretty friendly. Always hugging."

"So if you were reading the cues correctly, you wouldn't have needed ketamine to—" He hesitated, clearing his throat. "Well, to have an affair."

Gabby shook her head. "The problem with the ketamine is that you had access to the drug through your work." She added stew to her empty plate. "You could choose to give a DNA sample. They could compare it to the semen sample found in Anita Franks. That could exonerate you."

Jace stopped pacing in front of his little sink. He looked out the window to the night beyond. "Or prove to everyone, even me, that Jace Rawlings isn't the altruistic surgeon that he wants everyone to believe, that Jace Rawlings is nothing more than a manipulative cheat, running from scandal."

20

The next morning, Jace headed to the HDU before sunup. When he approached Beatrice's bed, she made immediate eye contact, locking on Jace with an intensity unusual in the Kenyan culture.

Her wrists were tied with padded restraints, an effort to keep her from pulling out her endotracheal tube, the tube placed through her mouth that delivered oxygen straight into her trachea.

Jace went over her clipboard data, noting vital signs, ins and outs and oxygen saturation. Other than a tachycardia, which seemed to have developed since he arrived, her night had been perfect. When he looked up, she glared at him, her eyes unflinching and her brow beaded with sweat.

"Everything looks good, Beatrice," he said, taking her hand in his below her wrist restraint. Instead of a gentle squeeze, she returned a vice-grip on his fingers. He pulled away, shaking his hand. "Wow. Okay. Good grip," he said.

He studied her ventilator settings. Everything seemed to indicate that she was ready to breathe on her own.

He looked at her nurse. "Could you set up an oxygen facemask? I want to pull this tube."

While the nurse prepared, Jace asked Beatrice to lift her head from the pillow. One last test to see if she was strong enough to stay off the ventilator.

Beatrice lifted her head, still not averting her gaze.

Jace worked to free the tape holding in the tube from the patient's cheeks and generous lips. He used a syringe to pull the air out of the tube's balloon-cuff. "Cough," he said. As she did, he slipped the tube out of her mouth.

"Dr. Raw-Raw-Rawlings," she gasped.

"Don't try to talk now, Beatrice. Save your energy." He fixed her facemask in place, pulling a stretchy band around the top of her head.

He watched her a few moments while he freed her from the restraints. "That should be more comfortable."

When he turned to leave, she gripped the tail of his white coat.

He turned. Her face was etched with fear. "Beatrice, what's wrong? Are you in pain?"

She shook her head. "I have a message for you."

"A message?" He slipped his hand in hers again. "From whom?"

"Go see Michael Kagai."

Jace recognized the name of his bowel-perforation patient. "I don't understand. How do you know Michael?"

"I don't."

"Then how—"

Beatrice struggled to whisper. "Can't explain it." Her eyes seemed to be searching his face, obviously troubled. "Tell him to—" Her voice faded.

"Tell him what?"

She shrugged. "What a person should do to prepare for dying. You know. Like call a preacher or something."

Jace looked at the nurse. *Delirium?* "We see confusion after bypass sometimes."

"I'm not confused. Just warn him," she begged. "He is going to die tonight."

Naomi Wanjiku, Beatrice's mother, sat for two and a half hours on the worn wooden bench in the hospital corridor waiting for the nurse counselor to call her name. Then she listened as the kind woman explained the consequences of getting an HIV test.

For Naomi, it was old news. She'd been tested twice before. Miraculously, she'd always been negative. Now, she wanted to be tested again.

To prove Beatrice wrong. She'd visited her daughter, who had come out of surgery claiming some inside spiritual knowledge. She'd begged her mother to get tested again. "It's important, Mother. There are treatments that can help you."

After the counseling session, the nurse drew Naomi's blood. Then she waited, watching the little indicator in the circle on the test strip. If it showed a blue plus sign, it would mean Naomi was HIV positive.

She felt a little silly, really. But Beatrice had latched onto the idea with such vigor that Naomi had finally relented. "Okay," she said, "since there is a voluntary testing center in this hospital, I'll go. Besides, you need to get your rest."

A twinge of anxiety tightened her gut. *What if Beatrice is right?* Images from her past moved through her consciousness. Countless encounters for a few shillings. Men as desperate for her as she was for the drugs she would buy with their money.

She watched, her gaze fixated on the test strip.

A bright blue plus sign appeared and darkened.

HIV positive.

For the rest of the day, Jace was haunted by Beatrice's words, but discounted them as the product of some sort of paranoid reaction after cardiopulmonary bypass. Weird neurologic sequelae had been reported after cardiac bypass. This must have been just another unreported side effect. Maybe one small area of her brain wasn't perfused well during the bypass portion of the operation.

Nonetheless, Jace checked on Michael Kagai not once, not twice, but three times during the day. Each time, the man was jovial. He'd accepted, even anticipated his HIV-positive status. Jace had referred him to the medicine team that planned to start him on antiretroviral medications. He was eating and walking well enough for discharge. Jace promised Michael that he'd let him go in the morning. Unlike in America, where Jace constantly had insurance reviewers breathing down his neck and demanding patient discharges, in Africa, he often had to make sure his post-op patients were well enough to walk five or ten kilometers to get to their homes in the bush. And that meant extra days of recovery in the hospital—but at less than ten dollars per day for in-hospital room and board, no one was complaining.

Nairobi's top newspaper, *The Standard*, ran a story about Kijabe's heart program along with a picture of Jace at the bedside of Beatrice Wanjiku. The article was favorable, done in response to a press release by the hospital administration. Jace stood at the newspaper stand outside the front entrance of the hospital, thumbing through the article and smiling. For good or ill, the word was out: Kijabe Hospital was doing heart surgery.

Jace was just turning toward the driveway in front of the hospital and looking up at the many weaver birds' nests in the tree when his pager sounded. He returned to the guard station to answer. He punched in the number. Wairegi men's ward. "Dr. Rawlings. I was paged."

"Dr. Rawlings," the nurse gasped. "Please come back to Wairegi. Your patient is not breathing."

"Not breathing? Who?"

The nurse must have covered the phone with her hand. In a muffled tone, he heard her ask who was coding. He heard the answer. "Mr. Michael Kagai."

"I'll be right there."

He ran back up the sidewalk and into the building, rushing up the long graded hallway to the second floor. At the top of the ramp, he turned left onto the men's ward.

A full code was in progress. His patient had been intubated by the intern and a nurse was doing CPR.

"What happened?" Jace questioned.

"He walked up to the nurses' station. Then he collapsed when he turned to go back to his bed. He grabbed his chest and fell to the floor."

"How long have you been at this?"

The intern checked his watch. "Ten minutes."

"What does the monitor say?"

"Asystole."

They continued giving two rounds of drugs.

No response.

How could this have happened? He looked fine an hour ago!

Jace immediately thought back to Beatrice's comments, now a prophecy fulfilled. He sighed and pulled out a pocket penlight. He shone it into the eyes of his patient. "It's no use. His pupils are already fixed and dilated. We've lost him."

"Must have had a pulmonary embolus."

"Or an acute MI."

Jace shook his head. "It was his time."

Wow. I'm thinking like a Kenyan.

He looked at his watch. "Let's call it. Time of death, seven ten."

He stayed a few minutes and filled out a death certificate. As he walked down the hallway a few minutes later, he paused. *I've got to talk to Beatrice. How did she know?*

This was something far deeper than the manifestation of post-pump paranoia.

He walked to the HDU, where he found Beatrice sipping sweet Kenyan chai. He nodded at her soberly. "Hi, Beatrice. Can we talk?"

She set down a steaming plastic mug. "Sure."

"This morning, you warned me about a man named Michael Kagai."

"Yes."

"Beatrice, he was my patient. He just passed away."

"I'm sorry," she said. "I knew it. I told you. Did you warn him?"

Jace shook his head slowly. "No. I checked on him three times today. He looked fine. I was planning on sending him home tomorrow."

"You should have warned him. He wasn't a Christian."

"Beatrice," he said, hesitating. "How do you know?"

"Surely your patients have told you stories."

"Stories?"

She shrugged. "Messages. Warnings."

Jace grew frustrated. "No one has ever sent me warnings before. Why do you think my patients would send me messages?"

"Tell me about my operation. You stopped my heart. I saw it. I was dead and yet I was not dead. I was watching you as you worked on me."

Jace shook his head again. "That's not possible. You weren't dead. Your heart wasn't beating, but we had a machine doing the work of your heart while your own heart was still. The machine kept you alive."

"Dr. Rawlings, I saw things. Heard things."

"What things?"

"Who was the woman? Gabby, you called her. You joked about finding her a Kenyan husband."

Jace drew back, lifting his head with a memory of the conversation. *You couldn't have heard that. You were under anesthesia.*

"I saw people in a new way. Some were filled with light. Some were dark. I saw Mr. Kagai." She seemed to hesitate. "He was dark."

"You saw light?"

"Inside of people. Christians."

Jace touched his hair. This was crazy. She couldn't know such things. "You predicted he would die."

"An angel told me. He said I was to give you the message."

"Why me?"

She shrugged. As nonchalantly as if they were talking about the weather. "Maybe they are sending you a warning."

"Warning me? Why?"

Beatrice bit the inside of her lip and looked away. When she looked back at Jace, she changed the subject. "When can I have this tube taken out?" She gestured toward the tube draining blood from her chest cavity, a mediastinal tube.

Jace frowned. "You didn't answer my question."

"Maybe you don't want to know."

"Don't want to know? Of course I want to know."

Beatrice eyed a Kenyan nurse who had joined Jace at the bedside. "Because, Dr. Rawlings, I did not see light in you."

21

Jace walked down the sloping hallway from the HDU, wanting only to be alone and get back to his house. He was almost to the door when he heard his name.

"Dr. Rawlings."

He looked around to see Naomi Wanjiku, Beatrice's mother.

Naomi ran off a phrase in the Kikuyu language.

Jace held up his hand and walked a few steps to the door where a hospital guard sat in a chair. "Can you help me understand her?"

The guard spoke to the woman. Naomi gesticulated wildly, waving her hands and pointing at Jace and back up to the HDU. Jace understood very little of what she said, except that he recognized his name and Beatrice's name over and over.

The guard shook his head and put his hand on Naomi's shoulder. Finally, she stopped talking. The guard looked at Jace. "She wants to know what you have done to her daughter."

Jace began explaining the operation, something he'd done before, though perhaps Naomi hadn't understood.

"No, no, not that," the guard said. "She knows what operation you performed." He seemed to hesitate, shuffling his feet. "She says that her daughter has powers now."

"Powers?"

"This woman says you have worked magic on her daughter, that you have turned her into a prophetess."

Jace squinted. He didn't like where this was going. "Look, just tell her that I am a scientist. I don't work magic. I merely performed a heart valve replacement. I'm sure there is some logical explanation for what she is seeing in her daughter."

"She says her daughter's face is brighter."

"Of course," Jace said. "She has normal heart function for the first time in a long time. She has more blood flowing to her body. Certainly she will appear more vital."

The guard explained in Kikuyu. Naomi interrupted with more emphatic words and hand waving. She motioned for the man to come closer, then whispered something in his ear.

The guard pulled back, again shaking his head. "She says her daughter awoke from the operation with special knowledge that you had given her."

"Tell her the daughter's mind is confused, a common occurrence after major surgery. I've ordered some medications that will help soothe her mind."

Jace listened as the guard translated, but after another exchange, the man shook his head. "She says there was no way that her daughter could have predicted her illness, but that her daughter told her about her HIV status."

Jace sighed. "Look," he said in a soft voice. "I'm not sure what you should tell her except to assure her that I am not a magic man. As far as her daughter's prediction goes, I can assure you that this woman's occupation puts her at risk for the disease you mentioned. It would not take a scientist to predict the outcome of such a test."

Jace turned to go, and left the guard talking rapidly to Naomi. As the door closed behind him, he heard Naomi repeat the English word *magic*.

That evening, Jace built a fire in his fireplace to chase away the chill. As had become their usual practice, Evan and Gabby joined him, and the trio sipped Kenyan chai and discussed the future.

Evan adjusted a small oximeter clip over his index finger. "See," he said to Gabby. "I'm two points lower at this altitude than back in Richmond." Then his demeanor shifted and he changed the subject. "I can't justify staying around if I'm not helping."

Jace frowned. "So help out with the general surgery load like I do. You don't have to do just hearts."

"I didn't come here to do anesthesia for general cases, Jace."

"After the newspaper article, I'm sure we'll get more cases. The word is just getting out."

Gabby added granular sugar to her mug. "Maybe you should advertise that we're giving magical experiences."

"Ha, ha," Jace responded. "Our patient just had some post-pump paranoia, that's all."

Gabby shifted in her seat. "So how do you explain that she predicted her mother's HIV?"

"Come on, Gabby. The woman is a prostitute in Kenya. How likely is she to be HIV positive?"

"Okay, I'll accept that. But what about her prediction about Michael Kagai?"

"She must have heard someone mention his name. I could look back, but I think they might have been in the HDU together. The place isn't exactly huge. It would be easy for one patient to hear what the nurses say about another. Again, he was HIV positive. He wasn't exactly low risk for dying. She just twisted something she was thinking into a paranoid delusion."

"Altogether," Gabby said, "you've got to admit, it seems pretty spooky."

"There is a reasonable explanation for all of that stuff." Jace stood and walked toward the kitchen. He didn't like Gabby giving credence to Beatrice's predictions. He was glad that he hadn't decided to share the description that Beatrice had given about him. The last thing he needed was Christian Gabby talking about the darkness of his soul.

But discount it as he tried, the description haunted him.

"Come on, Jace," Gabby continued. "You of all people should be open to this sort of communication from beyond the grave."

Jace stayed quiet, his hand almost involuntarily tracing the scar on his scalp.

"If you really think your sister sent you a message, why not Beatrice?"

Jace shook his head, aware of the irony. "I don't know." He paced back into the little den where his friends sat. "Okay, let's play this out. Suppose Beatrice did get a message from another realm. Why would someone ask *me* to warn someone about death? I'm about the least likely person to be able to help. Why not tell a chaplain?" Jace paused. "So why would someone want me to know this stuff?"

"Could you have prevented his death?"

"If I'd been there and witnessed it?" Jace shrugged. "I don't know." He sat on the couch and stared at his friends through the steam lifting off the mug in his hands. He didn't want to admit that Beatrice's prediction had any merit.

Because if that was true, he'd have to confront the darkness in his soul.

The phone rang. Jace was thankful for the diversion. "Yes?"

"Dr. Rawlings, we have another young patient with a significant heart murmur."

Jace recognized his intern's voice. "What is the situation?"

"Seventeen-year-old male. Very short of breath. Neck veins distended. Looks like heart failure."

"Use oxygen, give Lasix. I'll be over soon."

"We're in casualty."

"Okay," Jace said, hanging up the phone. Then, to Evan he said, "Looks like you might not have to wait so long for our next heart case."

In the HDU, a young man in a blue business suit identified himself to a nurse as Beatrice's brother and asked for an update.

A few minutes later, he slipped into the empty corridor to use his cell phone. "Dr. Okayo," he said quietly, "I'm calling for Minister Okombo. The American doctor's work is done here."

The rain started suddenly, prompting Jace to retreat back inside for shelter. Then, with his umbrella low and braced against the wind, he started out again, walking the slick path back down toward the casualty department. He jumped the quickly forming puddles, zigging a diagonal line, imagining himself a checkers piece, conquering his opponent on the way to being crowned.

His little game diverted his attention, and as he arrived at the guard gate, he collided with a young blue-suited man fending off the rain with a newspaper. They glanced off at the shoulders as the man began a reflexive, "Pole, pole sana." Sorry, so sorry.

Jace caught a glimpse of the man's face as they passed. Determined look, chin set and clean shaven, and dark eyes that flashed with an instant of recognition. It did not register for a moment, but then Jace remembered. *Samuel, Minister Okombo's driver.*

Jace stepped into a puddle, and muddy water ran into his shoe. He hopped quickly on and raised his umbrella, calling out to the man. "Samuel!"

But the man continued on, rushing away with his newspaper tented over his head. In the downpour, Jace's words dissolved away and the man was gone.

22

Jace's night was anything but routine. He started with the admission of a young Maasai man in heart failure, almost certainly another case of valvular destruction after an untreated strep infection. Before he left casualty, two victims of a traffic accident were brought in, one with a jagged and gaping laceration running ear to ear across the top of the head. Jace and his intern, Paul, worked in the theater for an hour just matching up the skin left behind. Then, when he thought he was done for the night, Jace got a call from the student health nurse up at RVA. She was escorting a student down, a senior with right lower-quadrant pain.

Jace suspected appendicitis. Unfortunately, it took the better part of the next hour to successfully contact the student's father by phone. The parents, missionaries in the bush near Dire Dawa, Ethiopia, gave consent. The mother would try to come down the next day.

By three, Jace plodded home, tired but strangely invigorated. Rather than being put off by his general surgery call duties, he found he enjoyed dealing with fixable problems. While not life-and-death like most of his heart patients, the general surgery problems were nonetheless serious, and tended to improve rapidly after an operation. There was something comforting to Jace about having done a neat operation on a kid who would get better and go back to school in a day or two. *Yes,* he thought, *I can still do general surgery.* He smiled and imagined himself like the first cardiac surgeons. He'd read stories of Michael DeBakey, the infamous heart surgeon from Texas. His operative schedule might include an open-heart case, a bowel case, and a hemorrhoid all in one day.

By three fifteen, Jace had stripped off his clothes, including the sock still damp from his encounter with the puddle, and collapsed into bed. He knew nothing after that until his alarm sounded at seven.

He met Evan Martin for rounds the next morning. Together, they used the ultrasound machine to look at the heart of young Joseph Ole Kosoi. *Ole* means "son of" in the Kimaasai language. Joseph had returned home from boarding school saying he had been unable to keep up with the other boys in rugby practice. Whereas in prior seasons he'd always been able to outperform his peers, now he became winded with a slow jog across the field. Jace traced the problems back to an episode of flu-like symptoms two months before. Now, the patient was exhibiting classic signs of heart failure: distended neck veins, shortness of breath, and difficulty breathing while lying flat on his back. Whenever he tried, he felt like he was drowning.

Which he was, his lungs filling with the fluid his heart was too weak to pump away. The patient coughed and spat the wet foam into a plastic cup.

Jace placed his stethoscope against Joseph's back and explained what he heard to his intern. "This is what rales sound like," he said. "The classic description is the crackling sound of hair being rolled between the fingers in front of the ear. The further up on the back you hear the rales, the worse the failure."

The intern listened, stepping the diaphragm of his stethoscope up the patient's back. His eyes widened as he reached the apex. "Here," he said.

Jace nodded soberly. No wonder the patient couldn't breathe.

Joseph wore a red-patterned shuka. Jace suspected that Joseph wore Western dress at his boarding school, but quickly reverted to traditional dress at home. He smelled of smoke, cow leather, and sweat. Jace had been in the small mud-and-manure dwellings of the Maasai tribe, so he understood. Inside, the huts were dark and permeated with the heavy odor of the open fires used for cooking. On either side of the cooking area were beds, leather stretched tight across a natural stick frame.

Evan repositioned the patient and scanned across the chest with the ultrasound. "Just what you thought. The aortic valve is destroyed."

Jace nodded. "Our next case."

Paul frowned. "The blood bank is exhausted. They warned me no more hearts until they can find donors."

Jace raised his index finger. "I've been thinking about that." He held out his hand to his anesthesiologist friend. "Let me see your wallet."

Evan handed it over. Naive.

Jace lifted a small handful of bills. "This ought to do."

Evan protested. "What are you doing?"

"Hey, you're the one who said you were leaving if you couldn't do hearts. Call this a loan. You want to do hearts, you may just have to pay."

Jace walked away, deaf to his friend's protests.

Fifteen minutes later, Jace made a deal with a local shopkeeper, the owner of the Supa-Duka, the colorful local general store. Jace paid the shopkeeper twenty thousand shillings to purchase forty five-hundred-shilling vouchers. His plan was to hand out vouchers to anyone willing to donate a unit of blood. In an economy where the hourly wage was closer to fifty shillings an hour, a five-hundred-shilling voucher would tempt anyone. To sweeten the deal, he paid for thirty lunches at Mama Chiku's so that the first thirty donors could eat stew and chapatis.

Jace went home to print vouchers, then paid a schoolboy fifty shillings to distribute them throughout Kijabe town.

By four o'clock, they had forty fresh units of blood in the blood bank. Ten units were compatible with Joseph Ole Kosoi's blood type.

By six, Jace was planning his next open-heart case. He looked at Paul. "We continue to diurese him for the next thirty-six hours. If we can stabilize him, I think we can operate."

The intern nodded. "I will be monitoring the urine output and his vital signs." He paused and touched a small bandage at his elbow crease.

Jace pointed at the bandage. "Are you okay?"

"Just donated a unit of blood for a worthy cause."

Jace smiled. "For a free meal."

Now the intern smiled back. "Sawa sawa," he said. The phrase was Kiswahili and meant, "Okay, okay."

That night, the phone woke Jace. He shook his head and mumbled, "I'm not on call," before forcing himself from the comfort of his chair in front of the warm fireplace. He winced as his bare feet touched the cool linoleum. Picking up the phone, he growled, "Hello."

"Dr. Rawlings." The voice was deep, male, and belonged to the MP. He cleared his throat. "Minister Okombo."

"I'm calling to thank you. I hear that your first open-heart case has been successful."

He didn't call her his daughter. Perhaps he was in a public place.

"I want to invite your team to my office. Dinner with the minister of health. I will be sending a car on Friday."

Jace rubbed his eyes. *Friday?* He sighed and collected his thoughts. "I am honored, sir, but I have another urgent case to attend to. Perhaps we can reschedule."

"It has to be Friday." Minister Okombo raised his voice.

Jace was tired. And he didn't feel like being manipulated by the politician. Again.

"Do I need remind you that your equipment is in Kijabe only because I arranged it?" Okombo said.

Jace reacted, speaking without restraint. "Do I need remind you that your daughter is alive because we were able to help her?"

Jace listened to the sound of breath blowing into the phone. "Look," Jace said. "Could we come this weekend? I really do have an urgent case to attend to."

"Fine."

Silence followed his cryptic response. Jace worried that he had offended the powerful man. He wasn't sure how to respond.

"I'll send a car. Ten a.m. Saturday morning."

Before Jace could thank him, he heard the noisy clunk of the phone slamming into its cradle.

In Richmond, Heather Rawlings sat across from Detective Steve Brady as he looked at the report lying on the coffee table between them. Steve's wife, Carol, balancing a toddler on her hip, set a mug of coffee in front of her husband. He touched her hand gently as she lifted it from the mug. Their eyes met.

Jace used to look at me that way, Heather thought.

Heather had called Steve and Carol, who attended her church, to ask if she could stop by their home and ask a few questions.

Her detective friend loosened his tie. "Where'd you say you got this?"

"Got it in the mail. Is it legit?"

"It might be."

"There was ketamine in her blood."

The detective sighed.

"I don't need to tell you what that implies," Heather said.

"You want me investigating this? Heather, you're putting me in a funny—"

"No," she said, shaking her head. "I don't want to cause Jace trouble." She hesitated. "I just need to know the truth. Can't you just ask some questions for me?"

He shook his head slowly. "Look, this may not even be legit. I can check with the medical examiner's office and see if I can find the original. I'll keep it off the books for now, but the presence of ketamine complicates things a bit."

"I'm not sure why your department wasn't aware of this report."

"Mrs. Franks's death was not being investigated as a homicide. She was struck by a passing motorist. It was a pedestrian accident."

"But if the governor's wife had been raped, wouldn't you want to know that?"

"Heather, you can't believe Jace could—"

"I don't know what to believe anymore. Jace has no memory of that night. He doesn't remember being in a car with Anita Franks at all." She hesitated. "But I want to know the truth. I want to know why someone thought this information was important enough to send to me."

"We don't even know if this is a real document. Someone could have easily forged it. Sent it to you to make you doubt your husband." He tapped a pencil against his desk. "Who would want you to think Jace was unfaithful?"

She cleared her throat. "No one. I mean, the media went crazy with speculation about his relationship with the governor's wife, but Jace assured me it was all talk."

Steve shrugged and straightened a small picture frame containing a shot of himself and Carol standing in front of an ocean. "So you believe your husband?"

"I want to believe him." Heather took a deep breath and touched the corners of her eyes with a Kleenex. She looked at Carol, who had positioned herself on the flowered couch beside her husband. "There are moments when I know I should throw my doubts away and believe that Jace is the man I love. But then, other times ..." Her voice weakened.

Carol reached over and squeezed Heather's hand.

"I'll find the true ME's report, see if this is valid," Steve said.

"If it is?"

"I'm not sure it means anything. Ketamine in the blood doesn't necessarily mean foul play. It may only mean that Anita Franks had a penchant for illegal drug experimentation. I hear ketamine and LSD share similar qualities."

"Ketamine is a date-rape drug."

"I know that. But the presence of the drug itself means nothing. Anita Franks was not known to be raped."

Heather pointed to the report. "There was evidence of recent intercourse."

"Exactly. Intercourse isn't sexual assault."

Heather sighed. "I'm not sure that news is any comfort to me now."

"What exactly do you want me to do?"

"I'm not sure. I'm just looking for advice. I'm trying to find out the truth."

23

Two days later, Jace's team gathered in the theater for an aortic valve replacement. The room had been fumigated for mosquitoes; the blood bank was ten units ahead; monitoring lines were in.

Game on.

Jace sutured in the atrial and aortic canulas. "Let's go on bypass," he said to Gabby. "I'm opening venous line to you."

"Venous line open. We're on bypass," she echoed.

Two minutes later, the electricity failed. Gabby scrambled to operate the pump by hand.

Jace looked around the room. The overhead lights were off, the operative field dim. A moment ago, with his attention only on his operative field, he could have believed he was anywhere in the developed world. With the electricity off, he was brought back to reality. *TIA. This is Africa.*

In thirty seconds, the generator kicked on and the lights returned. Jace breathed a sigh of relief. "Let's cool."

After a few minutes, Jace used the cardioplegia, stopping the heart during diastole. "Knife."

"Wow," Jace mumbled as he looked at the patient's valve. "No wonder he was in heart failure."

For the next two hours, they worked with orchestrated precision. When the patient's temperature was three degrees below normal, Jace put the paddles against the heart muscle. "Charge to twenty."

"Twenty, charged," Gabby said.

"Clear."

At the head of the bed, Evan compressed both carotid arteries on the side of the patient's neck. This was a protective measure to prevent the first blood pumped out of the heart from going to the brain, just in case all of the air hadn't been removed from the heart before restarting it. Air left in the heart, even in small amounts, could cause a stroke if allowed to reach the brain.

The heart began a fine quiver. "We've got fibrillation. Charge again to twenty."

"Twenty, charged."

Crisis.

Jace depressed the buttons on the end of the defibrillator. This time the heart began to pump. Once, twice, then jumping into a regular rhythm.

Evan counted five beats, then opened flow to the brain by lifting his fingers from the carotid arteries. He studied the echo and then looked across the drapes into the open chest. "Looks like he could use a little volume."

"Agreed," Jace echoed. "Give me a hundred."

Gabby nodded and turned a dial. "One hundred, in."

"Better," Jace said. "Dial back the bypass to fifty. Let's get out of here."

Jace spent the first eight hours post-op at Joseph's bedside, doing what he could to keep his anxieties at bay. Give a bolus of fluid. Titrate in a little morphine. Wean down the oxygen. He relished the predictability of physiology at work.

But that night, he lay on his bed and sighed, unable to escape the oppression of Beatrice's revelation. *I did not see light in you.*

Her words didn't really surprise him. He would have predicted he would be dark. But his patient's words unroofed old hurt, a bellyful of pain that he knew he needed to face but didn't know how.

If I am dark, he thought, *my sister was light.*

He remembered how intense she was in the weeks leading up to their graduation.

A youth minister from New York had given an emotional plea for students to make a commitment to Christ on the final day of spiritual emphasis week at Rift Valley Academy. Day after day, Janice had responded, weeping for herself and her friends at the altar. Jace had sat in his chair, dry-eyed and unmoved.

Afterward, they walked together down the rocky path toward their house.

"I've decided to stay an extra year in Africa," she said. "I'll work as a surgical tech for Dad in the theater and volunteer at the children's hospital. It will give me a chance to beef up my résumé for medical school application."

Jace said nothing. He couldn't wait to get to America and start a life of his own.

"Jace, why don't you stay? You could work in the physical therapy department or—"

"What's this about? I'm going to college, Janice. I need to find a life outside this bubble."

"Don't you see? This bubble has been protecting us, Jace."

"Restricting us, more like."

She shifted her backpack to the other shoulder and sighed. "Why didn't you respond to the message? All your friends were at the altar, yet you stayed in your seat."

He shook his head. "It's not my thing."

"Your thing? Is that what you think this is? My thing?"

"I don't know. We've always been different that way. We hear the same message. You believe. I doubt." He shrugged.

"You could believe."

"You could doubt."

She shook her head. "No, Jace, I can't. Look around. The world is amazing. Everything speaks of a creator. I feel Him. He loves us, Jace."

"Jacob have I loved," he mumbled.

"What?"

"Nothing."

"Say it, Jace. You're quoting the Bible."

"Yeah. Spiritual me."

They walked along in silence, but Jace knew his twin was boiling. Finally, when they reached the turnoff leading to their house, she spoke. "Do you think that's us? Jacob and Esau?"

"Maybe," he said. "I hate that story."

"You're not Esau."

"How do you know? Why do you cry when you hear about the cross and I don't?" He paused and shrugged. "Jacob have I loved. Esau have I hated." He touched her shoulder. "Janice have I loved."

"No, Jace. Listen to what He says to you. Jace have I loved."

"I wish I believed it. It sounds nice."

"It doesn't just sound nice, Jace. It's truth."

"Is that why you don't want me going off to America?"

"I'm afraid for you. You need to make a decision before you leave this place. Decide to live your life for something bigger than yourself."

"God."

"Yes, God."

"You're afraid I'll get away from the bubble and never come back."

"Jace, I just want you to respond to God's call."

"What is it with you? Why the God-talk all the time?"

She shook her head. "This isn't something to joke about. You know what happened to Timmy. You never know what will happen. You heard the chapel speaker. We could have an accident and be standing before the throne of judgment tonight. Or tomorrow."

"That's just it. Timmy dies. And it makes you think we should make a decision to follow God. But for me, it just makes me want to doubt that God loved us in the first place. How could God let that happen to him?"

"We can't know why. We just know He loves us."

"Well, maybe He loves *you*." *Jacob!*

Jace walked into the house and up to his room. He wished he believed.

But faith just didn't seem like something he could psych himself into, as if he were preparing for a rugby match.

God, if You're really there, show me.

24

Jace fell into a fitful sleep after midnight, rousing at six when the ibis squawked a proclamation of the dawn.

He drank Kenya AA coffee prepared in a press and wondered how he'd survived in America without it. He showered, dressed, and hurried to the ICU. It was Saturday, and the team was supposed to join the minister of health for lunch in Nairobi, but Jace wanted to check on his post-op valve patient and be sure everything was stable before he left.

Jace found his patient, Joseph Ole Kosoi, awake and with a familiar face of terror.

Jace winced.

Just like Beatrice.

He told himself it was just the patient's unfamiliarity with his high-tech surroundings. If you were used to sleeping in a mud hut, the environment of the high dependency unit at Kijabe Hospital would certainly be a scary place. With the lights, monitors, electronic alarms, and physical restraints, who wouldn't wake up afraid?

Jace studied the numbers. Blood pressure, check. Ins and outs, check. Central venous pressure, check. Ventilatory mechanics, check. It was time to remove Joseph's endotracheal tube and let him fly on his own.

He looked at the monitor. "He's a bit tachycardic," Jace said, referring to his fast heart rate. "When is the last time he had pain medicine?"

The nurse, a young Kikuyu woman named Dorcas, responded. "He has not received pain medication."

He frowned. "Nothing?"

The nurse checked his bedside chart. "He is Maasai."

"Maasai have pain."

"But they never want pain medication."

"That's crazy. Maasai have pain like everyone else."

"This young man was circumcised without anesthesia and would not dare to whimper or show pain."

"Look at his heart rate. I think he is having pain."

"Look at his face. I do not think it is pain driving up his heart rate."

Jace inhaled. In spite of all Joseph had been through, including a Betadine chest scrub in preparation for surgery, the distinct scent of charcoal lingered.

After the nurse prepared an oxygen mask, Jace told Joseph, "I'm going to take this tube out of your throat." He removed the tape holding the tube in place. He pulled the air out of the balloon with a syringe. "Now cough!"

Joseph obeyed and Jace pulled out the tube.

"Rest, Joseph," he said as he pulled an oxygen facemask over his nose.

His patient struggled to talk, his eyes locked onto Jace's.

Jace sighed and leaned in close to his patient. "Okay, what is it?"

"Your patient, Anthony Kimathi."

He thought through his patient list. He didn't know anyone named Kimathi. "What about him?"

"He's going to die."

"Rest, Joseph," Jace said as the heart-rate alarm sounded. One hundred twenty. "Relax. I'll look into it." He put his hand on the young man's shoulder. He'd get the details when Joseph was stronger. "We'll talk more later."

Jace took a step away from the bedside and pulled a white index card from his pocket. On it he'd written the names of all the patients he'd seen. Not one Anthony and no Kimathis.

He took a deep breath and blew it out slowly, unsure how to react. He hadn't come to Kenya to deal with weird messages from the next life. He was a scientist. Heart surgery was supposed to be predictable. Cardiac output was based on stroke volume and heart rate. But the comforting sameness of physiology hadn't given him a framework for understanding spiritual problems. This experience called him to look back to his Christian roots, the God of his sister, and pushed him toward painful territory.

He checked his watch and looked over at Dorcas. "Do you know Anthony Kimathi?"

"No."

He looked at Joseph. "Do you know him?"

The patient shook his head.

Dorcas seemed to be taking it all in stride.

"Doesn't this strike you as unusual?"

Dorcas wrinkled her nose.

Evidently not.

Jace frowned. "My first two open-heart patients survive to give me spooky messages. Why am I the only one to think this is weird?"

Dorcas lifted her stethoscope from around her neck, preparing to examine the patient. She paused, looking at Jace. "The world you see is not the only reality, Dr. Rawlings. Does this collide with your culture?" She waited for an answer, but when he stayed quiet, she added. "This does not surprise me. What surprises me is that we don't hear about it more."

He walked away thinking that he had traveled across an ocean expecting to arrive in Kenya, and had landed instead on a different planet. Here, young men lived in mud huts and were initiated into manhood by circumcision without anesthesia. Here, witch doctors spoke to the dead, herbs made bruises disappear, and the unseen and seen blurred together in daily life, all accepted as a part of normality. He muttered something about the Twilight Zone and thought ahead to his lunch meeting with the minister of health.

Jace wasn't looking forward to it. In spite of the honor, walking the tightropes of political correctness and cultural appropriateness deflated any air of joy in the experience for him.

When he gathered with Gabby and Evan to wait for John Okombo's driver, Jace warned, "I haven't figured Minister Okombo out. During my first meeting, he drops our governor's name, calling him Stuart as if they are the best of friends. He has me brought to Nairobi to see him as if he is sizing me up, wondering whether I can be trusted. Then, he tells me that Beatrice is his daughter and he wants me to operate—and then orchestrates the hang-up of my equipment in customs, demanding a large tax. Finally, he accuses me of playing games, leveraging his daughter's health to get my equipment through, but then drops the tax altogether and even donates more equipment for us to use in our program."

Evan adjusted his tie, looking unhappy about straying from his normal wardrobe of scrubs. "Sounds like the politician wants to secure your loyalties."

Gabby asked, "How does he know our governor?"

"It seems he was somehow in the middle of a trade deal with the Franks administration: Kenyan tea and coffee for Virginia tobacco."

Evan nodded. "I read about that. The deal is worth millions."

Jace frowned. "Sounds like Virginia gets the sweet part of that deal. We get coffee; the Africans get cancer."

Evan continued fumbling with his tie. "Tobacco growers predict they have another twenty years to flood the African continent with cigarettes before the legal system clamps down with restrictions on advertising and lawsuits over health issues."

Gabby made a final adjustment of Evan's tie and patted his chest. "It's fine."

He frowned. "It's too long."

"Button your coat," Jace said. "No one will notice."

The sound of gravel crunching in the driveway signaled the arrival of their driver.

Jace looked out a window to see a well-dressed Samuel exiting the Land Cruiser. "Let's roll."

In Richmond, Detective Steve Brady circled the back parking lot of the medical examiner's office to see if the service entrance was crowded with funeral-home vehicles. If his morning report predicted correctly, the ME would have plenty of business—there were two fresh homicides, victims of drug-related gang violence.

He parked and walked into the front office. A middle-aged woman sat at a desk behind a counter, looking up as the door opened. "Morning, Steve. Haven't seen you since you left Homicide. How's your new bride?"

He smiled. "Great. Carol's working for Heatwole and Granstead." He lifted a travel mug of coffee in a pretend toast. "Maybe I should retire."

"Fat chance of that," she said, laughing. "You're a crime junkie."

"Always looking for my next fix."

"So what can I do for you?" she said, standing and doing a pirouette. "I know you didn't come by to congratulate me on my new figure."

"Wow," he said. "What did you do?"

She smiled. "Weight Watchers."

"You look great."

"I've lost thirty-eight pounds." She smoothed her skirt and sat back behind the desk. "So what's up?"

"I need to know about an ME report on the governor's wife. Can you check your records to see who might have accessed her autopsy report?"

She shrugged. "Sure." She tapped on a computer keyboard while he waited. "Here it is," she said. "It's confidential information, so our list is pretty short. We released it to the governor's office for his eyes only. Other than that, the report only goes out to her physicians."

"I need a list."

"Well, it looks like only one."

Steve picked up his pen. "And who is that?"

"Dr. Jace Rawlings."

25

At Dagoretti corner, John Okombo's driver exited the highway.

Jace looked out at the crowded shantytown and motioned for Evan to lock his door. "Samuel, why are we going this way?"

"We need to avoid Uhuru Highway because of protests today. I'm taking you in the back way."

The Land Cruiser slowly parted a sea of street children and men pushing carts laden with vegetables. The crowd separated, but quickly pressed in around them with children holding out their hands to the white faces on the other side of the glass windows.

Jace shifted in his seat and looked into the eyes of several teen boys standing next to a burning trash barrel.

The driver picked his way among the frequent potholes, following a colorful matatu covered with paintings of young African men heavy with bling and ghetto attitudes.

Samuel lurched forward, cutting left around a bright orange duka painted with the slogans of a cell-phone company. The Land Cruiser sped down the rutted dirt road, a thick forest on the left and a jumble of tin-roofed shacks on the right.

As they approached a blind corner, Samuel eased the accelerator, but not enough. The Land Cruiser splashed through a puddle, spraying the windows with black water, and careened past a speeding matatu. He rounded the corner, which was crowded by a grove of eucalyptus trees on one side and a billboard for Kenya Airways on the other. Perhaps predictably, right beyond the blind corner, the police had set up a roadblock. Extending well into both lanes from opposite sides of the road were two spiked metal strips that forced the traffic to slow down and detour through a narrow opening after being inspected by the police.

Samuel slammed the brakes, skidding to a stop, but not before the right front tire rocked over the spike strip. The tire exploded and Samuel cursed. A moment later, he was out of the vehicle, gesturing wildly and yelling at the police, pointing to the writing on the side of the government vehicle.

The police made a show of loud speech, but then dragged the metal strips from the road, loaded them in the back of a blue truck, and retreated.

While Samuel changed the flattened tire, Jace and his friends walked across the street to stand beneath the grove of eucalyptus trees. A minute later, a speeding matatu suddenly appeared, rounded the corner, and fishtailed, splashing water in their direction. Jace felt his breath catch. "That was too close," he said, taking Gabby's hand and backing away from the street.

"Ugh," she moaned, "my dress."

A few minutes later, a trio of young men appeared from the other side of the Land Cruiser. The tallest wore a long coat, an odd sight on the warm day. He yelled something at Samuel and placed the heel of a black boot against his back as Samuel knelt to remove the lug nuts from the wheel.

Samuel shook his head and pointed across the road toward the forest. The trio was obviously upset about something and yelled at Samuel again. The tallest stuck his hand inside his coat and began to walk across the street, his eyes now fixed on Jace.

There was something about the young man's expression that tightened Jace's gut. He looked around for a rock or stick. Just as he leaned over to close his hand around an apple-sized rock, a second matatu roared around the blind corner, dust cloud trailing. The eyes of the man in the road were still fixed upon Jace. At the last moment, he turned toward the matatu.

The matatu swerved. The man jumped for the side of the road.

Too late. The van struck him head-on in a sickening crunch of bone meets metal, skin meets windshield.

The man cartwheeled off the edge of the road, his arms rag-doll limp and his raincoat flapping. Some sort of automatic weapon flew out of his coat, skidding to a halt across the road. After a moment's shock, Jace sprang to action, running to the victim.

Airway. Fortunately, the man was already on his back. Jace put his fingers behind the angle of his jaw and thrust his mandible forward. The man gasped.

Breathing. The man took a second breath, and then fell into a pattern of rapid, shallow gasps.

Circulation. Jace pinched just over the radial artery at the wrist. Nothing. When he laid his fingers at the side of the trachea, he could feel a weak pulse.

He looked over at Evan. "His pressure is low, probably sixty-range. We need to get this guy to a hospital to have a chance."

Jace looked around. A crowd had started to gather.

That made Jace worry. Crowds in Kenya have a reputation for turning violent, seeking someone to blame for whatever it was that started the gathering.

"We need to find a way to move him," Evan said.

Jace kept one hand on the man's forehead to keep his neck from moving, and one on his jaw to keep it thrust forward, keeping his airway open. "Look at this," Jace said. "His neck veins are up."

Evan looked worried. "I need a stethoscope. He either has cardiac tamponade or a pneumothorax."

Jace looked up to see Gabby flagging down a passing pickup truck.

An angry man straddled the victim, looking down at Jace. He pointed at the Land Cruiser. "Is that your vehicle?"

Jace shook his head and looked around for the matatu responsible for hitting the pedestrian.

Gone.

Jace kept his concentration on the victim. "The vehicle that struck this man has fled."

The angry man spoke again. "The van had to swerve because of your vehicle beside the road." He closed his fist.

Jace scanned the crowd and the road. The other two youths who had accompanied the victim seemed to have disappeared. Along with the gun.

"This is your fault," the man said, pushing Jace backward, out of contact with the victim.

Suddenly, Gabby was in the angry man's face, screaming and motioning wildly. "This man is a doctor! He is the only thing keeping this victim alive. We need to move him to a hospital so he will have a chance. Now get out of the way!"

Surprisingly, the man backed away from the crazy white woman. The pickup truck backed up so that the bed was a few feet from the victim. Gabby began shouting orders for the occupants to get out, like a sergeant ordering the evacuation of a bunker. "Now!"

Reluctantly, more than a dozen men began to hop out. When only one man remained, Jace looked at a few men standing quietly beside the road. "Help me move him," he said. "We need to move him all at once. Head, chest, hips, and legs all together. Try not to bend the spine."

The men seemed to understand. Jace supported the head and neck. Evan took one side of the chest, Gabby the feet. Three other men joined and followed orders. "On three," Jace said. "One, two, three!"

When they had the victim in the back of the truck, Jace pulled his hand away from the man's hair. Blood. Jelly-like and matted on the back of his head. He wiped his hands on his pants and wished for a pair of examining gloves, pushing a threatening thought aside. *HIV is everywhere.*

"What's this?" Evan said, picking up a paper that had fallen from the man's front pocket during the transfer. He unfolded what appeared to be a photocopy of a newspaper picture.

Jace looked at the paper with his heart suddenly in his throat. The image was unmistakable. The man in the picture was Jace Rawlings.

26

As he approached the Rawlings home, Steve Brady thought, *Jace Rawlings must have been running from some pretty powerful demons to want to leave all of this.* Stone foundation, covered porch, tan siding, and a yard with dogwood and azaleas—the home could have graced the cover of *Architectural Digest*.

He rang the doorbell and waited.

Heather answered. Even in a jogging suit, she was attractive. Steve was pretty sure she had at least ten or twelve years on him, but she was aging well. He found himself thinking again that Jace Rawlings was either running or a fool.

Or both.

Heather's face brightened. "Hi, Steve."

He nodded and stood quietly for an awkward moment until she added, "Would you like to come in?"

He followed Heather into the formal living room and sat when she gestured toward the couch. She sat opposite him in a leather chair, with a large coffee table between them. "I've done a little snooping," he said.

"And?" She waited.

Steve cleared his throat.

"Tell me it's a fraud. Tell me I shouldn't be doubting Jace—"

"The copy of Anita Franks's autopsy is legitimate. It appears to be a photocopy of the original."

"Okay, how does that help me?"

"That doesn't. But what may help is tracing who had access to the document."

She waited until he continued.

"Since it is officially a part of her medical record, it is protected. The only people with access are the next of kin and her doctors."

"That doesn't really help. There is no reason for the governor to send me the information."

"So perhaps we need to think about Anita's physicians."

"Do you know who else the ME's office sent the report to?"

"Only one doctor's office." He paused. "Your husband's."

"Jace? Why would his office request her records?"

"He must have had a file on her. Otherwise, the state wouldn't have released the records."

"This makes no sense. Jace was the governor's doctor."

"Would anyone at Jace's office want you to know this information?"

Heather stood and began to pace. "Not that I know of." She turned and faced the detective. "So what's next?"

He held up his hands. "I know things don't add up, Heather, but we really don't have any evidence that Anita Franks was sexually assaulted. Maybe she was using ketamine as a recreational drug."

"That's crazy."

"I'm sorry. But this is good news, in a way. Right now, we don't exactly have solid evidence to indicate a crime."

"If the governor's wife was using ketamine illegally, that sounds like a crime to me."

"Maybe it was," he said slowly. "I want you to consider another possibility." He took a deep breath. "Maybe Jace sent that autopsy report to you."

"Jace? Why would he want me to know this?"

The detective shrugged. "Maybe it's his way of coming clean," he said. "Maybe it's a confession."

"Tell him to drive us to the new hospital in Karen," Jace told Gabby, naming a Nairobi suburb.

The driver heard. "It's too expensive."

Jace sighed. "It's the closest. Don't worry about the money." He looked at Gabby. "Ride up front with him. Evan and I will ride with the patient."

They knelt beside the man as the driver sped away, leaving a thick trail of dust and Jace and Evan grabbing for the sides of the pickup.

Evan shouted, "Just keep his head from rolling around."

When the driver slowed behind another truck, Jace addressed the elephant in the room. "So why does a man carrying a gun have my picture in his pocket?"

His friend kept his hand locked on the side as they swayed and bumped along. "Seems like you were just spared a bit of serious trouble of your own."

"The guy was coming over to kill me."

Evan squinted into the sun. "Evidently."

"So was that whole thing set up? Was our driver in on it?"

"How else would the guy have known we'd be there?"

The thought sent a chill down Jace's back. "Let's just keep this guy alive so the police can question him."

The pickup truck slammed through a series of potholes, then ran off the road onto the shoulder, since it appeared smoother than the road itself. Speeding, passing a matatu, and weaving back into the left lane again, the driver of their pickup kept up a brutal pace, knocking Jace and Evan side to side and prompting Jace to cry out. "Slow down!"

The driver ignored him. Or didn't hear.

By the time they pulled into the hospital parking lot ten minutes later, their patient was gasping, with a thready pulse of 120.

Jace called to Gabby. "Go ask them for a stretcher. I don't want to move him twice."

She disappeared and came back a minute later with a nurse pushing a stretcher.

The nurse was a light-skinned Kenyan of about twenty-five. "I am Dr. Rawlings," Jace said. "This is Dr. Martin. We were traveling from our home in Kijabe when we witnessed this pedestrian accident."

She nodded soberly. "You are welcome to help."

Wow, Jace thought. *That was easy. No complicated application or a critique of my case log. Just a Good Samaritan agreement. Welcome.*

They maneuvered the stretcher against the tailgate and moved the patient. As they were pushing the stretcher toward the casualty entrance, Jace looked over his shoulder to see Gabby laying shillings in the open palm of the driver. She made quick eye contact with Jace. Clearly, it was not her idea, but what could she do?

The emergency-room facility was better equipped than their department back in Kijabe. Jace asked for IV equipment as another nurse began cutting off the victim's clothing with a large shears. Evan lowered a cushioned mask over the patient's nose and mouth and began bag ventilation. "I'll need a laryngoscope and an endotracheal tube," he said.

A nurse responded by wheeling up an emergency cart. She quickly broke a seal and pulled open a drawer. Evan grabbed an Ambu bag and sealed the mask over the patient's mouth. After another thirty seconds of ventilation, Evan inserted the tube. "I'm in," he said.

"Here's a sixteen-gauge IV," Jace said, taping down the tubing to the canula just below the patient's elbow. "Do we have blood available?"

A young nurse in a white coat scurried toward a desk. "I'll call the lab to see."

Jace connected a bag of saline. "Squeeze this in as fast as it will go."

Evan placed a stethoscope on the chest. "The lung sounds are absent on the left," he said. "And I can feel the crepitance of broken ribs here."

"He's going to need a chest tube." Jace looked at the nurse. "Do you have a tray or some sort of kit for the placement of chest tubes?"

An older nurse, a heavy-set woman with white hair, shook her head and looked at the dial on a manual blood-pressure cuff. Her accent was distinctly Kenyan. "Blood pressure is sixty."

Jace opened another sixteen-gauge IV needle. "Here," he said, swiping the skin with an alcohol swab. He shoved the needle into the patient's right chest. Air and blood sprayed through the needle, relieving the buildup of pressure.

In the minutes that followed, Jace made a small incision over the patient's right chest and inserted a clear tube the size of his index finger. Immediately, the tube turned red, colored by a continuous flow of blood from the chest. Jace quickly attached the chest tube to a clear plastic collecting chamber to record the output.

A nurse returned holding a single unit of blood. "Our surgeons were up late last night operating. This is all we have in the blood bank."

Jace looked around. "Anyone here have O negative blood?"

The chest tube collection system continued to fill. One thousand ccs. And rising.

Gabby touched the patient's abdomen. "Look at this. It seems to be expanding."

Jace ran his hand over the lower ribs. "Most of his injury seems to be on the right side. His liver is probably lacerated."

Evan asked for a flashlight and looked in the patient's eyes. "His pupils don't respond."

"What's the pressure?"

"I can't measure it."

Jace made eye contact with Evan. "Could he be in cardiac tamponade?"

Evan examined the neck. "Neck veins are flat. That means he needs volume. If his neck veins were up, that would mean tamponade or pneumothorax."

Jace looked at the chest-tube container, now containing almost two liters of blood. "We start CPR or we call it."

Gabby frowned. "We can't save him, Jace. Let him go."

Jace nodded. "We have no more blood."

Evan stepped away from the table. "Time of death, eleven thirty-two."

Jace felt like cursing. If they'd had an emergency prehospital system, if they'd had more blood, if they'd had access to equipment in the field … He looked around the room as the nurses began cleaning up. There was no emotion, no tears, just the everyday let's-get-the-work-done attitude.

In emergency rooms in Africa, death was a frequent visitor. There wasn't time to mourn. Only time to prepare for the next victim transferring from life to somewhere beyond.

Jace needed air and space to think. He sighed deeply, frustrated by his inability to turn the tide against the enemy of death. As he walked toward the entrance, he heard the voice of the nurse. "Who is going to pay his bill?"

He felt an immediate stab of anger. How could they be thinking of money when a man's life had just been lost?

He turned to see the face of the light-skinned nurse holding up a chart. "I'm going to need you to fill out a report."

Jace nodded. "Maybe there's some next of kin. Perhaps he has a family who can help with his bills."

"Doubtful," the white-haired nurse mumbled. She rifled through a discarded pile of bloodstained clothing, lifting a wallet from the man's pants. "He has an ID," she said. "His name is Kimathi."

Jace froze.

"Kimathi," the nurse repeated. "Anthony Kimathi."

27

Jace and Evan split the six-thousand-shilling bill for the supplies they used in their resuscitation attempt of Anthony Kimathi and walked out into the parking lot.

Gabby followed, rubbing dirt from the front of her dress. "We need to talk to the police, Jace."

He shook his head. "I've been rethinking this. I think we ought to keep this quiet."

"Jace," Evan said, "that guy, Anthony whoever, clearly had ideas about doing you harm. Don't you think the police need to hear about that?"

"That might not be a smart move," he said. "Think about it. How would that guy have known we would be at that exact spot? Obviously our driver told him where we would be stopped."

"Unless they were following us," Gabby said.

"They were on foot," Jace answered. "So it all had to be planned. The driver had to know exactly where he would run into the spike strip to flatten a tire."

Gabby frowned. "So you assume the police were in on this too?"

"I think so."

"What if our driver just knew where the police were going to be setting up a roadblock?"

"Unlikely," Jace said. "You saw that place. It was a crazy place to put a police checkpoint. They were endangering their own lives, setting up just beyond a blind corner."

"This is Africa," Gabby said.

Jace squinted toward the sun. "Still, I don't think we can afford to go to the police. They may be in on this."

Gabby touched his shoulder. "This is crazy, Jace. Who would want you dead?"

"I don't know."

"So what's our next move?" Evan asked. "Should we call our MP friend and give our regrets for lunch?"

"I'm sure he has already heard," Jace said. "The driver would have phoned him." He looked at Evan and Gabby, making eye contact with them both. "Besides, I'm a little concerned that he may have been in on all of this. He insisted we come on a certain day. He arranges for his driver to pick us up. We just happen to flatten a tire on a police spike strip ..."

"Does seem like a lot of coincidences."

Gabby scratched another blob of dried mud from her dress. "Okay, if the MP set this up, why?"

"Who would benefit from you being gone?" Evan asked.

"Someone afraid I might take their business?"

"And the minister of health would be in on it?"

"If someone paid him enough." Jace paused, rubbing his blood-stained shoe against the curb. "I'm just guessing. I really have no idea."

Evan looked over his shoulder at the Karen Hospital looming over them. "If there were surgeons behind such an attack, I'd suspect they'd be at a place like this, somewhere you could attract private patients and charge them Western prices."

"It really makes no sense. I'm only taking care of the poor patients these doctors wouldn't want anyway."

"Then who wants you dead?" Gabby asked.

"I have no idea. Really. No idea."

"Here comes a matatu," Evan said. "Let's catch a ride back toward Kijabe."

One day, a month before Jace's graduation from Rift Valley Academy, he had walked into the kitchen and startled his father and sister, who spilled a glass of tea onto the table.

As she scrambled to clean up the spill, Jace studied them for a moment. "What's up? You guys look like you were solving the world's problems."

He watched as Janice and his father exchanged looks.

His father took a deep breath. "We should tell him."

Jace squinted at them, feeling a knot tighten in his throat. "What?"

His father gestured toward a chair. "Sit down, Jace."

He obeyed.

"This may be nothing, Jace."

Jace stared at them. Janice had her hand over her mouth.

"But it may be a legitimate warning."

"A warning?" he asked.

Janice spoke. "I've had two very vivid dreams, Jace." She halted a moment. "About you. It's one of those weird dreams where you wake up and you've been crying."

He wasn't sure what to say. "Okay."

"Both times, I was talking to Pastor Wally."

RVA's minister for the student body.

"Both times it seemed so real."

"What did he say? Something about me?" Jace shifted in his seat, wondering just what sin he'd committed that was about to be publicly discussed.

"Yes, something about you," she said. "He told me to invite you to follow Christ. He told me I wouldn't have many more chances."

"What?" he said. "What are you saying? I'm going to die or something?"

"I—I don't know. I just know it seemed so real. I had the distinct feeling that I wouldn't have many opportunities to talk with you again."

Jace stood, squeaking the feet of his chair across the floor. "That's crazy."

His father nodded. "Sounds crazy, doesn't it?" He stood to face his son. "But what if Janice has been warned for a reason?"

"It was a dream, Dad. Nothing else. Janice has dreams like this because this is what she thinks about during the day. We just had spiritual-emphasis week. We've been talking about this stuff, so she dreams about it, okay? It's nothing."

Jace went to the refrigerator and poured a glass of mango juice.

His father spoke again. "Maybe it *is* nothing, Jace, but there is little of greater importance for you to think about than the eternal destiny of your soul."

The phrase ticked him off. "What is that?" he mocked, raising his hands to make air quotes: "'The eternal destiny of my soul.'" He set down his glass on the counter. "That sounds like flaky stuff to me."

"You know what it means, son. You've been around this kind of talk all your life."

"And all my life I wished we could just talk like normal people."

"How can I say it so you will hear what I'm saying?"

Jace shook his head. "I don't know." He turned and faced away. "It's not that I don't want to believe," he said. "But it just seems like a fairy tale."

"Too good to be true?"

Jace felt the knot in his throat begin to melt. "Kind of, yes."

"It's the gospel, Jace—it *is* too good to be true," his father said. "But that doesn't make it any less true."

Jace looked at them. They stared back with pity on their faces. And at that moment, he pulled away. He didn't want their sympathy. "I'm Esau, don't you get it?" he shouted. "I hear the stories, but they don't matter to me. They are just stories."

He took a step toward the door, but Janice moved into his path. "You need to hear it again. Maybe you'll believe."

He shook his head. "I've heard it a thousand times," he said, pushing past. "Lay off!"

That evening, Jace sat across the table from Evan, eating stew and chapatis at Mama Chiku's.

Jace pulled a generous portion of white ugali through his stew and kept his voice low. "When I went to see Joseph Ole Kosoi this morning, he told me a patient of mine was going to die."

Evan huffed, "Again?"

Jace nodded. "He gave me a name. I blew it off because it wasn't the name of any patient I recognized."

"So, he was wrong. It's postpump paranoia. Maybe it's the drugs we're using here."

"No," Jace said, shaking his head. "The name of the patient was Anthony Kimathi."

Evan's jaw slackened as he stared at Jace. "Good one. You almost had me on that one."

Jace leaned forward. "I'm serious, Evan. I didn't say anything back in Karen because I didn't want to get Gabby started. You know how she is on all those spooky spiritual things."

"Joseph Ole told you that Anthony Kimathi was going to die?"

Jace nodded. "I need to know what you're doing. None of my patients back in America experienced this stuff."

"I'm doing exactly what I do in America." His voice trailed off and he shifted in his seat.

"What?"

"We've been a bit short on the inhalant anesthetics during the first two cases, but I gave Versed hoping to wipe out their memory."

Jace sighed. "It didn't work."

Evan folded a chapati into a triangle. "You've got to admit, this is pretty spooky. How do you explain Beatrice predicting that Michael

Kagai was going to die? Or that her mother had HIV? Or now, this?" He cleared his throat. "Maybe God is trying to get your attention."

Jace shook his head. "What? Are you going to get all spiritual on me too?"

"I'm just saying it all seems pretty weird." Evan held up his hands. "Maybe there's something to this."

Jace stayed quiet and looked away.

"Jace, how long have we known each other?"

He looked back. "Eight, maybe nine years."

"And I'm out here supporting you, right?"

Jace nodded.

"I've never been one to talk about my faith. But this—this is hard to explain."

Jace pushed his plate away.

"Listen, Jace. Someone apparently wants you dead. And for some reason, you're getting these weird messages. I'd start paying attention if I were you."

"What am I supposed to do?"

"Things happen for a reason, Jace."

"So what am I to make of this, Evan?"

"Pay attention. Pray." He shrugged. "If your life is in danger and you've got faith issues to work out, I wouldn't waste a lot of time."

Jace stood up and tossed shillings on the table to pay the bill. *I've heard these warnings before.*

And that didn't work out so well, did it?

28

As Jace walked up the path toward home, he heard his name and looked back to see his intern. "Hey, Paul, what's up? How are the heart patients?"

"They are doing fine. But I need help in casualty."

"I'm not on call, Paul."

"Dr. Fitzgerald is already in surgery with a head-trauma patient."

Jace sighed. It wasn't like he had a wife to go home to. "Okay, what is it?" He reversed direction and started down the path toward the casualty department.

"Ten-year-old boy fell from a tree. He had rib fractures and a pneumothorax. I put in a chest tube and got out a little blood, but the patient is still hypotensive."

Jace quickened his pace. "Which side?"

"Left."

"Left-sided rib fractures are associated with what abdominal injury?"

"Ruptured spleen."

"That's right. Have you assessed the abdomen?"

"He is tender."

They pushed through the casualty door. The scene was all too familiar. A crowd of relatives surrounded a bed where a young boy lay beneath a red wool blanket. Other patients filled the stretchers, while still more sat in chairs waiting to be seen. Saturday night in Kijabe.

Jace nodded to the family. Paul said something to them in Kiswahili. They parted to let Jace approach the bedside.

Jace spoke to the patient, rehearsing Kiswahili words he had spoken as a child. "Jina lako ni nani?" What is your name?

"Boniface," he said. "I'm cold."

Jace looked at his intern. "A sign of shock."

Pleased that the patient spoke English, Jace continued. "What happened?"

"I was climbing a eucalyptus tree and put my hand right on a green boomslang."

A tree snake. Jace nodded.

"He struck at me, but I ducked. Then I lost my balance."

"Where do you hurt?"

"Here," he said, placing his hand over his swollen abdomen.

Jace looked at Paul. "Can you bring me the ultrasound machine?"

Paul nodded and disappeared. Jace looked around for a nurse. There were two on duty, but both were talking to other patients. Jace pumped up the blood-pressure cuff and listened just above the patient's elbow. He ran the cuff up and down three times before laying aside the stethoscope and using his fingers to palpate the pulse.

Too low to hear. Must be sixty or lower.

He opened up the little roller on the IV tubing to increase the drip rate and began to squeeze the plastic fluid bag to speed the fluid administration.

When Paul returned, rolling the ultrasound machine, Jace frowned. "His pressure is down. He needs blood."

"I didn't get that much out of the chest."

Jace squirted ultrasound jelly onto the patient's abdomen and stroked the probe across the skin beneath his ribs. "Here's the problem. See that?" He pointed to an image at the bottom of the screen. "That's the spleen, what's left of it." He moved his index finger on the screen. "All of that is fluid."

Paul nodded. "Blood?"

"Blood."

Jace looked at the family. "We are going to need to operate to stop the bleeding."

Paul spoke in rapid Kiswahili.

"This is his mother. She does not wish an operation. She is afraid he will die."

"Tell her if we do nothing, he very well may die. He is bleeding inside."

Paul spoke again to the mother, a Kikuyu dressed in a red-patterned dress, orange headscarf, and purple-dotted sweater.

The woman answered softly.

Paul translated. "She says you are the doctor. She will trust you." He looked at his watch. "I need to arrange for a second team in theater. The first team is already working with Dr. Fitzgerald."

"Okay, tell them to hurry. We've got a real emergency on our hands."

256 · HARRY KRAUS

Twenty minutes later, Jace helped transfer the boy onto the operating table.

The nurse anesthetist, a young woman named Grace, pulled down on the patient's lower eyelid to examine the sclera behind the lid. "His hemoglobin is under seven," she said.

"You can tell that just by looking?"

"In an African, yes."

Jace shrugged. "Heart rate is one-sixty. He needs blood."

Paul shook his head. "The blood bank is out of his type."

"Get O negative then," Grace said. She worked to place a second larger IV while the intern went for blood.

Jace scrubbed his hands, gowned, gloved, and waited for a signal from anesthesia that he could start. He dipped a gauze in brown Betadine and began painting from the middle of the abdomen in larger and larger circles.

Drape towels were squared off against the prepped abdomen.

Grace frowned. "We need blood now. His pressure is down."

Jace hurried ahead. "I'll open and pack. Maybe I can slow the bleeding until you get caught up."

He opened through a midline incision, immediately releasing the floodgates. A river of heme spilled over the patient's abdomen, down the drapes and onto Jace's shoes. "I need more packs," he said, his own pulse quickening.

Grace leaned over the drape screen separating her from the surgeon. "What do you see?"

"Blood. Lots of blood." Jace fought a rising tide of panic. "I need more packs!" Over and over he shoved large white absorbent gauze packs into the abdomen to seal off the bleeding. Within a few moments, the white was painted crimson. "What's the pressure?"

"Below measurement."

Paul returned to the room empty-handed. "There is no more O negative blood."

Jace's throat tightened.

Paul shook his head. "This patient is the same blood type as Joseph Kosoi. We used all of the blood for him."

"I can close over the packs. We'll resuscitate him and come back when he has stabilized."

Jace watched as Grace pushed back the drapes to get access to the patient's chest.

"What are you doing?"

"Chest compressions. The boy has no pressure!"

"Squeeze in the IV fluids, Paul." Jace looked at his assistant. "Give me a zero Prolene suture. I'll close the skin over the packs to tamponade the bleeding."

Jace sewed as quickly as he could, shoulder to shoulder with Grace, who was rhythmically pumping with the heel of her hands on the boy's sternum. He looked at the monitor. *Ventricular fibrillation. The heart doesn't even have enough blood to pump oxygen to its own muscle.*

Jace looked at Grace and felt the accusation in her stare. "Do you have a clamp you can place on the aorta?" she asked.

Jace shoved his hand back into the abdomen, feeling for the patient's aorta as it entered the abdomen through the diaphragm. "It's flat, Grace. Clamping it will not help."

She stopped compressions and locked eyes with Jace. "We shouldn't have started without blood. Opening his abdomen allowed him to bleed out!"

"I thought we had blood."

Grace peeled off her examining gloves and threw them to the floor. "You cannot assume anything around here! You bring me a patient and turn me into an executioner!" She stormed from the room.

Everything fell silent except for the swinging of the theater door, flopping back and forth, accusing Jace of failure … failure … failure!

Jace continued to sew the skin. "It was his only chance of survival. If we'd been able to operate sooner, we could have stopped the bleeding."

Paul leaned against the wall and slid to the floor, his tall frame folding like a chair. "I told his mother to trust us. I told her we would save her son."

Jace looked over and saw tears in his intern's eyes.

Dave Fitzgerald walked into the room, stripping off his sterile gown from his case in the next room. "What happened here?"

"Ruptured spleen," Jace said mechanically. "No blood. Dead patient."

Dave picked up the chart. "Boniface? I know this kid. He's always at the front entrance selling mangos for his mother."

"I don't understand," Jace said. "I thought I'd solved the problem with our blood bank shortage."

Dave coughed. "You really don't get it, do you? You think you can throw money around and solve all of Africa's problems?"

Taken back by Dave's harsh tone, Jace didn't reply.

Dave continued his tirade, a flood unleashed. "After your little plan to bribe donors, we couldn't talk anyone into giving for free. Everyone wanted a free lunch and a store voucher!" He shook his head. "You didn't solve this problem, Jace. You caused it. You and your wonderful open-heart program." He paused and threw the chart back on the anesthesia cart. "Okay, you saved two heart patients. At what cost?" He turned and walked to the swinging door. "The cost of one ten-year-old boy!"

29

That evening Heather put on a black cocktail dress and her pearl necklace and let the valet park her car at the Jefferson Hotel in downtown Richmond. Known as Richmond's finest historic hotel, its opulence was forever marred in her mind as the place her husband reportedly met up with the governor's wife.

Heather came here to see for herself. She wanted to absorb the atmosphere and observe. *Did Jace come here because he was out of love with me? What do these walls know about my husband that he can't or won't tell me?*

She walked into the lobby, admired the marble statue of the third US president, the faux marble pillars, and the multicolored rainbow of the Tiffany stained-glass skylight. She strolled through Palm Court, the historic location where live alligators used to swim in the decorative pool.

The marble staircase was said to have inspired the infamous scene in *Gone with the Wind*. She let her hand glide along the railing as she climbed. After walking through the Rotunda lobby, she decided to have a drink in the lounge at TJ's restaurant, the less expensive of the hotel's dining options, known for its single-malt scotches and over-the-top wine and beer selections.

She sat in a leather chair overlooking the lobby. A young waiter appeared. "Will you be dining with us tonight? Perhaps meeting someone?"

"I'm fine here," she said. "Bring me a glass of your house white zinfandel."

She sipped it slowly, taking in the downtown atmosphere and eavesdropping on yuppies and their dates.

She was halfway through her glass when she heard her name. "Mrs. Rawlings?"

A man in a gray business suit, black shirt, and silver tie nodded at the empty chair next to hers. "Expecting someone?" He smiled. Gorgeous. "Perhaps someone to accompany you while your husband is so far away?"

She shook her head. "Do I know you?"

"No, but I know you. May I sit?"

The man didn't wait for her answer. He held out his hand. "Allow me to introduce myself. I'm Ryan Meadows."

"Of course," she said, realization dawning. "I've seen your picture in the paper."

"So what brings you downtown?"

"Can't a woman just enjoy a drink without a reason?"

"Not you."

She smiled uneasily. He was spot on.

"You didn't answer."

She took a deep breath. The wine had already loosened her tongue. "I just wanted to see this place."

He nodded and stayed quiet. After a moment, he swirled the golden liquid in his glass. Single malt. "Quite a place for a rendezvous, don't you think?"

She sipped her drink and stared over her glass at the governor's chief of staff. She shook her head. "Am I supposed to find that endearing? A reference to my husband, perhaps?"

"I read the papers too."

"Don't believe everything you read."

"Why did you want to see this place? There must be closer places to buy a drink."

She looked around, listening to the murmur of conversations around them, the clink of ice against glass and the quiet sounds of a piped-in symphony. "This place is just so not Jace."

"Not Jace?" He smiled.

"Not at all. He may have operated on the rich and famous, but he was such a wog at heart."

"A wog?"

"A slang term thrown around at his Kenyan high school. An American who adopts local customs and cherishes a simple life."

Ryan sipped his drink and motioned for a waiter. "Another," he said, "for myself and the young lady."

Heather smiled at the compliment and reminded herself that she was a lightweight.

Ryan smiled back. "So Jace is a wog. I guess he's found his home again, huh?"

She sighed. "I don't know." She held up her drink in a mock toast. "Here's to my husband, off to save the world." She felt the wine beginning to make her lips tingle. "Jace used to sleep outside in

264 · HARRY KRAUS

our backyard when he was in medical school. No sleeping bag, just a few blankets laid out by a campfire the way the Maasai would." She shrugged. "A true wog."

Ryan gestured to the opulent lobby. "I guess his tastes must have changed."

Heather felt a stab of remorse. Or guilt. Sitting there talking about her husband with Ryan felt unfaithful somehow.

But more than remorse, she felt a growing apprehension. There was something unsettling about Ryan Meadows. He seemed so … *political*. Yes, that was it. More concerned about image than substance.

She paused as a second realization dawned. This man was exactly the opposite of Jace. Jace cared little for image.

A waiter delivered their drinks. Ryan took another swallow. "So you are a woman looking for answers?"

She nodded. "Perceptive, Mr. Meadows."

"Anita had an agreement with the hotel management. They kept a suite available to her, so that she could entertain guests."

Heather leaned closer. "You mean they kept a suite available for the governor and his wife."

He smiled sweetly. The kind of smile that you give to a child who just failed an algebra test. "This one the governor didn't know about."

She sat back. "I see."

She watched as he appeared to be scanning the crowd. "I'm sure someone on the staff could answer your questions." He paused, looking back at her and crossing his legs. He leaned forward until his knee just grazed hers. "I'll ask a few questions. I know how to be discreet."

"It's just that my husband can't tell me. He suffered amnesia after his accident." It sounded so lame, so contrived when she spoke it aloud.

"Of course." Ryan tugged on the sleeve of his black shirt. "It's only natural that you would want to know."

"Why are you here?" she asked. "Meeting with the governor?"

He shook his head. "I'm just winding down after being at the office."

"On a Saturday no less."

He shrugged. "Politics." He rattled the ice in his glass. "After a day in the mansion, I stop here to relax."

"How is the governor?"

"Recovering. That goat can't be killed."

"I thought you were friends."

"Ah, yes, we're best friends. But we fight like brothers." He fell silent staring into his glass. After a moment, he added, "I was supposed to be the party's nominee. But Stuart gave my stump speech when I got the flu." He held up his glass to mimic the mock toast Heather had given. "Stole the whole show, he did. Here's to Stuart Franks."

She smiled. "Big of you to support him."

"Hey, he was electable. You need a few gray hairs to be successful." He raised his eyebrows below a perfect head of thick hair and winked.

She suppressed a sudden urge to throw her drink in his face, and she smiled as she imagined doing just that. When she saw his positive response, she realized he must think she was enjoying his flirtation.

Perhaps Mr. Meadows has his own Achilles' heel, she thought, setting her glass aside. As much as she bristled at his arrogance, he might be a useful source of information. She put on her best I'm-just-an-innocent-schoolgirl smile. "Will you do it?"

"What?"

"Ask a few questions for me? Find out what happened the night of my husband's accident. Is it like the media says? Was he meeting Anita Franks in this hotel?"

"Are you sure, Heather?" he said, dropping her name like they were old friends. "What if it's painful?"

She lifted her glass again. "Especially if it is painful."

That evening, Heather headed for home after dark, unhappy about the rain but happy that she'd made a contact who might assist her in her search.

As she drove, she sank back into the leather seat and thought about a similar summer evening when a sudden rain shower had sent her family running in from a picnic table in the backyard of her parents' home. She grabbed a casserole dish of baked beans, lifted the mustard, and followed her father into the house.

David Montgomery, her father, looked out the window. "I guess that's just Florida weather. Wait five minutes and it will change again."

Once they were gathered again at the kitchen table to continue their picnic, Heather looked at her mom, Trevor Anne, and smiled.

"What?" her mom asked.

"I've got something to show you," she said, hardly able to contain her excitement. She reached into her jeans pocket and pulled out a diamond ring solitaire. She slipped it on her ring finger and held it up for her parents to see.

"You—you're engaged?" Her mother's hand covered her mouth.

Heather watched as her parents exchanged "the look," a silent communication of alarm. Her gut tightened. "Jace asked me to marry him."

Her parents returned a collective blank stare.

"What?" she said. "Say something! Aren't you excited?"

Her mother wiped her mouth with a paper napkin. "Of course, dear." She hesitated before adding. "We hope you are going to finish college first."

"Mom, we've checked on married student housing on campus. It would be cheaper for us to live together than rent two separate places."

"He didn't ask me," her father said.

"Daddy!"

Her mother shook her head. "Your father is old-fashioned that way, you know."

"I'm sure he'll ask for permission."

Her father pushed back from the table. "A little late, don't you think?"

"He's planning a trip down during our Thanksgiving break. He can ask you then."

Her mom reached over and took her husband's hand.

Uh-oh. Whenever they hold hands it's a sign they'll make some proclamation they've agreed upon.

"We've talked about Jace, honey," her mother said. "He's a nice boy."

Heather felt her jaw slacken. "A nice boy?"

"I'm concerned about his ability to lead you," her father said.

"He's got his head on straight. He's taking his MCATs, he's going to medical school."

"I'm not talking about that kind of leadership. I'm talking spiritually. You need a man strong in his faith to lead."

"His family were missionaries, just like us!"

Her mom shifted in her seat. "Just what does *he* say about his faith? I, for one, haven't heard him mention it. Not even once."

"Jace is quiet about his beliefs. That's not a sin."

Her mother leaned forward. "That's called hiding a light under a bushel."

"If there is light at all," her father added.

"I don't believe this. You're judging him."

"And we're supposed to sit back and not have opinions about who our daughter marries?"

"Jace is a good man," Heather countered, feeling the tears that would soon flow. "I love him!"

Her father nodded. "Ah, love." He continued gripping his wife's hand. "Is that what is going to see you through hard times?"

Heather nodded.

"I'm afraid," David said.

"Afraid?"

"The Bible teaches that the husband provides a spiritual covering for his wife. We need your husband to be that for you."

"Jace is strong."

"But is he spiritually strong? If he is not a believer, you won't have the spiritual protection you need."

Heather crossed her arms. "Spiritual protection?"

"We saw things," he began, "during our time in Mozambique."

Her mother nodded. "Spiritual attacks. Warfare."

"You're weirding me out," she said.

"Remember, reality isn't only the things you can detect with your five senses."

Trevor Anne released her husband's hand and reached for Heather. "We just want our baby to be safe. Take it slow, honey. If Jace is the one, a little extra time isn't going to change that."

"Maybe you just need to ask him a few questions. He'll tell you about his faith if you let him."

Her parents nodded.

Disaster averted, she thought.

For now.

A short tap of a car horn snapped Heather back to the present. She'd been sitting at a traffic light, a green one, and the guy in the car behind her wasn't happy. She sped off. *How long had I been sitting there?*

But her memory of her parents' judging of Jace made her wonder about her own attitudes. *Am I becoming my parents, too quick to judge?*

She thought about Ryan Meadows. *That guy doesn't hold a candle to my Jace.* Jace never seemed complicated. He'd always been an up-front, what-you-see-is-what-you-get kind of man. He would have been much more comfortable in a small-town diner than the Jefferson Hotel.

So why did I let little doubts take hold?

Have my parents' doubts become my own?

Is this really about Jace—or about me?

Can I ever trust him again without knowing all the facts?

30

Jace walked toward the surgery waiting room. His intern, Paul, touched his arm. "Dr. Rawlings. It would be best if you changed your scrubs before talking with the family."

He looked down. He was so taken by his own grief that he hadn't thought about his appearance. His scrub pants were crimson, his shoes tracking blood with every step. "Thanks."

He changed and returned to talk to the crowd. Paul stood by. Boniface Kabochi was dead at age ten. His mother stood, her face alive with alarm.

"I'm so sorry," Jace began.

The Kikuyu crowd understood. "Eh."

The mother began to shake her head. "No. Noooo!"

"We did everything we could," Jace said.

Paul interpreted, speaking in Kikuyu for the mother to understand. She began to wail, swaying at the hips and stomping first one foot and then the other. She cried, pummeling her fists into Paul's chest.

Jace stepped forward, intervening and grabbing the woman by her wrists as she continued to cry. Then, he moved her hands over his chest, directing her to strike him instead. She dropped her fists onto his chest, pounding out her sorrow, before another two women joined her at her right and left, hugging and crying in unison. Her fists slid from Jace's chest, and she collapsed to the floor, wailing and pulling at her sweater. "Boniface, Bon-i-face," she sobbed.

This was Kikuyu grief, extravagant and expressive.

Jace watched with his own heart breaking. Grief, he understood, took many shapes. The Maasai would hear bad news and not frown, not flash the emotion of pain across their faces. The Kikuyu, like some Hispanics Jace had observed back home, were loud, a fountain of tears.

Beyond her tears, though, he knew that she would not accuse him.

Jace stood, not knowing what to say and knowing his words would do little to comfort the woman.

A Kiswahili phrase came back to him. I'm sorry. So sorry. "Pole. Pole sana," he repeated.

After a few minutes, Paul tugged his sleeve. "Let them grieve alone."

Jace walked back to the theater desk. "Do I need to fill out any paperwork?"

"Just fill out an operative report and do the charge for the operation. I'll do a death summary."

"Charges?"

"Yes. I'm not sure they will release the body from the morgue until the family has paid."

Jace looked at Paul. As broken as the American health system was, it was generations better than Kenya's. "Tell the mother not to worry about the costs. I will cover the bill."

"Okay."

Jace quietly wrote a report and recorded a charge. With that, he left the theater and headed home. He thought about his offer to pay the boy's bill. *Dave was right. I'm throwing money around, thinking it will solve problems ... even if all it does is quiet my conscience.*

The next afternoon, Jace ate a quiet American lunch classic: a PBJ on white bread. It came in a colorful wrapper emblazoned with the words "Supa Loaf."

Then he walked down the hill, beyond the hospital, and past the cemetery to the doorstep of the hospital chaplain, John Otieno.

The chaplain's wife answered the door. "Dr. Rawlings, what a nice surprise." She held out her hand. "I'm Lydia, John's wife. Come in."

"Is your husband in?"

"Yes, he's in the back. I've just put on water for chai. Can you join us?"

"Yes, yes," Jace said. Beyond the kitchen counter, he could see the chaplain sitting in an easy chair with three large books open on the table in front of him. His Bible was in his lap, and he had a pencil behind one ear and a highlighter in his hand. His face brightened when he saw Jace.

"Daktari Rawlings, I've been waiting for you to come and visit me. Karibu." Welcome.

Jace took the chaplain's hand and grasped it around the thumb before falling into a normal handgrip. The Kenyans often alternated between the two grips several times depending on how vigorous and happy the greeting. Jace smiled. "Hi, Pastor. I hope I'm not interrupting."

"Just my favorite thing in the world," he said, his eyes beaming. "I was just dissecting the book of Romans."

"Dissecting. Sounds like surgery," Jace said.

"It is … of sorts. I peel away one layer only to reveal something deeper that feeds the layer on the surface, dissect that away, and yet another aspect of truth is revealed." He gestured toward a worn green couch. "Have a seat. What's on your mind? You look—" he hesitated—"troubled."

Jace sat and took a deep breath. *Where to begin?* "I need some advice."

"I'd be honored to listen."

Jace leaned forward and narrated the confusing events of the past few days: Beatrice's claim to have talked to some sort of angel during her open-heart surgery, the accuracy of her predictions of her mother's illness, and her knowledge that one of Jace's patients would die. Jace didn't mention what she'd told him about seeing light in certain people—but not in Jace.

The chaplain sat, mesmerized, pausing only to sip the sweet chai.

Jace finished by telling him of Joseph Kosoi's prediction and how that had also come true just the day before.

His story complete, Jace picked up his chai for the first time. "What do you make of this? Do you really believe my patients have communicated with angels?"

"What do you believe, Jace? Do you believe we can communicate with the dead?"

"You've been talking to my father."

He nodded. "Before you came, we talked. He told me of your sense that your sister wanted you here."

Jace rubbed the back of his neck. "Okay, so two months ago, I would have completely discounted this, but after my ..." He paused and made a gesture of quotation marks as he continued: "vision or whatever it was, I've been forced to rethink a few things."

"So why do you discount your patients' experiences?"

"When I saw my sister's face, I was close to death."

"And your patients, they were close to death as well?"

"Not exactly, but suspended with their hearts not beating."

"You haven't told me why you are questioning your patients' experiences."

"When it was only Beatrice, I thought she must have just over-heard my other patient's name and repeated it to me. And it would be easy to predict her mother had HIV. But when my next patient gave me another name, and his prediction also came true, I came face-to-face with things I just don't understand."

"Things that you'd rather not believe. You're a scientist, so natu-rally, you are looking for a rational explanation."

"Exactly."

"And yet you had an experience yourself."

"Something I am still trying to understand."

"You believed somehow that returning to Kijabe might help you resolve your feelings about your sister's death?"

"Look, to be honest, I think I was scared. I almost died. It was only natural for me to dream of my dead sister. It was the only time in my life when I was so close to the death of someone I loved. So I tell myself it was a dream, perhaps an important one, something of some significance to help me refocus my life around what is important. So as I processed it, I felt like I wanted to do something of lasting value before I died."

"And you thought starting this heart program to help poor Africans was it?"

Jace nodded. "Basically."

"But now, you're faced with even more bizarre spiritual events, stuff that you can't explain away as only a dream anymore."

He hesitated. "Exactly."

"It will be difficult for me to make a judgment without further study." Otieno opened the leather Bible that he had laid aside when Jace arrived. "I believe strongly after listening to the accounts that your patients have had encounters with spiritual beings of some sort."

"Spiritual beings?"

"Angels." He paused. "Or demons."

"Okay, I'm at least open to that idea. I have no other explanation."

"The Bible teaches us that we are in a spiritual war."

"I thought that just meant good versus evil."

"It is not only metaphorical, Jace. There are many verses that teach of ministering or accusing spirits."

"Angels or demons."

"Exactly," the chaplain said, clasping his large hands together. "Perhaps this does not sit well with your Western scientific bent."

Jace nodded.

"I know for a fact it's true, Jace. I've seen evidence of the battle, both sides, during my years on this continent. I'm sure your father could tell you stories. Unfortunately, your country's missionaries are reluctant to share their experiences with angels and demons. They are afraid that their supporting churches will think they've fallen off the deep end, and so they don't tell the stories that might enlighten the church to the battle." He sipped his chai and continued. "These stories often come out at missionary gatherings late at night, when friends begin to swap personal accounts around campfires and over chai." He smiled.

"You said you've seen evidence?"

He nodded. "When I was just a boy out in Kisii town, there was a witch doctor who lived in a mud hut in the center of the village. He kept snakes in his house to use in casting spells. They lived in special baskets fastened on the walls. The man would come out in his yard and call the snakes by name and out they would come, a black mamba slithering down the side of the doorframe, and then a cobra."

He sat back. "One time a man became convinced that my father had spoken an evil word behind his back, so he asked the witch doctor to place a curse upon my father." John shook his head. "The witch doctor refused, saying he was unable to successfully curse my father because he was protected by God. My father was the village pastor."

"Interesting." Jace shifted in his seat and set aside his empty cup. "But there is something I don't understand. Why are these patients bringing messages to *me*?"

"I do not know. I need to interview your patients about what they saw and felt. It is possible they are dealing with a demonic spirit of some sort."

"Beatrice called it an angel."

"Could be a disguise." The chaplain shrugged. "Listen, if I can discern that it is angelic, we need to figure out just what God is trying to do here."

"And if it's not?"

"It is possible that this isn't angelic at all."

"A demon?"

"Yes. Listen, if this is some sort of satanic attack, then we'll need to figure out why. Let me ask you something, Jace. Certain activities can open you up to the Devil's handholds. Have you been involved in any dark activities?"

"I don't understand."

"Séances? Ouija board games?"

"Of course not."

"Have you been in contact with a witch doctor? Used a witch doctor's cure? Had a witch doctor work a spell on your behalf?"

"No."

"Okay," John said. "Listen, Jace, if this is a demonic attack, you need to take precautions to protect yourself."

Jace shrugged. "I'm not sure what you mean."

"Just like the old witch doctor couldn't curse my father because of his faith, the Enemy can't attack Christians without some opening. The Bible says it like this, Jace: 'Greater is He who is in you than he who is in the world.'" He shrugged. "If I were you, I'd make sure I was in the camp."

31

Jace no sooner got inside his little house than he heard pounding at the front door. "Karibu!" he called.

Jace opened the door to see two uniformed men, Kenyan police, about thirty years old, standing shoulder to shoulder. "Dr. Rawlings?"

"Yes." Jace held out his hand.

The officer on the right had a scar with a heaped-up edge on his chin. Jace recognized it as a keloid, a common problem in the healing of dark skin. "We are investigating a hit-and-run," he said, shaking Jace's hand. The scar dimpled when he spoke.

The second man was of very dark complexion, a Luya perhaps, maybe Luo. "Yesterday," he said. "Near Dagoretti corner."

"I was there."

"The man who was killed was Mungiki."

Jace said nothing.

Keloid-chin spoke again. "Why would you be associating with him?"

"I only happened to be there at the time."

The second officer consulted a notepad. "We have witnesses who say you were at the scene with the Mungiki."

"I was traveling with my friends to have lunch with the Honorable John Okombo, the minister of health. I'm sure he can verify this. Our driver, a man named Samuel, who works for Minister Okombo, ran over a spiked barrier at a police stop. We had to repair the tire, and so we were waiting at the side of the road when this man showed up. As he crossed the road, he was struck. I wasn't with the man. I only attended him."

"Yet you traveled with him to a local hospital and paid his bill," the scarred man said.

The second officer backed out into the yard to use his cell phone. When he returned, he frowned. "Perhaps we should talk of this further. Our records show no plans for a police stop anywhere close to Dagoretti yesterday."

"It was there. Ask the driver. He was the one who repaired the tire." Jace paused, squinting at the two officers. "I thought it was an odd place for a police check, just around a blind corner like that. Our driver yelled at the men at the stop, pointing at our official government vehicle, and they pulled out and left."

"Did you see the vehicle that struck the pedestrian?"

"A matatu. Bright green, I think." Jace shrugged. "That's all I know. How did you track me down?"

"A white doctor travels with a victim to a local hospital, then signs the record after caring for a criminal. It wasn't hard."

"A criminal?"

"Mr. Kimathi is suspected in the burning of a Luo church in western Kenya after the last election."

"I see."

"Why did you pay his bill?"

"The nurses at Karen asked who was responsible. I felt bad that I had used their supplies on a case that turned out to be hopeless." Jace shook his head. "The man didn't look like he had the means, so I just paid it."

"You felt guilty?"

"Not exactly. Responsible." Jace paused. "What else do you know about the victim?"

"Why do you ask?"

Jace wondered how much to tell the officers. If the police were involved in setting up a hit, he would be wading into murky waters.

The trio stood silently for a moment. Finally, Jace spoke again. "I think the victim may have been looking for me."

The officer touched his chin scar. "And why is that?"

"My friend found a photocopy of a newspaper picture, a picture of me."

The second officer laughed. "Maybe he was a fan. Maybe he wanted surgery."

"Seriously," Jace said. "The man was crossing the street, staring at me, not paying attention to the road. When he was struck by the matatu, some sort of gun came flying out from under his coat."

"No one else mentioned a gun."

"It was taken from the scene."

"And how do you know this?"

"I looked for it a few moments later. It must have been taken."

The darker-skinned officer made a note. "This complicates things."

"Look, this whole thing bothers me."

"As it should." The man paused. "And yet you neglected to inform the police."

"Because I was afraid. Look, put yourself in my shoes. A man with my picture in his pocket shows up with a gun. Why would he be looking for me there unless he knew I would be there at a certain time? And how would I be there at a certain time without it being set up with the police checkpoint?"

"You think our police set this up?"

"Maybe not the police. Maybe our driver. He had to have me at a certain place at a certain time."

"You are accusing a government official?"

"I'm not accusing anyone," Jace said, immediately regretting the loud volume of his response. "Look," he said, lowering his voice, "I didn't know what to do."

The man with the scar studied Jace for a moment. "You will need to come with us to the station to give a formal statement."

"I'm not interested in trouble."

"I know, Dr. Rawlings." The man smiled, revealing a perfect row of white teeth standing out against his black skin. "But we are." He paused before adding, "We are very interested in trouble."

Two hours later, Jace sat in a small room in the Uplands Police Station answering questions from Detective Ndemi, a man of medium stature, with a shaved head and teeth etched brown from too much fluoride as a child, an endemic problem in Kenya.

The detective leaned back in his chair, linking his fingers behind his shiny head. "It seems that what began as a simple hit-and-run investigation has raised more questions than answers," he said quietly. "You know, Dr. Rawlings, that police corruption is a problem very difficult to root out because the wages are low."

Ndemi's cell phone rang. He looked at the phone and sighed. "Hello," he said, punching a button.

From that moment on, he listened, saying "Eh ... eh ... eh ..." every few seconds, the Kikuyu way of saying *yes, I'm getting you*. After two minutes, Ndemi switched off the phone and smiled at Jace. "My wife," he said.

Jace looked around the room. Painted a drab gray, the walls were bare except for a picture of the Kenyan president, a requirement for all government buildings.

"Where was I?" the detective continued. "Oh, yes, the corruption of our police. It would not surprise me that our police could be bribed to set up a checkpoint in a particular location." He paused, leaning forward and pointing at Jace. "But I would be very careful about lodging complaints against government officials, especially a man of national reputation like the Honorable John Okombo."

"I am not accusing him. I was afraid. Maybe I've let my imagination run away with me."

Detective Ndemi paused, thinking. "Yes, of course." He tapped his pen on the metal table that separated them. "The Mungiki are a troublesome group, and they have connections. If they had a reason to target you, they could have bribed the police themselves." He hesitated. "Of course, we will question Minister Okombo's driver and see what we can find out. Perhaps the Mungiki only wanted the police to stop your vehicle long enough to do their work. The flattened tire may have been coincidental."

"I hadn't thought of that."

"Of course not. It is not your job."

"I am afraid of stirring up trouble." Jace shrugged. "That's why I didn't go to the police in the first place. I thought if the police or someone inside government was involved, it could be dangerous for me to raise concerns."

"It seems you have no choice now."

Jace nodded.

"Minister Okombo's influence reaches beyond his role as the minister of health. He has traveled widely, securing trade deals even with your country. His father was the ambassador to the US, I believe, so the role was a natural one for him."

"I do not want to disrespect Minister Okombo."

"Of course."

"Why would the Mungiki target me?"

"They may not have had a motive on their own, but money is a powerful motivator. Perhaps someone else paid them to do it. Unfortunately, the man who knows why he was targeting you has been killed, and we have failed to identify his accomplices."

"How can I protect myself?"

The detective ignored Jace's question, only giving him a look of sympathy and continuing. "Tell me about the police at the checkpoint. Were they uniformed? Did you see badges, official papers?"

"They were wearing blue uniforms and police hats. They appeared legitimate to me. I didn't see any papers."

"They may not have been police at all. We've had some thievery of our metal spike strips."

"So perhaps the police aren't involved at all."

"A possibility." He made a note on the paper in front of him. "Some Luos used our equipment to set up blockades after the last election, stopping cars and threatening the Kikuyu." He shook his head. "They claimed Kibaki stole the election from Odinga." He slammed his hand on the table. "Foolishness!"

From what Jace had heard, the claim was far from foolish. To see that the conflict between the tribes was still able to stir such an emotional outburst from the Kikuyu detective demonstrated that the rift in the culture was deep and ongoing.

"You may want to stay in Kijabe for a while. My people will investigate this," Ndemi said.

Jace shifted in his seat.

"Don't worry, Dr. Rawlings. I can be discreet."

"I don't need any more attention. I just want to do my work as a surgeon without disturbance."

The man smiled through brown teeth with an expression that made Jace shudder. "I hope that works out for you." He paused. "You can catch a matatu back to Kijabe. I'll be in touch if I have any more questions."

With that, the man walked out, leaving Jace alone.

Alone was exactly what he felt.

32

Heather picked up the phone, noting the caller ID: "unrecognized number."

"Hello."

"Heather, Ryan Meadows here."

"Yes," she said, her stomach beginning to churn as soon as she heard his name. Ryan had promised to call her with information about the night of Jace's accident.

"How are you?"

She bristled. She wasn't interested in small talk. "Fine. Did you find out any information for me?"

"I'm fine too, thanks for asking. I was hoping we could meet for lunch. The Tobacco Company is close for me. Is that too far out of your way?"

"I'm really just interested in what you found out."

"I'd rather discuss this face-to-face. Shall we say noon?"

Heather shook her head. "What did you find out?"

She listened to Ryan sigh. "Heather, some of this stuff may be difficult to hear. You didn't let me buy you dinner the other night.

Can we meet for lunch? Having a friend may make bad news easier to take."

A friend? Is that what you are now? "I appreciate your concern, Mr. Meadows," she said. "But I am prepared to hear whatever you tell me."

Another sigh into the phone. "Okay, but I'll take a rain check on the meal together." He paused.

She imagined he wanted a hopeful response, but she wasn't about to give it.

"The hotel manager, Mr. Baker, usually took care of Mrs. Franks personally. I asked him about the night she died. He remembered a few things, even made a few notes so he could tell the police if they ever questioned him. Fortunately, they haven't."

She waited and finally prompted, "Well?"

"Let's see," he said as if he were reading. "At approximately nine p.m., Mr. Baker assisted Mrs. Franks with her bags, taking them to her suite. At ten p.m., he received a call from her asking him to escort up her physician. Dr. Rawlings arrived a few minutes later."

"The news said they were seen leaving together at eleven thirty."

"Heather, I'm so sorry." Ryan paused. "Listen, I hope you won't think I'm too forward. I know that you've separated from your husband, but this must be horrible for you. I do hope you'll let me take you to dinner sometime."

"Why don't we keep this just business?" she said. "Thank you for the information." With that, she hung up.

Ten p.m.? Heather walked to a calendar on the wall of the study and paged back. *I was with Jace at ten p.m. that evening. We got out of the theater at ten forty-five. We'd driven separately because he came straight from the hospital and went back there after the film.*

Something just doesn't smell right.

Is Mr. Meadows lying? Or just misinformed?

Jace arrived back in Kijabe after two crowded matatu rides from Uplands. He stared at his refrigerator and sighed. A wilted head of lettuce, a half-empty can of tuna, some grape jelly, an overripe mango, and some carrot sticks stared back at him, an offering fit for the starving, but not for Jace. He couldn't face another PBJ. What he wanted was stew and chapatis, but he didn't have the energy to walk down to Mama Chiku's.

After morning rounds, the day had been a whirl. His conversations with Chaplain Otieno and the police had left him uneasy. He hated the unknown. If he didn't know the source of a threat, real or perceived, how could he do anything about it?

What disturbed him most was a sense of déjà vu. The warnings the chaplain gave him sounded eerily like those his sister had issued in the weeks before her death.

During Jace's last weeks in Kijabe before leaving for college, Janice's urging had become stronger, prompted by a sense that her chances to warn him would soon pass.

As it turned out, she was right. But it was her time that was short, not his. He'd wondered about it later. Could she have had a premonition of death, yet misunderstood?

He remembered how she'd pleaded with him to join her and some friends for a last campout at Malewa River before their graduation. He should have known it would be another spiritual ambush.

She had rolled the red-checked Maasai blankets the day they left, tying each one with a short segment of rope. "I'm glad you're coming, Jace," she said. "Most of the station kids are going. Bruce, Mark, Eric, Joel, Stephanie, and Linda."

He nodded. "I want to roast a goat. I can slaughter it with the guys the night before we leave. We can roast the meat at the campsite."

She smiled and shoved a rebellious strand of blonde hair behind her ear. She picked up a pen and added something to a list of supplies before pausing. "Jace, Bruce is bringing his guitar. He wants to lead a time of prayer and worship, kind of a dedication—a send-off, since we're not going to see much of each other after grad."

"We'll see each other."

"Not so much. Our group is going to be everywhere. Air Force Academy, Wheaton, University of Virginia, John Brown University." She seemed to hesitate. "I just don't want you to feel weird."

"Janice," he said, trying to hide his irritation, "I'm fine, okay? I've been around this stuff all my life. It's not like I'm gonna get all weirded out because of some songs." He put his hand on her shoulder. "I told you, it's not that I don't like it. I just wished I *believed* it, like you and Bruce." He looked away. "I'm just not going to fake it anymore."

"No one's asking you to fake anything."

"Besides," he said, "if there's any place where I feel close to the Creator, it's sleeping out under the dust of the Milky Way."

"I know," she said, smiling. "I know." She took a deep breath. "Just promise me you'll ask God to make Himself real to you."

"You still think I'm going to die?"

"Jace, I don't know what to make of my feelings. I've never felt this way before. Like I know I'm supposed to get you a message, 'cause I might not have many more chances."

"I'm not going anywhere," he said. "Except America." He made a popping sound with his mouth, implying a popping of the Christian bubble he'd lived in at Rift Valley Academy. The students often complained about the restrictive bubble when they were at RVA, but graduates would come back and tell them how comfortable the bubble really was. "Bye-bye, RVA," he said.

"Promise me," she said.

"Just lay off, Janice. You are not me."

The Honorable John Okombo pressed his stomach and wished he could belch away his pain. He found some antacid tablets in his top desk drawer and shoved the day's copy of *The Standard* aside. He'd been quoted on the front page as saying a Mungiki leader, Anthony Kimathi, had met a just end. In truth, he *had* said that, but as quoted it seemed out of context. A reporter had implied that the Kenyan police were incompetent, since they had been searching for Kimathi for quite some time. Another reporter had linked Okombo to the story and asked for his comment because his vehicle was at the scene of Kimathi's death. What he'd actually said was, "What we couldn't do, God intervened and did. Kimathi may have escaped the police, but he couldn't escape God."

Okombo knew that his comments would be distorted. Kikuyu-Luo tensions were bound to escalate in the wake of the Mungiki leader's death, and Okombo didn't need the negative attention. He cursed his luck and called Simeon Okayo.

While the phone on the other end rang, Okombo stood and shut the door to his study. Alone, he waited.

"Hello."

"Simeon, did you hear about Anthony?"

"He was an idiot."

"Perhaps." He sighed. "We've got other problems."

"We?"

"Rawlings told the police about it. They are asking my driver questions. Seems like some Detective Ndemi is concerned about police corruption."

"Maybe he wants to run for Parliament," Simeon said, laughing at his own joke. "But I don't see this as a problem, especially not my problem. Anthony is dead. He can't talk."

"You need to help me here. Now there is double reason to take care of Rawlings. You should have never bragged to the governor's staff."

"He only asked me what kind of work I was capable of. He seemed fascinated with curses."

The MP listened to what sounded like liquid sloshing in a jar. He imagined the witch doctor mixing a potion. "Westerners always find black magic exciting."

"I had no idea the man would ask for a favor," Simeon said.

"Well, he did. And if we want to keep our trading partners happy, we're going to have to follow through."

"Certainly you have other contacts."

"I thought you'd do what you do best," Okombo rejoined.

"Curse him?"

"Exactly. Instead you hire a Mungiki friend."

"He owed me a favor."

"I counted on you."

Okombo listened as the old doctor's breath blew into the phone. "Okay," he said. "I'll take care of it."

"A blood oath."

"Better if you don't know."

That night, Jace found Evan Martin eating in the little restaurant within the hospital grounds. Catering mostly to employees and patients' families, the service was friendly and the food fried.

Jace saw Evan attacking a plate of chicken and chips, a cup of sweet chai in front of him. Jace fetched a mug of tea from the counter and sat on a white plastic chair opposite Evan. "Keep eating like that, and you're going to need me."

Evan shook his head. "I have GPS in my cell phone. There's this cool app that tells me how far I walk every day. I'm doing at least three miles more here than I did in Virginia."

Jace leaned forward and kept his voice low. "I talked to the chaplain about our patients' experiences. He thinks they may have been contacted by some sort of spirit."

Evan raised his eyebrows. "A spirit?"

"You know, an angel." Jace studied his friend for a reaction. Nothing. So he added. "Or a demon."

Another subtle raise of the eyebrow, but no comment from Evan.

"I know it sounds weird, but Africans have a bit more respect for this kind of thing." He paused. "He seems to think I might be under some sort of attack."

"An attack?"

"Spiritually. Like a curse."

"I don't like it, Jace." Evan sipped his tea. "Look, this is all getting to be a little much for me." He lifted his index finger. "We have a pretty good idea that this Anthony guy had you in his sights." He held up a second finger. "And now you're talking about weird spiritual stuff."

"You're the one who told me I should pay attention."

"Sure, but this whole thing is getting out of hand." He set down his mug and shook his head. "I've got a family, Jace. I came over here to do a few cases, get you started, test the waters. But this—well, this is getting a little scary."

"But I need you here. At least for another case or two."

"If we even get to keep doing this. I heard about how mad Fitzgerald was after that kid died of a ruptured spleen." He sighed heavily. "We're taxing an already overloaded system, Jace. I think it's better all around if I go home where I know what to expect."

"Evan," Jace said, trying to keep his voice from showing the urgency he felt. "What if someone really is trying to get a message to me?"

Evan raised his eyebrows. "This from my friend the scientist?"

Jace sighed. "Maybe I'm changing."

"If someone is trying to send you a message, you don't exactly need me for that."

"You're wrong. I need you. I need you to do exactly what you did in the first two cases."

"And what—you're going to hope your patient contacts the great beyond and gives you whatever message you came here for?"

Jace sat back. "It sounds stupid to have you put it that way, but yes." His eyes bored into his friend's. "I don't get what's happening either, but ..." He stopped talking while a Kenyan mother carrying a baby passed their table. "But something is clearly going on here. Someone—" he paused— "or some *thing*—has a message for me."

"Maybe I have a message for you," Evan said. "You need to stop chasing weird messages and go home to your wife."

Jace shook his head. "I just need you to reproduce everything you did in the first two cases."

"Better find your case soon," Evan said. "Because I'm going home."

"Scared?"

Jace expected defensiveness. Instead, he got honesty. "Yeah, Jace, I'm scared." Evan paused and leaned toward his friend, his eyes glistening and his voice etched with tension. "Scared for you."

33

On his next call night, Jace started at the sound of his pager and groaned. Two thirty. *This had better be good.*

He picked up the phone and dialed the number.

"Casualty."

"This is Dr. Rawlings. I was paged."

"Dr. Rawlings, my name is Charity. I'm the medical intern on call."

"What is it?"

"I am seeing a twenty-two-year-old Somali man. He has been having fevers for a week. He was injured three weeks ago in fighting in Mogadishu."

"What kind of injury?"

"He was shot in the left groin. He says there was a lot of bleeding and that a doctor there sewed him up." She paused. "Now he has a fever and an elevated white blood cell count to nineteen thousand. I'm wondering if the wound might be infected."

"Are there signs of infection?"

"Tenderness."

Jace yawned. "When was the injury?"

"Three weeks ago."

And why am I getting up in the middle of the night to see him? Jace hid his sarcasm. "I'll be right there."

He dressed, splashed water on his face, threw on a white lab coat, and plodded down the path to the hospital. A few moments later, Dr. Charity N'ganga introduced him to his patient.

"This is Mohamed Omar Abdullahi," she said, pulling back a curtain to reveal the young man. "He speaks good English."

Jace studied him for a moment. "Al-shabaab?"

"No, sir. I went to school in Minnesota and returned to Mogadishu to work with the World Food Bank." He shrugged. "I was in the wrong place at the wrong time."

Jace lifted the blanket. "May I see the wound?"

He nodded.

Jace put on an exam glove and carefully palpated the length of a four-inch surgical scar. "How old is your wound?"

"Three weeks tomorrow."

"And how long have you been having fever?"

"Ten days."

"Any abdominal pain? Painful urination? Cough? Pain over an IV site? Skin rash?"

To each question the patient answered no.

Jace looked at the intern. "This wound doesn't look infected to me. You have to look elsewhere for a source of infection." He asked the patient, "Are you taking any drugs?"

"No."

Jace explained. "You must always consider drug fever."

The surgeon gently squeezed the patient's calf on the side of his injury. "No signs of deep venous thrombosis."

Jace lifted his stethoscope and laid the bell on the man's chest. After listening a few seconds, he asked, "Have you ever been told that you have a heart murmur?"

"No."

He nodded at the young Kikuyu intern. "Charity, listen here. Sounds like tricuspid regurgitation."

"What are you suggesting?"

"He needs to be treated for endocarditis."

"A heart-valve infection."

"Exactly. Something seeded his blood, perhaps the bullet fragment, and the bacteria have decided to rest on a heart valve. I'll do an ultrasound tomorrow to look for vegetations. I'd like you to get two sets of blood cultures and a chest X-ray tonight. Start him on broad-spectrum antibiotics."

The intern took rapid notes.

Jace headed for the door, but stopped and turned around when he'd gone only a few steps. "Get the first dose of antibiotics on board stat. If he has clumps of bacteria on the valve, they could embolize and give him a pulmonary abscess."

The patient's eyes widened.

Jace nodded. "Unlikely, but possible." He turned to the patient. "We are going to do everything we can for you."

And now, I need some sleep.

300 · HARRY KRAUS

The following morning Jace threw Mohamed Omar's chest X-ray on the view box and smiled. He'd just found his third open-heart case.

"Hey, Paul," he called to his intern standing a few feet away at the theater desk. "Look at this."

Paul squinted toward the film.

"Presented last night. Twenty-two-year-old Somali male with a three-week-old shrapnel injury to the left groin, fever, and a new tricuspid murmur."

"What is that?" Paul pointed to a bright white irregular object overlying the heart shadow.

"Yes, what is that?" Jace stood back.

"It's a trick," Paul said. "It's on his skin, right?"

"Nope." Jace threw up the lateral chest film. "Here it is again," he said, pointing.

"He was shot in the chest?"

"No. His injury is in his thigh near the inguinal crease."

"It looks like a bullet."

"Exactly. But how did it get there?"

Paul scratched his head.

"It's called a bullet embolis. The bullet entered his femoral vein through an open wound, then escaped up the vein and traveled to the heart where it appears to have lodged in his right ventricle." He paused. "He seems to have endocarditis, so the bullet must have carried bacteria to the heart valve, causing an infection."

"What do we do?"

"Treat his endocarditis with antibiotics, then operate to remove the fragment when the infection clears."

"Will the bullet move out into the lung?"

"Not likely. It's stayed put for three weeks. It must be stuck."

Paul's eyes brightened. "Cool."

"For us," Jace said. "Try being the patient. Now," he said, "let's go get the ultrasound and confirm my suspicions."

Twenty minutes later, he did just that. Scanning over the precordium, Jace demonstrated the bullet lodged next to the valve. "It appears to be entangled in the tendinous insertion of the valve leaflets. The murmur could be coming from dysfunction of the valve, but also because the bullet could have carried bacteria and infected the valve." He paused. "The good news is that I don't see any significant bacterial vegetations on the valve leaflets."

Paul pointed at the screen, an area of apparent turbulent flow. "What's that?"

Jace moved the scanner. "Looks like a small atrial septal defect. Probably something he was born with."

Jace turned to Mohamed. "You've got a bullet fragment that traveled from the vein in your leg and has become trapped in your heart. If we do nothing, it could cause continued infections of the valve, or even infect the lining around the heart. There is a small chance the bullet fragment could travel out into the lung and cause death to a portion of lung or an abscess." He paused. "Or it could cross the small hole between your heart's upper chambers and cause a stroke."

"Meaning?"

Jace shrugged soberly. "Paralysis. Maybe death."

"So what are you recommending?"

"An operation to remove the bullet, repair the valve, and repair the hole in the heart."

A look of fear spread over the patient's face. "Here?"

Jace nodded. "We have a program to do this right here. I have brought the necessary people over from the United States to do the surgery."

"Or I could go back to the US. I live in Minnesota. I could go to the Mayo Clinic."

Jace nodded. "You could. It is possible that with the proper equipment, the bullet could be retrieved with a catheter threaded up from a vein in your leg, but that is not something we can do here."

"What would you do?" The patient looked at the Kenyan intern.

"Delaying to travel to America could be risky." Paul put his hand on the man's shoulder. "Dr. Rawlings is one of the best. He operated on the governor of Virginia."

"I can't lie. There are possible complications," Jace said.

"I will stay here. I will be okay. *Insha'Allah.*" It was the mantra of Islam: If Allah wills.

Jace understood.

He looked up to see one of the hospital security guards lingering on the other side of the patient's bed. Jace made eye contact.

The security guard, a man not much older than twenty, nodded seriously. "Dr. Rawlings, the Kenyan police visited us this morning. They are insisting we escort you when you are on hospital grounds."

"Escort me?"

"Yes, sir. They seem to think you are in danger."

Just then, Dave Fitzgerald walked up. "What's going on, Rawlings? There's a huge crowd of unhappy people at the gate. The police have set up a perimeter and are insisting that we revise our visiting policy: no one but family members, and they want everyone to produce a doctor's note to confirm that they are needed inside."

"I don't know," Jace said. "I didn't know anything about this."

"Well, I need you to go out there and straighten things out."

Jace hesitated.

"Now!" Fitzgerald said.

On Sunday morning, Heather planned a late arrival and early departure from church. She loved hearing Pastor Ken exposit the Scripture but disliked the judgmental looks of the church members.

I'm reading too much into their expressions, she told herself. *Maybe it's pity or concern and not criticism for separating from Jace.*

Jace. He was the congregation's favorite son. Famous surgeon. Missionary family. Rich enough to help the budget stay in the black.

Sunday mornings with Jace were always a zoo of old women fawning over him, thanking him for operating on this relative or that. One woman had even pulled aside a pearl necklace, pointed to the scar starting on her upper chest and disappearing into her cleavage, and gushed, "He saved my life."

Sometimes, Heather wondered just who was being worshipped, Jace or Jesus. She'd brought it up only once, and Jace's reaction was a flippant, "You're crazy!"

But since she'd dared to return after a month's hiatus, the attention was gone, replaced by silent nods and expressions that threw scalpels of judgment—or an avoidance of eye contact altogether.

So she opted to slip into the last row after the first hymn at six minutes past the hour. Sadly, the service was that predictable. She wondered how they would handle it if God showed up and requested a change in the program. *Not allowed. You are scheduled for 11:20 to 11:40.*

It didn't seem to matter that the media had painted her husband as the unfaithful one. Heather felt just as guilty when she walked in alone under the stares of Richmond's upper crust.

She moved toward the center of the pew, an antique wooden structure with red upholstery, and sat. A second hymn. Announcements. Offertory. Dismiss the children. Responsive reading. Morning scripture reading. A sermon by Pastor Ken. Closing hymn.

Time to escape.

When everyone stood to sing, Heather slipped quietly out the back. She made it as far as the parking lot before she heard her name. "Heather."

She turned to see Lisa Sprague, the feature writer for the *Richmond Times Dispatch.* "Hi, Lisa."

Lisa looked around. They were alone. "Can we talk?"

Heather studied her expression. "Something wrong?"

"Maybe." Lisa wore a dark skirt, a designer blouse, and a bit more jewelry than Heather's taste would allow, but her makeup was perfect. And unnecessary, given Lisa's youth and the blonde hair that fell in ringlets to her shoulders. She probably looked just like that when she woke up.

"I talked to Steve Brady," she said. "He's a friend." She paused. "We share stories. Sometimes, when he doesn't have the time or authority to look into something, he throws me a bone."

"He told you about Jace?"

"A few things. Can we talk?"

"I'm not really interested in splashing our story in the papers."

"But you are interested in what happened to Jace."

"Yes."

"Then we should talk." She smiled. "Let's do lunch. I have connections. I can help you learn the truth."

Heather smiled back. "The truth." She gestured toward her car. "For that, I'll drive."

34

Heather and Lisa sat in a booth at Applebee's. Lisa looked at Heather's bacon cheeseburger and shook her head.

Heather understood the unspoken question. "I walk a lot."

Lisa pushed her chicken Caesar salad around the bowl and leaned forward. "How are you doing? You and Jace seemed so—" she hesitated while she searched for the right word—"comfortable with each other back when I did the story on his career."

Heather nodded. "That pretty much sums it up. But this whole Anita Franks thing and his accident seem to have shaken everything up."

"What happened? I would have thought you guys had the faith foundation to weather just about anything."

"I thought so too. But after his accident, Jace didn't seem sure about anything." She took a bite of her sandwich. "Especially his faith."

"What gives? I thought his faith was important to him."

"Me, too. I tried to talk to him about it, but he just kept pulling away. It was as if his accident brought back something horrible from his past. He just kept talking about his need to go back to Africa."

Heather hesitated. "He was very close to his twin sister, but she died in an accident shortly before they graduated from high school. He never talked to me about it, but I know Jace was there when his sister died, and he felt responsible because he couldn't help her. I think it's why he became a doctor."

"Guilt?"

Heather nodded again. "A powerful motivator."

Lisa leaned forward. "In spite of knowing the gospel, many Christians struggle with guilt."

Heather stared out the front window at the busy street. "It's weird. Jace and I were both from missionary families, so I always assumed that Jace was a true believer. He was always quiet about his faith. He went with me to church, but he never talked about it. Then, after his accident, he started talking about needing to go back to Africa, and I thought it was just a crazy idea, but then he up and resigned his practice and expected me to jump on board."

"But you didn't see it his way?"

"He said he thought his sister would have wanted him to come. He claims he saw a vision of her on the night of his accident. He said he saw her face, asking him to 'come back to me.'" Heather shrugged. "He couldn't articulate it, but I think he felt so guilty about having an affair that he ran off to Africa for penance."

"So you believe the rumors?"

"I'm not sure what to believe." Heather sipped her tea and told Lisa the whole story, beginning with Jace's accident and including the findings of Anita Franks's autopsy.

"Steve Brady mentioned that." She paused. "So Jace doesn't remember anything?"

"Jace and I were out to see a movie that night. I know we didn't get out until at least 10:45. But that doesn't jive with what the manager of the Jefferson Hotel told Ryan Meadows. Ryan reports that the manager took notes to document the evening after the accident, in case the police questioned him. He claims that he escorted Jace to Mrs. Franks's suite shortly after ten."

Lisa raised her overly plucked eyebrows and wrote something on a notepad. "What is Jace's blood type?"

Heather shook her head. "Not a clue. Why?"

"I've learned a little bit following the crime beat in this town. If the autopsy had a semen sample, it could be easier to rule Jace in or at least out by analyzing it. You see, eighty percent of males are secretors. That means they secrete their blood-type antigens in their body fluids, including semen. If the semen sample has blood antigens that don't match Jace, it could get him off the hook."

"But if they match Jace ..."

"Well, it doesn't prove it's him. But a DNA study would be conclusive."

"I asked Gabby Dawson, his pump tech, to bring me some of Jace's blood."

"It wouldn't even take blood. It could be a cigarette butt or a glass that he used, anything with DNA."

Heather sighed. "I'm not sure she'll do it. She's very loyal to Jace and doubts he is guilty of adultery."

"But you're not so sure."

Heather shifted in her seat. "You've seen pictures of Anita Franks. She was gorgeous. And you know my husband. I think Anita could have seduced him."

"So what's with the ketamine?"

"I don't know. But I don't think my husband was capable of rape. Falling for a beautiful blonde, maybe, but not rape."

"So you want his blood to prove …"

"I want to prove he's innocent."

"But you're scared."

"Wouldn't you be?" Heather felt tears welling up in her eyes. "I'm not sure of anything anymore. I used to think I married a reliable Christian man. Now I'm not sure who I married."

Lisa reached over and squeezed Heather's arm. "Let me do some snooping. I'll see if I can get more information out of the ME's office about that sample. In the meantime, see if you can find out Jace's blood type."

"The medical examiner won't give out information on Anita to anyone except next of kin."

"I have a friend or two who owe me favors. Let me see what I can do."

When Jace walked home, he was escorted by two security officers. Near his house, two baboons ran from the corner of the small carport back toward a trash pit where they joined another pair looking for food. Overhead, the leaves of the eucalyptus trees clapped with the breeze, a constant in Kijabe.

Just as he was unlocking the door, he heard the crunch of gravel and the familiar clicking drone of a diesel engine. He looked to see the Toyota Land Cruiser used by the minister of health.

Samuel, the driver, did not smile, but exited quickly to open the passenger door.

John Okombo stepped out into the afternoon sun, looking even more massive than when Jace had met him face-to-face in his office.

Jace's gut tightened. He whispered to the hospital security, "Stay close." Then louder, he said, "Minister Okombo, I didn't expect to see you."

The MP held out his hand and engulfed Jace's. "I wanted to check on your safety."

"You didn't need to come all this way for me."

Minister Okombo smiled. "I wanted to see you. You didn't call after you failed to keep my invitation."

Jace opened his front door. "Will you come in? I should explain."

The tall man nodded. "Perhaps you should."

They entered the small kitchen. Minister Okombo's driver stayed outside with the hospital security guards.

Jace motioned toward a small couch and selected a chair for himself. "It became pretty obvious that someone was coming after me. What I didn't know is who I could trust."

"So you suspected my driver?"

Jace shifted uncomfortably.

"And you suspected me?"

Jace swallowed.

The large man laughed. Loudly, he slapped his knee. "Of *course* you didn't know who you could trust!"

Jace nodded and forced a smile.

Okombo leaned forward. "When the police informed me of the plot on your life, I assured them that my office would cooperate with an investigation." He paused. "And I have asked the police to provide additional security measures for your protection."

"Unfortunately, the security measures are disrupting the flow of visitors, and hospital security is already stretched thin."

"My concern is for your safety. And I will send extra help from the Kenya police to speed security screening."

Jace shook his head. "If you want this heart program to succeed, you will have to make this all go away."

"Of course I want the program to succeed."

"I'm not a very popular man around here just now. It seems like my efforts are just making problems. Honestly, I'm not sure the system can support it."

"You saved my daughter."

Jace nodded. "Yes." He folded his arms across his chest. "I'd prefer a low profile. I won't hold you responsible. Please don't make my life harder by tightening security."

The man shrugged. "As you wish." He lifted his cell phone. "But I will insist on personal guards here. We want to watch your house at night."

Jace sighed. "Fine."

Minister Okombo folded his hands. "Don't forget who your friends are, Dr. Rawlings." The man stood, towering for a moment above Jace. "I'll have my men in place before night. They will report directly to me."

"Why are you doing this?"

"I am the minister of health. I am only looking out for one of my own."

Jace didn't like it. He wasn't sure Okombo could be trusted, but he couldn't exactly voice his concerns. Instead, he just mumbled "Thank you" and followed him to the door.

As Okombo reached the Land Cruiser, Jace stepped up beside him and spoke quietly. "Would you like to visit Beatrice?"

The man looked away, his face sober. After a moment's reflection, he turned back and nodded. "Okay."

Jace smiled. "Let's go. I'll take you there." He motioned for the hospital security. "We're going down to the hospital for a few minutes."

As they approached the pull-down bar at the entrance to the parking lot, a hospital security guard held up his hand. "Hi, Dr. Rawlings." Then, he looked at Minister Okombo. "Sir, I'll need to see some identification. We're restricting access to patients and patients' family members only."

Minister Okombo didn't smile. He moved closer to the man and spoke in a quiet voice. "I am John Okombo, the minister of health. It was my department that requested this additional security." He made a move to step around the bar.

"I'll still need to see an ID."

Jace shook his head. Maybe this was good. Okombo might be frustrated enough to stop all the bother.

The MP huffed and pulled out his wallet. "Here," he said, shoving a card under the man's nose.

The security official waved them through. Okombo flipped open his phone. In a moment, he spoke loudly. "Captain, I want you to tell your men to notify Kijabe Hospital of a relaxation of our previous request. Remove the visitation restriction. But leave two men to guard Dr. Rawlings's house. I want them in place by dark."

He closed his phone.

"Thank you, sir," Jace said. He lifted his hand and ushered Minister Okombo through a crowd near the entrance. "This way."

As they walked up the long hallway toward the HDU, Jace closed his eyes for a moment. There was no other smell like the hospital—too many bodies in one place, clinical aseptics, and floor wax seemed to permeate every inch. The surgeon looked at his guest. The MP didn't seem to mind. Probably every hospital in Kenya that he'd visited smelled this way.

Jace pushed open the door to the HDU. "This is our high dependency unit," he said. "We have the latest vital-sign monitors, continuous oxygen saturation monitoring, and a very favorable nurse-to-patient ratio."

He waved his hand from left to right. "We have six beds here." He sighed. "If our program takes off, we could easily use three times that amount."

The MP smiled. Jace introduced him to the three nurses in the unit. Okombo made a joke. "Why are all the nurses Kikuyu? We need some good Luo nurses here."

He then walked to the bedside of Beatrice Wanjiku. "Now this one has a Kikuyu name, but she looks like a Luo!" He looked at Beatrice. "Hello, Beatrice. Congratulations on your surgery. Dr. Rawlings has told me that it was a ringing success." He paused. "Forgive me for not introducing myself. I am John Okombo, Kenya's minister of health."

Beatrice remained sober. "I know who you are."

"You've read the papers."

She shook her head. "No."

"How do you feel?"

"Nzuri." Fine.

"Then you will be going home soon?"

Beatrice looked at Dr. Rawlings. "Let me stay. I don't want to go back to Kibera."

Jace forced a smile. "We'll see. I want you to stay here for a bit longer."

They chatted for a few minutes as Minister Okombo shuffled around her bed, unable to be still. They talked of schoolwork and of Beatrice's hopes to make good grades. When it was apparent that they had little more to say and the MP was about to leave, Beatrice asked, "Why did you come here?"

He smiled. "I wanted to see you."

"Then it *is* true."

"What is that, Beatrice?"

"You are my father."

Okombo jerked upright and looked around to see if the nurses were listening.

They were.

"What would make you say such a thing?" he gasped.

Beatrice shrugged. "An angel told me."

35

The following night, Jace looked out the front window to see that his police guards had settled in for the night, one leaning against a tree, the other resting against a small shed on the other side of the carport.

He looked up at the full moon and allowed it to take him back to that camping trip just before his graduation from RVA. He remembered sitting with his friends around a campfire, stirring a long stick in the coals, occasionally taking it out to allow the smoke to curl toward the moon. He and his friends talked of their future, college plans, America … and God.

They talked of a desire not to be absorbed into the emptiness of the American dream, of their ability to make a difference, of a calling to be light and salt for the One who loved them.

Jace looked at the moon and remembered the emptiness he felt then, and how it mirrored his feelings now.

They speak with such confidence of God's love, he'd thought back then, *and His calling on their lives. Why don't I feel the same?*

Will I always feel like I am looking in from the outside?

Will I ever believe?

Will I ever feel the call of the chosen?

Jace, too, looked forward to going to America, but for different reasons. He wanted to escape the bubble, the exclusion of other faiths, the restriction of so many rules.

He'd been excellent at compliance. He knew how to look good. But inside, Jace felt unchanged and unredeemed.

When Janice talked with passion about being loved, Jace felt curiously neutral.

When Janice whispered "grace," as if it was the most precious concept in the universe, Jace was unmoved.

Grace. Yawn. *Yes, I've sung the song. But if it is wonderful and amazing, why doesn't it move my heart? I must be Esau.*

Jace listened as his classmates sang songs of unending love. But for Jace, their words were soon melted in the vastness of the African sky. The moon beckoned. He stood and slipped away from the fire, preferring the solitude of the wilderness.

He walked a hundred meters into the bush, stopping to lean against a tree. In the background, he could hear the mix of his friends' worship and the cicadas. As he looked at the sky, the expanse seemed to echo from within his own emptiness.

If You are real, why can't I feel You like Janice does?

If You love me, why can't I believe?

His heart was stone.

He wanted to be loved.

He wanted to believe.

Is she right? Do You love me?

Show me, God.

He searched the sky, waiting for the writing of God.

Nothing.

He was alone.

With his heart aching, he formulated the essence of his heart-cry. "Choose me, God," he whispered. "Choose me."

In western Kenya, Simeon Okayo led a cow into the forest. His path lit only by the moonlight, his progress was slow but steady. Serenaded by a chorus of crickets, he prodded the animal forward.

By midnight, the altar was built, a fire started, and flames licked the cloudless sky as smoke from the green wood curled upward.

Simeon killed the animal by stabbing its neck, slicing through the right jugular vein and carotid artery. He collected the blood in a large wooden bowl.

Then, he lifted the bowl to the sky and set it in the fire. Before the blood could boil, he painted his hands and face.

Jace awoke and pushed back the thin blanket. *I'm burning up.* He touched his forehead and rubbed his fingers against his thumb, lubricated by the generous sweat. *Malaria?*

But there was something else.

Evil.

Fear.

I am going to die.

He puzzled over the thought. *Where did that come from?*

He pushed the thought away, struggled to his feet, and stumbled toward the bathroom, where he pulled the mirror forward to open the medicine cabinet. He dropped four ibuprofen tablets and a Malarone antimalarial pill into his hand, threw them to the back of his throat and drank water from the faucet, lifting it to his mouth with his hand. He splashed water onto his face, wanting to wash away the sweat. He closed the door to the medicine cabinet as he lifted his face to look at his reflection in the dim light of the moon coming through the window.

His face was dripping wet. *With blood!*

He gasped and looked at his hands. *Blood!*

He fumbled for a towel with shaking hands. He took deep gasping breaths, exhaling into the cloth to suppress his urge to scream. With the towel over his face, he found and snapped on the light. It took a moment for the overhead fluorescent bulb to ignite, flicker, and then stay on.

Slowly he lowered the towel to study his reflection.

The blood was gone.

He looked at his hands, the towel, and the wall where he'd left a trail of wetness searching for the light switch. *Just water.*

But the fever consumed his face. He knelt by the tub and lowered his head beneath the faucet there.

He stood and towel-dried his hair and went back to bed.

There, he was aware only of heat.

In minutes, his body and bed were drenched.

Again.

Simeon Okayo placed the cow's heart into the boiling blood. Then, eyes focused on the unseen, he chanted and lifted an object toward the moon.

Slowly, he lowered an instrument into the fire, allowing the tubing to coil snakelike into the coals.

Dr. Jace Rawlings's stethoscope. Smoking. Melting.

Okayo began to scream.

Jace tossed, finding sleep impossible as his body pulsed with fever.

He stared at the ceiling with a weird but distinct sense that he was not alone.

His heart began to race, galloping within his chest. He looked down, alarmed, sure that he would be able to see the pulsation.

His chest tightened.

He fought for breath.

The night sounds of crickets disappeared into the thunder of his heart in his ears.

His throat began to close.

Instinctively, he reached for the ceiling, one name on his lips.

"Janice!" He tried to scream, but his voice choked without air.

The room began to swim. Searing pain ripped his chest. He was sure of death.

And then, with his fingers drawing across the skin of his chest as if he could peel away the pain, he managed to whisper.

Not his sister's name this time.

But a name he knew from his childhood. The one he thought had betrayed him. Left him on the bench unchosen. Unwanted.

"Jesus!"

Barely a whisper.

But as he fought for air, a whisper was all he could manage.

Simeon lifted his head. Something was wrong. The moon was gone, obscured by the sudden appearance of clouds.

The fire provided the only light, revealing the trees as dancing spirits against the clouds.

And then, lightning. Violent. Stretching from east to west across the sky. The finger of God.

Rain began to fall, big drops sizzling against the glowing coals. A few at first, and then his fire began to wither.

Jace gasped as the weight lifted from his chest.

"Jesus!"

This time, the word came louder as his lungs relaxed to receive desperate breath.

The heavens opened. Rain fell as a sheet. Within moments, Okayo's offering was doused.

Coals smoldered. Okayo brushed wetness from his face and looked at the ruined altar.

Lightning revealed the unburnt carcass and reflected off something metallic. Okayo lifted the small object from the soggy ash.

He weighed the disk in his hand, the remnants of Jace Rawlings's stethoscope.

Okayo cursed, threw the object into the forest blackness and began to pick his way through the trees toward home.

Okayo shook his head. *Someone is praying.*

Jace dressed and slipped out his front door. He quietly stepped past a sleeping Kenyan policeman leaning against a tree in his front yard. Jace waited until he was a few yards past the man to pick up his pace and switch on his flashlight to illuminate the path.

His heart was full.

Could it be that God had intervened on his behalf?

He bypassed the hospital. Only an emergency could beckon him there at that hour. Instead, he walked the rocky road toward the cemetery.

There, he knelt at the small memorial stone for Janice Rawlings to pray. His words echoed an old plea from deep within the recesses of his soul. "Please, God, choose me."

36

Lisa Sprague smelled a story. It had all the elements. A famous person, now dead. Mysterious autopsy findings. An accident. Or something more sinister?

A local surgeon, a family man, suspected of betrayal. A rich doctor turned hero? Or a surgeon running from the truth?

Lisa started at the scene of the accident, downtown Richmond at the intersection of Lombardy and Broad, where a drunk driver in a Ford pickup had T-boned Jace's Lexus. Lisa had reconstructed the scene from the police report.

Anita Franks had been a passenger on the side opposite the impact. She'd made the 911 call, reporting that the driver was unconscious. She'd opened his door, and Jace had tumbled onto the road. As she knelt over him, she was struck and killed by a third vehicle, driven by a VCU student.

The VCU student had not been drinking. No charges were filed in the pedestrian accident.

The driver of the pickup was charged with DUI, his second offense, and was now wearing an orange jumpsuit in a city jail.

Lisa turned right off Broad Street and made a mental note to obtain a copy of the 911 call.

She parked two blocks from the Jefferson Hotel. On the sidewalk, she purchased a copy of the *Richmond Times Dispatch*.

The headlines splashed the latest in a story being rooted out by one of her colleagues. "Tobacco for Tea: A Conflict of Interest for Governor Franks?"

She scanned the article that pointed to family ties to tobacco money for Ryan Meadows, architect of the trade deal and Franks's chief of staff. Ryan's maternal uncle, longtime CEO of Landtower Tobacco Company, stood to gain a half-billion dollars for his company in the next decade, the price of selling carcinogens in a continent years behind on tobacco injury liability.

Good job, Rebecca. Looks like you're really onto something here. Lisa smiled. Rebecca Smythe and Lisa had started at the *Richmond Times Dispatch* within a few months of each other three years earlier and had cut their teeth reporting on local Richmond politics.

Lisa walked toward the hotel, wondering how she could win the manager's confidence. If he had been loyal to Mrs. Franks, he might not speak.

She looked around the expansive lobby, a testimony to extravagance in architecture of an era gone by. She stepped up to the concierge's desk and spoke to a bottle brunette with gray roots. "May I speak to Mr. Baker?"

"Is he expecting you?"

"No."

A man in a three-piece gray suit and white shirt with a striped blue-and-red tie approached, evidently pleased that a young lady would be asking for him. "I'm Mr. Baker."

Lisa smiled and extended her hand. "Lisa Sprague," she said. She kept her voice low. "I have a few questions of a sensitive nature. Could we find a private place to talk?"

He shrugged. "Sure," he said, "the bar is quiet."

She followed him to TJ's, the hotel's namesake restaurant on the second level. He gestured toward a corner booth. "How's this?"

"Fine," she said. They sat.

He looked thirty-five, fighting an extra pound for each year, but mostly hidden beneath the expensive suit. "What can I do for you?"

"I'm looking for information about someone who stayed in your establishment."

He smiled. "We serve many famous people. Who are you interested in?"

"Anita Franks."

He squinted behind gold wire-rim glasses. "Are you a reporter?"

"Yes." She hesitated. "But I'm not writing a story. At least not yet."

He folded his arms across his chest. "But whatever I say will be quoted."

"Why don't we just keep everything off the record? I'm not interested in damaging her reputation."

"So why ask questions?"

"I'm trying to find out information for a friend."

He stayed quiet.

"Look, Heather Rawlings, the surgeon's wife, is a friend of mine. She doesn't know what to believe. She's read the media speculation, saw the pictures of her husband out with Anita Franks around town. What she doesn't know is what to believe. Was Anita Franks having an affair with Jace Rawlings?"

"Why would I know this?"

"I was told you made arrangements for a suite for Mrs. Franks."

"Sure, but the Frankses kept a suite here, mainly for guests, political figures, and others who preferred to stay out of the public eye. Many people have stayed in the suite rented by Mrs. Franks."

"Many?"

He pointed to the front-page story. "Even these Kenyan visitors."

"Did Mrs. Franks stay there too?"

"Occasionally. Mr. Meadows always called ahead to make arrangements."

"Mr. Meadows?"

"The governor's chief of staff."

"And what about the night she died? Was she staying here then?"

He seemed to hesitate. "Yes."

"What can you tell me? Help me out here. Did Jace Rawlings spend time with her here?"

"I can speculate, that's all. Nothing can be quoted."

"Okay."

"Mrs. Franks liked to drink. But she didn't like drinking in public, so she'd have our bartender mix her favorites and I'd take them to her."

"Was she drinking that night?"

He nodded. "She'd talk when the alcohol started. I'd sit and listen. She said she'd made mistakes, but was going to take care of them that night. She told me she loved her husband and didn't want to hurt him."

"What do you think she meant?"

"I took her to mean that she had regrets." He shrugged again. "An affair, perhaps. But she was going to set things right that night."

"She was going to break off an affair?"

"A guess, that's all."

"Did Jace Rawlings visit her room that night?"

"She asked me to show him to her room, which I did."

"What time was that?"

"Just before they left. After eleven."

Lisa checked her notes. "I was told it was ten."

He shook his head. "No."

"How can you be sure?"

"Certain things stick in your mind after a tragic death."

"Did you make notes?"

"Of course not."

Lisa gazed at him across the table, trying to read him. *Ryan Meadows claimed that the manager of the hotel made notes in case the police asked any questions. He also claimed that you let Dr. Rawlings into the room at ten p.m.*

"Could it be that Mrs. Franks was trying to end an affair with the doctor?"

"I wasn't privy to their conversation. They certainly didn't stay long."

"Perhaps there was no reason to after that."

"Again, I'd only be speculating."

"Yet she left with him?"

He nodded.

"Pretty odd that she'd choose to leave with him if she'd just ended an affair."

"Again," he said, shifting in his seat. "I'd only be speculating."

She nodded. "Thanks for your time."

Jace knelt over his sister's grave, whispering to a God who for most of his life had remained outside. Someone else's Father. When he lifted his head, there were no waves of peace, no glory filling his soul. The terror that he'd experienced in the night was gone, but beyond that, his soul felt wooden. Untouched by the greatness that always seemed to overwhelm his sister.

Why couldn't he sense the Spirit the way his old friends at RVA claimed?

Guilt.

The mountain that had sat immovable on his chest since a fateful day just before high school graduation. For years, he'd pushed ahead, ignoring its whispers, accepting that life was like that. Everyone had baggage. Everyone had *issues.* But a dullness settled on his soul that seemed to keep events from having a sharp edge.

He trudged home, aware that for a brief moment that night, he'd felt a hint of relief. It had been in the seconds after calling out the Savior's name. Jace shook his head. Maybe the sensation of the lifting of the weight was only an illusion, a realization that he could finally breathe. Whatever or whoever had been stealing his breath had been swatted aside.

Had he imagined it? In the absence of any glorious change in his feelings, he began to doubt. Perhaps it had simply been a recurrence of some childhood asthma compounded with the high altitude of Kijabe.

No. He'd felt something. *A presence.*

Evil.

He'd felt heart-pounding, choking terror. As clearly as anything he'd ever known, he'd sensed that he wasn't alone. And whatever had been with him had wanted him dead.

He walked on, carefully keeping to the rocky path in the dark. He knew little of the warfare that Chaplain Otieno had spoken of. But he did understand that whatever power had faced him had slithered away in response to the whispered name "Jesus."

His inner scientist argued. It had been asthma. Perhaps stimulated by a little extra smoke in his small house from a faulty chimney. Of course he'd felt evil. It's evil not being able to get a breath.

As he passed the morgue, a small block building at the back of the hospital, he thought about the boy who'd died after falling from a tree. He'd died because there wasn't any blood, and there wasn't any blood because Jace had interrupted normal donations with his scheme to get enough blood for open-heart surgery. Jace looked back at the cemetery and thought about Timmy O'Reilly. He remembered listening to his father explaining to Timmy's parents. *The antivenom goes bad too quickly. It was too expensive to keep on hand.*

In Jace's memory, Timmy's parents and Jace's father stood in the dingy back hallway of the hospital, their forms silhouetted by the sun coming through a doorway beyond them. He could not see their faces, but the sound of the parents' pain had seared its way into his memory. *"No! No! Nooooo!"* Mrs. O'Reilly cried with her rhythmic sobs muffled into her husband's chest.

Jace's father's decision had condemned a little boy to death.

And Jace's actions had resulted in the death of another.

He thought about his reaction to Timmy's death, how he had blamed his father. Now, with the shoe on the other foot, he'd begun to understand. Perhaps he'd been too quick to judge. He was beginning to understand that nothing about hospital care in Kenya was straightforward.

And that meant that more money didn't necessarily solve the problems.

Once at home, he slipped past the still-sleeping guard, sat at the kitchen table, opened his laptop, and accessed his email account. He found a new message from Heather.

Jace, I'm sure by now that Gabby has told you about Anita Franks's autopsy report. I can't figure out why someone would want to send this to me, but the document is accurate (I had a detective at Richmond PD confirm), and it certainly raises more questions than answers. Jace, I need to know what you know. It doesn't work for you to just retreat and say you don't remember. The medical examiner's office says they released the autopsy information to only two sources: the next of kin and your office. Why would you be requesting this? And if you requested the autopsy report, was it because you were seeking answers yourself? Did you send it to me? (The Richmond detective seems to think so, and feels you are "confessing" to me in this way.) A blood test could clear things up, Jace.

Why don't you send a sample home with Gabby so we can compare the DNA with fluid collected from Anita Franks's autopsy?

How is your work going? If I know you, you've probably changed the name of the hospital. By now, it's probably Kijabe Heart Institute.

Keep safe. I'm praying for you. I confess, praying wasn't my first response when we first faced all of this mess. But maybe I'm understanding my role a little better. I have a feeling that things between us will never be resolved until you resolve things between you and God.

Heather

Jace sighed, closed his laptop, and tromped back toward his bed, shedding his clothes onto the floor as he went.

Heather hadn't said all was well.

But she did say she was praying. *Hmm. Like the Heather I knew in college.*

And for now, that was enough.

37

In spite of the cool Kijabe night, Jace tossed in a restless slumber punctuated by sweat and a return of his earlier terror. It wasn't so bad this time, but enough to interrupt his rest with troubling dreams.

Sometime in the early hours of morning, Jace dreamed of the doctor he'd met when he first came to Kijabe. The face of Simeon Okayo seemed to float just above his bed, hovering out of reach. At first, he appeared in a suit, looking like a modern professional. Then, as fear slowly tightened around Jace's chest, the doctor's face morphed into something tribal. His teeth were pointed and his face striped with red paint. *Blood?*

The floating face seemed to delight in the knowledge that he was scaring Jace. He curled back generous lips to reveal teeth, white and sharp. The picture expanded, giving Jace a full view of the man. He wore little more than a loincloth, flapping below his waist. Around his neck was a necklace of bones, irregular and worn.

Then the necklace began to change, blackening and lengthening, turning into a stethoscope, much like the one Jace used. The tubing began to smoke, then melt, dripping hot plastic onto Jace's skin. Suddenly, the stethoscope burst into flames, becoming a necklace of fire around Okayo's neck, but the doctor didn't scream. He only laughed, watching in delight as the stethoscope dripped its melted contents onto Jace.

Jace writhed with the sensation that he was being burned. His heart quickened and he awoke gasping for breath. He rushed to the bathroom sink, washed his face, and stood looking at himself in the mirror.

On his chest, where the drips of plastic had fallen, a pink blister had formed.

He went back to bed and fell into a fitful sleep again, with the dream recurring several times. He tossed until the desire to escape the night terrors drove him to the kitchen in search of coffee.

Standing at the sink, he paused, sensing that he needed to do something in response to the vivid dreams. But what? He felt as if there were something just beyond his remembrance, something he needed to act on, but for the life of him, he couldn't come up with it. It was almost like the sensation he'd had in the past after awakening from a dream, knowing he'd been dreaming, but not knowing what had prompted his heart to race.

He shrugged. The sensation that he needed to do something wouldn't pass. But he came no closer to recalling what.

"Coffee," he muttered. Maybe the caffeine would wake up his brain and nudge him in the right direction.

Back in Richmond, Heather knelt by the king-size bed she used to share with Jace. "Father," she prayed, "I want to learn to trust you with my husband."

She waited, unsure how to continue. After a few moments, she spoke again. *Is Jace in danger?* "Protect him. Reveal Yourself to him. Give him a new love, not for me, but for You."

She rose and walked to the kitchen, thinking some warm milk might help her sleep. Her sleep had been fitful lately because of her intense focus on Jace. It seemed that everywhere she turned, painful memories surfaced. Even ordinary events seemed to bring up haunting conversations, ones she wished she could forget. As she reached for the refrigerator door, she remembered confronting Jace after he'd come in late from work one night not long before.

She'd entered the kitchen silently, having risen when she heard the garage door. Jace's head was in the refrigerator, his back to her. When he emerged, he held up the milk jug, about to take a swig. When he saw Heather, he smiled sheepishly and opted for a glass. "Sorry," he said. "Did I wake you?"

"Jace, it's one thirty! I've been worried."

"I told you I was going to see the governor."

"You didn't answer your phone."

He extracted it from his coat pocket and frowned. "Dead battery."

"It doesn't take two hours to see the governor."

He sighed and moved toward her. She knew she wouldn't stay mad if he swept her into his arms. Instead, he stopped with his hands on her shoulders. After kissing her forehead, he spoke, "You worry too much, baby."

She pulled back, sampling the air around him. "You've been drinking. Where else did you go?"

He shook his head. "Nowhere." He took a step back. "I had a drink at the governor's mansion."

She glared at him.

He shrugged. "Maybe two." He swirled the milk in his glass. "The governor has quite a collection of single-malt scotches."

"You let the governor drink? I thought he was on blood thinners."

"He is. I had a drink with Anita."

Heather forced a smile, a plastic one. "How nice. How is Anita? I'm glad that her concern over her husband hasn't gotten in the way of her being the perfect hostess."

"Heather, jealousy isn't attractive on you."

"Wait until the morning paper." She swept her hand in an arc to display the imaginary headline. "Famous cardiothoracic surgeon leaves governor's mansion at one a.m. Governor's health isn't his primary concern."

Jace slapped the milk jug onto the kitchen island. "It isn't like that. For one thing, they have an unmarked side exit that the media can't see."

"Convenient."

"It was just a drink."

"I don't like it, Jace. You aren't supposed to be having midnight cocktails with her." She tried to keep her voice steady, but knew it was on the verge of cracking. "What has happened to you? The Jace I fell in love with was happy not knowing a thing about single-malt scotches."

"She was just being kind. She appreciates the close care I've given her husband."

"I'll bet she does." Heather shook her head and reached for her husband's hand. "Jace, what is going on?"

"I told you not to pay attention to the tabloids. They just want to sell papers."

"I'm not reading the tabloids. I'm just watching you from the sidelines. You seem to have forgotten that I'm in the game too."

"You don't understand." He pulled away. "It was just a drink."

"Just a drink. A powerful one. With a beautiful ex-model with augmented anatomy. After midnight." She raised a finger. "And I'll bet you were alone."

"There were staff everywhere."

Heather put on a southern drawl and said, "Nothing good ever happens after midnight." The phrase had become a joke for Jace and Heather during their courtship. Heather's mom, Trevor Anne, was the originator of the phrase, and Heather had imitated her whenever the hour was late and Jace wanted more than a good-night kiss. But now, Heather spoke it in all seriousness.

Jace rolled his eyes. "Thank you, Trevor Anne."

"She's right this time, Jace. And if you ever need to make a late-night trip to the governor's mansion again, I'm coming with you."

Jace looked incredulous. "You? My little guardian." He shook his head. "I'm a big boy." He put the milk in the refrigerator. "Don't push me away, Heather."

"I'm not pushing," she said. "I'm holding on to what is mine."

He turned to face her. "It feels like pushing," he said.

With that, he plodded off to the bedroom.

Heather didn't follow. She slumped onto a kitchen barstool and began to cry.

Now, Heather realized the truth behind her husband's statements. She hadn't meant to push him away, but to Jace it had certainly felt that way.

"Oh, God," she whispered. "How can I learn to trust?"

Later that morning in Kijabe, Jace stopped at the small counter that made up the nursing station on the Wairegi men's ward. "Anyone seen my stethoscope?"

He was met with blank stares. *Maybe I left it down in theater.*

A few minutes later, Jace stood beside his patient Mohamed Omar. "We need to talk," Jace said.

The young Somali man nodded. "I am ready."

"I need to have blood set up in order to do your surgery. But we're facing significant shortages. Do you have friends or family who can donate on your behalf?"

His patient smiled. "I am Somali."

Jace didn't understand. "I know that."

"Just listen to my name. Mohamed Omar Abdullahi. Mohamed is my name. Omar is my father's name. Abdullahi is my grandfather's name." He held up his hands to explain. "We are all connected. I can find many, many cousins willing to help." Smiling, he added. "I can name my father's father's father back twenty-seven generations." He paused. "I have friends who can name one hundred. How about you?"

"My father's name was Lloyd. His father was Peter." Jace scratched his head. "I think his father was James."

Mohamed shook his head. "How can you know who you are if you don't know where you came from?"

Jace thought for a moment before mumbling, "Americans seem too caught up in their own lives to care too much about yesterday."

His patient scoffed. "Idiocy."

"Perhaps." Jace shifted uncomfortably. "Listen, I don't need to tell you that waiting too long could be dangerous. We can only pray that the bullet fragment doesn't move beyond our reach."

"A stroke?"

"Yes."

"I'll get you the blood," he said, flipping open his phone. "How many donors are needed?"

"Ten."

The Somali smiled. "I'll have twenty by dark. It will be a good deed for my Muslim brothers."

Jace understood. Muslims live in awareness of opportunities to put checks in the positive column. "We operate in the morning."

"*Insha'Allah.*"

38

That evening Jace stopped by Gabby's little duplex apartment to discuss plans for the next day's case. Evan Martin met Jace at the door. "Come in," he said, his voice urgent. "We need to talk."

Jace stepped into the little kitchen. Two suitcases sat next to the table. "What's up, Gabby?"

She shook her head. "We need to leave, Jace."

He traded looks with Evan and raised an eyebrow, mouthing, "What's up?"

Evan held up his hands. "Talk to him, Gabby. I know things have gotten a little weird around here lately."

"A little weird?" Gabby started to pace around the apartment. "Strangely enough, when I thought someone might have been trying to kill you, it freaked me out a bit, but I told myself it was just a case of a thug trying to rob a rich American doctor. But all these weird encounters your patients are having, along with the messages—" She paused. "I had a dream last night, and I'm afraid."

"A dream?" Jace stepped forward. "What kind?"

"Scary. I don't remember it all, just that I woke up feeling terror."

Jace looked at Evan. "You?"

Evan nodded. "I can't shake a feeling of dread, Jace. Something about this place. I'm with Gabby, I think we've given it an adequate trial. It's time to go home and regroup."

Jace pulled up his shirt. The skin over his chest was still red and blistered. "Look at this."

Gabby stopped pacing and frowned. "Jace, what happened?"

"A dream last night. I saw a man I met during my first day back in Kijabe. He called himself a doctor. Simeon Okayo. In my dream, he was dressed like a witch doctor with a necklace of bone. The necklace morphed into a stethoscope that burst into flame and melted, dripping hot plastic onto my chest. When I woke, my skin looked like this."

"What do you know about this Simeon?" Gabby asked.

"Only that he said he was a consultant. I haven't seen him around Kijabe since."

Gabby frowned. "I don't like this, Jace. It's like you are the focus of some intense spiritual war."

"War?" Jace took a deep breath. "Now you're sounding like Chaplain Otieno." He moved slowly to a kitchen chair and took a seat. "When I explained what was happening to my patients during surgery, he said the same kind of thing."

Jace stood again and paced. "I need you guys to stay for one more case. Mohamed Omar is ready. He's counting on us."

Evan shook his head. "Why is this so important, Jace? He's connected. He could even return to the States."

"No. He could stroke."

"Is that it, Jace? Is it really about him? Or is it about you? You've become obsessed with the messages."

"I need to know the truth."

"So why don't you just pray like the rest of us?" Gabby asked.

Jace shook his head. "You wouldn't understand." He looked down. "I can't."

"Jace, everyone can—"

"No!" he shouted, immediately regretting his volume. "No," he repeated more quietly. "I really can't pray. I can't ask God for this."

The sound of a siren interrupted their conversation.

Evan walked to the window. "What's going on at the hospital?"

Gabby pointed. "Flames!"

Jace, Gabby, and Evan ran down the uneven sidewalk past the hospital to the gravel parking lot bordering the cemetery. Flames danced above a small building on the west end of the hospital complex. Partially blackened wooden coffins lined the edge of the lot. Hundreds of patients in pink hospital-issue pajamas shuffled over the gravel in orange shower shoes. Inside the chain-link fence bordering the pediatric play area, the able-bodied patients pasted their faces against the fence to *ooh* and *ahh* as the roof collapsed.

"It's the morgue!" someone shouted at Jace. "Help us, Daktari!"

They followed, weaving between the onlookers who were either silent with mouths agape or loudly pacing about with arms flailing toward the sky, begging God for rain.

The fire rose through the roof of the small structure, the flames dancing into the night. A man in a security uniform sprayed water from a garden hose—David versus a fiery Goliath. The American trio joined a line passing plastic buckets of water forward.

Gabby struggled to pass a bucket forward without spilling the contents. "What's that smell?" she asked.

Burning flesh. Jace recognized it from his use of the cautery unit in the operating rooms. "Gabby," he said.

She looked up, her mouth twisted as if she tasted something sour.

He shook his head to communicate the message. *Don't ask.*

They worked on, muscles aching, as shouts for water and speed rose above the prayers for rain. Heat and smoke drove the workers back. Sweat and determination drove them forward.

At the edge of a parking lot, a woman moved from coffin to coffin, clutching at her neck and crying out above the crowd.

In the end, all that stood were the stone walls. The roof and everything inside had been destroyed. For another hour, water doused the smoldering wood. Jace joined an elderly man, the white-haired mortuary attendant, as he picked through the remains. His eyes met Jace's. "It was my fault," he said slowly. "The refrigerator keeps me cold, so I came out to stand next to the barrel where I keep a small charcoal fire."

Jace nodded. He'd often passed the mortuary at night and smelled the kerosene used to keep the fire burning. The barrel was old, rusted, and smoldering against the stone wall.

Mthanga continued, "The barrel tipped when I added charcoal."

Jace walked toward the doorway, now a blackened hole. "Did you get all the bodies out?"

The old attendant sighed. "Only two remained. The flames were too strong for me."

Two hospital workers fought to keep the crowd back, shouting loudly in Kikuyu. The woman who had been checking the coffins was now the point of the spear, anxious family members pushing forward to see.

Jace asked the morgue attendant, "Do you know who they were?"

Joel Mthanga nodded and wiped at a blackened streak running across his forehead. "They were yours, Daktari."

"Mine?"

"Your patients. Michael Kagai and the young boy."

"Boniface?"

"Yes."

A knot tightened in Jace's upper abdomen. The boy who sold mangos for his mother at the hospital gate, the boy who'd fallen from a tree and died from a splenic injury when no blood was available. "Why were these bodies still here?" He looked at the crowd. *The crying woman. Boniface's mother.*

"The families leave them until they are able to clear the hospital charges."

Jace was incredulous. "But the boy ... his bill had been paid." He knew this for a fact. He'd paid it himself, paying homage on an altar of guilt.

"Yes, but the family had no money for a funeral. They left the body here while they worked on raising money."

Jace looked away, unable to meet the gaze of the crowd.

But soon, they swarmed in around them, ignoring the few security guards imploring restraint. Men kicked away the smoldering wood and soon, the gruesome remains were exposed, two unfeeling black skulls, bone bearing teeth draped with burned flesh now barely able to cover the skeletal support.

Jace watched the morgue attendant, a grandfather who'd aged a decade in an hour. He stood stoop-shouldered and defeated with a penance of ash on his forehead, and began to weep. The attendant touched the shoulder of the sobbing woman and spoke in hushed Kikuyu before she wailed in fresh pain.

The grief over losing her young son was renewed as she stumbled forward to glimpse the charred remains. Her agony was loud, acute, and each cry was a stake pounded into Jace's chest. She turned from the blackened body in front of her, reaching out to Jace. "Daktari! Daktari!" She lurched forward, swinging her fist at his chest.

He reacted, lifting his hands in front of his face, warding off the blows of the heartbroken mother.

Two other women in orange and purple sweaters came alongside the crying woman, pulling her back from Jace, yelling in their tribal tongue.

Jace lowered his hands. *I deserve this,* he thought. He stood exposed in front of her. For a moment, beneath a waning moon, with the acrid smell still hanging thick around them, he thought her fury had quieted.

But then, the woman broke free from the women restraining her and with a cry, carried her fist through a high arc ending in Jace's teeth. He stumbled back, tripping, landing in the warm ash next to the charred remains. He stood and faced the woman. She clutched her arms across her chest, a futile attempt to protect her broken heart. The women at her side coaxed her into their arms, and soon, the trio moved away, their cries mingling and soon lost in the noise of the crowd.

"Jace! Here!" It was Evan Martin.

Jace looked toward the voice and retreated to the edge of the parking lot into the company of his friends. His eyes met Gabby's. "I can't watch," he whispered. He spat and wiped his chin. Blood.

"What's going on, Jace? Another coincidence?" Her eyes bored into his, asking, *Why your patients? Is this another message? A warning?*

Jace brushed back tears. "I don't know."

"We need to leave this place," she said.

"One more," Jace responded. "Please."

Gabby began walking away. Her posture was set as she struggled forward against an unseen wind.

"Gabby," he called after her.

She turned. "One more, Jace. For the sake of our Somali patient. Then I'm gone."

Jace nodded, though he knew she did not see. Gabby was already moving across the parking lot, weaving her way through a sea of dark faces.

From the crowd, a large man emerged. Chaplain Otieno passed Jace without speaking, pausing only briefly to place his large hand on Jace's shoulder before moving on in the direction of a Kikuyu mother's painful cry.

Jace nodded at Evan Martin. "See you in the morning," he mumbled. He turned up the rocky path toward his house, feeling like Jonah in the hold of the ship about to capsize. *It's my fault. I'm the one they should throw into the sea. I'm the one who has brought terror to this town.*

Because I killed my sister.

He walked alone, away from the cacophony of African tongues that wagged in excitement over the fire.

Tomorrow, he promised himself, he would operate again, hoping to make up for the misery that seemed to follow him.

Is it possible to atone for all that I've done?

39

Alone in his house, Jace Rawlings missed his wife. They'd been separated for more than six weeks. Over that time, anger had given way to sorrow, and sorrow to remorse. He didn't blame Heather for their problems. In fact, in light of his current difficulties, he felt that he was getting just what he deserved.

He thought about Anita, how he'd been swept up in the emotional tangles of desire. She'd *wanted* him. It was fresh. New. Fun to be wanted in a way that Heather seemed to have lost.

He thought back to the night he first felt he'd crossed a previously impenetrable barrier. The governor had suffered a postoperative pneumonia, then a deep venous clot led to a pulmonary embolus and need for another period of time on the ventilator. The governor had survived, and after his discharge, Jace had adopted the practice of slipping by the governor's mansion at least once a week to check on his patient.

It was on one of those late-night visits that Anita took his arm and led him toward the door, thanking him as they walked. She turned toward him, and in a gesture that seemed accidental, her breast brushed across his arm.

Accidental or not, Jace was aware of every firing nerve ending. He gently pushed back, allowing the touch to linger a moment longer. An accident. Nothing more.

"Stay for a drink."

He was helpless. "Of course."

She selected a white zinfandel for herself, allowing Jace to select his own poison. He lifted an expensive scotch. She poured three fingers' worth into a glass and added ice.

They sat in leather chairs set at ninety degrees that allowed their knees to bump. Another accident of course. She slipped off a pair of red heels and crossed her legs, brushing his thigh in the process.

He cleared his throat.

She smiled. "I'm sick of the media," she said. "Sometimes I just want to escape the circus." She paused. "How about you? Do you enjoy the attention?"

"No." He sipped his drink, already feeling his anxiety slipping away.

"Do you want children, Jace?"

Her use of his first name had become a practice whenever they spoke alone.

"I always thought so. My wife … we've struggled a bit in that area."

"Stuart always wanted children, but his sperm counts are low."

Jace shifted in his chair. This felt like too much information.

"Finally, last spring, I got pregnant, but I lost the baby after three months. Stuart was devastated. I'm not sure if he told you."

Jace shook his head. It hadn't come up. And evidently, if the media had heard, they'd exercised a rare bit of courtesy in not reporting it.

"Now I'm afraid that Stuart isn't up to the task." She paused again, making eye contact until Jace looked down, feigning interest in his drink. "Jace," she said, leaning forward.

Jace diverted his eyes from her cleavage.

"When do you think it will be safe for us to try again?" She smiled. "I don't want to hurt him."

Jace tried to swallow. "The governor is a strong man. He'll be back in the saddle soon enough." He blushed, immediately regretting his choice of words.

Anita giggled. "I certainly hope so," she said.

He sipped his drink and protested lightly as she poured a bit more.

She talked of her modeling career, of the endless stressful hours of a life in New York City before being rescued by Stuart Franks. She told of her desire to be a background compliment to Stuart, but knew the media couldn't resist her charm.

"How do you deal with the pressure?" he asked.

"I drink," she gushed. "Seriously? I exercise. You wouldn't believe how hard it is to stay in this kind of shape." She straightened her posture and placed her hands against her petite waistline.

"Something I need to do more of myself." He took a deep breath. He should leave. "I've got surgeries in the morning."

"You should leave through the service entrance."

He stood and set his glass on the table.

She walked him to the door, glancing behind to see that they were alone. She turned, allowing her chest to contact his.

"Good night, Anita." He opened the door, greeted by Richmond air, damp from spring rain.

As he walked to the car, he wiped his mouth, still smelling her perfume.

He didn't notice a car following him until he'd traveled three blocks. Then, at a red light, a BMW with tinted windows moved within inches of his back bumper. The driver seemed to want Jace to know he or she was there, following him away from the governor's mansion.

Down Broad Street toward the interstate, the car kept itself pasted to his bumper.

Jace looked around, wishing for police. Nothing. He took a quick left and accelerated, then suddenly braked and made a U-turn at the next red light.

The car followed.

Jace lifted his cell phone to his ear. As he did so, the car dropped back.

A coincidence?

Had someone followed him from the governor's mansion?

Jace made two more detours before getting onto the interstate. The other car faded.

He checked his watch. It was past time to be home.

John Okombo loved his job, relishing the attention, the power, and the beautiful people who orbited around politicians. What he didn't like was the critical attention that Luo politicians suffered under a Kikuyu president. Today was an example of the kind of attention the

MP didn't like: an interview with the president's anticorruption czar. He tried to smile, but was sure his perspiration was giving him away.

Across the table, Mr. Kithingi sat smugly shuffling papers, reading snippets to Minister Okombo and questioning the large man in front of him. "I think it would be helpful if you didn't speak to the media about Anthony Kimathi."

Okombo folded his arms. "I think we can all agree that Kenya is a better place without him."

Kithingi was a short man, clean cut and wearing a blue business suit. He raised his eyebrows at the suggestion. "Perhaps. Will you go on record to explain just how your vehicle ended up at a police check where apparently an ambush was to take place on the American doctor?"

"I've already done so. I know nothing other than the fact that my driver was bringing the Americans to dine at my house. The police stop, as far as I know, was a random event."

"I've spoken to the heart surgeons at Nairobi Hospital and at Aga Khan. They have contributed heavily to your party, have they not? Perhaps you were trying to keep them happy by having the American surgeon taken out of the way?"

"Ridiculous!"

Kithingi smiled. He enjoyed needling the older man.

Okombo opened his phone.

"What are you doing?"

"I'm going to call my attorney. I won't answer any more questions without him. This is an outrage!"

Kithingi gathered his papers and placed them in a mahogany-colored leather briefcase. "I think you should be happy I

356 · HARRY KRAUS

haven't leaked this to the media. *The Standard* would love this stuff."

Okombo stayed quiet, stewing.

Kithingi smiled again. "I'll let myself out. President Kibaki will be briefed. And I think I'll need to talk to this American surgeon."

The minister of health waited until after Kithingi was out of his office before calling Simeon Okayo.

Simeon answered after three rings.

"Simeon." John Okombo kept his voice low. "What is happening? Kibaki's man was just here."

"Kithingi?"

"Yes. He's digging."

"Of course he digs. You are Luo. He's Kikuyu. A chance to make a Luo politician look bad makes men like Kithingi happy."

"He wants to talk to Dr. Rawlings."

"So? All Rawlings has is suspicion."

"I'm afraid he will talk to the media. I thought you were taking care of him. You had a deal with the Americans. Now more than ever, I need you to follow through. Finish this."

"Look, I underestimated the power of a place like Kijabe. It's as if the Christians there have laid down a blanket of prayer that rendered my curse ineffective."

"So what will you do?"

"He needs to be taken out of Kijabe." Simeon sighed. "I'll have him brought to Kisii town. The American surgeon will disappear."

Back in Kijabe, Jace knew he needed sleep but feared a return of the terror. Finally, after midnight, he collapsed in exhaustion, only to rise a few moments later as the troubling mental puzzle piece finally clicked into place.

The mysterious medicine given him by Dr. Okayo. Seeing Okayo's face in his nightmare brought it back to him, but just what was troubling him stayed out of reach until he lay down to sleep. Then John Otieno's questions came to him. The chaplain had asked him about contact with a witch doctor. *"Certain activities can open you up to the Devil's handholds. Have you been involved in any dark activities?"*

Jace rose and flipped on the light to his bathroom. In the cupboard below the sink, he found what he was looking for. A small bottle and a crumpled white cloth that contained a purple circle.

He wasn't sure what connection he had to Okayo, or even if he was indeed a witch doctor, but in light of his dreams, he wasn't taking any chances. He threw the small glass bottle into the trash and carried the cloth to the fireplace. There, with the assistance of some fresh kindling, Jace prepared a small fire.

When he tossed in the cloth, the circle of purple ignited, hissing vigorously and spewing a wavering tail of black smoke. Jace jumped back. It reminded him of the infamous smoke monster from the television series *Lost*. The middle of the cloth seemed to evaporate, leaving the white edge that melted and finally burned.

"There," Jace whispered. "Stop haunting me."

He plodded back to bed, shaking his head, wondering just how far off center this trip to Africa had taken him. A month ago, he would have scoffed at such talk.

Now, he just wanted to survive a night without terror.

And after that, do his work undisturbed by crazed Mungiki, angry politicians, or mothers crying for their dead children.

He sighed. He knew better.

This was Africa.

40

Heather stared at the screen waiting for her email to load. Still no word from Jace. Not that she blamed him. They hadn't really parted on the best of terms.

She picked up a leash and clipped it to Bo's collar. The English mastiff easily outweighed her by a hundred pounds, but she didn't worry about him trying to pull away. He was fiercely loyal.

"Let's go for a walk," she said.

Bo tilted his head.

"Okay, you win." She reached in her pocket and pulled out a small doggy treat. Then, balancing it on the top of his nose, she commanded, "Wait."

The dog's breath came fast.

"Now," she said.

Bo flipped back his head and snapped the treat out of the air as it slid from his nose.

"Good dog," she said, scratching behind his ears. She swiped at a string of saliva on the door, evidence of Bo's quick action to obtain his snack. "Ugh. Do you think you could drool a little more?"

Heather was glad for the diversion. But even a walk with her favorite dog couldn't keep her from mulling over regrets.

Such as her regret over how she'd handled the week just before Jace's accident, when she'd come upon him in his study. He'd snapped his phone closed just as she entered.

He seemed flustered. He made his way to the window and peered out, standing in the shadow of the curtain.

"Who was that?"

He acted nonplussed. "The governor's wife. She was calling for advice about his Coumadin dose."

"She calls you at home on your day off?"

He shrugged. "He is the governor."

"I don't like it. You shouldn't be making special allowances for her."

Jace ignored her. "Have you ever seen that black BMW before?"

Heather lifted apart the blinds to get a better look, but Jace pulled her aside.

"Stand back," he said. "I don't want him to know we are watching."

"Who?" Heather couldn't hide her irritation. "Jace, what's this about? Why would someone be following you? Why all this talk about being tailed late at night?"

He shook his head. "I don't know. Do you have a pair of binoculars? I want to get the license plate number."

"I'll just go out to get a better look."

He clamped down on her arm. "No!"

"Jace! Let go!"

"Don't go out there."

"He's not exactly hiding."

"Maybe he wants me to see him."

"You are acting paranoid." She stepped back and looked at her husband. This was so unlike him. Normally confident, the typical surgeon, now he was slinking around in the shadows talking quietly on his phone and telling her he was being followed. "You know what I think? I think you have a guilty conscience." She moved to his side and placed her hand on his. "Tell me what's going on. If you are being tempted by this woman, I need to know it. I'm your wife. You can talk to me."

He pulled away. "Don't be silly. Anita Franks is the governor's wife."

"And he is a powerful man who happens to be very sick. She's a young, vibrant woman. Has she been too forward with you?"

Jace stayed quiet. Heather sensed she was pushing the right buttons.

"I've seen the way she gushes over you."

"Gushes? When?"

"After the news conference on the day of the governor's discharge. You were the knight in shining armor, Jace. She held your hand and posed for pictures." She shook her head. "She looked like the prom queen smiling with her date."

"That's crazy."

"No, it's not. And you can talk to me."

"There's nothing to talk about."

"And what about all this fear of being followed?"

He shrugged. "Maybe an angry family member. Perhaps family of an old patient who died."

"Your patients think you walk on water."

He squinted at her. "And I guess you know better, huh?"

"I took your shirts to the cleaners, Jace. You had lipstick on your collar. Not my shade."

"So, a patient is grateful. I get hugs."

"Old women, I can take. I don't want you hugging Ms. Ex-Lingerie Model."

"You need to stop. I'll let you know if she crosses the line."

"No, Jace, you need to open your eyes. That woman is bad business. I can feel it."

"Intuition, I suppose."

"Call it what you want."

"I'd call it nagging."

"You can sleep on the couch!"

"Fine," he said, stepping back from the window. "At least I can monitor how long the car stays here."

Bo nuzzled Heather's hand, nudging her out of her memory, but not out of the gnawing sense of guilt over her behavior. She scratched the dog behind the ears. "What was I to do, Bo? I hated what that woman did to him." She paused. "What do you think? Did I nag Jace too much?"

The dog growled.

No, she told herself, *I was just looking out for what was mine.*

I still need to fight for Jace.

"Come on, Bo," she coaxed, tugging at his leash. "I can pray as we walk."

The next morning in Kijabe, Jace rose, stoked himself with Kenyan AA coffee and set off for the hospital. He was pleased to find Mohamed Omar in the pre-op holding area and his promise to find blood fulfilled. Twenty-two units had been donated, and eight were suitable for transfusion.

Jace smiled. Mohamed's Somali clan had come through just as he'd promised.

As the team readied the room and supplies, Jace touched Gabby's shoulder. "Thanks for staying."

She nodded.

"Gabby," he said, "have you been communicating with Heather?"

Gabby nodded. "She asks about you." She paused. "Why don't you write?"

Jace sighed. "I'm still searching for answers, I guess. I've got nothing to say."

"Tell her you love her."

Jace mumbled, "I've got a funny way of showing it, huh?"

He assisted Gabby in rolling the bypass pump into position. "I've been thinking about something Heather mentioned. She said Anita Franks's autopsy report was requested by my office. That's just routine. Any time one of our patients has died, the front office requests the report. I didn't have anything to do with it." He shuffled his feet. "You can tell Heather that much."

"Anita was a patient of your practice?"

He nodded. "She had an episode of atrial tachycardia. I ran an EKG one night, so we had a small file. Turns out she was just anxious."

Jace walked to the window and stared out at a poinsettia tree, remembering the evening months before when he had left his office late after finishing up his charts. He was exiting the back door when Anita came running across the parking lot toward him. *Had she been waiting for me?*

Her face was twisted in worry. "Jace, I didn't know who to call."

"What's wrong?"

"My heart is pounding. It won't quit."

He took her wrist. The rate was 140. "Let's go inside."

"Are we alone?"

"My staff is long gone. I was catching up on paperwork. Why didn't you call an ambulance?"

"I couldn't. I just knew the media would be all over it, so I snuck out the service entrance and came here."

"I need to do an EKG," he said, leading her to an exam room. He flipped on the light. "Could you lie down up there? I'm going to get my EKG machine."

When he came back, she was wearing a hospital gown. "I thought you'd need me this way."

He tried not to stare. "Of course." He hesitated. "When did this start?"

"Right after supper. Stuart began having chest pain and took some nitroglycerin."

"Is he okay?"

"It went away, but I worry about him so. I tried to calm down, but it feels like my heart is running away."

He prepared the electrodes. "I need to place these to obtain a cardiac tracing."

She bit her lower lip and nodded.

He placed leads on her shoulders and legs first and lastly applied a series of leads across her chest. She seemed eager to provide him adequate exposure. He swallowed, turned, and fumbled with the machine until the paper emerged to reveal the heart's electrical tracing.

When he turned around, she grabbed his hand, guiding it to her chest, just over the sternum. "Here," she said, "you can feel it."

"Yes," he replied, withdrawing his hand. "We call that the PMI, the point of maximal impulse." He paused. His palm was sweating. "Have you ever had this before?"

"No."

"Are you in pain?"

"None."

"I need to set you up for a few tests. Is it possible that you've just become worked up over all the stress?"

"Can you help me?"

"I think I can find some samples that will help." He turned toward the door. "You can dress again. I'll see what I can find."

She pulled down the neck of her gown. "Shouldn't you take off these sticky things?"

"Uh—you can do it."

He left her alone for a few minutes, hoping she would be entirely clothed when he returned. He wasn't sure he was up to resisting what he thought was being offered. As he walked down the hall, he looked at his palm, still warm and alive after touching Anita's bare skin. In the pharmacy cabinet, he found a few diazepam samples.

"Here," he said, returning to the doorway of the exam room. "I have some Valium. It will help you rest."

She immediately popped two of the tablets from the foil-backed packaging and threw them to the back of her throat.

"You shouldn't take those and drive," he said.

She smiled. "Too late." She touched his arm. "Can you give me a lift?"

He looked at his watch. "I'll drop you on the way."

She giggled. "My hero."

Jace's memory of the event vanished at the sound of Evan's voice. "Jace!" He turned from the window. "Jace, I've been asking you a question."

"Hmm? Sorry."

"Can we bring in the patient? Are you set?"

He looked at Gabby and Evan. They didn't look happy. "Uh, sure. I'm ready. Let's rock and roll."

Monitors were fixed, intravenous and arterial lines placed. The patient was anesthetized, prepped, and draped. Jace and his intern, Paul Mwaka, scrubbed, gowned, and gloved.

Jace looked over the drape separating the operative field from the anesthesiologist. "I need you to reproduce everything exactly, Evan. If someone is trying to send me a message, I want to hear it. Loud and clear."

Evan nodded. "Game on."

41

Heather pulled back on Bo's collar as she saw the old pickup truck slow. Two teenaged boys leaned from the window, tangled blond hair trailing. One just yelled. The other made a squeezing gesture with his hands.

A little early to start drinking.

Glad for the large dog at her side, she ignored her oglers and continued to her neighbor's house. She didn't release the leash until she was inside the enclosed backyard. Bo could be ultraprotective, and if a loyal friend was to be had, it was the mastiff.

It hadn't been that long ago that Bo had sensed the tension in a moment she'd shared with Jace.

It had been a Friday, and Jace, taking a rare day off, had slept in. Heather was up, grooming Bo, readying him for a walk. Jace appeared in the doorway to her "dog room," looking sleepy.

Heather tried to keep her voice calm. "You were out late."

"My office charts took me longer than normal."

She kept brushing through the mastiff's hair. "I've already put in a load of wash, Jace." She studied him for a response, feeling anger rise within her.

He rubbed the back of his neck.

When she spoke, she couldn't keep the spite from her voice. "I could smell her on your shirt."

He shook his head. "Smell her?"

"The governor's wife. She uses that expensive French perfume, her signature aroma."

"I hadn't noticed."

"You deny you were with her?"

"For Pete's sake, Heather, back off!"

Bo growled. Heather closed her hand around his collar.

"Haven't you ever heard of confidentiality? It's not like I can tell you about patient encounters."

"Oh, so now she's your patient?"

"She came by the office with a tachycardia. I did an EKG, okay?"

"I thought you had nurses for that."

He stepped forward, raising his voice. "This has got to stop! You're acting crazy!"

Bo leapt at him, tearing free from Heather's handhold on his collar. He knocked Jace against the wall. Jace's head bounced with a thud against the doorframe, then his feet slid out from under him, and he sank to the floor. The dog growled, baring teeth, inches from Jace's nose.

"Bo, no!" Heather commanded, bounding around the grooming table to grab the dog's collar.

Bo backed off a step as Heather moved in, evidently satisfied that the threat had been neutralized.

"Jace," she cried, picking up his head. She looked into unfocused, glassy eyes. "Jace!" She pulled her hand from the back of his scalp, already sticky with blood. "You're bleeding."

She grabbed for a towel and pressed it against the wound as Jace aroused and his temper flared. "Don't use that drool towel!"

"Do you want to bleed to death? This is all I've got."

He stared at Bo. "Get that monster off me!"

Jace struggled to his feet, exploring with one hand a gash on the back of his head. "I'm going to need suturing!" He frowned and stumbled out into the hall, pushing the drool-slinger towel against his scalp.

Once he was out of earshot, Heather handed Bo a doggy treat and scratched behind his ears, marveling at the speed and efficiency at which he'd come to her aid. "Good dog, Bo," she whispered. "Good dog!"

Now, in her neighbor's backyard, she unclipped the leash from the dog's collar.

Her cell phone signaled an incoming text message. She fished the phone from her pocket. It was from Lisa Sprague.

Making progress on fact finding. Some things don't add up. Can we meet for lunch to discuss?

Heather felt her stomach tighten. *Now that I'm closing in, I find myself fearful of the truth.*

She reminded herself of the woman she wanted to be. *Trusting. Forgiving.*

She typed a response.

Strawberry Street Café. Tomorrow. Noon. Okay?

She wound the dog leash into a small circle. "Bye-bye, Bo."
She turned to leave. *God, give me grace to accept the truth.*

Jace finished the surgery on Mohamed Omar, deftly going on and off bypass, removing the bullet fragment, and patching the small hole between the atria in a time that would rival the best of cardiac teams in the United States.

He took a deep breath as he tied the last knot in the skin suture. "There. What's the time?"

Evan looked at the wall clock. "A quarter past," he said. "No worries."

"When can you pull his tube? I want to talk to him."

Evan shrugged. "He's young and strong. The pump run was brief. I'd say, give me an hour or two and I might have him off the ventilator."

Jace pulled off his gloves, folding one inside the other and stretching the latex out to slingshot the gloves across the room into a trash receptacle. "Nice work, Gabby."

She looked at him in all seriousness. "Now, Jace, I've done what you asked. I'm calling British Air."

"You have to stay tonight. What if there is a complication and I need you?"

"Okay," she said slowly. "But tomorrow, I'm on a plane."

"Fair enough."

She shook her head. "You two need to come with me. Something bad is going on in this place. I'm afraid for you."

Evan spoke to the intern. "See if you can find an extra person to help lift him." He turned to Gabby. "I'm with you." He paused. "Jace, you need to come with us."

"So you're afraid for me now too?"

He nodded. "Frankly, yes. Things have gotten too weird for me. Someone or something isn't happy about you being here."

Jace finished applying a dressing over his patient's sternum. "I can't just operate and run."

"You can if you're in danger," Gabby said.

Jace touched his patient's shoulder. "Maybe this guy will give me an answer."

"So now you're expecting messages from beyond?"

Jace threw up his hands. "I don't know what to expect anymore. But I'm listening."

"I'm calling about flights. I'm going to reserve three seats."

Jace sighed. "Maybe you're right." He paused, looking out the window toward the cemetery. "But I can't help feeling I haven't done what I was supposed to do here."

"You've got one night," Gabby said, forcing a laugh. "Whatever business you need to settle, you'd better do it fast."

"Okay," he said. "I'll go with you. Buy the tickets."

Governor Franks waited until Ryan Meadows sat before closing his office door. "So what is so urgent that you needed to see me face-to-face?"

"It's about Jace Rawlings."

"You found a way to get a DNA sample?"

"Not exactly. At least not in the way you'd expect."

Stuart Franks hadn't been happy thinking that he'd let Jace Rawlings slip through his fingers. And Ryan Meadows hadn't been successful in figuring out a way to force Kenya to extradite him. "So what's the situation?"

"Did you know that Rawlings had his own ID badge so he could get in and out of here through the service entrance?"

The governor shrugged. "I knew. Jacobs from security asked me to sign off on it. I wanted my physician to have easy access to me."

Ryan smiled. "Or Anita."

Stuart Franks sighed. "Maybe some of that was my fault." He stared from the window. "But this office is so demanding."

Ryan leaned forward and ran his fingers over the back of a large mahogany carving of a Cape buffalo, a gift from the Kenyans. It stood two feet high, and the governor had placed it next to his desk.

"So what did you need to tell me?" Franks asked.

"Rawlings is coming home. Airline security notified me this morning. He has a reservation for a flight to Heathrow tomorrow and on to Dulles the next morning."

"Call the chief of police. Have him contact the magistrate with what we know. I want him arrested on arrival."

Ryan raised his eyebrows. "What about if I tip off the paper?"

Franks sighed. "One person. Do you owe someone an exclusive?"

"There is a young lady I'd like to please."

The governor huffed. "I don't want a circus."

"Oh no, sir," he said. "We wouldn't want that at all."

Stuart Franks chuckled. "Welcome home, Dr. Rawlings."

With that, Ryan Meadows slipped quietly from the governor's office, leaving him alone.

That evening, Jace studied the bedside chart of his most recent open-heart patient, Mohamed Omar Abdullahi. Everything was "euboxic," as they liked to say, meaning every value was inside the normal "box."

He leaned close as his patient began to speak. Mohamed's voice was weak, and Jace strained to hear among the beeping of the monitors and the clamor of clinical noise in the HDU.

"I had a dream while you were operating."

Jace nodded.

"I saw Issa, the one you call Jesus."

"Yes."

"He was not dressed like a prophet, but came as a God."

"Did He speak to you?"

Mohamed shook his head. "He only touched my heart. I believe He has brought healing to my body."

"Okay," Jace said.

"Muslims are taught that Issa was a prophet, not God, and certainly not above our Muhammad, peace be upon him."

Jace nodded, and his patient continued. "I have friends, smart Muslim men, who cannot be converted to Christianity through intellectual arguments, but this—" He halted, breathing deep behind his oxygen mask. "This dream has made me think of Issa differently." He looked about, as if nervous that his Muslim friends may be near. "I think Issa wants me to be a Christian."

The surgeon shifted on his feet.

Mohamed touched Jace's hand. "Can you pray for me?"

"I—uh, no." Jace shook his head. "I'm afraid I'm not the one for that."

"Issa also had a message for you."

"I thought He did not speak to you."

"He didn't, but He showed me something, and I feel I am to tell it to you."

"What it is?"

"I saw the minister of health, a man named John Okombo."

"I know him."

"Warn him," Mohamed said. "I saw him giving a speech, and he was shot."

"What about me? Wasn't there a message for me?"

Mohamed shook his head. "Only what I have said. Will you warn him?"

Jace mumbled a response, but did not share his true feelings. *Maybe I would be better off if Minister Okombo were dead.*

42

Lisa Sprague leaned toward the waitress across the small table at the Strawberry Street Café. "I'll have the quiche."

Heather smiled. "Just salad bar for me."

The waitress, a student at Virginia Commonwealth University, sported three earrings in her left ear. She pointed at an old porcelain bathtub that housed the salad. "Feel free to get your salad anytime."

Heather waited until the waitress retreated toward the kitchen. "So what have you found out?"

"A little." Lisa shrugged. "I interviewed the hotel manager down at the Jefferson. His timeline is a bit off from the one Ryan Meadows gave you."

"How so?"

"Mr. Baker said he escorted Jace to Anita Franks's suite after eleven. You said Ryan Meadows said ten."

"I thought his timing was off," Heather responded. "I remember because Jace and I had been to the theater that evening and we didn't even get out until after ten."

"Mr. Meadows must have been confused."

Heather nodded and stayed quiet. She thought about canceling her order for salad. She wasn't hungry anymore.

"There is something else," Lisa added, twirling her blonde hair and lifting it behind her ear. "I talked to a friend at the ME's office." She slid a piece of paper across the table. "Anita's sexual partner was a secretor."

"So…"

"So we need to know Jace's blood type to know if he is ruled in or out."

Heather studied the paper. "I'll contact Gabby. Maybe she'll know. Jace hasn't been responding to my emails."

Lisa nodded and sipped her water.

Heather kept her voice quiet. "I remember the night of the accident like it was yesterday. Jace and I had a real blowout."

Lisa kept quiet and Heather kept talking.

"Jace got a text as we were exiting the theater. The movie was romantic, and I wanted him home with me." She dabbed at the corners of her eyes. "I could tell by the way he acted that the text was from *her*. He wouldn't let me see it. He said he needed to swing by the office and would be late.

"I grabbed his phone and turned my back to him. We were in a crowd in front of the theater, so he couldn't make a scene. I read the text." She imitated Anita's feminine voice. "I need to see you tonight. I need help. Call me."

"What happened next?"

"He exploded. He grabbed my elbow and forcibly walked me away from the crowd. It's the first time he ever laid a hand on me like that. Jace was always so gentle." Heather's voice thickened. "He wrenched the phone from my hand and blamed *me*. He said I didn't trust him. It was patient-related, and he would be home soon. I looked at him and told him not to bother. Why keep acting out a lie?"

Heather stopped talking while the hostess passed with a young couple. They were twenty-somethings and seemed totally absorbed with each other.

"I don't curse, Lisa. But that night, I watched Jace stomp off toward his car and I sat in mine and just pounded the steering wheel and let it fly. I didn't even know I knew how to say those words, but I managed. And you know what? They tasted like they belonged there. I was just so bitter."

"Did he come home?"

"It was the night of his accident. I'm not sure he even remembers our fight." She paused, folding and refolding her napkin. "I went home and packed. I was leaving. I couldn't stay with him another day. I had my keys in my hand, Lisa. I was on my way out the door when my phone rang. It was the hospital. 'Your husband's been in an accident.'" Heather's voice choked and she halted.

Lisa reached for her hand. "You couldn't have known, Heather."

"You know what's horrible?" She paused and stared past her friend. "When they told me he'd been in an accident, my first thought was, *I hope he dies.*"

Lisa squeezed Heather's arm. "That's normal. Just because you're married doesn't mean you're going to feel the love all the time, especially after a rocky time."

Heather shook her head slowly. "I never left him. After the accident, I felt so bad for him that I decided to stay a few more weeks.

Then he started talking about leaving for Africa, and I knew that would be it. At that point I was too hurt to want him to stay. I asked him not to come back."

"So much for that, huh?"

"What do you mean?"

Lisa squinted. "You don't know?"

Heather shook her head.

"Jace is coming home. He's flying to London tomorrow, then on to Dulles the next day."

"He's coming home?"

Lisa nodded. "Ryan Meadows tipped me off. He said the police will be waiting for him at the airport. They're going to arrest him, Heather."

Heather covered her mouth. "For what?"

Lisa leaned forward again. "For an attack on Anita Franks. Maybe they know something we don't, but the governor is supposedly behind this. He wants Jace in custody."

That evening, as Jace approached his house, he noticed the front door was already open. He looked for his guards, unsure whether they would be around before dark.

He slowed and placed his hand against the front door. "Hello?"

As soon as he stepped inside, someone appeared in the doorway behind him, a tall uniformed man. Jace turned toward the sound.

"Dr. Rawlings, we were expecting you."

Jace backed into his kitchen. "Who are you? What do you want?"

In the living room, his guards sat on a small couch, at the will of three other men, all uniformed, muscular, and carrying automatic weapons.

Jace looked right and left. "What's going on?"

"We need you to come with us."

"Where? Who are you?"

"We are men with the job of keeping you safe. You are in danger here. We need to take you to a secure location."

Jace shook his head. "I don't feel unsafe." He paused, looking at their weapons. "Your guns make me feel unsafe."

"Get your things. We're leaving now."

"Have you talked to my medical director? I've got responsibilities. I'm on call."

An older man stepped forward. "Shut up and pack a bag."

Jace pointed at his guards, the police officers that the MP had arranged to watch his place at night. "These men can guard me. I need to stay here for my work."

"We cannot ensure your safety here any longer."

"Who is behind this? Who are you working for?"

A muscular young man with a large gap in his lower teeth grinned. "We are under orders from the minister of health."

That jolted Jace's memory. "Is the minister of health giving a speech any time soon?"

"Get packing. What is that to you?"

"I need to speak to Minister Okombo."

"Move, Dr. Rawlings. We need you to move."

Jace stood his ground. "I need to get a message to Minister Okombo."

One of the men came out of Jace's bedroom. "I packed your things," he said, throwing a suitcase onto the floor.

"Someone is going to shoot Minister Okombo during a speech. You have to warn him."

"Shut up." Jace felt a sharp sting on the back of his head. He stumbled forward, watching in horror as one of the new men moved behind the guards sitting on the couch and quickly slit the throat of the first guard and shoved him sprawling to the floor. The second guard leapt to his feet, only to be clubbed by the attacker with the butt of the automatic weapon. The guard staggered, and the man slit the guard's throat just as he had the first one.

Jace made a break for the door, but was tackled onto the kitchen floor, slamming his head against a chair as he fell. He felt searing pain and then ... nothing.

In the hospital casualty ward, Dr. Paul Mwaka worked through his own call load. He'd done a spinal tap on a young man with cryptococcal meningitis and HIV, performed a C-section, and was now examining an old man with severe abdominal pain. He didn't mind the heavy load. Many of his colleagues from medical school had accepted internships at the large government hospital in Nairobi. But even in Kenyatta, their experience wasn't as hands-on as his was in Kijabe. He knew in Nairobi he would not have been able to first assist on an open-heart case as he had that morning. He still couldn't believe it. Dr. Rawlings had taught all the way through the case, showing him detailed anatomy and instructing him on technique.

He looked at the old man's face as he felt his abdomen and asked him in the Kikuyu language, "Are you having pain here?"

Paul felt his own heart quicken as he slid his hand over the patient's upper abdomen. There, feeling as if it was just beneath the skin, something pushed back against his hand. The intern paused. No, something was beating, pulsating. Paul probed gently, outlining a pulsatile mass. He'd not felt anything like it before, but was sure it was a swelling of the aorta known as an aneurysm. If this was responsible for the patient's pain, it was a clue that the aneurysm was about to rupture or perhaps already beginning to rupture. He may only have a short time before the old man bled out.

He walked away from the stretcher and talked quietly to the nurse. "Could you start an IV on the patient in bed two?"

Purity, an experienced nurse, nodded.

"No," Dr. Mwaka responded. "Start two IVs. Large gauge, one in each arm. I'm going to call Dr. Rawlings."

He picked up the phone, dialed, and let the phone ring ten times.

After that, he asked the operator to page.

He walked to the HDU, thinking Dr. Rawlings might be visiting the open-heart patient.

But Dr. Rawlings wasn't there.

He walked back through casualty.

"Dr. Mwaka," Purity called, "the old man's blood pressure is falling. Only eighty systolic."

"Okay," he said. "Don't try to get it too high. The patient will bleed. I'm going to run up to Dr. Rawlings's house. Maybe he has his headphones on or something."

Paul felt certain the patient was close to death. He needed to find the surgeon stat. He ran up the hill, thankful for a clear night.

Strange. There are no guards outside his house.

He knocked, and then banged on the door, calling for the doctor. "Daktari Rawlings!"

Finally, in frustration, he tried the door. It wasn't latched; it slid open. He stepped into the kitchen, calling "Daktari!"

He gasped. On the kitchen floor were two bodies, both male. Both African. And both in a sea of blood. He knelt to take a pulse but pulled away before touching them. Both throats were sliced and their eyes were open, their chests unmoving.

Paul began to yell for help. He stumbled out of the house and ran down the hill, screaming for the security officer in the little guard station beside the hospital entrance.

At the guard station, he pointed back up the hill. "Just there," he gasped. "There's been a slaughter!"

43

Jace opened his eyes. He was in the back of an old car traveling somewhere fast. How long had he been out? The sky was dark, and he'd gone home just before sunset, so it had to have been at least thirty minutes. He studied his surroundings. He was unrestrained, but didn't move as there was a large African man on the bench seat beside him, carrying an automatic weapon, like something Jace had seen on cop shows in America. The man didn't seem to know that Jace was awake. He stared out the window at passing trees in a thick forest. *Are we on the highway yet?* There were two men in the front seat, arguing loudly in Kiswahili, saying something about a payment.

If Jace was to take advantage of the element of surprise, he'd have to do something quickly before they knew he was conscious. Could he jump from the vehicle? No, they were traveling too fast. He closed his eyes, in case his captors looked at him—then risked a quick glance at the weapon. The man held it loosely, unsuspecting.

Jace lunged for the gun, bringing his fingers over the man's within the circular guard over the trigger mechanism. The gun's barrel swung in an arc across the floor away from Jace as it began to fire. The sound was deafening and soon accompanied by the man's screams as he shot himself in the left foot. Reflexively he dropped the gun. Jace popped open the door on the other side of the man.

The men in the front seat screamed as the injured captor dove forward in an attempt to grab Jace's neck. Jace evaded him by sliding off the seat onto the floor. The man toppled into the space of the open doorway. Jace kicked hard and connected with the man's butt, sending him tumbling onto the pavement. Next, Jace reached forward and grabbed the driver by his hair, snapping his neck backward. The car careened from the road, crashed through a roadside fruit stand, and dropped into a ditch. Jace bounced off the ceiling, then the backseat.

He took a quick inventory of himself for injuries, then lifted his head and looked around. The two men in the front seat were now half in and half out, sprawled awkwardly through the broken windshield onto the hood.

Jace's door had slammed shut and was lodged against a stump. He crawled through the open window and glanced up the street. A woman ran in his direction and would be at the car in a few moments. He squinted toward the forest. *Time to get out of here.*

He ran into the trees, pausing to get his breath and listen to the growing crowd only after he was sure he hadn't been followed.

He looked at the moon. For now, he was on the run.

And alone.

Back in Kijabe, Dave Fitzgerald picked up the phone. "Calm down, Purity. What's the problem?"

"A mzee with low blood pressure. I know you are not on call, but we have tried over and over to raise the surgeon on call and have no response."

"Dr. Rawlings?"

"Yes."

"He's probably up in the HDU with his heart patients."

"We've checked. Meanwhile, I fear for this patient. I cannot find a pressure."

Dave sighed. "On my way."

In four minutes, he entered casualty. "Where's Mwaka? The intern needs to be with this patient."

"He left to find Dr. Rawlings," Purity answered. "He thought this was an aneurysm."

The surgeon stepped to the bedside. The patient moaned. Dave looked at his eyes. His conjunctiva were pasty pale, a sign of severe anemia. He laid his hand upon the belly and felt the pulsatile bulge above his navel. "Yes, Dr. Mwaka is right." He looked around. "Call blood bank. Tell them I will need as much blood as they have available."

Nearby stood an elderly woman in an orange sweater and a purple headscarf. The patient's wife. Dave spoke to her, using Purity as a translator. "Your husband's condition is very critical. He has one slim chance for survival. That chance is surgery." Deciding that it was better to skip the details of what he needed to do, he said, "The only other option would be to give him pain medication to keep him comfortable, and let nature take its course."

"Let him die?"

Dave nodded.

The woman shook her head. "Save him. He isn't ready to die."

"We will do all we can. Please pray."

Dave called an emergency team, including Evan Martin to do anesthesia.

"Have you seen Jace?" Dave asked.

Evan shook his head. "Not since leaving the HDU about an hour ago."

Ten minutes later, they were just rolling the patient into theater number one when the medical director walked up, looking pale.

"Hey, Blake, good timing. I could use an assistant. Ruptured aneurysm. Can't find Jace."

"I can't," Blake said. "We've got a real bad situation here, fellas. I just came from Jace's house. He's gone, and two police officers are dead, with their throats slashed."

"What?"

"I came to see if anyone knows where Jace is. He's disappeared."

Dave tied the strings of his mask behind his head. "What's going on? Where's Jace?"

"I don't know what to think. He's gone."

Evan spoke up. "Someone wants him dead. They've taken him. Where are the police?"

Blake shrugged. "We called them. They are walking up. They don't have a vehicle."

Evan looked back at Dave. "We've got to do this operation now if this guy is going to have a chance."

Dave nodded. "Get me some help, Blake. I can't do this alone."

Gabby sat alone in her Kijabe duplex wishing she could will the clock forward and leave for the airport now. She opened her laptop and connected to the Internet to get her email. There was a note from Heather, frustrated at Jace's poor communication. She'd done a little digging. She knew something about Anita's sexual partner. Could Gabby ask Jace about his blood type to see if he's a match?

Gabby scrolled down to see an attachment, the data on the semen analysis on Anita's attacker.

As she read, her throat went dry. *Oh, Jace!*

She needed to talk to him.

She picked up the phone and dialed. He didn't answer.

Oh well, he probably crashed after his big day in the OR. I suppose this can wait another day. It's not like he's going anywhere tonight.

Jace pushed on into the forest, pausing occasionally to look at the stars. He thought he must be on the west side of the highway that led north out of Nairobi toward Nakuru. He'd hiked these woods a hundred times growing up. He knew the waterfalls and the caves like his own backyard. If he continued, he should hit the railroad, the infamous line that had stalled at Tsavo during its construction because of the man-eating lions.

He limped on, stepping carefully, looking for a trail. So far, all he'd found were the crisscrossing paths of the ruthless men who illegally cut timber for the charcoal industry. *That's all I need,* he thought. *A run-in with the charcoal burners.*

He listened to the sounds of the night. Everything was alive. As he moved forward, branches overhead swayed from scampering colobus monkeys. After thirty minutes, he stopped, leaning against a tree. The sounds of the highway had vanished; only nature spoke to him now.

He closed his eyes, trying to rid his memory of the gruesome images of his guards killed without mercy. As a surgeon, he was accustomed to blood, but not the uncontrolled release he'd witnessed. He took a deep breath. *This is all my fault. It began on a fateful night in Richmond when I walked away from Heather.*

He lifted his face toward the night sky. *Are You punishing me because of Janice? I thought coming here would make up for my sin.*

Jace ran his hand over his right hip where a deep pain seemed to originate. He hadn't done a proper inventory since crawling from the car. *How long ago was that? Are they after me still?*

The bone seemed intact, but there was sharp pain every time he pressed against the ligaments of his right hip. *A strain. I deserved worse.*

A twig snapped nearby. Something moved in the distance, something heavy. *A baboon? A man?*

A volley of automatic-weapon fire cut through the night. Jace pressed his body against the tree and held his breath.

They were looking, trying to scare him into running.

He heard voices. Shouting. Kikuyu, he thought.

I must get to the railroad. Or to a stream. I can follow it west toward the escarpment over the Rift Valley. Then I'll know where I am.

The voices passed to his left by fifty meters. *They don't know where I am.*

He waited a few moments, then doubled back, limping away from the voices. Tree to tree. *Stay in the shadows.* He winced when his weight broke a stick. The voices halted. Another burst of gunfire. This time, with bullets spraying the tree above his head. Monkeys squealed and fell silent.

He smelled charcoal. Or was it from the gunfire?

Why does someone want me dead?

Jace crawled away, beneath banana leaves, his clothes now damp with sweat and moisture from the forest floor. He stood again, leaning low, and stumbled onto a path. After a few steps, he came to a mound of fresh dirt. Smoke seeped from several small openings.

A charcoal burning spot.

A rough voice greeted him. "Habari."

He looked up to see a boy holding up a machete. His teeth were yellow, visibly stained even in the moonlight.

The boy pressed the tip of the machete to Jace's throat.

Jace lifted his hands in surrender. "Don't hurt me," he whispered. "I have money."

44

Dave Fitzgerald worked quickly to get the abdomen open, relieved to see that the aortic rupture had been confined to a small area next to the aorta known as the retroperitoneum. If there had been a free rupture, he was sure he'd have been doing an autopsy rather than an attempt at saving the patient's life.

"Wow," Dr. Mwaka gasped. "It's huge."

The surgeon felt the area above the aneurysm. "We are fortunate. I think it starts below the takeoff of the renal arteries. Here," he instructed, "give me counter traction on the duodenum. I need to dissect it away so we can get this baby clamped."

The duo worked on. "This is a big day for you, huh?"

The intern nodded. "An open-heart case and an aneurysm in one day. Unbelievable."

"Believe it," Dave said. "This is Kijabe."

Evan's voice was etched with concern. "The pressure is sagging again. Have you clamped the aorta?"

"Working on it."

Evan stood up and squeezed a bag of blood. "Work faster."

Gabby was undressing when a knock interrupted her preparations for bed.

"Just a minute," she called.

From outside the door, she heard the Australian accent. "It's just me, Gabby, Blake Anderson."

She pulled a robe around her and unlocked the door, and pulled it open to stare at the medical director through the second barred door. "What's up?"

"Have you seen Jace?"

She shook her head. "No. I mean not since shortly after our case."

"He's missing, Gabby. The guards at his house were killed. He's nowhere to be found."

Gabby swallowed hard. *No!* "I was afraid of this."

"Why?"

She squinted at him. "Hasn't he kept you in the loop about his misery?"

"I guess not."

"Hang on," she said, unlocking the bars. "Let me dress. We have some catching up to do."

"The gunfire," the boy chuckled. "I thought they were coming after me." He smiled with a row of uneven teeth. "But they are after you."

Jace nodded. "Yes. Please keep your voice down."

It was too late. He heard voices and movement crashing through the trees.

"Lie down," the boy said. "I'll cover you with sticks."

Jace obeyed. He had little choice. The boy pulled branches across Jace and sat down, machete in hand.

Jace looked out from beneath the pile of cut branches, the discard that was too small to make good charcoal. His young partner was tapping the machete against a worn pair of Bata Bullets, the Kenyan version of cheap Converse court shoes.

Two more men appeared, one carrying an AK-47. They spoke to the boy in rapid Kikuyu.

Their voices rose. Arguing. The boy gestured with his knife, shaking his head.

The man shoved the boy to the ground. More arguing.

Finally, a deal. The man pulled out a stack of bills and peeled off three.

The boy pointed at the sticks.

Jace had been sold out for three thousand shillings.

Back in Kijabe, the night turned to morning, and word of Jace's disappearance traveled fast. Gabby paced her small apartment and prayed, while wondering, *What do I really know about this man?*

She pulled an old RVA yearbook from a shelf and turned to the index. After a few minutes, she found what she'd been looking for.

There, on page 72, were the senior pictures of the Rawlings twins, Jace first, sporting a serious pose, and then Janice, smiling as if she were a sunbeam ready to light the world.

The thing that struck Gabby was the girl's eyes. And the more she stared, the more she saw another face. Anita Franks.

Wow, Gabby thought. *Subtract a few years and Anita was Janice.*

The phone rang. It was Chaplain Otieno.

"Hello, John."

"Sorry for the early hour," he said, skipping the routine greetings. "I wanted you to know that a group is gathering for prayer. We need to lift up Jace. We will be at station hall in one hour."

"I'll be there."

She looked at her suitcases. All that remained was to put in her toothbrush. *Oh, God,* she prayed silently, *I so want to be on that plane.*

Dave tied the last suture knot to close the skin. His patient was alive. "Stay with him in HDU and monitor his urine output every hour. If he falls below fifty ccs per hour, let me know. Give him morphine liberally. Cover him with Kefzol. And don't even think about extubating him until morning."

Paul smiled in spite of his fatigue. He couldn't wait to call his mother. He was sure his village would all know of his exploits by lunch.

The intern looked at Evan Martin. "Ready to move?"

Evan nodded. "Let's roll."

His captors kept Jace in the back of a village duka stockroom until a car arrived just after sunrise.

This time, Jace was restrained, bound hands and feet, and dropped into the trunk.

For the next four hours, all he knew was road noise and his bruised body flopping about over merciless potholed Kenyan roads.

After two hours, his captors opened the trunk and allowed him to drink water from a cup. He was so thirsty, he didn't worry about amoebas or the dysentery sure to follow. A large man scoffed at him. "I'll bet you are praying, huh, Daktari?"

Jace shook his head. "No. I'm not much for that anymore."

The man's face changed, an inquisitive look replacing his smile. "Maybe you should learn," he said.

Then the trunk slammed and the journey continued.

In the darkness, Jace reviewed his life, a life he wasn't sure would continue beyond that day. In spite of his present danger, the hours of captivity seemed to prod Jace into an inspection of his past. *Funny,* he thought. *All the significant plot points in my life story revolve around death.*

Timmy O'Reilly.

Janice.

Anita Franks.

Michael Kagai. Anthony Kimathi. Boniface.

He thought about praying. And he remembered the day he promised never to talk to God again.

It had been on that final campout on the Malewa River for Jace and Janice and their RVA friends before they all left Kenya. It was their last day, and they'd returned to a favorite spot with high cliffs to swim.

Janice had always been afraid to join the others in a daring leap from the top into the water below.

Jace dared her, taunted her, telling her it was her last chance before college. He jumped, screaming as he fell. The water was cool. Refreshing.

And that day, deadly.

Everyone else had jumped. Some were swimming in the water below. Others sunned themselves on flat rocks on the other side.

Jace climbed back to the top where Janice sat judging his jumps.

"Seven point two," she said.

"Oh, come on. That was a nine!"

He walked to the edge again. The rocks were getting slick because of everyone's dripping bathing suits.

A straight jump wasn't really that daring. You needed to clear a distance of only three feet to avoid the jagged rocks below. But Jace wanted a higher score, so he did a handstand on the edge of the cliff.

"Stop, Jace, you'll fall!"

"I'm not going to fall. If I just lean over, I'll clear it easy."

"Jace, no!" She walked over and pulled on his shorts.

He collapsed his handstand. "I'll do a flip then. You'll give me a ten for a flip."

"Stop."

"Why?" He looked at her, then remembered. "You think I'm going to die, don't you? You think I'm going to miss my chance to be saved, don't you?"

"Jace, don't." Janice looked over her shoulder at their classmates, who seemed uncomfortable at the twins' exchange.

"You do it then. Jump. Jump or I'll flip."

She edged closer and stared down at the water.

"It's only twenty-five feet, give or take." He smiled. "Less than a second."

He snuck up behind her, meaning only to give her a scare. He only intended to shove her shoulders and then pull her back.

He yelled as he grabbed her by the shoulders. She gasped and immediately pushed back, but lost her footing on the muddy cliff edge.

Her foot slipped over and Jace lost his grip. Her head bounced off the rocks as she went over.

Jace heard, rather than saw, her descent. Thud. Scream. Thud. Silence.

He'd heard that scream in his head a thousand times since that day.

He looked over the edge. Her body lay mostly in the water, having rebounded off the unforgiving face of the cliff.

He jumped immediately, yelling her name, "Janice!"

He swam back to her and turned her face toward the sky. Her neck bent at a sickening angle. Blood and bubbles came from her nose and mouth.

"No!"

The others came.

No one could help. Janice gasped. Once. Twice. Three times.

And then she died in Jace's arms.

That afternoon, he took the small wooden cross his sister had worn around her neck and tossed it into the campfire. He whispered,

"I asked You to show me if You love me." He paused. "So now, I guess I know."

He spoke the next words crisply. Each was a stake pounded into the dry earth of his heart. "I. Will. Never. Serve. You."

Midmorning in Nairobi's Uhuru Park, the Honorable John Erastus Okombo was set to take the stage at a political rally. The air was electric. Some were comparing him to President Kibaki and wondered if a Luo could do a better job of uniting a country separated along so many tribal lines. Certainly his success negotiating exports of Kenyan coffee and tea were examples of his smooth tongue. Okombo's future could only be bright.

But rising to power in Kenya took many friends in the right places and a willingness to be ruthless to one's enemies. He couldn't have Jace Rawlings talking to Kibaki's anticorruption czar, raising questions about his driver or his loyalties, could he?

Soon, he thought, *Jace Rawlings will be out of my way forever.*

Okombo looked out over the crowd, scanning for friendly faces. There was the group of some of Kenya's finest physicians he'd invited to brag of their modern facilities. Even the heart surgeons, his generous benefactors, were there to cheer.

Once introduced, it took but three Okombo-sized strides to reach the podium.

He raised his hands to silence the crowd.

He waved at a television crew.

At first, the shot sounded like fireworks. The crowd cheered, expecting a colorful display.

Okombo felt the impact without conscious recognition of pain. Instead, as he stumbled backward, clutching his chest, his only thought was that he'd been shot.

A man in a dark suit dove to protect him, shielding the minister's body with his own. Okombo tried to speak, but he couldn't get his breath. He tried to push the man away. *Dr. Rawlings, you were right.*

Chaos. The crowd stampeded away.

Okombo heard officers shouting his name. Screams erupted from the crowd. He felt pressure in his chest. *Am I dying?*

In Kisii Town in western Kenya, Simeon Okayo watched footage of the shooting and cursed. He flipped off the television. *This can't be happening! He was a trusted ally.*

He paced his little shop and tried to think. The witch doctor needed friends in powerful places. With Okombo dead, he would have to step carefully. Life in Kenya was a balance between old ways and new. It wasn't uncommon to see a traditional Maasai tribesman with a cell phone. Likewise, political leaders vacillated between using the witch doctors to curse their opponents and denouncing witch doctors as ludicrous followers of outdated superstitions. While other politicians had supported witch hunts, Okombo had allowed Simeon a new status and access to powerful people previously unknown to practitioners of traditional magic arts. Okombo had taken Simeon with him to bless his trade missions. And he'd rewarded him for his faithfulness.

What would he do with Okombo gone?

He couldn't think of that now.

He'd made a promise to take care of Jace Rawlings. The American surgeon had become a political dead weight.

And Simeon had made a promise, a blood oath, and he feared the consequences if he failed again. Even without Okombo around to pull the puppet strings, Simeon would have to follow up on the oath. He feared dark consequences if the spirits were angered.

He picked up his phone, punching a number. "Have you seen the news? John Okombo is dead. Bring Dr. Rawlings to the warehouse. I'll have things set up there. No one will care about a little smoke out there."

45

Gabby punched in the long series of numbers to make the call from Kijabe to Virginia. After a few moments, she was rewarded with the voice of her friend. "Heather, it's Gabby."

"Gabby? Where are you? Are you back?"

"No, still in Kijabe. We're leaving tonight." She hesitated. "But there's a problem. Jace is gone."

"Gone?"

"Look, things have been weird since the moment we arrived. Jace is missing, Heather. Someone broke into his house, killed his guards, and Jace is gone. I can't tell you everything right now, just that we think someone tried to target Jace."

"Gone? Where is he?"

"That's just it. I think he's been abducted."

"I don't understand. Why would someone target Jace?"

"I can't explain everything. Just that Jace is in trouble."

"I don't understand. What's going on?"

"I'm sorry, Heather. I can't explain what I don't know. It's confusing to me, too. I'll explain as best I can when we get back to Dulles.

Can you meet us? It will be Saturday afternoon at four. The BA flight from Heathrow."

"I know. I heard Jace was coming."

"You knew?"

"A friend of mine was tipped off." Heather's breath was heavy into the phone. "Gabby, the police are going to be there. They want to arrest Jace for attacking Anita Franks."

"What? That's crazy."

"They have collected some sort of evidence that links him to her."

"No," Gabby said. "You sent me the information on the semen analysis." Gabby shook her head, even though her friend couldn't see. "The attacker was blood type A. Jace is type B. He didn't have sex with her, Heather. It was someone else."

Silence.

"Heather?"

She listened as Heather broke down. "You're sure?"

"According to what you sent me, it's impossible. Our first patient was type B, and Jace donated blood for her."

Heather sniffed. "I'd stopped believing him."

Gabby listened for a moment before Heather continued. "But now he's gone? Where?"

"The police think someone has abducted him. You need to pray." She hesitated. "Heather, I'm not getting on that plane without Jace. I'll call you and let you know."

"I'll be praying."

"The staff is gathering here in a few minutes. We'll be praying here, too."

Jace rolled from side to side in the car trunk, feeling every bump in the road, unable to find a square inch of skin that didn't hurt.

I am going to die. He'd seen the brutal way his captors dealt with his guards back in Kijabe.

He quieted his mind, resigned to the inevitable. *If only I had a chance to do things over.*

He thought about the messages, how he'd waited anxiously for the last one from his patient, Mohamed Omar. Yet he hadn't really had time to process what he'd heard. As soon as he got back to his house, he'd been abducted for this death ride.

What was it he said?

Something about Issa coming as God.

I've heard that story before.

It always seemed to affect everyone around me, but not me.

But now, I'm face-to-face with a realm scientists can't test. Far away from my scientific comfort zone in America, where everything is predictable.

Here, in Africa, I've seen things, heard things, I can't explain any other way.

There is no way my patients could have given truthful predictions of the future without the reality of a spirit world.

So was Janice right?

Is Chaplain Otieno correct when he speaks so passionately about the power of Christ in us? The power of the cross?

Did Jesus come as God for me?

He thought about the vow he made in bitterness, a vow he'd sealed by burning a wooden cross.

There, bound in the trunk of a car, Jace realized the truth. He knew the story. The incarnation. God made man. A cross to pay an impossible debt.

And he believed.

He couldn't put his finger on the moment he moved from doubt to faith. He knew only that now, when he considered the story in light of everything happening in his life, he believed.

He believed.

Jace began to weep. He was not afraid to die. He knew he deserved death.

Did I cheat on my wife? I'm still unsure, but I know I'm not worthy of Heather. I've never been able to lead her as I should.

The highway noise disappeared. The car had turned off the main road. Jace began to smell dust, the red dirt of Kenya. He bounced along, trying to ignore the pain in his head, neck, back, legs, and shoulders.

He decided to try the taste of prayer on his tongue.

Overhead, at twelve thousand feet in a Cessna Caravan, John Okombo rubbed the bruise inflicted by the bullet that had slammed into his Kevlar vest.

He delighted in his situation. His apparent rise from the dead would do wonders for his political aspirations.

But now, he had a date in Kisii with the American surgeon.

Jace Rawlings had saved the life of Okombo's daughter, yet the MP had been willing to sacrifice him along the political trail. After all, a deal was a deal.

But Rawlings had come through again, sending a message, warning him of a plot, an impending attack, allowing him to protect himself and prevent his untimely end.

So now, if Okombo could pull off a favor for the surgeon, he suspected he would win a valuable ally.

He thought about the Virginia politicians. The jealousy. The dirty laundry of personal favors for promises of deals worth millions.

Screw them, he thought. *The American has become valuable to me.*

He moaned and looked at his useless cell phone. He'd tried to reach Simeon a half-dozen times before takeoff without success. *He's probably too busy preparing for the sacrifice.*

The plane raced along, diverting around threatening weather.

John Okombo folded meaty hands in his lap and sighed. *If I know Simeon, I may well be too late.*

Heather Rawlings paced and prayed, lifting her phone to her ear. "Mr. Meadows? Thanks for taking my call. I hear you are looking forward to my husband's return."

Ryan Meadows said, "Something like that." He chuckled. "I guess he called you."

"No."

"Then how—"

"Doesn't matter. I need you to listen to me. And if you've got an ounce of dignity or an interest in your own political future, you'll convince the police to back away from their plans to arrest Jace."

"Why would I do that?"

"Because he's innocent."

"You're naive. Not that I blame you. Dr. Rawlings is quite the ticket to the good life, is he not?"

"He's working for the poor in Africa, not exactly my definition of the good life." She paused. "Don't have him arrested."

"Oh, I'm going to have him arrested. And if you think the commonwealth attorney is going to be satisfied with a sexual assault charge, think again. Jace Rawlings is going to pay for her death as well. Poor woman was drugged, don't you see? Couldn't get out of the way of the car that killed her."

"Ridiculous," Heather said.

"Is it?"

"It is. Ask the ME."

"I've seen the autopsy report. It's quite alarming. Perhaps you've seen it?" He laughed again.

"The semen analysis doesn't match my husband. So whose was it? The governor was out of town." She hesitated, but decided that if she'd come this far, she was going all in. "What about you, Ryan? My sources tell me you were quite close to Anita Franks. Nice thing about DNA," she said. "A glorious one-of-a-kind fingerprint."

"I'm not sure what you're implying. It was my job to be close to the first family."

"Of course." She paused for effect and to still her racing heart. "Go ahead and arrest the wrong man. I'm sure the governor will reward you for it."

She closed her phone and her eyes, pinching back the tears that had lived just below the surface since hearing the news from Gabby.

She backed up against the kitchen wall and slid to the floor, praying again that she'd have the chance to fight for a husband she'd pushed away.

"Oh, God," she whispered. "Give me another chance to believe him."

Lisa Sprague spread the photocopies across the table in front of her. A photo of Virginia's first lady hugging Jace Rawlings, her husband's surgeon. An article Lisa had written on the grueling training of a modern heart surgeon. Jace addressing the media at the hospital after the successful valve replacement.

She shook her head. Something was bothering her.

Why would Jace suddenly give up everything when he was just riding the wave of unequalled popularity and success here?

Was he really trying to escape a dangerous affair?

But Anita Franks was dead. Didn't that close the chapter?

Or did he need to atone for sins we didn't understand? Just because it wasn't his sperm found on the autopsy doesn't mean his relationship with Anita was good and proper, does it?

Something else bothered her. But what?

She picked up the picture of Jace and Anita captured in an embrace. This time, she focused not on the duo, but on the background for something she might have missed.

Behind them were a few bodyguards wearing dark suits and wires in their ears. And beside them, Ryan Meadows.

She studied him for a moment, noting his scowl. This guy was unhappy about something.

Maybe he didn't like the first lady hugging the doctor.

Her phone rang. It was a friend who worked as a 911 operator. "I've emailed you the MP3 file you wanted."

"I owe you." Lisa closed her phone, went to her computer, and clicked on the file.

Then she listened.

The 911 call from Anita Franks.

"This is 911. Please state the nature of your emergency."

"There's been an accident. Oh, God! Oh, God!"

"Ma'am, please calm down. Where are you?"

A pause, then Anita's frantic voice, "Lombardy and Broad. A man is bleeding. Oh, there's blood coming from his nose and ear." The voice quieted, as if she'd pulled the phone away and was talking to the victim. "Jace, Jace, come back to me. Come back to me."

The 911 operator's voice again. "Ma'am, help is on the way. Is the man breathing?"

"I think so. Oh, God. He's moaning."

In the background, she heard Jace's voice. "Janice?"

Again, Anita's voice. "Jace! Jace! Come back to me."

"Stay on the line, ma'am. Is he conscious?"

The sound of squealing brakes and a loud cracking sound ended Anita's communication.

"Ma'am? Ma'am?"

The 911 operator cursed and the tape ended.

Lisa replayed the file three times. She nodded slowly.

Jace didn't hear from his dead sister. He heard from Anita Franks.

46

It was nearly dark again by the time the trunk opened. Even so, Jace squinted in the dim light. The men jerked him up and out of the trunk and onto his feet. In spite of Jace's restraints, it felt great to be anywhere except the trunk.

He looked around. "Where are we?"

His captors looked at each other before the older and larger one answered. "Kisii. Witch doctor capital of Kenya."

Jace nodded, feeling good in spite of his captivity. His spirit was free for the first time. "Wonderful!"

"Shut up."

Jace looked around. They appeared to be in a back alley. He heard distant voices, but couldn't see anyone but his captors. "I'm thirsty."

They ignored him. Someone slammed the trunk lid. Someone else from behind put a sack over his head. Then Jace felt he was being carried by three sets of arms. Beneath his chest, hips, and feet. A door closed. More voices. The creaking of stairs. Darker now, with no light filtering through the sack. His head was lower than his feet.

We're going up a flight or two of stairs.

He listened. He heard the squawk of ibis. They always sang at dusk. A car engine sputtered, and he thought he heard the clank of metal and the clicking sound of a socket wrench.

He dropped onto a hard wooden floor. It echoed more than concrete. Jace smelled charcoal. Smoke.

Communication in a tongue he didn't understand.

Soon, they lifted him again, his arms stretched above his head, far out to either side, and tied tightly around the wrists. His feet still touched the ground, but barely. The rope binding his ankles was left in place.

Finally, the sack was lifted from his head.

In his face was Simeon Okayo. It was not the Dr. Okayo he'd first met in Kijabe, the one in a business suit who claimed to be a consultant; this was the Simeon Okayo from his dream, the witch doctor with devilish plans. Jace felt his heart quicken. He attempted to calm himself with the words of the Kijabe chaplain: *Greater is He who is in you ...*

Jace was in what appeared to be an abandoned warehouse. The ceiling was incomplete, revealing rafters beneath a metal roof. There was a single window around thirty feet away. Jace was tied to metal circles fixed to a wooden wall. In front of him, eight feet away, was a small wooden table on which sat a raised metal dish. A fire was burning in it.

Jace tried to relax, but found it difficult to breathe if he didn't push down on his toes. His calves began to cramp.

Simeon nodded at the men, who disappeared down a set of stairs, leaving Jace alone with Simeon.

"Nice digs. This your office? You must give me the name of your decorator."

Simeon ignored him. His face was striped with some sort of white paint. Loose animal skins hung around his waist. A series of raised scars looped around his neck and upper chest like a necklace. He danced in a circle chanting and threw liquid from the tips of his fingers, splashing Jace's face and chest.

At his feet lay a gutted animal, the size of a young goat. The organs were lined up on the table next to the fire.

"Did you invite me for dinner?" Jace asked.

Simeon halted. "You might say that." He smiled. "You are the main course."

Jace felt his bravado fleeing. He'd heard tales of African leaders actually consuming the hearts of their enemies, something that was said to help them gain strength.

"It is time you learned a few things, Dr. Rawlings. There is a world out there, one you cannot see."

Jace sighed. "I know."

"You know?" The man scoffed. "But do you even know why you are here?"

Jace didn't answer. He wasn't sure.

"I speak to the dead. Janice—"

"I don't know who you talked to, but you didn't speak to Janice."

"But you yourself heard her calling."

Jace shook his head, trying to process.

"It was me all along, Dr. Rawlings. The spirits were bribed, and they worked this all out."

"Why would you do this?"

"Our people want to be rich, just like yours," he said. "And my services are valuable, are they not?" He walked to the fire and used a stick to stir up the flame. "There are powerful men in Virginia that you have angered. A man who wanted you out of the way."

"Who?"

"A confidant." He added a white powder to the fire. When he did so, it snapped and popped; sparks danced in the air above the flames.

Simeon continued. "You were misbehaving. I bragged that I could lure you away."

"I was stupid."

"You are a mortal."

"You are going to kill me?"

"Balance needs to be restored."

"You can't kill me."

"This is my town. I make the rules here." He picked up the leg of the slain animal, waving the hoof over the flame.

Jace jerked his feet off the wooden floor, lifting himself by his arms. He screamed.

Simeon smiled. "Now do you believe?"

Back in Kijabe, Gabby excused herself from the small circle of believers who had gathered to pray for Jace.

While the group continued praying, Evan stood and met her at the door. "A car is waiting for us," she said. "But I can't just leave Jace."

Evan shook his head. "You need to go." He spoke with a whisper. "Get out of this place, Gabby."

She began to protest, but he stopped her with a finger to his lips. "What good are you here? I want you safe."

"And you?"

"I'm staying until ..."

She nodded and took his arm.

"Until I know how this ends," he continued.

"I made a promise to Heather."

"Tell her I made you return." Evan hesitated. "There is nothing you can do here but pray, and you can do that on the plane to somewhere safe."

Gabby smiled. The gadget geek turned hero.

"Go!" he said, more forcefully. "I'll stay here. I'll come as soon as I know ..."

She understood what he didn't say. *As soon as I know Jace is dead.*

"Be safe," she said. "I'll call once I get back to the US." She shoved a cell phone into his hand. "This is the phone I purchased in Nairobi. You can buy a card to load more time onto it at the duka here in Kijabe." She motioned toward the praying circle. "How are you with all of this?"

Evan looked over his shoulder at the small group circled in front of a stone fireplace in the gathering room of station hall. Everyone took turns praying. Sometimes loudly, binding evil in the name of Jesus, and sometimes quietly, earnestly praising the One who gave His blood to pay the price for their sin.

Evan raised his eyebrows. "It's new for me." He paused, his voice thickening. "I've played on the edge of faith for a long time. It's time for me to get serious. Africa has demanded that of me."

"I understand," she whispered.

"Pray as you go," he said. "Jace and I will follow when we can."

The tears in her eyes betrayed her thoughts. She didn't believe Jace was alive.

She turned to go, but halted. "Call Heather. She is going to meet me at the airport."

Gabby watched as he returned to the circle. There was nothing they could do.

Except pray.

And in a way, she felt that was enough.

She hesitated at the door and listened.

Chaplain Otieno was leading. "In the mighty, merciful name of Jesus, the Lamb that was slain from the foundation of the world ..."

John Okombo leaned forward and yelled to his pilot, "I thought you were going to land."

"Too many animals," he said. "I'm going to come in low one more time and buzz the strip to chase them away."

Okombo looked at the dirt strip below them, receding into the distance. In the moonlight he could see that a herd of zebra had taken up the job of mowing the grass around the edges of the runway.

He looked at his watch and sighed. *Dr. Rawlings will be dead before I get to Kisii.*

47

Jace lost track of time as the witch doctor continued a feverish dance around the fire.

One by one, Simeon roasted the inner organs of the slaughtered goat, and Jace felt a burning within him, a searing pain like a stake being driven through his stomach.

Yet Simeon did not seem satisfied. "Something has changed," he said, pointing a bony finger at Jace's forehead. "The Christians in Kijabe have gotten to you, have they?"

Jace watched as the old man ran his fingers over the goat's intestines, apparently searching for an answer.

Finally, he looked back at Jace. "You must deny this Jesus." He shook his head. "He cannot save you."

"I deserve to die."

"Curse Him!"

Jace stayed quiet. He found it increasingly hard to breathe.

Simeon walked to a large leather satchel and retrieved a wooden cross. He walked toward the fire.

"No," Jace said. In his mind, he saw the cross in his own hand, as he vowed to God that he would avenge his sister's death by never serving him. "I was wrong," Jace gasped. "I love Your cross."

"Shut up!" Simeon said. He laughed and dropped the cross into the fire.

Jace watched as Simeon's anger grew. The cross, nestled in a bed of hot glowing coals, refused to burn.

Simeon grabbed another twig and shoved it into the coals by the cross, where it instantly flared. He withdrew it, swinging the smoking stick beneath Jace's nose. He moved it to Jace's left arm and rested the stick against his elbow.

The skin sizzled. Pain!

Simeon laughed.

Behind him, heavy footfalls on the stairs.

John Okombo appeared with two uniformed men carrying guns. "Simeon," he said, his voice deep and resonant. "He's passed your test." He gestured with his hand. "Leave him to me."

"You are a ghost," Simeon said. "What do you want with me?"

"I'm no ghost."

"I saw you die. It's all over Kenyan news."

"You saw me fall. You saw me being loaded into an ambulance. You did not see me die."

"But—"

"This man, this doctor sent me a warning." Okombo paused, stepping forward with the guards. "I owe him my life."

But Simeon shook his head. "The spell is working. He feels the pain I inflict upon the proxy."

"Stop."

"It was you who paid me," he sneered. "You had to please the Americans."

"Stop."

"The gods will not wait. I've promised them blood." Simeon picked up a knife, still dripping with blood from the animal sacrifice. "I will finish him. He is nothing to you."

"We will stop you," Okombo said. He motioned to the officers, who lifted their weapons and trained them on the witch doctor.

Simeon knelt at the table, the fire flickering in front of him, dancing in the slick of sweat on his forehead. He lifted a small wooden cup above his head. Then, holding the knife high in the air, he aimed the tip of the dagger toward Jace's chest.

"No!" Okombo shouted.

Simeon threw the contents of the cup into the fire. Immediately, a cloud of red smoke enveloped the witch doctor, so thick that Jace strained to see only a few inches in front of him.

Jace screamed.

He heard a shot, then footsteps running toward him.

"Fool!" cried the MP. "You've shot the daktari."

"I was aiming at the witch doctor."

Jace fought for breath and looked down at his chest where a ring of red was spreading. *Weird, I don't even feel it.*

John Okombo waved his arms through the smoke. "Where is Simeon?"

The officers coughed. "He's gone. Disappeared."

Jace felt faint. The room was darkening.

He looked at the floor in front of him, noting what appeared to be the seam of a trapdoor beside the goat. *What a charlatan—he only made it look like he disappeared.*

Then, blackness.

Okombo pointed to the knife Simeon had apparently dropped as he made his exit. "Cut him down."

The two officers cut the ropes binding the American surgeon's wrists and lowered him to the floor.

John Okombo knelt over Jace Rawlings, placing his fingers on his neck. "He has a weak pulse." He ripped away the shirt to expose a wound entering the chest a few inches below the clavicle. "It must have missed the heart or he would be dead by now." He motioned with his head. "Call the pilot. Tell him to ready the plane. We need to take him to Bomet."

"Why not the district hospital? It is closer."

"There is a Christian mission hospital in Bomet, Tenwek. They will know how to treat him."

"They can treat him at the district hospital."

"They will not know how to deal with Okayo's curse. At Tenwek, they can battle not only for his body, but for his soul."

The officer nodded and made the call.

"Let's get him outside. The car should be in the alley."

John Okombo lifted Jace like a child in his arms, cradling him and carrying him down the wooden stairs.

Once outside, Jace started coughing, spraying blood onto Okombo's shirt. "Open the back door," he said. "And get a blanket. The night is cold."

In Nairobi, at Kenyatta International Airport, Gabby took her seat on British Airways Flight 61 bound for Heathrow. She sat next to a white-haired woman, who smiled and extended her hand. "Tilly Brown," she said.

"I'm Gabby. Looks like we're going to be seatmates."

The woman nodded. "I've been on safari. I was diagnosed with breast cancer last year. I looked at my bucket list very seriously and decided it was time to visit all those places I'd never been."

Gabby smiled. *Please don't tell me about your chemo.*

Too late.

"My surgeon said he could save my breast if I had chemo and radiation. It nearly killed me, but I made it. My husband wasn't so lucky. He died of lung cancer last year and made me promise I'd take a safari to Kenya like we'd always talked." She paused, fastening her seatbelt. "Were you on safari?"

"Not exactly."

The woman didn't take the hint that Gabby didn't feel much like talking. "So why were you in Kenya? I'll bet you have a boyfriend in the Peace Corps, don't you?"

"I was helping in a mission hospital. I'm part of a cardiac surgery team."

"Oh, my, that must be something! I've always thought medical mission work would be the most glamorous life imaginable."

Gabby sighed. *Not exactly glamorous in the way you might expect.* She smiled at the old traveler and wondered what she would think if she told her the truth, that her friend may have been killed after they'd encountered a vicious spiritual war, that they'd been caught up in dirty Kenyan political games, and that she was on her way home to lick her wounds.

Instead, she just nodded. "Oh. Well. Yes. Glamorous."

"I'll bet. Did you see any breast cancer? I hear that women in Kenya have little access to mammograms. You know, if it wasn't for mammography, I would still be walking around with cancer in my body and I probably still wouldn't know it. Why, did you know that by the time a breast cancer is the size of a pea that it's likely been in your body—"

Graciously, the woman hushed while the flight attendant explained emergency procedures in case of a water landing.

Gabby used the opportunity to slip on a sleeping mask to cover her eyes and pulled a blanket up under her chin.

Before she slept, she prayed for Jace Rawlings.

48

Jace fought for consciousness. He wanted to tell them he was alive, not to give up, but the nurse didn't seem happy about his blood pressure. In fact, he'd heard her tell the doctor that she couldn't find it.

He tried to breathe, but it felt as if some giant hand was squeezing his chest. The harder he fought to breathe, the more it felt as if movement of any kind was impossible. *Am I strapped down?*

He moved his tongue against a hard object. *Am I entubated?*

For a moment, he saw, first from below, and then *from above* that a young Kenyan doctor was pumping on his chest.

No wonder I can't breathe.

"He's been down for thirty minutes. How long was the flight from Kisii?"

The nurse didn't know. No one seemed to know anything.

"How about drugs? When is the last time we gave epinephrine?"

Jace looked at the vials of drugs on the top of a rolling cart. A half-dozen little glass vials.

It comes down to this. I'm naked down there and I can't even cover myself.

I wanted to tell Heather that I loved her.

"His trachea is shifted." The doctor grabbed a stethoscope. "No breath sounds over here."

I've got a pneumothorax from the bullet ripping through my lung.

A being of light appeared to Jace's right. An angel?

They communicated without speaking.

Are you here for me?

No.

Then why—

You are Jacob.

Jace understood. *Chosen.*

He watched as the Kenyan intern splashed Betadine across his chest.

Funny, I can't feel you touching me.

"I need a knife." He paused and then instructed a nurse. "You need to do chest compressions until I get this tube in. If that doesn't work, I'm calling it."

Jace watched as the intern made a cut on his left chest lateral to the nipple line. He pushed a clamp into the chest.

That sure looks like it should hurt.

The intern inserted a clear tube that flashed with blood. A lot of blood gushed from the end of the tube, spraying the stretcher, the floor, and the intern. "Wow. Get me a collection chamber."

"I've never seen so much blood."

"Call the blood bank."

"They only have two units of O negative. I just called them a few minutes ago for Dr. Samuels."

"We need it." He appeared to be sweating. "Now!"

The intern pushed a stitch through Jace's skin next to the tube.

Hey! I felt that!

The young doctor secured the tube and felt for a pulse in Jace's neck. "Weak," he said, "but I think better."

He reached up and squeezed an IV bag, quickening the transfer of its liquid contents into a vein in Jace's arm. "Come on," he said. "Come back, Dr. Rawlings."

Another man arrived, this one Caucasian. He wore a white coat. Jace thought he looked like a missionary. "What's up, Peter?"

"This guy was shot in the left chest. Came in a few minutes ago without a pulse. We coded him. It looks like he had a pneumothorax. Once I put in this tube, he started to respond."

Immediately, Jace lost the experience of floating. Now, all he was the firmness of the stretcher and a sensation of being cold.

Hey, guys, I'm freezing!

Jace reached for the hand of a passing nurse and squeezed. "Hey," she said, "he's responding!"

The white doctor's face appeared over his. "Get him a blanket. Poor guy's blue."

"What's wrong with his feet? They're blistered."

"They look burned." The male voice paused. "And just look at that arm. Looks like someone burned the flesh right down to the muscle."

Jace listened as a new male voice entered the conversation, English, but with a distinct Kenyan accent. "Daktari, we rescued him from a traditional sacrifice ritual in Kisii. The witch doctor was boiling the organs of some sort of proxy animal."

The Kenyan intern's voice. "He may have internal damage."

The missionary spoke again. "Go see if you can find our chaplain, Kiploni. Tell him to bring the anointing oil. I want him to do a prayer of deliverance."

The following morning, Evan Martin awoke to the sound of someone pounding on his door.

His first thought was that the vegetable ladies were getting an early start. *Go away. I don't want to buy any more mangos.*

He cleared his throat and ran his fingers through his bed-head hair. "Coming!"

He stepped across the cool floor, still amazed that equatorial Africa could be this cold. He slipped on a pair of jeans and a T-shirt and plodded toward the sound of the knocking.

"Daktari Martin!"

"On my way," he said.

At the door, he fumbled with the keys and unlocked it. He stared at John Otieno across the metal bars. "Morning, Chaplain."

"Evan," Otieno said. "They've found him."

"Jace?"

The chaplain nodded. "Dr. Thomas over at Tenwek called. They have Jace in the hospital. He was shot, but he's alive."

Evan unlocked the bars.

The chaplain smiled. "Hallelujah!"

Evan returned a grin and allowed himself to be enfolded in the big man's arms. "Yeah," he said, finding himself buried in the chaplain's chest. He managed a muffled "Hallelujah" of his own.

When the chaplain released him, he asked. "How can I get to Tenwek?"

"You can hire a driver. Elisha will take you."

By late afternoon, Gabby was bone-tired and stepping off the plane in the US.

After passing through passport control, she picked up her luggage and headed for customs.

A few minutes later, she passed through the doors marked "No return after exit." She pulled out her cell phone to call Heather Rawlings. Two men in dark suits approached and addressed her. "Ms. Dawson?"

"Yes."

"Officer Jackson," the shorter man said, flashing a badge. "Virginia State Police. Is Dr. Jace Rawlings traveling with you?"

She shook her head. "No. He was unable to make the flight from Nairobi to Heathrow. He's still in Kenya."

The men looked at each other. Evidently, this was news.

"I'm sorry," she said. "Now, if you'll excuse me." Gabby walked off as the men flipped open their phones.

She waited until she was a few feet away to dial Heather.

"Hey," she said. "It's me."

"Gabby!" Heather said. "I just got off the phone with Evan Martin. They've found Jace. He's alive!"

The following afternoon, Evan sat at Jace's bedside in the men's ward at Tenwek hospital, feeling far from alone. The large room housed twenty-two beds, each with a patient in various states of ill health.

Jace was pale and appeared to be the center of a tangle of tubes giving or receiving fluids. A urinary catheter drained the output from his kidneys. A tube drained bloody fluid from his stomach, another blood from his chest .

Two IVs were Y'ed into one, joining to give Jace a mixture of electrolyte fluids, sugar, and antibiotics.

Evan studied the chart in his hand. "Your liver functions are improving."

"How's my hemoglobin?"

"Down one since yesterday. Drop any lower and you're going to need another transfusion."

Jace groaned. He didn't want another transfusion. With HIV running at fifteen percent in the general population, he didn't want blood, even if they claimed they screened every unit.

"What did they do to you, Jace?"

"Not sure. Seems like they scalded me inside and out."

"I'd like to get you back to Kijabe. Dr. Thomas said I could take you once the chest tube is out."

Jace nodded. "Say, Evan, help me sit up, would you?"

Once he was sitting on the side of the bed, Jace motioned for the other men in the room. "How many of you understand English?"

Six men responded in the affirmative.

He looked at Evan. "I think there are a few plastic chairs at the nurses' station. Can you help gather these men around? I want to talk to them."

Evan was surprised, but did as Jace had asked.

Once the chairs were gathered, two men sat on the chairs, two on Jace's bed and three more stood against the wall between the beds.

"Men," Jace began. "I want to tell you my story.

"I came to this country expecting to do good works, hoping I might win a few points with God. I've done some pretty bad stuff in my life, and I knew I was long overdue for some changes. What I found is that the cross has taken care of my sin, and that my works can't add one little bit to what God has already done."

The men nodded.

"For a long time, I doubted that God wanted anything to do with me. But what I've found out in the last few weeks in Kenya has convinced me that God has been in my corner all along, loving me, forgiving me, and fighting a real war on my behalf.

"I'm here to tell you about encounters beyond the grave. My patients', and my own.

"You can write me off as crazy, but what I'm going to tell you is absolutely true." Jace smiled. "Strange, but true." He pointed at the men. "I know now that God is alive and loves each one of you."

Evan Martin looked at his friend. "Jace," he said, his voice etched with concern, "you've been through a lot. You may not be thinking clearly."

Jace shook his head and ignored his friend's concern. "My story starts the day I arrived in Kenya and saw a goat that had been raised from the dead. It ends with an angel who told me I was chosen ..."

49

Heather pulled the brush through the thick hair of the mastiff. "Good dog."

She'd been working steadily for twenty minutes when the doorbell interrupted her attention.

She scratched the dog behind the ears. "Stay, Bo."

She walked down the hall, through the kitchen, and out to the entrance foyer. She looked through the window. *Ryan Meadows.*

She put her hand in the pocket of her shorts to check for her cell before opening the door. "Mr. Meadows."

"May I come in?"

She shook her head. "What is your business?"

"I hear that your husband decided to change his plans and delay his return."

She put her hands on her hips. "So?"

"How convenient," he said. "Did you tip him off that the police would be waiting for him?"

"No," she said, "I've not spoken to Jace. I hear he's recovering from an assault. He should be home soon." She paused. "I would hope the police would rethink the decision to arrest him."

"Mrs. Rawlings, I'm sure Jace wants you to be convinced of his innocence. Perhaps you'd like to look at some other evidence that will help you see things more clearly."

She stepped back. "Perhaps."

He put his hand against the door behind her, pushing it open. "Shall I follow you?"

She sighed. "Sure."

Inside, Ryan Meadows sat on the couch and opened his briefcase. "You're going to want to look at this with me," he said, patting the couch cushion next to him.

Irritated, she complied.

As she did, he shifted his open briefcase to hide its contents. His demeanor changed, darkening. "You just had to start snooping, didn't you?" Before she could react, he pulled out a syringe and plunged it into Heather's left thigh just below her shorts. She screamed and stumbled to her feet. "What are you doing?"

"Ketamine," he said, smiling. "Nice to have a brother in the veterinarian business. You may want to sit before you fall. Don't worry," he said, loosening his belt. "You won't feel a thing."

She stumbled into the kitchen, leaving Ryan on the couch. She pulled out her cell and, turning her body so that he couldn't see, punched 911. Feeling her head begin to swim, she placed the open phone behind the toaster before collapsing onto the floor.

"Bo," she gasped. "Help! Bo!"

She heard footsteps and then saw Ryan leaning over her. He whispered, "When you wake up, you can call Jace for help, just like Anita did." He laughed. "Except you're not going to wake up."

The last thing she felt was Ryan ripping open her blouse. "Too bad you won't be around to see your husband go to jail."

The 911 operator frowned. She usually received a dozen mistake calls a day, many of them from elderly patients who dialed emergency services by accident. But this was different. The line was still alive. There were sounds, but they were faint.

She listened as a woman called for help. A man's voice was next, too quiet for her to hear.

Unfortunately, the location wasn't easy to trace. She heard a dog barking, then a man screaming, "Hey, get off me! Ow!"

The line was still open when a second call came in. She left the first line alive and answered the second call. "911. Can you state the nature of your emergency?"

A man's voice. "I've been attacked by a dog. He won't let me get up. I'm bleeding."

"Can you give me your location?"

"124 Dogwood Lane."

"Help is on the way."

Six minutes later, Nathan Gilson and Ginny Tannous knocked on the door at 124 Dogwood Lane. Hearing a weak, "Come in," they entered.

A man was leaning against a kitchen island, holding his right hand over his left forearm. A large dog lay at his feet.

"Careful," the man said. "The dog is protecting the woman."

They looked to the man's left. A woman lay sprawled on the floor, eyes open, snoring. Her blouse was ripped open.

The man looked desperate. "She collapsed, fainted or something. I went to help and thought she didn't have a pulse. I ripped open her shirt to start CPR when the dog attacked. He won't let me touch her."

Ginny approached the dog, holding out her hand and handing him a doggy treat she kept on hand for unruly dogs they encountered on the job. "Good boy," she said calmly. "Good dog."

"I'm okay," the man said. "Please attend to her."

"How's your arm?"

"Bleeding, but I think it will be okay. I called because he wouldn't let me up."

The dog stood and emitted a deep growl.

Ginny tugged on his collar. "Easy, boy."

"What's her name?" Nathan asked.

"Heather Rawlings," the man said.

"Is she diabetic? Does she have a known seizure disorder?"

"Not that I know of. She came out to the kitchen to prepare drinks. The next thing I heard was a thud. I came out to find her right here."

The duo turned their attention to the woman. Nathan knelt over her assessing her airway, breathing, and pulse. He noted a small drop of blood on her thigh.

Ginny tilted her head. "Do you hear that?"

"What?"

"Someone is talking. Like a radio," she said, standing, "or a phone." She leaned over the island counter, listening. There, behind the toaster, she saw a small cell phone, the source of the voice.

She lifted it to hear, "Hello! Hello!"

Ginny said, "Hello?"

"This is the 911 operator. Is there an emergency there?"

"This is EMS. We are on scene."

"How did you know where to go? I've been monitoring this call, but haven't had communication to know where to send a crew."

"Wait a minute," Ginny said. "You directed us here, said a man had been attacked by a dog."

"That wasn't *this* call," she said. "That was a second call. This call was a woman screaming for help. Then I heard a man and a dog. Then the second call came in."

"Well, don't worry," Ginny said. "We're here now. The man came to help her."

"Okay, carry on."

Ginny closed the phone. "Where is that guy?"

Nathan looked around. "Sir?" He walked into the front room, returning a moment later. He shrugged. "He's gone." He looked at their patient on the floor. "Let's move her. I'll bet she's a druggie. Just look at those eyes."

50

Two days and two international flights later, Ryan Meadows stepped out into the Nairobi sunshine, grateful that he'd cultivated a contact who owed him a favor. He checked into the Stanley Hotel downtown and dialed a number on the phone in his room.

"Minister Okombo, it's Ryan Meadows."

"Mr. Meadows. I didn't expect to hear from you. Are you calling for an update on our business arrangement?"

"Not exactly. I'm in town. Just arrived at Kenyatta an hour ago. I'm at the Stanley."

"Did you see Dr. Rawlings? He is flying out. You must have passed him in the airport."

Ryan huffed. "He's alive?"

"Yes."

"We had a deal."

"The doctor became useful to me. An ally, even."

Ryan sighed. He couldn't worry about that now. He listened as the African exhaled into the phone. "So what brings you to town?" Okombo asked.

"I need a little favor. Perhaps you know of a place I can rest for a while—someplace private. No one can know that I am here. I'm so tired of the media attention from my job. You understand."

"Of course. I'll send a car for you. Can you leave first thing in the morning?"

"No problem. Thank you for being discreet. Perhaps you know of someplace on the coast?"

"I'll make all the arrangements."

John Okombo picked up the phone. "Simeon," he said. "I need a favor."

He listened as Simeon sighed. "You call me for a favor? Your goons tried to kill me!"

"Not kill you, just prevent you from killing." Okombo began pacing around his desk. "We had a misunderstanding. You were carrying out my orders, but once I realized that the American doctor had saved my life, I didn't have time to notify you to stop." He paused. "I'm sorry about my officers. They were too trigger-happy, that's all. Besides, we can still be valuable allies."

"And if I don't do this favor?"

"You realize that the MP from your region is still under pressure to eliminate the witches? You need a friend."

Another sigh. "But you don't really need me. You've risen from the dead in the eyes of the public. They love you." Simeon paused. "Does this concern the American surgeon?"

"In a way. He has become an ally to me, so his enemies are now mine."

"What do you need?"

"An enemy of a friend of mine has come calling. I know how disappointed you were not to be able to complete your last assignment, so I'm willing to give you another chance."

"Regular price?"

"Sure."

"Can you deliver the man to my place in Kisii?"

"Of course. There won't be any trouble this time. He thinks he's going to a private getaway for a holiday."

Okombo listened to what sounded like something rattling in a glass bottle. *Probably the bones of his last sacrifice.*

"I'll be waiting."

Two days later, Jace and Evan walked through the doors of no return at Dulles International Airport outside Washington, D.C.

Jace scanned the crowd and leaned on his cane, a mahogany stick with a handle decorated with Maasai beads.

A moment later, he heard his name and the voice he'd longed to hear. "Jace!"

Heather came to him slowly, with open arms. She folded them around him and buried her face in his neck.

"Careful," he said.

He smiled in spite of the pain in his chest.

He was home.

When the hood was snatched from his head, Ryan saw that he was in some sort of old warehouse. He was tied against the wall, arms outstretched in a crucifixion pose, so that he could barely reach the floor.

The man in front of him looked like something out of *National Geographic*, a tribal monster dressed in an animal loincloth. His face was vaguely familiar. When he smiled, the red stripes painted on his face seemed to dance.

The man picked up the hoof of an animal and moved closer, peering into Ryan's eyes. "Do you not recognize me, Mr. Meadows?"

I know the voice.

Ryan squinted. *Dr. Okayo?* He shook his head. The man looked nothing like the professional he'd met back in Richmond. But the voice was identical.

The man laughed and each deep, mocking, hideous note escalated Ryan's fear.

"No!" he cried. "I've got money."

The man held the hoof over a small fire.

Ryan's feet began to blister.

The witch doctor danced.

Ryan screamed.

And everything went dark.

That evening after dropping Evan Martin off at his house, Jace and Heather were finally alone. They had covered a lot of Jace's African journey during the drive down to Richmond, but Jace knew a hard discussion was still ahead.

Jace turned to Heather, took her hands and led her to the couch. He felt his voice began to tighten. "There are tough things I need to say."

Heather's eyes glistened. "Jace—"

At first, he tried to fight the tears. He pressed his fist against his quivering chin. He sat on the couch and began to weep. "I can't believe how stupid I was with Anita Franks."

She sat beside him. "Jace, it's okay."

"No, it's not. I was unfaithful."

"Why do you say that? Did you remember something about the night of your accident? You told me you hadn't slept with her, but that the night of your accident was blank."

"I remember going to her room."

"Of course. I know that."

"But the autopsy showed that she'd been with a man."

"Jace—it wasn't you."

"But how do you know?"

"You did go to her room, but only because she called you for help. She called you because she'd been raped. I suspect she didn't call the police because Ryan Meadows had threatened to expose their affair." She paused and looked into his eyes. "You don't know, do you?"

He shook his head.

"The analysis of the fluid taken from her revealed her partner as someone with type-A blood. You're type B. It couldn't have been you."

"But who—"

"Ryan Meadows. The ME has matched it against his DNA."

He took a deep breath. "My relationship with her was still wrong. I was a fool for putting myself in such a place where it would be easy to cross a line."

"Jace, you've learned." She paused. "But I was at fault too. I should have trusted you."

"Where is Meadows now?"

"He escaped to Kenya. Evidently he has friends there."

Jace leaned his head against Heather's shoulder and let the relief that he hadn't slept with Anita Franks begin to settle upon his soul.

After a few moments, Jace spoke again. "Kenya can be a scary place if you don't know the Savior."

... a little more ...

When a delightful concert comes to an end,

the orchestra might offer an encore.

When a fine meal comes to an end,

it's always nice to savor a bit of dessert.

When a great story comes to an end,

we think you may want to linger.

And so, we offer ...

AfterWords—just a little something more after you

have finished a David C Cook novel.

We invite you to stay awhile in the story.

Thanks for reading!

Turn the page for ...

- **Discussion Questions**

DISCUSSION QUESTIONS

1. The novel opens with heart surgeon Jace Rawlings in strange territory: a world hinting at reality beyond what he can see, feel, and quantify. He is challenged with the thought that a spiritual battle is present and may be reflected in the physical. While Jace's circumstances certainly are extraordinary and not typical, in what ways have you seen evidence of spiritual reality beyond this visible world? Can you think of biblical accounts where a spiritual battle was raging while people remained innocent and unaware?

2. As a fiction writer, I love using memory loss as a way to create mystery, and suspicious circumstances that look one way on the surface, yet are revealed to be something else entirely. But what we love in fiction can be disastrous for intimate relationships! Misunderstanding, jealousy, and suspicion were key elements that drove a wedge between Heather and Jace. If you had a chance to sit with them as a marriage counselor, are there ways you would suggest to regain a pathway to trust? In what areas did Jace fail as a husband to protect his marriage? Heather?

3. When Jace's self-sufficient world begins to implode, he finds himself searching for the truth at his boyhood home of Kenya. Although he seems to have rejected the religion of his parents, when times get tough, Jace runs to the familiar. In spite of his search for his own way, Jace ends up looking a lot like his earthly father. Can you think of similarities?

Why does Jace return? Do you believe that the "cry" from his dead sister was spiritual? Psychological projection based on some inner need? Misunderstanding orchestrated by God to bring Jace back to faith?

4. To some degree, Jace was on the run from a host of real miseries. Are you like Jace? Do you have a tendency to run from pain, while all the while telling yourself that you are really running toward answers?

5. I'm currently working at Kijabe Hospital, just like Jace. I used the example of a decision not to stock snakebite antivenom to represent the reality and complexity of decisions we face here. In fact, we've decided *not* to stock life-saving antivenom here because of the expense and infrequency of use. That means someone may die someday. But we can treat so many cases of malaria successfully because of our decision to save money. Put yourself in my shoes (or the shoes of Jace's father). What would you do? Can you justify putting a snakebite victim at risk just because of money?

6. Jace ends up in the middle of Africa, and right in the center of God's plan. But he got there for a variety of reasons, none of which could be considered particularly noble. Do you think God can use our less-than-noble motivations (guilt, fear, desire to run away from difficulty) to help steer us toward faith? Again, imagine that you are Jace's counselor back in Virginia and he asked for your advice after telling you of his desire to return to Kenya. Once he explained his honest motivation, what would your counsel have been? Would you have been correct?

7. Jace and Heather grew up as "third-culture kids." These are citizens of one nation who have grown up in a foreign country. They are often caught in the middle, unsure where they fit. In a sense, that describes all Christians. We find ourselves in this world, but longing for a heavenly home. We don't "fit" here. Can you relate to this longing or this kind of identify confusion? Do you ever have a sense that you just don't belong?

8. While this story is fictional, I pulled from research into actual witchcraft practices in this country, some of which are very mysterious and colorful. For some reason, things that would be laughed at in American culture are accepted here. Post-Christian America is in some way becoming more "spiritual" while at the same time, less Christian. Do you see evidence of this? Why do you think witchcraft flourishes in a place like my home in Kenya?

9. What do you think about modern nonfictional accounts of experiences beyond the grave, either in heaven or hell? Are these real? Psychological projections? Spiritual … demonic perhaps? What's your explanation? Are you a scientific skeptic like Jace?

10. In the end, Jace makes this statement: "Kenya can be a scary place if you don't know the Savior." Do you agree? If you were advising me on writing the sequel to this novel, what should be the next challenge for Jace and Heather?

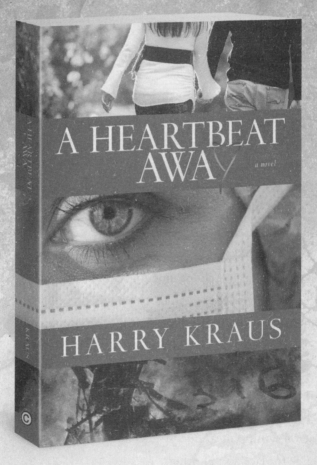